THE BOOK OF LOWMOOR
JEWEL
AND
THORN

THE BOOK OF LOWMOOR
JEWEL AND THORN

Macquarie
Regional Library

RICHARD POOLE

SIMON AND SCHUSTER

For Will –
onlie begetter;
tough critic,
brilliant son.

SIMON AND SCHUSTER

First published in Great Britain in 2005 by Simon and Schuster UK Ltd,
a Viacom company.

This paperback edition published in 2006

Simon & Schuster UK Ltd
Africa House, 64-78 Kingsway, London WC2B 6AH.

A CIP catalogue record for this book is available from the British Library.

ISBN 0 689 87290 9

1 3 5 7 9 10 8 6 4 2

Printed and bound in Great Britain.

www.simonsays.co.uk

CONTENTS

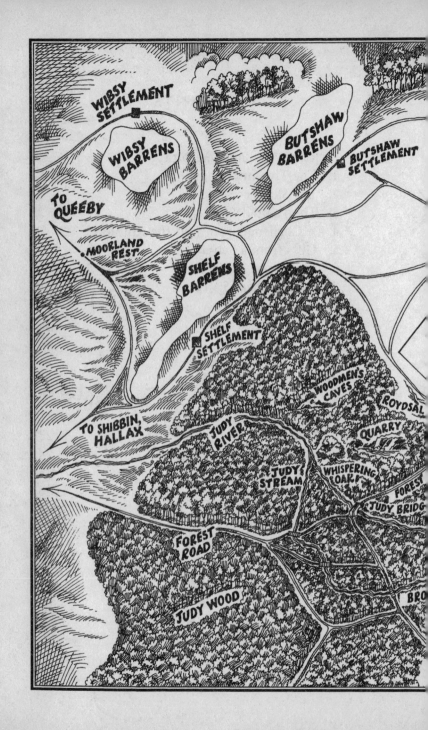

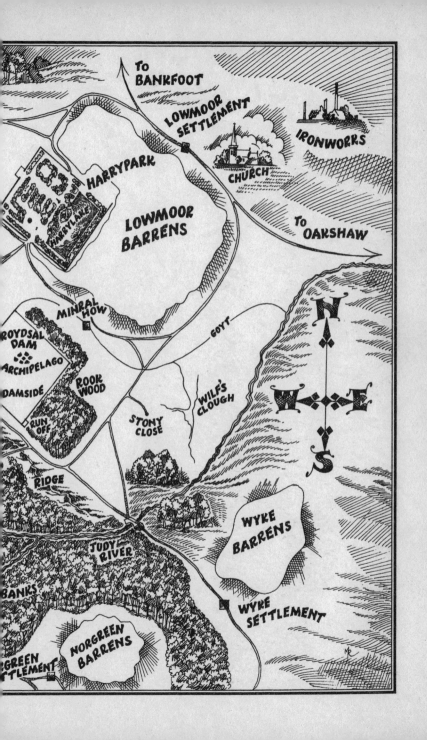

PROLOGUE
THE EMERALD POOL

The girl pushed into the screen of reeds, making their stems crackle and rasp. The tallest were three feet high, more than six times her own height, and grew so close together that passage through them was difficult. The last thing she wanted was for a broken stalk to spring back and poke her in the eye. Nevertheless she harboured no ill feelings towards the plants – nor the soggy ground underfoot on which they thrived. A formidable barrier, they guarded the pool's secrecy.

The reed-patch came to an end, and the girl emerged onto a flattish stretch of bank – a three-foot-wide strip of sward the neighbourhood rabbits kept close-cropped. She advanced a little way, then sat down cross-legged, her back to the tangle of undergrowth that enclosed the pool.

On any other day, she would have been happy to be here: happy to stare at the still water with its clots of duckweed, to scan the far, bush-hung, rocky banks, or to follow the stop-start flight of some midge-hunting dragonfly, its thin body impossibly blue as it flashed in the sunlight. Happy simply to dream. But, although the sun was out and her surroundings seemed to throb with the fecundity of springtime, she wasn't able to raise even a wraith of a smile. Frown lines creased her unblemished forehead. Something, it seemed, was worrying her.

After a time she reached forward and plucked a single stalk of grass from a tuft on the edge of the bank. She put one end into her mouth and sucked on it thoughtfully, her eyes seemingly fixed on nothing.

She sat like that for quite some time, oblivious of the outside world. Until, out of nowhere, an arm came snaking around her and a hand clamped on her mouth. Swung up into the air, she kicked out, but now her legs were also seized, cutting short her brief struggle, and she was carried into the undergrowth.

Tranquillity resumed its interrupted sway at the pool. Time passed, the sun strengthened. A buck rabbit hopped into view and, spotting the tuft from which the girl had plucked her stalk, began to nibble. He knew nothing of the girl, and cared as much about her fate.

1

THE TREASURY

Grass blades were tickling Thorn's nose. This was always how it was when you were crawling on your belly. And often how it was when you were standing up too.

As Thorn's nose twitched, he gripped it between finger and thumb. There was a muffled *snuffle-squeak*, and the sneeze subsided. He released the offended organ, and massaged it ruefully.

If I give myself away now, I'm done for, he thought. Today's the one day of my life when there must be no mistakes.

He peered through a fringe of grass into the gathering gloom. There it was. Wyke settlement, with its forbidding palisade.

Come on, Taylor, do your stuff. Then I can do mine.

The gate-guard looked bored to tears. Toting his iron-tipped pike (complete with wickedly curving prong, all the better to disembowel you with a jab, a twist and a jerk), he took a few paces down the track and aimed a kick at a loose pebble. It skittered away, hit a bigger stone and bounced into the grass.

No one else was in sight.

What did *you* do, wondered Thorn, to earn your passage from boy to man?

Wyke, Wyke, where they're all alike! The children's chant rang in his head. He seemed to have known it since before he'd started to talk. But Wyke had its reply: *Norgreen's a has-been, a has-been, a has-been!* A has-been, eh? Well, here was one Norgreener bent on proving otherwise. Quite simply, he *had* to. Prove himself now, today, on his sixteenth birthday. To Haw, Taylor, Morry, yes, to everybody in Norgreen. Prove himself to himself. Failure was unthinkable. If he dragged himself home empty-handed, his name would be mud. Girls would shy away from him. Look at poor Raggy Wilks – he'd be lucky to marry a hedgehog.

Better to get caught and end up in Brear Marsh. Head down; end of story.

Thorn sniffed the air. Taylor had said that it would rain. But not, they both hoped, before—

At last! There they were – tongues of fire in the twilight! There, flickering orange-yellow a little way to the north, not far from the rim of the ditch that circled the wooden palisade. Fire rising from a patch of last summer's crushed bracken. Fire – the thing above all else that every settler feared. Fire could leap spaces, fasten its fangs in anything, reduce a settlement to charcoal . . .

He'd spotted the fire before the gate-guard. But then he was looking for it. Now the guard saw it too. Dropping his pike in his excitement, he whirled round, seized a rattle from a hook near the gate and began to twirl it. As its jagged cogs set up a racket, "Fire!" he shouted. "Fire! Fire!"

All settlements had contingency plans for such an event. The double doors of the gate were drawn back; Wykers erupted from inside and rushed off towards the flames. Some carried buckets, others poles tipped with flattened metal blades for beating. The humans looked tiny beside the leaping flames that lit them. Two cranked open a sluice, and water came pouring into the ditch to form a natural barrier. Those with buckets dipped them and tossed water on the palisade. Wet, the walls wouldn't catch fire so readily. Those with poles beat bravely at the edges of the flames.

But the oldest inhabitants, too decrepit to contribute, milled about, gesticulating and shouting at one another. Children, more excited than frightened, scurried about, yelling and getting underfoot. The gate-guard stood in their midst, his eyes on the conflagration. In the commotion and half-dark it was easy for Thorn to get to his feet, cross the ditch, move quickly along the palisade and slip through the open gate.

The settlement seemed deserted. Soon, Thorn was deep inside. But he was far from lost. Norgreen kept ground plans of neighbouring settlements, continually updating them as new information came in. Wyke's he had studied, committed to memory and – in his imagination – moved about in a hundred times. Now, navigating as much by his mental grid as the physical structures around him, he knew exactly where he was going. A left here, a right there; now down behind this smelly row of privies, now past this carpenter's yard. And there it was.

The building proclaimed its specialness not only by its shape – it was circular, one of a kind in Wyke settlement – but by the ornamental work that had been lavished upon it. The jambs and lintels of the doorway were carved with abstract patterns; sinister gargoyles were mounted at intervals round the eaves; and from the middle of the door itself there jutted a wooden knocker in the shape of a rat's head, its jaws bared to reveal teeth that could tear off your head. The real thing, he thought, inset by some cunning hand.

The door was merely latched. Crime wasn't tolerated in the settlements. Theft was punished by banishment, a fate tantamount to death. Yet Thorn didn't hesitate to lift the metal hasp: to steal from other settlements was virtuous, and applauded; tradition sanctioned it. The door opened; he went in.

And knew, straightaway, that Lady Luck was with him. For, in the centre of this windowless room, suspended from the ceiling, a single oil-lamp burnt. Without it, he'd have had to grope his way about in the dark. He pulled the door shut.

Wyke's Treasury wasn't so very different from Norgreen's. It was crammed with artefacts created in The Dark Time. He'd been allowed into Norgreen's Treasury on no more than two occasions, always under supervision, and not allowed to touch. Now, entering a Treasury alone – albeit a rival settlement's – he felt an immediate thrill mixed with a sudden sense of transgression. All about him artefacts loomed, a strange and silently threatening gathering of objects whose original purposes were, for the most part, lost in the mists of time. Painstakingly collected by intrepid foragers from the massive but ruined or dilapidated structures that dotted the landscape, they were fragmentary remnants of the giant civilisation that many believed had once filled the world – or that tiny part of it Thorn Jack and his kind knew. What the foragers could shift, of course, was limited by size, but Thorn, forbidden as a minor to enter – even to closely approach – those crumbling and dangerous buildings, had heard astonishing tales from other Norgreeners of the amazing objects they'd seen. How he'd ached to grow up, so he could share their experience. And now here he was, his passport to adulthood within his grasp . . .

But what to take? It had to be something compact, to fit into his backpack. And he must be quick: sooner or later the Wykers would realise that the fire was a diversion.

Larger artefacts stood on the floor or marched along the sturdy shelves that lined the wooden walls. Many were bigger than Thorn, and some were twice his size. One, a couple of inches shorter than himself, consisted of a circular superstructure set firmly on a flat base. Around the rim of its moon-white face, behind a frontage of clear glass, ran a sequence of black markings; from a small, central hub stuck out two slim black pointers, one longer than the other. The markings, he thought, might be numbers, but, like everyone else in Norgreen, he'd never learned to read, there being no call for it.

Next to the first object, and of roughly his own height, stood a slim, rectangular object with rounded corners. Some three times as long as it was broad, it had been propped against the wall on one of its narrower sides. A stubby projection stuck up from one corner. It was made out of some shiny greeny-grey metal. Inset high on its front was a dark, glassy blank rectangle; below were a host of whitish studs of various sizes, most of them oval in shape and all of them carrying black markings – some identical to the ones on the other object. These two things Thorn saw at a glance – but neither was what he was looking for. Even if he'd wanted to, he couldn't have carried either one.

Smaller, still more precious items would be carefully stashed away. Directly beneath the lamp in the centre of the room, a big, circular chest of drawers occupied pride of place. Stepping up to it, he unhooked his backpack, placed it on top and unstrapped it, fumblingly.

He wrenched open the topmost drawer. A jumble of battered objects. He shut the drawer and opened another. Disappointment again. He tried another five before he struck lucky.

Two gold rings, giant-made!

Gripping with both hands a shank as thick as his thigh, he hefted out the first. A single enormous diamond glinted from its setting. That would do for the settlement. He loaded it into his pack. But he wasn't finished yet: he wanted something for his sister Haw as a memory of his triumph. The second ring – whose little claws clutched an emerald – was certainly attractive, but there was one more drawer.

It held a greenish bundle of cloth. He was about to settle for the emerald when he thought: Not so fast – there must be something inside there . . . He was right. Swaddled in the soft nest was a crystal half the size of his head. Its surface was irregular, all pits and jags and edges – quite unlike those of the diamond and the emerald with their symmetrical, polished facets. It wasn't really pretty, yet there was something about it . . . something that drew him towards it. A brooding blood red, it seemed to emanate darkness . . . How could that be? And why the wrapping? He reached into the drawer, gripped the object – and let go of it. For, up from his hands, down his arms and into his body, so that his whole frame quivered in the instant he held the thing, had shot a bolt of energy. And the thing had seemed to pulse with a crimson radiance, as if, deep inside it, beat a strange crystalline heart.

He stared at the object. It had sucked back its brilliance and now seemed almost black. This was beyond his experience. Still, so were many things. For a moment his will faltered: better take the emerald. Then the devil-may-care attitude of youth reasserted itself. He'd be damned if he was going to be so easily defeated. If the Wykers had moved the thing, which they had, so could he. But how? There was nothing here but the crystal and its wrapping . . .

The wrapping! Throwing the flaps of cloth back so that they cloaked the thing, he touched the bundle with the tip of a finger. Nothing happened. Experimentally, he told hold of it again. Nothing happened. This must be the way to lift it, then. It proved surprisingly light. Into his pack it went.

And now the pack was on his back, and he was out in the open air, coolly latching the door of the Treasury behind him.

So, to his escape strategy . . .

Down this alley. Right – left – right. Rounding a potter's kiln, he bumped straight into a man. The pair of them went sprawling, hitting the ground like a pair of wrestlers. Thorn recoiled from the other's clutch. The Wyker was old and bald, and wore a hide jerkin over his shirt and trews. A lump the size of a thumbnail bulged from his chin.

"What the hell—" he gasped.

But Thorn was already on his feet –

"Hey, you, stop there!"

– and around the next corner.

Quickly, his mental map took him to the outer wall. Like

Norgreen's, Wyke's palisade was a foot in height, its uprights roped together by twisted lengths of fibre. Around its inner perimeter, again just as at Norgreen, ran a raised platform for observation and defence. A short flight of steps led up to the platform.

No one was about. Hampered by his bulging pack, he struggled over the palisade and dropped to the ground. The earth was hard, he landed unevenly, lost his balance, toppled over and slid down into the ditch, where he was greeted by a good half inch of muddy water. His trews were soaked through, but he grinned in the gloom. If this was the worst of it . . .

He'd emerged from the settlement on the opposite side to the fire. Now to put some distance between himself and the palisade. From time to time he looked back, trying to penetrate the darkness. As far as he could tell, nobody had followed him. Taylor, he must find Taylor. A dim glow in the sky revealed the location of the fire, declining but still burning. In truth, there had been little danger of it spreading to the settlement. It had never been their intention to set Wyke on fire. So – their agreed meeting-point had to be somewhere in this direction . . . He circled the settlement, maintaining his distance from the ditch.

Without a brand to light the way, the going was slow. The ground was rough and, though the grass here was still fairly short, his knees would catch in tussocks, or he'd be surprised by a dip or hollow. After three successive trips, the last of which pitched him onto his face, so that he scratched his cheek on a bramble and bruised one hand against a stone, he caught himself in mid-curse.

He lay still, listening. Around him, night was deepening its blankets of black. But no voice came to his ear, and he got to his feet and plodded on.

At length, from somewhere to his right, came a low whistle. Taylor's signal. He returned it – or, rather, tried to. Tension had dumbed his lips. It took him half a dozen attempts before a sound emerged – a pathetic one at that.

"Thorn?" came a low voice.

"Taylor?"

And then his uncle was with him, and their arms were around one another.

"You made it, then?"

"Sure. You should see what I've got – a diamond ring!"

The theft of the ruby crystal was for Haw's ears alone.

"Wonderful – you'll be a hero. But first we get away from here. Run into any problems?"

"I bumped into an old man – I think he knew I wasn't a Wyker."

"Then they'll be after us. Come on, no time to spare."

They moved off, but hadn't gone far when brands appeared ahead, flickering in the distance. Like the will-o-the-wisps he'd once seen, dancing over the stagnant, weedy ooze of Brear Marsh . . .

Taylor caught Thorn by the arm.

"This way," he whispered urgently.

They changed direction, tracking away from the lights. But the brands were moving faster than they were, stringing out in a line.

"Look!" hissed Taylor.

Thorn turned, and saw a second skein of torches bobbing along to their rear.

"Damn it! They're outflanking us!" said his uncle anxiously.

They tried to quicken their pace but they were lightless and burdened and however fast they went, the brand-bearers were much faster.

The two of them hunkered down on their heels. Grass brushed against Thorn's cheek. In front of and behind them, the lights came ever closer. They could hear quite clearly the Wykers shouting to one another.

"There," breathed Taylor. "Look."

Thorn looked. And saw, in the cordon that was closing in behind them, one gap between the brands a little bigger than the others. They began to edge towards it. The slight breeze was in their faces, and they could smell the pitch-soaked rags that the Wykers had set alight.

Voices came to their ears. Two of the Wykers were arguing.

"You sure this is the right direction, Jed?" one was saying.

"I reckon. Got a better notion, Tom?"

"Further west, to my mind."

"Who's Head Tracker – me or you?"

"You. But for how long?"

A third voice broke in on them: "Shut it, you two. Get your minds on the business."

Rufus Crabb, the settlement's Headman. Taylor had met him a couple of times in formal contacts at Council level: a tough nut, as hard as flint. The pair could expect no quarter if Rufus Crabb got hold of them.

The two Wykers had shut it. The lights moved on without further ado, dipping and lifting with the terrain. Thorn and Taylor could make out the faces of the nearer men, glimmering behind the flames of the brands they held. But the Norgreeners had got themselves just where they wanted to be – positioned midway between the two more widely spaced lights. Thorn crouched still closer to the ground. The smell of loam rose into his face. If he could have burrowed down, like a mole, and disappeared, he'd have done so. His pack dragged on his shoulders. He steadied himself with outstretched fingers, ready to move at his uncle's signal.

"Hey you two! Close that gap!"

The voice was Crabb's. The cordon in front was almost upon them.

"Come on!" Taylor hissed.

He and Thorn sprang to their feet, moving as swiftly as they could towards the gap. But it was closing.

"Right ahead!" a voice shouted. "I heard something, Rufus!"

"Close in!" commanded Crabb.

One of the Wykers came straight at them. The man was armed with a cudgel. But even as he saw Taylor and raised the weapon to strike, Taylor leapt forward, butting the man in the stomach and knocking him off his feet. The Wyker grunted, and his brand went spinning. Taylor punched him for good measure, snatched his cudgel from his grasp, then quickly gathered up his brand, which lay flickering in the grass.

"Come on," he gasped.

They began to run. Over the tussocky ground they flew, grass whipping their thighs and elbows, Taylor's flame shedding flakes of fire as they bounded along. But now they could see the ground before them, and they managed to stay on their feet. In their wake, the Wykers also ran, their lights funnelling together as if drawn to a common centre.

Something struck Thorn on the forehead. What on earth . . .? It happened again – on the cheek. A third time – his upper lip. He opened his mouth and a drop of water ran in. He caught it on his tongue.

Rain!

And within seconds it wasn't just raining, it was teeming, as if all the water in the clouds above had decided, there and then, that it had to make a getaway. Taylor's brand fizzed and fizzled, as random raindrops struck it. Thorn risked a glance back; one by one the torches of their pursuers were going out. There were ten; then there were nine. Taylor's brand hissed and died. He threw it aside. Black dark ahead.

"Keep going!" Taylor urged him. "This rain could save our skins!"

Thorn's lungs were protesting. He was muscular, fit and strong, a natural runner and jumper. But the pack on his back . . . It dragged at his shoulders, a dead weight.

He threw a glance back again. Just three lights behind, and a ragged volley of shouts and curses. Then two – then one –

None.

Rain beat down on his head, plastered his hair to his skull. But he'd never been so thankful in his life for a downpour.

"Which way?" An anguished cry now some distance to their rear.

"Spread out," came the Headman's voice. "We can still run them down."

There was a tug on Thorn's arm. Taylor was pulling him sharply left, at a right angle to the direction they'd been going in. Thorn tripped, lurched to one side and almost fell, but managed at the last moment to recover his balance. Then he was running flat out again, the grass beating against his knees. Something whacked him on the hand, stinging his clenched knuckles. A nettle. His pack jounced against his back, it must be beating him black and blue.

Around them, excited voices rang and ricocheted, some nearer and clearer, some less so – half-smothered by rain or distance.

This is a dream, he thought. I'm running, but going nowhere. Whatever's behind me will sink its claws into my back and pull me down.

His legs felt heavy as logs.

"Taylor," he panted. "Finished. Can't keep going. You go on."

His uncle grasped him by the arm.

"Don't give up. Can't be far now – can't be far."

Astoundingly, nor was it. All of a sudden, they were in thicker undergrowth, then overgrowth. Vegetation pressed against their knees, their chests, their faces. Their rush had slowed to a walk. They forced their way in amongst dry, bent bracken stalks, brambles, and a mass of other growth.

Taylor halted. "Gloves!" he whispered. "Masks!"

As one they reached into the long side-pockets of their trews and pulled out the protection they carried there. Soon, double-skinned in tough mouse-hide mittens and headgear against nettles, thorns and briars, they were able to press ahead.

"Let them follow us if they can!" whispered Taylor. "I'll lay a gold piece to an acorn that they're not equipped like us."

The rain drummed above and around them, then thinned to a patter. A pleasant, familiar sound. Drops fell through from time to time. Thorn threw back his head and caught a few in his mouth, grateful for the liquid. His shoulders were wet and sore – the straps of his pack had rubbed them raw. But so what, so what? Occasionally, behind them, they heard a loose shout or whistle: frustrated, forlorn.

And after a time, nothing at all.

2

THE SHAPES

"Jewel! Jewel!"

The voice broke across her dream. Across the blue lake, the sailing boat, the mysterious – but surely masculine – figure standing on the prow, his face too distant to make out.

She stretched out an arm, but the craft was receding beyond her. Fading. Gone.

"Jewel! Jewel!" The voice jangled insistently. "Do you intend to sleep all morning? Get up, lass, there's work to be done."

She opened her eyes – grey like her father's, not blue as her mother's had been. Forget-me-not blue . . . She would never forget. Jewel herself loved that colour, but you don't get to choose.

Grey eyes, then . . . Cold eyes, self-possessed eyes, calculating eyes. She was her father's daughter all right. Elliott's one and only child. She poked sleep out of their corners with a careful fingernail. The Sandman rarely forgot her. Warm under thick blankets, she lay gazing at the roughly-rendered ceiling of the poky room. Though many things about her father exasperated her daily, there was more of him in her than she cared to admit . . .

She'd been trained in the right school, which meant no school at all. Her mother, she thought, would have sent her, but her father kept her with him. What! – stick her among a rabble of kids in some tin-pot settlement, where they'd fill her head with the rudiments of pottery, weaving, needlework – the cultivation of all the varieties of edible grass? Prepare her, in short, for a life of servitude, which would be topped off by marriage to some brainless, brutal yokel: thereafter a wholly delightful package encompassing daily drudgery, childbearing, child-rearing, old age (premature) and, soon enough, death? Had he named her Jewel for nothing? Should he deposit his gem in a mud-patch? What could any school teach her that she could possibly need to know? Better by far an education in the schoolyard of the world, by which he meant the realm of trade, of buying and selling – the school of no favours, sharp bargaining, hard knocks. And along with it, inevitably, a life of travel, new encounters and the stimulation of the unexpected: free, proud, and beholden to no man.

Well, she couldn't say he was wrong, that she regretted the way they lived. When she thought of settlement people, tied to one place for a lifetime, there was no way that she could wish to exchange her life for theirs. And yet, hadn't she too become a creature of routine? Wasn't she hemmed in by her father's way of life? Hence her dream of the morning and similar dreams that had gone before. But if her life lacked something, she couldn't have told you what it was.

There was a bang, the door flew open and her father strode in. Yes, *strode*. He liked to stride about – as he liked, when he was standing still, to strike a magnificent pose. And Elliott Ranson, bearded, handsome and more than seven inches tall, had what it took to cut a figure. Never tell him he was nothing more than a jumped-up pedlar, a hawker of women's clothing and assorted fripperies—

"Jewel! Do I have to *drag* you out? Move your backside, girl! The world's hanging fire for us!" His voice boomed in the cramped space, which he almost overfilled.

"Yes, Father." Time to play the submissive daughter – a role she knew well enough.

"Good. Breakfast's a-waiting, lass." He turned on his heel and strode out. Behind him the flimsy door swung shut with a clap.

She sighed and threw back the bed-covers. A couple of paces took her to the window, where she drew back grimy curtains. It was a cloudy, unpromising morning. The inn stood on a little hill, and her room was on the second storey, but even combined these facts weren't enough to afford her more of a view than a rabbit sitting on a rock. Still, she knew what she'd have seen had she been standing at a height of sixteen feet above ground level. Beyond the narrow track that wound round this side of the inn, rugged moorland stretched to the horizon, dropping gradually away. As, of course, rugged moorland did on the other three sides. Here and there, the contents of an undernourished stream sought an escape route from it all, a faster way of getting wherever water wants to get to – which in a stream counts as anywhere but where it already is. A few stunted trees, presently struggling into leaf, stuck up pathetically, their angles of growth testimony to the whipping winds that ruled this landscape.

On a table beneath the window stood a jug of water and a bowl. She stripped off her nightshirt and began, with a burst of energy but no enthusiasm, to soap her body with the chilly liquid. Comic as her father's behaviour now often seemed to her, she had to admire his resilience, zest and bottomless optimism. One day, he was convinced, he would pull off the big deal that would make their fortunes for them. Quite what this deal would be, and how he'd contrive it, remained unclear. When was it – she cast her mind back – that she'd ceased to credit his dreams of wealth, begun to view him not with a child's unquestioning deference, but a woman's wry detachment? Perhaps a year or more ago, when she was turning fourteen? By then her mother had been dead for five years. She'd died of a fever in some shanty in a hole-in-the-wall settlement whose name time had erased from Jewel's memory. But the images of her mother's passing remained as fresh as yesterday in the girl's mind. She saw again the pathetic pallet on which her mother had breathed her last. Saw again too the local woman (the settlement was too mean to possess a Syb) whose much-vaunted expertise had failed to save her own head from the fate of going bald – or virtually bald, for (as Jewel couldn't help but remember) only a thin scrub of hairs grew on the shiny dome of her scalp. This woman had coaxed her mother to drink a series of obscure concoctions, and applied cloths soaked in one herb or another to her burning forehead, whilst assuring father and daughter that, no more than a few months before, she'd brought a man "in just such a fever back from the very brink of death". An empty brag. Her mother, after passing effortlessly from delirium to unconsciousness, died soon after sun-up on her fourth day of confinement. For some time after that, one settlement seemed to Jewel (and Elliott too, if truth were told) much like another. They came and went in an endless, befogged succession as she and her father, haunted by the memory of what they had seen and could never forget, ate, slept, bought and sold goods and travelled on, though never to any destination: for a destination is somewhere you *have* to get to, not just the next place after the last.

Of course, she'd never told her father that his grand conceptions held no more substance for her than a wisp of dissolving smoke. When he was in his cups, which he not infrequently was, and spinning out like a money-spider his ever more elaborate visions of how they'd live when they were rich – with a fine house (stone-built, of course), a rattery of superior animals to ride, servants to wait on them, the best clothes, every luxury – she kept her own counsel, murmured nothings, played along. While his dreams weren't beyond the utmost bounds of realisation – for her mother's death had taught her that nothing is for ever, that circumstances can alter in the time it takes to snap your fingers or wink a knowing eye – that same death imported a cloud of darkness into her mind that the winds of time could never sweep away.

She put on her travelling clothes – jerkin and trews of rough cloth, and hide boots – and tied up her black hair – her mother's hair, not her father's, she had at least inherited that – under a coarse green cap. So kitted out, she could pass for a boy, and indeed sometimes did. Downstairs, in what passed for the dining room of the inn (it would be a drinking room more often, as it had the previous night), her father, sprawled in the biggest chair, was holding forth to the landlady.

". . . Yes indeed, Mrs Dracup, it's trade what makes the world go round."

"My husband, God rest his soul," Mrs Dracup observed dryly, "was of the opinion that it's *wickedness* what makes the world go round."

"Ah, good morning, my dear," said Elliott.

It was a comfortable room. There were a number of settles and tables, a dresser with blue plates on the narrow shelves, and pictures of moorland landscapes on the walls. In the fireplace, crackling merrily, was a generous log fire.

"Sit yourself down and help yourself, love," said Mrs Dracup to Jewel. "A growing lass like you needs a full belly of a morning."

Jewel smiled in reply and took her place at the table. From the plates in front of her she took a slice of hard-boiled duck-egg and a round of oaty bread. She'd follow it, she thought, with some of the honey from the cruet: it was the colour of old gold. And to drink, to judge from the pleasant odour that rose from the pot, crab-apple tea. Not a bad start to the day . . .

"Your husband," continued Elliott, addressing the landlady, "was a man who looked at life from what I'd call a dark angle: *unduly* dark, not to put too fine—"

"A rat-squeak for your angles and undulies!" said Mrs Dracup. "You can't get away from wickedness in this world."

"Well, your late husband and I will have to differ. I confess to being something of an optimist myself."

"Then good luck to you, sir. My husband was killed over Wibsy way after a difference of opinion over the merits of a barrel of ale. May you never be given reason to change your mind."

"I hope not. I am, of course, very sorry to hear about the manner of your husband's death. Unfortunate things can happen among men who've drunk too much."

"That's very true, Mr Ranson. Why, you yourself were chattering away nineteen to the dozen in your sleep last night. I could hear you through the door. After you'd drunk a good few pots of my best ale."

"Ah, yes. Well, very fine ale, it was. I can honestly say that I've never drunk a better. Dark and sweet – just the way I like it."

Mrs Dracup smiled, mollified by the compliment. "Most kind of you to say so, sir, most kind."

A cunning rogue, my father, thought Jewel, as she plastered another slice of bread with honey. Just when he's on the back foot, he goes and delivers a knockout punch.

"And where are you off to now," continued Mrs Dracup, still glowing, "if I may be so bold as to enquire?"

"Where would *you* go, if you were me?"

"If I was a trader? Shelf Fair."

"Shelf Fair?"

"Once every month, from April to August, there's a big fair in Shelf," said the landlady. "Come from far and wide, they do. And the first one of the year is always a cracker."

"Is it indeed . . ."

"Aye. Spend money like water, some folk. All to do, I reckon, with being cooped up over the winter. The winters round here, they seem to last a lifetime. Nigh drive some people out of their minds."

"Well now," said Elliott, striking while the iron was hot, "perhaps you can advise me on the best route to Shelf. I've got my wagon, of course – I'm not on foot like a common pedlar."

No, thought Jewel: though once you were.

"Let me see," said Mrs Dracup. "Today's Thursday, the Fair's Saturday . . . Now there's a thing. I hadn't reckoned it properly before, but it doesn't look to me as though you'll get there in time. If you could travel as the crow flies, you'd be fine, but you can't. You have to go round Shelf Barrens. The Barrens, you see, at this end, is long and thin, kind of *stretched out*. If you could cut across you'd be there Friday evening, but even the crows won't fly across, and as for humans – well, I don't think I need say any more to a travelled man like you."

"I see," said Elliott shortly, and lapsed into gloomy silence.

Seeing her father so suddenly downcast instantly washed away all Jewel's critical thoughts about him.

"If we got off straight away—" she began.

"It's no good." Her father cut her short. "Mrs Dracup's perfectly right. We'll never get there in time."

"Not even if we took advantage of every last bit of daylight?"

"At this time of year? Exactly how much daylight do you think there is, daughter?"

Silence fell. Her father was in that mood where arguments count for nothing against the strength of a made-up mind.

"Well," said Mrs Dracup after a while, "time and tide wait for no man. I must get on."

And getting up, she began to clear away the breakfast things. Soon the table was empty, and the sound of dishes clattering as they were vigorously washed and stacked came from the kitchen next door.

Elliott was staring into the fire. A log flared, spitting a burning splinter out onto the hearth. There it sent up a thread of smoke and quickly turned from red to black.

"Father," ventured Jewel, "what if we *did cross* the Barrens?"

Her father stared at her.

"*Cross* the Barrens? Are you crazy, girl? Nobody crosses Barrens."

"Then we'll be the first to do it, won't we? Besides, Mrs Dracup says that this one isn't wide."

"Narrow or wide, it's impossible."

"Is this Elliott Ranson talking? The salesman who lets nothing stand in the way of his next sale? How many times have you told me, Father, 'Nothing's impossible, girl'?"

He managed a faint smile. "Quite a few, I imagine. But sadly, some things *are* impossible. *Nobody crosses Barrens.*"

"Do you know anyone who's tried?"

"Of course not. That's why we know it's impossible."

"Is it? What we know is that it's *said* to be impossible. Said by people who've never tried it."

"Jewel, you simply can't question the wisdom of generations. One of the first things you learn as a child, almost before you can walk, is: *Keep Away From the Barrens.* It's like learning not to stick your hand into fire, or mess with a wild rat. We wouldn't learn these things if there wasn't good reason to – even when the reasons, as here, are lost deep in time."

"So deep that whatever caused the taboo is known to no one? What if the whole thing is just superstition?"

"That hardly seems likely, since the taboo is so strong."

"What if the conditions that caused the taboo have changed over time, and it's outlived its usefulness?"

Elliott stroked his beard – a sure sign that his daughter had at last got him thinking.

"You're a clever girl, Jewel. You'd argue the tail off a magpie. Once you get your teeth into something, you never let go of it, do you? Mark my words: one of these days it will be your undoing. But – but . . . I have to admit that *this* time you might have a point." He paused for a moment, then went on: "And I have to admit that it goes against the grain of a lifetime's practice to pass up the opportunity of trading at this Fair . . . It sounds like a gold mine . . . I'll tell you what: let's get on the road and weigh up the situation when we reach the edge of the Barrens." He got up from the settle. "I looked in on Smoky earlier. She's fine. You harness her up, and I'll settle the bill."

When the rat saw Jewel, she reared up on her hind legs to greet her; then dropped down again and opened her mouth so that Jewel could drop into it a titbit saved from the breakfast table. Then Jewel scratched the underside of her jaw – a form of attention that gave pleasure to both of them.

"How's my beauty this morning?" Jewel enquired.

Smoky nuzzled into her hands. Her muzzle was moist and cool. She was the sixth rat they'd owned, but the most affectionate. Sometimes it seemed to Jewel she could almost talk, so eloquent were her black, intelligent eyes. She was named for her light grey colouring – a speciality of the breeder from whom they'd bought her.

"We're off to Shelf Fair, Smoky. What do you think about that?"

Smoky uttered a high squeak, as if to say: Fine by me. Jewel backed her between the shafts and harnessed her up. The Ransons' vehicle was a wagon or wheeled van, a kind of closed crate on wheels that kept out the rain. In front was a two-seater box where the driver rode. Inside the wagon were Elliott's stock and his and Jewel's personal effects. On each side, on a green background, the legend **RANSON AND DAUGHTER** stood out boldly in scarlet letters and, beneath this, GARMENTS OF QUALITY. The fact that almost none of Ranson and Daughter's customers would be able to read the words mattered not to Elliott. He couldn't read himself, nor could Jewel. A literate Ranter (itself a rarity) had written the words for him, then he'd painted them himself. It was the *impression* that mattered, not the substance of the thing.

As the girl led Smoky out of the inn yard, Elliott came out carrying their bags, with Mrs Dracup behind him.

"That's a fine animal you've got there," she said appreciatively. "A doe, if my eyes don't deceive me. How old is she?"

"Umm . . . Thirteen months," said Elliott.

"Ever littered, has she?"

"No. We don't have time for that. Though we've had offers for her from ratmen from time to time – for breeding stock."

"I'm not surprised. My husband had a keen eye for a saddle-rat, God rest his soul. Loved the racing, he did."

"Well, time to be off," put in Elliott, before the landlady had time to launch into further reminiscences.

27

Elliott mounted the box and picked up the reins, which Jewel had left hooked over the brake handle; Jewel climbed up beside him. Then, with Mrs Dracup's farewells ringing in their ears, they went rattling off down the road.

It was gone noon the following day before they reached the edge of the Barrens. Rain had thrashed down overnight, making sleep difficult. The sky had cleared during the morning, but a chilly breeze neutralised the rays of the sun.

Jewel and Elliott sat on the box gazing out into the Barrens. But what, in all honesty, could one say there was to see? *Something* certainly, but just as truthfully – *nothing*. All Barrens looked much the same – at least all those that Jewel had seen, and she'd seen plenty of them – and all were equally bare. Here, where one might have expected to see moorland, still bleak perhaps but – to her mind at least – not without a certain beauty, stretched an expanse of white earth. Well, "white" was the word you'd settle for in the absence of a better, but "white" implied colour of a sort, and Barrens were really *no* colour. It was as if some crazy god had hovered over the body of the land and scraped away the skin and flesh of every last natural feature with a massive knife-blade, until only bone was left.

So close to the Barrens – closer than Jewel had ever dared to venture in her life – its width was impossible to estimate. But this morning, sighting the Barrens below as they reached a point where the moor dropped away in a steady slope, they'd paused to climb a convenient rock for a better view. Mrs Dracup had spoken the truth. Away to the north the Barrens was a broad and bulbous clot, a meaty fist, but directly ahead it extended a narrow finger, pointing firmly south and disappearing into the distance. To go all the way round would swallow up a day or more.

Now father and daughter stared in silence. The enormity of what they had in mind to undertake seemed to have robbed them both of speech. Jewel could feel – almost hear – her heart tapping like a soft hammer against her breastbone.

Only Smoky seemed undisturbed by the prospect in front of her. What did she know of Barrens? They were no more than another kind of country to be traversed.

Elliott moistened his lips. "Well, daughter mine, is your mind still set on this thing?"

"Yes, Father. If I back down now, I'll never forget my cowardice."

Elliott smiled. "One man's cowardice is another man's prudence. There will be other fairs. There's still time for us to change our minds."

"Not for me there isn't."

"So be it," he murmured.

She looked at him for a moment, then flung herself into his arms. They held each other tightly.

After a time: "I love you, Father," she said.

"I know. And I love you – more than anything in the world. More, even, than I loved your mother." He kissed her lightly on the forehead.

At last they pulled apart. Elliott gave the reins a shake and the wagon moved forward. Its front wheels rolled onto the Barrens and were followed by its rear. Nothing happened.

On they went.

Still nothing happened.

But the difference between the moorland terrain and that of the Barrens! Luxury after ruggedness! The wagon was rolled forward as if on freshly oiled wheels. The ground seemed almost to propel them ahead.

After a time Elliott said, "Well, it looks as though you were right. There's nothing here to be frightened of."

"What did I tell you?" Jewel grinned. "Old wives' tales – nothing more!"

But now the light intensified. Sunrays bouncing back off the ground? Jewel had never known such brightness. She blinked, and rubbed her eyes. It's hot too, she realised. Morning's chilly breeze had altogether died away. Waves of heat were swimming up from underneath their wheels.

"How hot it is," she said.

"Ignore it," advised Elliott. 'We must be halfway across."

"But look at Smoky!" she exclaimed.

The rat was moving her head in a slow weaving motion. As they watched she stopped dead. She was jerking her body to and fro and squeaking in alarm.

"She's distressed," said Jewel. "I'll see if I can calm her."

She jumped down from the box but fell forward and went sprawling.

Winded, she lay catching her breath. The ground felt odd, both soft and firm at the same time. She'd flung out her arms as she landed, and now, as she pressed against the whiteness, it felt almost springy.

Elliott was calling to her. "Jewel? Are you all right?"

"Yes, I think so," she answered; then got to her feet. She was unharmed – neither bruised nor grazed where her limbs had struck the ground.

She turned to look at Smoky, and the rat was a grey smudge on whiteness, her outline indistinct against the depthless background. Was she still jerking her head? Yes, and squeaking too, though the sound was somehow muffled. Jewel took a step forward and the air appeared to tremble. Light danced before her eyes. The atmosphere seemed flawed, shot through by tiny seams, stitches of sharp brightness that flashed, twisted and disappeared – to materialise elsewhere in her field of vision. Her head had begun to ache.

She stumbled forward to the rat and put a hand on her flank. Reaching Smoky's restless head, she flung an arm around her neck.

"Easy, girl, easy now."

It seemed to work. The rat quietened, pressing against her as if thankful of her presence, until only the occasional twitch conveyed her discomfort.

Elliott's voice seemed to travel to her across a great distance. "Stay with her. Hold the harness. Try and get her moving again."

Jewel murmured in Smoky's ear. And her cajoling seemed to work: the rat shuffled forward again, pulling the wagon behind her. Jewel walked by her side, one hand on her neck. On the elevated box, Elliott sat redundant.

Sparks drifted and jittered in Jewel's restricted field of vision. Her eyes were watering, and she wiped them with her sleeve. But

31

they'd gone no more than a few yards when the rat came to a halt and began to jerk her head again. Jewel tried again to calm her, but the animal shook her off with a sudden heave of her shoulders. As the girl staggered backwards, Smoky got up on her hind legs and uttered a piercing squeal. She was pawing at the hurtful air.

"Father, Father, I can't hold her!" called Jewel desperately.

"All right, girl, I'm coming."

Elliott's head bobbed into view on Smoky's far flank, and together they tried to calm her. But when Elliott grabbed the harness the rat snarled, lowered her head and butted her master in the chest. Elliott tottered backwards and measured his length on the earth.

Then, before Jewel could react, Smoky leapt forward. She was off like a racing rat, making nothing of the wagon's weight. Jewel made to follow, but the wagon's vivid colours jabbed painfully at her eyes.

Her head swam. I'm going to faint, she thought.

Then an arm encircled her waist.

"It's all right, I'm here now." Her father's reassuring voice.

"It's so bright," she cried, "so bright! The air seems to be alive . . ."

"Yes, girl, I see it too."

But it wasn't just tiny faults. Slabs of light flashed and glittered. Rat and wagon had disappeared.

"The wagon," she groaned. "Smoky . . ."

"Don't worry about them. We've got to look to ourselves now. Gird up your loins, girl. We've got to get to the other side."

They moved forward, clutching each other. Unable to bear the dazzle, Jewel shut her eyes. But there it was on their inner side. She forced herself to trudge forwards, lifting one foot, then the other, and setting them down ponderously. They seemed to get heavier step by step, as if weights were stuck to the soles.

All of a sudden, a massive shape rushed at her out of nowhere. As it shot past, narrowly missing her, she lurched to one side, pulling her father to the ground. They fell awkwardly and their heads clashed. They lay for a time, recovering.

"Something came at me," she gasped. "Some weird shape – it was huge."

"I saw it too." Elliott's voice was trembling.

He helped her to her feet. Neither of them was very steady. Elliott's eyes were watering too; damp streaks marked his cheeks.

They got themselves in motion, but hadn't gone far when it happened again. This time, as Jewel shrank back, the shape passed right through her. Her chest and stomach spasmed, as if that part of her had been stretched before snapping back. She ran a hand down her body: it seemed impossibly intact.

And now the shapes came at them thick and fast. She staggered as a succession of violent tremors struck her body.

The two of them sank to the ground, clutching wildly at one another.

"Why did I bring us here?" she wailed, all her resolution gone. "I'm a fool, a little fool."

"That makes two of us," gasped Elliott. "No fool like an old fool."

But the attack seemed to have ceased. Panes of light twisted and slid before their streaming eyes.

"Which way?" she cried. "Which way? How will we ever get out of here?"

"Courage, girl," said her father.

Somehow he got her to her feet and, with his arm around her waist, they lurched along – a pair of drunkards staggering home from a heavy night at the tavern.

We're going to die here, she thought. The sun will burn our flesh away and only our bones will remain . . .

A host of shimmering pillars now came marching towards them, seeming to tower up into the sky. They rammed into and through her body in a bright, relentless succession. Each impact seemed to tear some vital piece from Jewel's body. She was being ripped apart. She gasped for breath, but could find none. Then, from amongst the pillars, a gleaming ghost-animal ten times the size of a rat came bounding towards her. Jaws agape, it leapt at her through the spinning shards of light.

She jerked back and her knees buckled. She felt herself drooping, fainting, slipping away from her father's arm. Merciful darkness swallowed her up.

3

THE PAINTED FEATHER

It was late in the afternoon of the third day following the raid on Wyke when Thorn Jack and Taylor Flood came at last in sight of Norgreen. How peaceful the settlement looked with smoke drifting from its chimneys into a cloud-puffed sky.

Thorn was expecting a hero's welcome. What recent rite-of-passager had brought off so audacious an exploit and returned with such rich spoils? Every boy would admire him, every girl worship him . . . But more than anything else, it was Haw's face he wanted to see when he unwrapped the ruby crystal and announced that it was hers. How radiant she would be! Much as he loved his aunt and uncle, who had always treated their nephew and niece as if they were their own children – the Floods themselves, as it happened, had never produced any offspring – Haw had always held first place in his heart.

He remembered clearly, although at the time he couldn't yet have been four, his mother nursing his infant sister: how Haw would suck away, with closed eyes, at his mother's plump breasts. Later he would stand by her cradle, charged by his mother to rock the baby to sleep. It was his favourite task. Sometimes, a wakeful Haw would guilelessly smile and stretch out a hand which Thorn would take in his own, marvelling at her fingers with their scarcely wrinkled knuckles and tiny pink nails. Haw would gurgle with happiness, and Thorn would smile down at her, feeling grown-up and responsible – just as an elder brother should. He could picture her infant face as if the between-years hadn't passed . . .

Which was more than he could say about his mother's face, to be truthful. Try as he might, he could bring no more of her to mind than a blurred, barely feminised oval lapped by waves of crow-black hair. Yes, her hair – he remembered that; but the shape of her nose or her mouth, or the colour of her eyes . . . No matter how deep he reached into the pit of memory, his mind's fingers closed on nothing – only those undulant swags of hair and the deft way she had of tossing her head to swing them away from her eyes . . . For, taking nothing more than a rucksack, a few clothes and a bow and quiver, his mother had upped and gone when Haw was only three months old. Even now, thoughts of Berry Jack had the power to provoke in Thorn a mix of bewilderment, guilt and resentment. Why had she abandoned him? Why did she hate him so much? In what way had he failed her?

Her disappearance intensified his bond with his little sister. It was true that the infant could hardly have been better provided for: the Headman assigned a wet-nurse to her, a bosomy fusspot called Dolly Puttock who nurtured her well; and then of course there were his aunt and uncle, who did everything they could to make up to the siblings for what circumstances had deprived them of. Still, Thorn's protectiveness towards Haw knew no bounds. Often, moved by some fear which had no rational motivation, he would sit by the sleeping girl until, limp with tiredness, he could barely keep his eyes open, and Taylor had to catch him up and carry him off to bed. When Haw found her feet, and began to toddle about outside, Thorn would follow her at a short distance to make sure she came to no harm. She never did, except once when she tripped over a stone and cut her face. He suspended these attentions only when his aunt finally rounded on him.

"You've got to let Haw have her head," Morry said. "She's got to discover things for herself. She won't come to any harm – people will keep an eye on her." And that was true: in the settlement people looked out for each other's children. Responsibility was communal.

Of his dead father, Thorn harboured no memory whatsoever. Davis Jack had been killed during a hunting expedition when Thorn was two by an arrow whose source was never determined. This was curious, for each hunter marked his arrows in a particular way. But the arrow that passed through Davis Jack's left ear into his brain, killing him instantly, carried no identification. Its fletching was unremarkable. The investigation that followed quickly ruled out the possibility of an accident: each member of the hunt was in view by at least one other, and none had fired a shot at that moment. Could Davis Jack have been murdered by a member of a rival community? This seemed a possibility. Yet there was no clue as to whom the assassin might be or for what reason the killing might have been done.

Everything Thorn knew of his father had been passed on to him by Morry, Taylor or some other Norgreener. What made the greatest single impression on the boy was the fact that his father had been a celebrated hunter, by some distance the finest archer in the settlement. It was said he could hit the eye of a sitting rabbit at fifty paces. When Thorn himself was old enough to take lessons in archery, he applied himself to the task with such ruthless dedication that Taylor – himself an average shot – could only surmise that the boy was trying to please his father's spirit. Not that Taylor believed in spirits: but who could say what might go on in an orphan's head, what forces might drive him, what powers he might feel an obscure need to placate? Happily Thorn had inherited his father's eye and at thirteen he stood out among the lads of his age. Now, as he turned sixteen, there was no finer shot in Norgreen. Exceptionally strong, he could string a full-size bow. He might not hit that rabbit's eye ten times in ten, but he rarely missed its head.

Taylor nodded at the gate-guard. "Peter," he acknowledged.

"Taylor . . . Thorn." Peter returned the nod. "So you're back," he added.

"We are," confirmed Taylor.

Peter was a man of few words. Almost any other inhabitant would immediately have quizzed them about their expedition, but Peter frowned and announced, "The Headman wants to see you both. Tomorrow at the latest."

Norgreen's Headman was Job Tubbs. He'd require a full report on Thorn's rite-of-passage.

Taylor nodded. Peter stood aside, and uncle and nephew went in through the gate.

When they were inside and out of earshot of the guard, Thorn said, "He didn't seem over-pleased to see us."

"That's just Peter being Peter. He can't help the way he is."

Taylor had said this of Peter before, but it didn't satisfy Thorn. He'd expected a lively welcome, not a wet blanket.

It was no better inside the walls. There was no rush of people towards them, no clamour to hear how things had gone. Those they saw acknowledged them quietly, barely uttering a word. Still more strangely, no one smiled: they might have been returning from a wake, or a funeral. A couple of small boys tagged along behind them, trailing them at a distance.

"Something's wrong," said Taylor. "I can sense it."

So could Thorn. He looked round at the children. Their faces were expressionless.

When they were no more than half a dozen paces from the house door, Morry erupted from it, face pale, features drawn from lack of sleep.

"Taylor! Thorn!" she exclaimed. "Thank God you're both back! The most dreadful thing has happened. I can't—"

"Morry, calm yourself," said Taylor, taking his wife by the arm and drawing her into the house.

As he shut the door, Thorn glanced back at the two little boys who'd trailed them. Silently standing against the white wall of the opposite house, they gazed at him with blank faces.

The latch dropped with a click. As he unhooked the straps of his pack, and set it down on the floor, Thorn glanced round the parlour, so familiar, so cosy. Morry hadn't yet lit any lamps (oil was a thing to be conserved), but a lively fire crackled in the grate.

There was the kettle on its hob, its sides blackened from years of use, its forked spout gently steaming. Nothing appeared to be out of place.

Thorn was seized by a sense of dread.

"Haw," he demanded, "is she ill?"

"Oh, Thorn . . ." Morry sank into a chair and burst into tears.

As Taylor knelt by her side and took his wife's hands in his, Thorn moved swiftly out of the room. The one internal door gave on to a dark passage and three bedrooms – his aunt and uncle's, and, opposite one another, his own and Haw's. Without knocking – a courtesy he'd never omitted before – he flung her door open and strode in. The bed was neatly made. Haw was not in her room.

Thorn retraced his steps.

"Haw," he demanded urgently. "Where is she, Morry? Tell me."

Morry looked up at him with tear-stained cheeks. "She's gone, Thorn, gone."

Morry told them what she knew. Two days after they left, Haw went for a walk and never came back. Morry tried her friends' houses. Haw was at none of them. Worried, she went to see Job Tubbs. When neither the duty gate-guard nor the one on watch before him reported her coming in through the gate – though the latter remembered her leaving – the Headman ordered a search. It drew a blank. Much of the night and all next day, search parties combed the surrounding area. Not a sight nor sign of her.

Meanwhile, the Headman began to ask questions, first of Morry, then Haw's friends. What state of mind had Haw been in? Had she been different from normal? A bit tense, Morry told him, but what sister wouldn't be with her brother away coming-of-age?

Could Haw have gone off after her brother? No, she was too sensible for that. She didn't know where he was going and she'd taken nothing with her – nothing was missing from the house.

Haw's a happy girl, said Morry. Popular. Dependable. Punctual. Never in trouble. Though she didn't like the idea, Morry could only think she was lying somewhere hurt, unable to walk.

The Headman's enquiries of Haw's friends drew similar answers: a blank. Meantime the search parties continued, but to no avail. The girl, it seemed, had vanished from the face of the earth.

When Morry had told her story, she burst into tears.

"I'm going to look for her," Thorn announced.

"But it's dark," Morry objected.

"So what? I'll carry a brand."

But it was now teeming with rain. The brand would have gone out before Thorn reached the end of the street.

That night, as rain hammered the windowpane, he lay in bed sleepless, turgid with thought. A variety of explanations for his sister's disappearance crossed and recrossed his mind. Amongst them was this: What if history was repeating itself? What if Haw had followed in her mother's footsteps? His sister was only thirteen, eight years younger than Berry had been when *she* chose to disappear. The notion was irrational, yet it gnawed away at his mind.

What price his triumph at Wyke now? What good was the ruby crystal, tucked away in his bedside cupboard? What good was the gold ring, which tomorrow he was duty bound to hand over to the Headman?

When at last he fitfully slept, it was to dream he was pursuing an elusive figure across a dark plain: from time to time this flitting ghost would be almost within his grasp, only to squirm away from him. He ran on through the featureless landscape, driven by a compulsion that was beyond explanation.

Dawn was breaking when Thorn, with a gruff "Good morning" to the gate-guard, passed out of the settlement. A quiver of arrows was strapped to his back and he carried a longbow. The sky was patched with cloud, but the rain had relented. He went some way down the approach road, then turned off down a narrow path. This was a region of rough grasses and bushes, also some smaller trees. Every plant, every leaf looked drunk with moisture. Dandelions as tall as himself held up their yellow heads in the eternal hope of sunshine. Alder and elder, newly in leaf, towered above his head. White blossom clothed the blackthorn bushes, spattering the dark twigs with clusters of tiny stars. The settlement was out of sight, its position revealed only by the smoke rising up from a clutch of early chimneys.

He went on, the path twisting and turning ahead of him. Rounding a bend, he came to a halt. Squatting no more than twenty paces away, in the middle of the trail, was a young rabbit, its fur a light grey, its height perhaps an inch less than Thorn's. Plainly it had never seen a human being before. Unafraid, it held

42

its position, gazing gormlessly at him from its trusting eyes, its nose gently twitching. He could have put an arrow through its brain then and there, before it could move, but he did nothing of the sort. He wasn't hunting today. In any case, hunters commonly travelled in parties, with pack-rats to carry the kill. Had he shot the creature, its carcass would have been spoiled by predators before he could return with transport. Even a small rabbit had to be properly skinned and butchered before it could be moved. The more you shot, the bigger the load. "What's killed must be carried; kill what you need," ran the maxim, and he'd long since grown out of the childish urge to shoot anything that simply happened to scuttle, hop or fly by. As he stepped forward again, the rabbit turned and, showing its white scut, hopped away into the vegetation.

What am I doing? he asked himself. In the uncertain light of dawn, the notion of searching for Haw seemed little less than ridiculous. What chance had he of finding her when the Headman's search parties had turned up a grand total of nothing? He knew how thorough Job Tubbs was. And if, by some vicious twist of fortune, he *did* find Haw, she would be dead – no doubt about it. It was cruel to contemplate, but he was too familiar with the realities of his world to imagine otherwise.

Yet to lie in bed thinking, or stay at home and sit still . . . Motion's better than immobility, so here he was – moving.

The path forked, and forked again. After a time, he turned off and pushed into the undergrowth. Whippy stalks of this and that tried to poke him in the eye, his trews rapidly got soaked, but he forged on till he came to a stream. Vivid green moss, dotted with small blue flowers, carpeted the bank. Rocks and snags obstructed the current, and water bubbled and chuckled between the low, loamy banks. Picking up a damp twig, he tossed it into the hurrying water where the current took hold of it and bore it off downstream until it stuck behind a stone.

He set off again, tracking the flow. At length the moss petered out. A dense stand of slender reeds many times his own height seemed to block further progress, but he dived into it. The stems rasped and crackled as he pushed resolutely through. When he came out into the open, the stream had expanded into a pool. Bushes and trees fringed it, and here and there rocks, scummed with lichen and furred with moss, had half-heaved themselves out of the water like great grey-skinned beasts before succumbing to sleep. Between two such boulders, barely visible from his position, the stream wound out of sight.

The grassy bank on which he stood had been cropped short by rabbits. He walked along it, scanning the water as if in hope – or fear? – that he would see Haw's body there, caught in a clump of duckweed. But no such horror met his gaze.

This – the emerald pool – was his and Haw's secret place. They'd discovered it years before and – as far as he knew – were its sole human guardians. No one but them came here. Brother and sister concealed its existence with jealous determination.

But today it was ashes in Thorn's mouth. Where was Haw? Until she returned, the pool would merely be a reminder of her absence. *If* she returned. What if she never did?

Abruptly he turned his back on the water. It was then that he saw it – a flash of something in the undergrowth where the cropped grass came to an end.

He walked over and picked it up. It was a young jackdaw's feather, no more than a couple of inches in length. But here was the curious thing – and the reason he'd noticed it: the middle third of the feather had been stained bright yellow – only the top and bottom were the rich blue-black of the natural bird. He thought he knew what it was. When on expeditions or parleys – or, in bad times, raiding or fighting parties – settlement men wore some item as a mark of identification. Norgreeners wore green neckerchiefs of a distinctive design. But if Thorn was right, and this feather was just such an identifier, how did it come to be here, so far off the beaten track? He knelt and studied the ground. Now that he was scanning for signs, he couldn't fail to see them: the undergrowth was trampled where brash feet had forced a way through – and more pairs than one. Haw was here! he thought. What he was looking at was evidence of his sister's abduction.

"Now," said Job Tubbs, "I know you've all studied the feather, and none of you has seen its like. The question is, therefore: how do we find out where it's from?"

It was early afternoon. The Grand Council of Norgreen was in extraordinary session. Clad in their formal jerkins, the six Councillors occupied a circle of chairs. Among their number was Taylor Flood. At their hub was a low table on which lay a carved wooden staff, the Council's symbol of authority. In attendance, sitting to one side of the circle, were Thorn Jack and Morry Flood. But they could only speak if invited to.

Thorn had never attended a Council meeting before. It wasn't unknown for non-members to be invited – or commanded – to sit in on part of a meeting, but rare for one so young to witness an entire session.

On finding the yellow feather, Thorn had taken it to his uncle. Taylor carried off feather and finder to Job Tubbs. The Headman summoned Shaw Flint, Norgreen's foremost tracker. After examining the spot where the feather had been found, Flint declared that Haw had been abducted by three men. The fact that they'd lain in wait for the girl argued foreknowledge of her habits and a carefully laid plan. Flint also tracked the route by which the men had come and gone until it petered out, obliterated by the recent rain. The trail led westwards away from Norgreen in the direction of Judy Wood.

The earlier part of the Council discussion had focused on the identity and motivation of possible kidnappers. But it had proved inconclusive. So now they'd come back to the feather.

"We need to consult someone who's travelled widely," said Drake Hackett. "How about a pedlar?" Drake was a ratman and, like many ratmen, considered a canny fellow. "Or a Ranter, when one calls."

"Good thinking," said Job. "But pedlars and Ranters are both irregular visitors. We may have to wait some time before any turn up – and they may not recognise it then. Time is precious."

"There is *one* man in Norgreen who's well-travelled," mused

Cooper Vetch, a silver-haired man with a reputation for clear thinking. "I'm sure you all know who I mean."

"Yes: Racky Jagger," said Barny Dodds, a Councillor renowned for his bluntness of speech. "Racky's a good man in a scrap, but a bit of a fly-by-night."

"Are you implying that Racky's unreliable, Barny?" questioned Job.

"I wouldn't fancy relying on him myself," was the reply.

"But it's not a case of reliance," Cooper Vetch observed blandly, "it's a case of identification. Surely that's simple enough."

"Is it?" Barny retorted. "I see Racky as the sort who'd say he knows where the feather's from when he hasn't got a clue."

"What a low opinion, Barny, of the human race you have."

"I speak as I find, Cooper Vetch. We're not all as trusting as you."

"I understand where Barny's coming from," said the Headman. "Even so, I think Cooper's idea is a good one. It may be our best shot. And what have we got to lose? Does the Council agree, then, that we call in Racky Jagger?"

Assenting voices only were heard. Even, a touch grudgingly, Barny's.

"Very well. Since this was Cooper Vetch's idea, I depute him to fetch Racky. In the meantime, a short recess."

Racky Jagger! thought Thorn. Now *there's* a surprise . . . But though Racky was an eccentric, he was a man to be reckoned with. Unusually for someone born and bred in Norgreen, he'd travelled a great deal, had in fact (if you believed the stories told about him) seen more of the world than any hundred other men. He'd disappear for months on end, then suddenly turn up again: but exactly what he did during these absences was a mystery: he never talked about them. Racky had never married, preferring casual liaisons with unattached women. He kept a few pigeons, caged, in a corner of the settlement, caring more for them, it seemed, than for any human being. He'd trained the birds to take food from his hand, and when they flocked round him, all you'd see were his head and shoulders as he muttered nothings to them. Before going off on a jaunt, he always made provision for them. Built on the short side, but stocky and muscular, he was a prematurely bald, round-headed individual with a swarthy face (invariably stubbled) and features that courted ugliness. Even so, he attracted women. Perhaps it was his mystique, his hard-bitten quality. Contemptuous of gossip, he fended off the curious with his air of superiority and dry, laconic drawl. Racky must have been with his birds when Cooper Vetch tracked him down, for he brought the whiff of pigeon dung into the Council room. Noses twitched but no one complained. You took Racky as he came.

Racky examined the feather for what seemed a long time. When he spoke, he did so in his characteristic drawl. "Hmm . . . Found, you say, at the spot where the girl was snatched?"

"That's right," the Headman said.

"Looks like a settlement emblem to me. But why on earth would a kidnapper wear an emblem he might drop?"

"Perhaps he always wore it and forgot to take it off."

"A stupid kidnapper, eh? Have you considered the possibility that it was left deliberately – to cause confusion or misdirect identification of the culprits?"

"Yes – but what else have we got to go on?"

"In *my* experience, things aren't always what they seem."

"True – but hardly original. So, Racky: any ideas where this feather might be from?"

Racky pursed his lips. "Something's tweaking the edge of my memory . . . Trouble is, there's a lot of tweakable stuff inside there."

He rubbed his cheek with a calloused hand.

Racky's enjoying this, thought Thorn: it's his moment of importance and he's revelling in it.

Again there was a pause. Racky stared at the feather. Job was opening his mouth to prompt him again when Racky said, "I *have* seen an emblem like this, I'm sure of it. And not just one of them . . . On the road? In some settlement? An inn? Aye, at an inn! It's coming back to me now. I was putting up overnight. There I was with a pot of ale, having just polished off a bowl of excellent stew. There were two parties of fellows in the room as well as the landlord, me, and a few odds and sods. One party was pretty drunk, and they started baiting the other one. You know how men get when they're out on the razzle, and full of themselves. The noisy party wore purple armbands; the others had these black and yellow feathers pinned to their quivers. They were minding their own business and looked a hard-bitten bunch; *I* wouldn't have crossed them. Anyway, for a time the feathers ignored the insults; but then the armbands got personal. You know, so-and-so's parentage, that sort of thing. One of the feathers told them to shut it. But they didn't. A bad mistake, because in the fight the feathers took the armbands apart. It was hand-to-hand stuff; no knives, fortunately. The feathers were outnumbered, maybe four against five, but they beat the armbands up and threw them all out of the inn. Then they sat down, called for more ale and continued their conversation as if nothing had happened. I had another drink and went off to my room."

This was the longest speech anyone had ever heard Racky deliver, but he'd told his story well. Thorn was impressed by the prowess of the yellow-feathered men. But then he thought: they took my sister! And his face became grim.

"Do you remember where this happened?" was the Headman's next question.

Racky scratched his head. "I think, yes, I'm pretty sure – the inn was on the Lowmoor road – way on the other side of Judy."

Judy – Judy Wood! *There* was a name to conjure with! Every child in Norgreen had heard tales of Judy Wood – tales of magic and savage animals, monstrous humans, ghosts and gremlins. Children were taught two things: stay clear of the Barrens, and never go near Judy Wood. The Wood had an evil reputation. To the west and to the north it stood gigantic and threatening – a darkly forbidding barrier. But travellers must pass through it – pedlars and Ranters, he supposed. As for Lowmoor, Thorn of course had come across the name, but Lowmoor was so far off it might as well have been on the moon.

Job Tubbs said, "So – were these men from Lowmoor?"

"No," Racky replied. "I've been to Lowmoor, and their

50

emblem's different. But they're from somewhere beyond Judy. Next morning, I asked the landlord – pretty casually, like – who the feathered men were. He'd been friendly up to then, but straightaway he became shifty. He said he'd never seen them before. He was lying. Why? Who knows? Prudence, perhaps? Fear? He didn't want to talk about them."

"And now, it seems, they've abducted Haw . . . And far from their home country . . . This is a puzzle indeed. Racky: any notion why they might have taken the girl?"

"I'm as puzzled as you are, Headman. *If* these men are responsible. There's no proof of that yet."

"That's true, Racky . . . Well, please take a seat with our other guests while we debate what response we might make to what you've said."

Racky sat down close to Thorn, wafting a strong smell of pigeon muck in the young man's direction. Thorn glanced at him, and Racky looked back. A corner of his lip twitched; then he turned his face away.

A fresh debate began. Taylor Flood, speaking with passion, proposed an immediate expedition: a strong, well-armed party to travel through Judy Wood and track down the kidnappers. Yes, thought Thorn: that's the thing – and I'll be one of them. But Taylor, it appeared, was in a minority of one. Led by Barny Dodds, the other Councillors counselled caution. Far too many unknown factors surrounded this issue. With all due respect to him, what Racky had said was vague. Could the settlement commit a large party on such thin evidence? It might turn out a wild duck chase. And was it wise at this time? Could Norgreen afford to reduce its manpower, denude its defences? And when Job Tubbs had his say, he took the view of the majority.

"Very well," declared Taylor, "I'll go alone, if I must."

Job Tubbs nodded. "Fair enough. You're the girl's guardian."

It was then that Thorn stood up.

"Haw is *my* sister," he said, his voice booming with pride: "I also claim the right to go."

"No, Thorn," exclaimed Morry, quickly rising to her feet. "It's far too dangerous."

"You forget, Aunt," Thorn replied, "that I'm a man now. I can choose my own way."

"He's right, Morry Flood," said the Headman. "I can't stop your nephew going and wouldn't choose to if I could."

"Then Thorn and I will go," said his uncle. "So be it."

"But the two of you will be travelling into unknown country. You are in need of a guide. Racky Jagger, you are the only man with the knowledge this task requires. Are you willing to be this guide?"

Racky grinned. "With respect to the Council and my fellow guests here, none of you can appreciate what this undertaking involves."

"But *you* do," said Taylor.

"You flatter me. I've no idea what we'll be up against."

"Yes or no, Racky Jagger," persisted the Headman. "You have the right to refuse. No one will think the less of you if you do."

"Is that right?" Racky's reply was heavy with irony. "Well, I'll say one thing: my curiosity's aroused. And when my curiosity gets aroused, it's the devil. If you'll guarantee my birds will be looked after, Headman . . ."

"You can be sure of that, Racky."

"Then I'll go."

There it was. The departure was fixed for the following morning, which would give the three men time to make preparations. As Thorn followed his aunt and uncle out of the Council room, he felt tense with anticipation. Judy Wood! And somewhere, invisible, Haw – and the yellow-feathered men . . .

"Don't forget to say goodbye as if you mean it, Thorn Jack."

Thorn turned to look at Racky Jagger.

Racky's mouth twisted in an unreadable smile. "It may be a long time, lad, before you're back – if you ever are."

4

A CHALLENGE FROM
RED THE RUTHLESS

Jewel opened her eyes. A dark shape hovered above her. Then something touched her forehead. It was cold and refreshed her.

"Jewel? Speak to me, girl!"

The dark shape defined itself. A familiar face hovered above her.

"Father . . . I'm so thirsty . . ."

Her voice was dry, reedy.

"Here, daughter: drink this."

Supporting her head and shoulders, he held a cup to her lips. She sipped the liquid, cool in her throat. Trickles escaped down her chin.

"Father, where are we?"

Elliott smiled. "We did it, Jewel – the impossible! We crossed the haunted Barrens!"

"But I fainted – I fell. How –"

"– did we get across? Listen. When you fainted I held onto you, but we finished up on the ground. And finished is how I felt. My body felt cut to ribbons. I thought I'd never get up again. I wanted to shut my eyes and sleep. But then the strangest thing happened. I heard this voice. 'You idle devil!' it said. 'What do you think you're doing down there?' Would you believe it, it was my father, though he's been dead these many years. His face was blurred, his outline wavered, but there was no mistaking him. He was as mad at me as I've seen him. 'Get up, you good-for-nothing! The world's a-waiting,' he said. Then he pointed at you. 'Look at this poor girl here. Call yourself a father? I brought you up to show gumption, not to be soft as a marshmallow!' He thrust his face into mine. It was so bright I could hardly bear it. He said, 'There's nothing wrong with you!' I was minded to protest, but he looked so incensed I didn't dare to say a word. He said, 'Get up and follow me.'

"Well, somehow I did. I lifted you up, off my father went and I staggered after him – this blurry shape made of light. It was weird, to say the least. Those marching pillars came at me again, but I stayed on my feet and kept going. Whenever I felt like collapsing, he'd turn back and glare at me. I started to wonder if I'd gone mad, or if the whole thing was a dream and any moment I'd wake up. Just one more step, I told myself. I took that step, I kept moving. Then the strange shapes were gone and I could see the edge of the Barrens. I pretty much fell over it, and passed out for a bit. Then I came to. And here we are."

Jewel threw her arms around Elliott's neck. "Oh, Father," she said, "you're a hero, truly."

Elliott chuckled. "Funny kind of a hero, if you ask me," he replied. "But you, love, how are you?"

She thought, I ought to be cut to pieces, but I can't feel any pain. "I feel fine," she said. "Fine."

"That's wonderful," he said.

"But the wagon – we've lost the wagon!"

"No we haven't. It's here – Smoky too."

"Smoky? But—"

"Yes. She was waiting. Calm as you like, right as rain. The wagon's not damaged at all. Now we shall make it to Shelf Fair!"

"Shelf Fair . . ."

"Yes. We can reach Shelf by nightfall. And tomorrow – rich pickings! Rich pickings, I'll be bound!" He touched her cheek with his fingers. "Rest a little, gather your strength. We'll have ourselves a bite to eat and then get on our way. Mrs Dracup told me there's an inn not far from the fairground: the Dewdrop, it's called. Let's see if they've some room."

A little later, as she nibbled a piece of bread, images from the Barrens began to come back to her. She saw, on memory's bright screen, the forms that had plagued her – the bright seams, the panels of light, the blocky shapes, the pillars; and last of all, and most terrifying, that monstrous, bounding creature. Her body remembered, too, the way the shapes had passed through her, each one with its sharp spasm; how, towards the end, each impact had seemed to tear something away, some vital thing, as if unmaking her. She shivered with remembrance. She could make no sense of it all. Yet she was sure of three things: that, as long as she lived, she would never forget the Barrens; that she would never speak of their crossing; and that all the gold in the world would never induce her to set foot on that bland, smooth, deceptively inviting surface again.

The light was failing by the time they drew up at the Dewdrop, one of the biggest inns Jewel had come across. Yet it was full, as they quickly found. People were sleeping three to a bed. First Fair of the year, said the landlord, it was always this way. No matter what the weather, people turned up in their droves. Everyone roistering, eating, drinking, keen to wring the last drop of pleasure from two nights and a day. And flinging about, enquired Elliott, their hard-come-by silver? That too, said the landlord. The trader's eyes lit up.

No soft beds tonight, then. But behind the inn, the landlord said, is a high-walled grassy yard; you can pitch your tent in that. And the Dewdrop had a rattery. When, amongst other rigs and tents, they'd sited the wagon, Jewel took Smoky there. The ratman seemed a caring sort; his stalls were clean and well-aired, with fresh bedding on the floor. Jewel gave Smoky into his charge.

After today, she'd have been content to settle for a quiet meal and climb into her sleeping bag, but her father would have none of it. They'd eat supper in the inn, then take a turn round the fairground, size things up, look out a good pitch for tomorrow.

Every public room was crowded. Nowhere a seat to be seen. But a chubby, red-cheeked woman on the end of a long settle took pity on Jewel.

"Sit yourself down by me, my love, you look proper worn out. Is this your father? You as well, sir. We can make room for two."

The man sitting next to her didn't look as if he agreed, but the woman would brook no opposition.

"Move your backside, Tom Snaffle, let these good people sit down."

Tom Snaffle grumbled, but indicated to the woman next to him to move along. The signal echoed down the row. Half a dozen people shifted, leaving just enough space on the end of the settle for the new arrivals to squeeze in. Elliott had already ordered their meal: game pie. And here it came, crisp and brown, piping hot and pungent. Jewel thought she'd never smelt anything quite so good, and attacked it forthwith – but she had to hold off, it was so hot. She watched the steam coming off it. The woman next to her laughed, and elbowed Jewel amiably.

"Makes a fine game pie, does Mrs Beck, but beware! If you're not careful, it'll have the roof right off your mouth." She laughed again.

After a cautionary wait, Jewel and Elliott tucked in. The pies were delicious: nuggets of meat in a rich gravy, laced with herbs, carrot and onion. They came with chunks of grainy bread and cubes of boiled potato.

Jewel had eaten all she could when their benefactress, who'd been studying her face, said, "I don't believe I've seen you before, love. I never forget a face – specially one as nice as yours. I'm local myself. Come far, have you?"

Jewel blushed at the compliment. It was Elliott who replied.

"Yes, indeed. A long way."

"Where are you from originally? Anywhere I know?"

Elliott laughed. "I wish I could tell you, madam, but to be honest I don't know."

"Don't know where you're from?" she said with amazement, and nudged the man next to her. "Do you hear that, Tom Snaffle? He doesn't know where he's from!"

"Doesn't know where he's from?"

"That's what I said, you duck egg. This here's my husband," she told Jewel. "Never once had a thought of his own. But that's all right – I've got plenty!" She laughed again.

Her husband looked peeved, but said nothing. Jewel thought that Tom Snaffle would do as he was told. Unlike her father, who would only ever do what suited him.

"So you're from nowhere," said Mrs Snaffle. "Come on – explain yourself."

"The explanation's simple. I'm a trader. My father was a trader. All traders come from nowhere."

"Come from Nowhere?" said the man opposite. He had an heroic wart on his chin, from which spurted a tuft of hairs. "That's impossible. No such place!" He laughed at his own wit, and Mrs Snaffle joined in.

"But that's not true," she said. "My Tom's been Nowhere many a time. He'll be there tomorrow morning, when he comes round after the bevies he's getting down himself tonight."

The whole table laughed at this, including Elliott and Jewel and the butt of the joke himself. His wife was dangerously infectious. All attention round the table was now focused on this end.

"Allow me to introduce myself." The merchant downed his fork. "My name's Elliott Ranson. This is my only daughter, Jewel."

"Jewel. What a lovely name," asserted Mrs Snaffle.

"She's your jewel then, isn't she!" announced Tom Snaffle triumphantly, and guffawed.

No one else thought this funny. Tom's grin quickly subsided.

"My name's Maddy," said his wife. And she proceeded to introduce the other people around the table. There were too many names to remember, and Jewel took in only two – those of the couple opposite. The man with the wart was Dunk Stott, the woman next to him Rona Futtock. Rona kept her arm entwined with Dunk's, proprietorially. She had a mole high on her right cheek. They were well matched, thought Jewel.

"So, now," said Maddy Snaffle, "you'll have a stall at the Fair tomorrow. And what is it you sell?"

"What is it you want?" asked Elliott boldly.

"Everything!" announced Maddy Snaffle decisively.

"Damn!" said Elliott. "That's the one thing I haven't got. But I'll order it for you. Then the next time I come round . . ."

"It'll be too late then. I want it now. Immediately."

"Well, much as it pains me to have to disappoint a lady . . ."

"Come on, now," said a man down at the far end of the table. "Drink up. It's my shout." He waved at the landlord, who sent one of his tapsters over. "The same all round," said the man. "And a drink there for Mr Ranson. And his daughter, if she'll have one."

Elliott asked for a beer, Jewel for an apple juice.

"You still haven't told us what you sell," said Maddy Snaffle.

"I never mix business with pleasure," said Elliott. "Rule of the road."

This was a fib, as Jewel well knew. Her father often mixed the two – more often than not, if truth were told. But traders weren't overmuch concerned with truth. He was playing hard to get, an old stratagem of his: whet their appetites, get them hooked.

"Oh, go on, give us an idea," implored Maddy.

"All I *will* say," Elliot said, as if relenting reluctantly, "is that I have an item in stock that would beautifully complement the rare colour of your eyes." He switched his gaze to Rona Futtock. "And for you, a little something that would set your hair off to perfection. Not that it needs it, of course."

You old charmer, thought Jewel. Trust you to pick on Mrs Futtock's best attribute.

"Indeed, I have something for everyone. But that's enough of that." And though pressed, he resolutely refused to say any more, other than: "Visit my stall tomorrow. RANSON AND DAUGHTER – GARMENTS OF QUALITY. Then you'll see."

He fell to asking questions about the Fair and the sort of people who frequented it, and Shelf settlement itself. Again Jewel recognised the tactic: he was doing what a good trader ought to do – gathering as much information about his customers as possible. The people around the table were keen to answer: they were, after all, talking about themselves, and most people are happy to do that, especially when their tongues have been loosened by a drop of hooch. Her mind wandered.

Suddenly people were rising to their feet. But it was early yet! Then she realised what was happening: they were off to the Fair.

Her father was speaking to her, "Come along, Jewel, time to have a look at the site."

Maddy Snaffle examined her.

"The fresh air will do you good, love. You come along with us. We know how to enjoy ourselves."

Outside, Jewel found herself strolling along with Maddy – herself on one of Maddy's arms, Tom Snaffle on the other. It occurred to her to wonder if the Snaffles had any children. But they'd be grown up by now, married with children of their own. Why hadn't she asked? She would if an appropriate moment presented itself.

The fairground was midway between the inn and Shelf settlement. If Jewel had been listening to the earlier conversation, she'd have known that Shelf was a community of around five hundred souls. Now that it was dark, the settlement couldn't be seen, but the fairground was lit everywhere by brands attached to poles or to the fronts of stalls and booths. At this time of night, no traders were to be seen. That would all change tomorrow; evening was traditionally a time for amusement.

Jewel had seen a good number of Fairs in her life, and their colourful, transient alleys never failed to lift her heart. Besides the atmosphere, the spectacle, she relished the sense of freedom the pleasure-seekers radiated. For one or two nights the shackles that bound them to their hard lives were off, and they could enter another world. Jewel knew well enough that there was fakery about: crooks whose sole aim was to con people out of their money. But fools and their gold are soon parted, as the saying goes. (Begging the question: How do fools come by gold in the first place?)

The first booths offered a series of cheap amusements: a penny-roll, a Hook the Duck, a Test Your Strength – that sort of thing. They were crowded with children. Further on, they came to some larger-scale attractions. Here was a shy: knock a target off a post with a wooden ball and win a prize. The men in their party decided to take up the challenge.

Elliott caught Jewel's free arm. "I'm going to take a look around. You stay here and have fun. I'll catch you up later."

He slipped away. Jewel watched the valiant efforts of her new friends. By luck or judgement, Tom Snaffle was the only one of them to succeed. He came glowing back to Maddy and presented her with a wooden bowl.

"That's my man!" said Maddy, and gave him a big, sloppy kiss.

Further along was a skittle-alley. The party decided to have a match. They were twelve in number, so that made two teams of six. Each contestant would have one roll. In Jewel's team were Maddy, Tom, Rona, Dunk and a man known as Rivet. Jewel, the tradesman's daughter, was deputed to keep score. She was as good at skittles as arithmetic, and scored nine out of ten. Only one other person (from the opposition) did as well. The competition was close, and the lead changed continually. Rivet was last of all to shoot. He needed seven to win. His ball clattered into the skittles, taking six out cleanly and leaving a seventh teetering. It looked as though it would right itself, but Jewel willed it to fall – and behold! It toppled over! They had won! The losing team bought them toffee treats from a nearby stall – but, of course, they had some too.

In the next lane they paused to watch a man sitting at a small table who was striving valiantly to "Find the Mistress", but the card-sharp's hands were too clever for him. The mark banged the table in his frustration, jumped up and strode away. Tom Snaffle would have sat down, but Maddy drew him away.

"There are better ways, love, of throwing your money away than that."

And now they were nearing the heart of the Fair. Here a number of sideshows featured human exhibits: among them a Luscious Eyeful, a Fat Lady, a Bearded Lady, and a human freak show. The party divided: the women to see the Fat Lady, the men the Luscious Eyeful. Enclosed in a rope ring, the Fat Lady occupied a stout, gilded throne, gazing balefully at the people walking round her, their eyes popping. Her flesh, astonishingly white, and even – to Jewel's mind – beautiful, bulged off her in swags and rolls. Were she to rise to her feet and walk, she'd wobble just like a gigantic jelly.

Next, some of the party opted to see the freak show, but Jewel stayed outside. She knew what such shows contained, and couldn't bear to think of the freaks trapped in their disfigurements, never mind gawp at them.

The open space at the hub of the Fair contained a host of attractions. There were three tumblers, a juggler, a fire-eater, a knife-swallower and, most arresting of all, a man who devoured glass. Glass not being easy to come by, he'd brought his own supply. If you purchased a piece from him, he undertook to eat it. People winced as he crunched up the glass and swallowed it down. You'd have thought he'd be cut to ribbons, but he seemed none the worse. He grinned, then amazed the crowd by gouging out his left eye. He held it up for all to see. The eye was made of glass! He would swallow and regurgitate it for a certain price, he announced. Keen to see this feat, people clubbed together to make up the fee. Pocketing the cash, the man tossed his eye in the air, opened his mouth and caught it again. His Adam's apple jerked: had it gone down his throat? He went round the audience, displaying his empty mouth. No, there was nothing under his tongue. Then he stood with hands on hips and, with a single mighty convulsion, vomited up his eyeball. He thrust it towards Jewel. There it lay, stickily glistening in the palm of his hand, insolently fixing the girl with its disembodied gaze until its owner whisked it away.

"Now I've seen everything," declared Maddy Snaffle, delighted and horrified.

The next performer to absorb Jewel's attention was the juggler – a good-looking young woman. She juggled balls, clubs and fiery batons, sometimes in combination. She threw them up from between her legs, over her shoulders and under her arms. She caught them at chest height, and behind her back. Once she seemed to lose track of one but, miraculously recovering, caught it just above the ground. Her wink told the audience the move had been planned. At length she announced that for her next manoeuvre, she required assistance – one member of the audience, please. When no one came forward, she called, "Hey, pretty girl over there!" Jewel looked round for the pretty girl, but there were no girls behind her. It was Jewel the juggler meant. Uncertainly she stepped forward. The woman gave her five silvery clubs and quickly whispered instructions. Jewel had to stand at a certain distance and, on a spoken command, throw her the clubs one by one. The task would have reduced most people to bundles of nerves, but the juggler had chosen well. Jewel was used to standing in front of people and keeping calm. One by one, as ordered, she tossed the clubs to the juggler, who then caught them deftly and incorporated them into the whirling fountain before her. To finish, she caught four clubs and lobbed the fifth to Jewel. The girl hadn't been expecting this, but fielded the club one-handed. The crowd applauded enthusiastically. "You're a natural," said the young woman. Jewel returned her smile, and dropped a coin into her bag. It seemed to be filling nicely.

The next alley was dominated by a boxing booth. Outside, a barker was at work: "Roll up, ladies and gentlemen. Tonight the Champion of Champions, veteran of a thousand bouts, fearsome and fearless, will take on all-comers for – yes! – a purse of gold."

A good-sized queue had formed. Unseen inside the gaily-striped, red and white marquee, people, clearly stirred, could be heard shouting and whistling.

"Why the excitement, Dipper?" Dunk Stott asked a man in the queue.

"It's Mick Flitch," said the man. "He's gone and challenged the Champion!"

"This we must see," said Dunk.

They joined the queue, paid their money and entered the booth. In the ring, Mick Flitch, button-nosed, stripped to the waist and loudly cheered by the crowd, was donning a pair of black gloves. He was young and well muscled, and looked full of himself. The Champion of Champions stood by the ropes, tattooed arms folded, staring slack-jawed down at the crowd. He had a pot belly, a broken nose, and two entirely dissimilar ears that vied in exoticism.

"Mick'll have him for breakfast," said a confident Tom Snaffle. "I've seen him fight; he's a holy terror."

"No, he won't," said his wife. "That bruiser will soon have him flat on his back."

"Rubbish," snorted Tom. "The Champion's living on borrowed time."

The MC introduced the fighters. In the blue corner, Mick Flitch, otherwise known as the Shelf Shaker. In the red corner, Dan Block, Champion of Champions.

The bout began. The Shelf Shaker clearly knew what he was at. He ducked and wove, jabbing away at the Champion's face with quick, rangy lefts whilst protecting himself with his right. The Champion moved clumsily, not doing much at all. When the first round came to an end, the crowd jeered the Champion back to his corner, where his second splashed water on his puce, perspiring mug. The Shelf Shaker strutted about, milking the crowd's enthusiasm.

The second round started similarly. But after Mick Flitch had landed a stinging left to the Champion's face, Dan Block woke up. He charged straight at the local man, swung his meaty right arm and hit Mick with a haymaker high up on the forehead. Mick flew backwards, bounced off the ropes and dropped to the canvas like a sack. Breathing heavily, the Champion of Champions gazed down at him for a moment, then sauntered back to his corner while the referee counted Mick out. If someone had dropped a pin then, you'd have heard it.

The MC re-entered the ring. "A big hand for the Shelf

Shaker!" Mick was helped to his feet. His eyes were rolling around in his head. He was away in dreamland.

"And now," continued the MC, "who will be the next to challenge the Champion of Champions? The purse stands at THREE GOLD PIECES!"

"He's got to be joking," said Tom Snaffle. "Nobody's going to go in there after what we've just seen."

He was wrong. Climbing into the ring was a man with flame-red, shoulder-length hair. He was dressed in a long black coat and had a silver stud in one ear.

"Me next, chief," he told the MC, and started to strip off his clothes, revealing a lithe but scarcely imposing torso.

A murmur went round the crowd. Who was this man? No one seemed to know. Not local, that was for sure.

Then Rona pointed: "Look there!"

A second man had appeared at the challenger's corner of the ring. He began to talk over the ropes with the flame-haired man. Their features were identical, but the second man's hair was blond. Later, Jewel would notice he wore his stud in the opposite ear.

"They must be twins, surely," said Rona.

"Sweetie, I think you're right," said Dunk.

But the MC's introductions left nobody any the wiser. The new challenger was billed as Red the Ruthless. Tom Snaffle was unimpressed.

"He hasn't a chance," he opined. "Look at his body: not a patch on Mick's."

"Wait and see," said his wife. "There's more to this fellow than meets the eye."

"In your dreams," said her husband.

The bout began. The two men moved warily around one another. Whatever you might say about Dan Block, he was cautious. But when the challenger seemed uninterested in throwing a punch, indeed to have nothing to offer, he became bolder. He landed a flurry of punches to the body of Red the Ruthless, who stepped back, winded. The Champion pinned Red against the ropes, and closed in for the kill.

What happened next happened fast. Red threw his arms around Dan and hugged him close. Their heads merged into one. There was an agonised shriek. Then Dan was staggering backwards, his gloves clutching his head. Red was swiftly after him; he struck with a low punch. As Dan sagged forwards, Red followed up with an uppercut right on the point of the Champion's chin. Dan's head snapped back. Then he crumpled forwards and slammed into the canvas like a block of wood. A Dan Block of wood, thought Jewel, oh dear! The referee stared down at the ex-Champion of Champions as if he couldn't believe his eyes; then, belatedly remembering his role, counted him out.

As this was happening, Jewel was watching Red, not Dan, on whom most eyes were fixed. He turned his head to one side and spat something out of his mouth. Then he walked to his corner, grinned down at his second self, and climbed out of the ring.

As the counting finished the noise began – a pandemonium in which cheers and boos were mixed in pretty equal quantities. As Jewel watched, the two men converged on the MC. It seemed as if the latter was reluctant to yield up the purse, but when the blond seized him by his collar and whispered in his ear, he put his hand in his pocket, pulled out a small bag and gave it to Red. Red quickly checked its contents, nodded to the blond man, and slipped it into his shirt. Jewel watched their heads bob away through the crowd. Then they were lost to view.

As the crowd dispersed outside the booth, Jewel looked round for her father. He was nowhere to be seen.

"I think that's it," said Tom Snaffle. "Who's for a drink?"

Everybody, it seemed.

"Right, back to the Dewdrop, then."

Maddy took Jewel's arm. "Come on, love, come back with us. Perhaps your father's at the inn."

All the talk on the way back was about the two fights they'd seen. Tom argued that Mick Flitch had been unlucky: he was out-boxing the champion when a lucky blow got him.

"If you believe that, you'll believe anything," was his wife's sarcastic comment.

Opinions differed as to what exactly had happened at the climax of the second bout. Why had Dan Block shrieked and staggered backwards, so fatally leaving himself wide open to attack?

"Red nutted him," said Dunk.

"Kneed him in the groin," said Rivet.

"Gave him a kiss," said someone else.

"You're all wrong," said Jewel. "He bit a piece out of his ear. I saw him spit it onto the floor."

This stunned everybody, until Maddy came out with: "Well, it *was* an inviting target. I've never seen such ears!"

Everybody laughed.

"What a callous woman you are," said Tom Snaffle admiringly.

"What sort of a monster would do that?" asked Rona Futtock.

"It's the red hair," said someone jestingly. "Never trust a redhead. They're completely unpredictable."

Rona flared up immediately – or pretended to. There was outrage and assent and a rush of stories about redheads. This passed the time pleasantly while they walked to the inn.

The Dewdrop was only a smidgen less busy than before. Jewel went from snug to snug looking for her father, but he wasn't to be seen. Well, she was tired, she'd go to bed. She said fond goodnights to the Snaffles ("We'll see you tomorrow, love," promised Maddy) and the rest of her new acquaintances, then made her way to the tent.

She wasn't concerned about Elliott. He sometimes disappeared like this. She had an idea what he was up to. He'd be here come morning.

She climbed inside her sleeping bag. It had been an amazing day. She didn't suppose she'd see its like no matter how long she lived. She fell asleep. In her dreams she wandered among a vague swirl of glass-eaters, fire-eaters, tumblers, jugglers and knife-swallowers. At last she found herself face to face with a man with red hair. He pulled a whole, enormous ear from his mouth and winked at her.

5

GIFTS FROM A SYB

It was mid-afternoon when the knock came at the door: three light taps, as if administered by the knuckles of a child. Taylor was out, gathering supplies; Morry and Thorn were trying to decide how much he could carry and what he should take.

It was Thorn who opened the door.

"Daisy Du— *Dutton*!" he said, correcting himself in the nick of time.

The young woman was thin to the point of emaciation. Under short mouse-brown hair, her pinched face contained a snub nose, a small mouth, tiny ears and two luminous eyes – eyes that were out of kilter with the rest of the assemblage. She had a way of looking at you askance that could be unnerving. Thorn had almost addressed her by the name Daisy Dumb – the name she'd earned in school, where her mind seemed anywhere but focused on her lessons, words hardly ever made their way through her lips, and "dumb" signified not only silent, but stupid. Like Thorn, she was an orphan. An outbreak of fever had claimed her parents when she was twelve. But unlike Thorn, Daisy had no kin to bring her up. To everyone's surprise, Minny Pickles, Norgreen's Syb, had taken her under her wing. Minny had no children of her own and needed, she gave people to understand, an assistant. Nobody thought the arrangement would last, but time went by and Minny and Daisy seemed perfectly happy with one another. Daisy, Thorn reckoned, must now be eighteen or nineteen, and had for a while carried out a number of the Syb's more public functions, such as ministering to the sick. Minny was getting old, and found walking increasingly difficult – especially in the winter months when older people's joints had a habit of seizing up. People had jibbed a little to begin with about following Daisy's somewhat peremptory instructions (she hadn't yet developed much in the way of a bedside manner), but when they proved to be perfectly sound, she grew in everyone's estimation. She was getting to be indispensable, and her nickname had long since ceased to be appropriate. But it stuck to her all the same, as nicknames do.

Head a little on one side, Daisy was favouring Thorn with one of her searching stares.

"Well," he said, "what can I do for you?"

"*You* can't do *anything* for *me*, Thorn Jack." Daisy paused, as if for effect. She'd spoken slowly as always, giving certain words particular emphasis. "*Minny* wants to see you. *Now*," she added, forcefully.

"*Minny?*" Thorn exclaimed, straightaway catching the habit. "*Minny* wants to see *me*? What about?"

But Daisy had already turned on her heel and was walking away. Thorn pulled a jacket on and hurried after her.

Minny and Daisy lived in a house just outside the settlement. It had belonged to a ratman, a fellow more at home with creatures of four legs than two. Thorn was about to knock when the door swung open.

"Come in," said Daisy Dutton.

As Thorn followed the Syb's assistant through the front door, the smell of herbs assailed his nostrils. The room was wonderfully cluttered. Cloudy festoons and leafy sprays hung dangling from the ceiling. Pots and bottles filled tables and shelves. Minny was a whiz with all kinds of jams and preserves: Pickles' pickles, as some were known. Larger kegs stood on the floor. Bowls, mortars and pestles, and other utensils and tools lay scattered about on a long table. Thorn had been here thrice before: the last time to collect an obscure potion for his aunt.

A fire leapt in the hearth. Minny sat near it in a chair, black shawl around her shoulders. Her long green skirt trailed on the floor. An empty chair faced her own.

"Sit yourself down, Thorn Jack," she said.

"You wanted to see me?" he enquired.

"You'll take a drop of elderberry wine."

This was not a question. From what looked like a heavy keg, Daisy poured two generous measures. Thorn got one mug, Minny the other. Daisy sat and transfixed him with her shining, exquisite eyes.

The Syb saluted her visitor. "Here's to your journey, Thorn Jack. May sunset never leave you with an empty stomach or an aching heart." They drank. "Though I fear," Minny added dryly, "that you won't be so lucky."

She gazed at Thorn. If eyes were knives, and could peel you bare . . .

No one knew how old Minny was or where she was from. She'd fetched up in the settlement thirty or more years before and taken a liking to the place. Norgreen's previous Syb had left in a huff a month before, after some not unfounded criticism of her medical abilities and her fondness for the bottle. Minny had been made welcome: Sybs didn't grow on trees. Quickly she demonstrated a mastery of herbal lore. Not only that: she possessed an uncanny sixth sense. She'd sometimes turn up at your door before you'd even sent for her, miraculously anticipating your need of her services.

Minny's figure was puddinglike, with plump arms and stocky legs – the latter most often (as now) out of sight beneath her skirt. Her grey hair was tied in a bun, but strands had escaped her attentions to straggle out over her forehead. Her face was puffy, her nose lumpy, her skin pale and blotched and, between her nose and upper lip, tightened by age and fuzzed with hair. All her life was in her brown eyes, which were liquid and penetrating: she might, perhaps, be short-sighted with the years.

"Well, Thorn Jack," she said at last, "you're turning out a fine young man. You'll be a big hit with the ladies." She chuckled wickedly, then switched on a stern look. "If, of course, you're alive then."

"Why shouldn't I be?" asked Thorn, somewhat thrown by this sally.

"Every possible event buds in destiny's deep womb," answered the Syb portentously. "Who knows why this thing comes to pass and that thing does not?"

Typical Syb-talk, thought Thorn. "But surely," he insisted, "at any given moment only one thing comes into being."

"So far as we know; but then, what do we know? If knowledge were water, scarcely enough to fill a thimble."

She's playing games with me, he thought. Why can't she tell me something useful, instead of talking in riddles?

"But *you*'ve no use for tricksy talk, have you, Thorn Jack?"

God, she's reading my mind.

"Tell me: what do you think of my elderberry wine?"

Thorn took another sip and swilled the liquid round his tongue.

"It's very good," he answered truthfully, "the best I've ever tasted. Funny, it's sweet on the tongue, but the aftertaste is dry."

"That's how it's meant to be. Sadly, too much of life follows the same pattern." The Syb took a sip from her mug. "So," she resumed, "the two of you leave first thing tomorrow."

"The two of us? I'm afraid, Minny Pickles, that for once you're ill-informed. There are three of us in the party – myself, my uncle and our guide Racky Jagger."

The Syb sniffed.

"If you say so, Thorn Jack. Well, I've got a few things for you." She motioned to Daisy, who fetched a cloth pouch from a shelf and handed it to the visitor.

"Empty it," said the Syb. "It won't bite."

Thorn reached into the pouch and took out a small, bulbous bottle filled with clear liquid. Then came a wooden box that rattled; one of its narrow edges possessed an oddly rough surface. Third was a curious object forged from silvery metal: it was tubular, long and thin, narrow at one end and round at the other; attached to it was a green ribbon. Last out, and the largest item, was a wrap of cloth containing a bundle of three brands. He thought of the Wykers, and how they'd pursued him and his uncle just days before. He'd handled such things himself, of course, but the stuff on the business ends of these particular examples wasn't like any he'd ever seen. It was dry, not tarry to the touch as it normally was, and of an unusual colour.

"Those, as you correctly guess, are brands," said the Syb. "Or, to give them the name I prefer, *links*. But they're special, they're long-burners. They'll come in handy when you find yourself in a tight spot. But remember: use them only with the earth above your head."

"With the earth above my head?"

"Your hearing is perfect, Thorn Jack. Ah, the wonder of youth! If I had ears as sharp as yours!" Thorn thought the Syb's hearing was quite good enough. He suspected she could hear things that hadn't even been spoken. "Now," she continued, "you open that box by pushing the inside out."

Thorn did as she told him, and found he was looking at a number of wooden sticks. Each was tipped at one end with a pink, bulbous lump.

"Those are lucifers," said the Syb. She was plainly enjoying herself. "To light one of the links, you strike the pink end of the lucifer on the rough edge of the box. Don't do it now, they're too precious to waste. The bottle contains a potion. But it's not for treating sickness."

"How shall I know when to use it?"

"Oh, you'll know, you'll know. Do you see the marking on the glass?"

Thorn looked more closely, and saw that the bottle was incised with a series of cuts – thus:

Z Z Z

Which left him none the wiser. He put the bottle aside.

"What about this?" he asked, holding up the silvery metal thing.

"*That's* the most remarkable item of all. It's a whistle."

"A whistle?" Thorn was puzzled. "But I can whistle myself." He pursed his lips and produced a piercing sound.

The Syb chuckled. "What a lot you have to learn! To make the whistle work, you blow though the narrow end. Go on, try it."

Thorn put the whistle to his lips and blew through it: once, twice, thrice. But no sound emerged.

"It doesn't work," he complained.

The Syb chortled again. "Yes it does, perfectly. But its sound is not for human ears."

She's crazy, thought Thorn. I'd best humour her.

"So, Minny Pickles: whose ears *is* it for?"

"Ears? *Ears?*" The Syb was in her element. "It's not meant for *ears* at all. Use it on water as a last resort."

"On *water?*"

"I don't believe it can be of use to you on land. There it will merely upset the neighbourhood rats. Now: the other objects can stay inside the bag, but keep the whistle around your neck. Hence the ribbon. Try it on."

Thorn ducked his head through the loop of the ribbon. Now, the whistle hung down against his chest.

"Tuck it inside your shirt. Don't advertise its existence. Guard it with your life, for you may need it to *save* your life. Now, whatever you do, don't show these things to Racky Jagger. Don't tell him you visited me. Tell him nothing, for you can be sure he'll tell exactly as much to you."

Thorn frowned in puzzlement. Riddles, riddles, that's all she was spinning him.

"But surely," he objected, "Racky's already proved helpful. Without him, we'd have no clue at all as to who's taken Haw."

"Racky Jagger is interested in only one person. That person is Racky Jagger." The Syb sighed. "Oh, Thorn Jack, you're so young. Your youth frightens me. The world's so old, so *very* old and so corrupt. The only advantage the young have is that they haven't yet discovered the terrible depths of that corruption. All the energy of innocence runs in their veins. If you knew what the world was like, your hair would turn grey and your skin grow wrinkled in a trice."

Like yours, I suppose, thought Thorn. He was getting a bit fed up with being patronised by the Syb. But he kept his mouth shut.

"Put the things away," she told him.

As he did so, Thorn said, "I'm grateful, deeply grateful for your gifts, Minny Pickles. I shall try to use them well. But your generosity begs a question: what have I done to deserve them? And why should *I* receive them, and not someone else?"

"That's *two* questions, Thorn Jack. The second is easily answered: the best gifts choose their recipients; these are yours because you'll need them. The first is not so straightforward. Perhaps in the past you've done nothing to deserve them, but will do so in the future. If you bring your sister home, that will be deserving enough." The Syb regarded him for a moment. "I knew Berry Waters and Davis Jack, I watched the two of them grow up. I liked Davis, he was always respectful to me. He used to bring me meat when he came back from the hunt: always the best cuts, too." She paused, and sipped her wine. "Ah, how the years pass. I wasn't always old, you know, and stuck in a chair by the fire."

"You speak of my father, Minny Pickles, but not of my mother. Have you nothing to say about her?"

"You're a sharp one. Your mother, now . . . Well, Berry Waters was very different from Davis Jack. Do you think fondly of her?"

"How can I? She abandoned me."

"It's not every woman that's cut out to be a mother."

"Then why did she marry my father, and go to the trouble of having children?"

"Having children isn't always a matter of choice. People do things without knowing why they do them."

"Do *you*?" This was bold, but the Syb smiled indulgently.

"Yes. Even *I*."

"But Sybs know everything."

"When people tell you that, take their words with a pinch of salt. It's commonly thought that people think with what's inside their heads. But they also think with their bodies. And that can make for trouble."

Thorn hadn't a clue what the old woman meant.

"You've still told me nothing about my mother," he said.

"What a persistent young man you are. Few dare to question me as you are doing today."

"I'm sorry, Minny Pickles. I don't mean to be disrespectful. It's just that – my mother's such a mystery to me."

The Syb pondered for a moment.

"Nobody should connive to turn anyone against his mother. Even when she abandoned him, as your mother did you. But then, as you've said, you think badly of her already . . . What can I say? That she was a mystery to herself? That in Norgreen she was a square peg stuck in a round hole? That she struck me as one of those people who'll never be satisfied, no matter what they do? That I perceived a darkness in her, a talent for self-destruction?"

Thorn was silent when she'd spoken: her last words were uncomfortable.

"Now, I think I've said enough. You'd better be on your way, Thorn Jack. I'm sure you've much to do."

Thorn knocked back the last of his wine, rose from his chair, bowed to the Syb and turned for the door. But he'd taken no more than a couple of steps when her voice halted him.

"Wait a moment."

He turned back to face her, but she was looking into the fire.

She grinned ruefully and began muttering to herself: "I'm starting to forget things . . . I must be getting senile . . . Is it the same for them, I wonder? They too must be getting old . . ."

For a while she seemed lost; then abruptly she roused herself, turned to look at him and said, "You brought a precious thing back from Wyke, Thorn Jack."

"A diamond ring – yes. It's gone into our Treasury to mark my coming-of-age."

"A diamond ring?" The Syb laughed. "I don't care about the ring. It's nothing more than a toy. You brought something else with you."

Thorn was flabbergasted. "How do you know that?"

"To know what *I* know you'd have to be me, Thorn Jack. Suffice to say, I *know*. Now, do *not* keep this thing in the house. Conceal it elsewhere, and conceal it well. Tell no one what you have done. Do it in secret and do it in haste. Now go, and may Fortune look kindly upon you."

Thorn bowed and left the house. He looked back after fifty paces. Daisy Dutton stood in the doorway, her eyes locked on him.

When he got home, Morry was out and Taylor still not returned. He went straight to his room. When soon after he came out, he wore a pack on his back. He went quickly out of the house.

Sleep played games with him that night. His body craved rest, but his mind took no heed, humming and buzzing like a beehive. When at last he drifted off, in his dreams huge trees towered blackly above his head, the screams of unseen birds rang through the treetops, and obscure faces peered at him through screens of foliage.

Morry was shaking him. "Thorn! Thorn! Come take a look at your uncle!"

He rubbed his eyes, climbed groggily out of bed and followed his aunt. His uncle lay swaddled in the sheets. His skin was frost-white, beaded with sweat, and his hand shook as he motioned to Thorn.

"Best keep your distance," Taylor croaked. "We don't need two of us down with this."

"I think it's the sweats," said his aunt.

Thorn was dismayed. "But – we're due to leave this morning!"

Taylor tried to say something, but instead began to cough. Morry held a cup of water to his lips and he gulped some down, then sank back onto the pillow, exhausted.

"I'm sorry, Thorn," he said, his face a picture of misery.

Morry drew Thorn out of the room.

"Will you go for Daisy Dutton? Let's see what she has to say."

For the second time in two days, Thorn knocked on the Syb's door. After a while, Daisy opened it.

"I thought it would be *you*, Thorn Jack," she said coolly.

"My uncle's ill," said Thorn.

"Then I'd better come with you, hadn't I? Wait a moment, I'll get some things."

Thorn sat tensely in the parlour while Daisy examined his uncle. When she emerged again, she said, "It's the sweats, your aunt's right. There's little anyone can do. Nature must take its course."

Morry looked at Thorn. "It's a bad attack, she says."

"But your uncle's a strong man," said Daisy. "He'll come

through it, but the sickness will drain his energies. It will take several weeks for him to get his strength back."

Morry returned to the bedroom. Daisy and Thorn regarded each other. Into his mind came what the Syb had said the previous afternoon, when he'd impudently corrected her on the number in the party: *If you say so, Thorn Jack.*

I should have known better than to question a Syb.

He was relieved on his uncle's part. Taylor would come through his attack. But he was dismayed for himself and Haw. He remembered more of the Syb's words: *Thorn Jack, you're so young. Your youth frightens me.* How would he cope without his uncle's strength and experience to support him? After what Minny Pickles had said about Racky Jagger, he knew he couldn't trust the man. He'd have to be on his guard against the fellow continually. All of a sudden the sheer weight of the task before him hit him. He felt like sinking to the ground, crawling into a corner and hiding. Who was he to take on the world?

He'd forgotten Daisy Dutton. But at this moment the girl reached out and took him by the hand, and he was aware of her again. Looking into her extraordinary eyes, too big for her face and yet in their own way beautiful, he saw she understood perfectly what he was thinking. And in that moment he saw that Daisy Dumb was a Syb. Not a stupid, pitiable girl but something out of the ordinary. Minny Pickles had chosen well. She must have known from the first, when she took Daisy into her house – but *how* had she known? Only a Syb, perhaps, could recognise another of her kind before her sister's powers developed.

Daisy broke the silence. "*Listen*, Thorn Jack. This is no time to falter. Think of your *sister*, who *needs* you. And *go* as you were going to go."

Thorn squeezed the girl's hand. "I *shall* go," he said.

At that moment, Morry came back into the room. If she was surprised to see the two of them holding hands, she didn't remark on it.

"Taylor's asleep," she said.

"I must go," said Daisy. "I'll call back tomorrow. *Fetch* me if you *need* me." Then she left without more ado.

"I've only just realised what she is," Thorn said to his aunt.

"Sometimes you're a bit slow on the uptake, nephew."

"When did you realise, Morry?"

"Perhaps a year ago."

"As long as that . . ."

"Well, I've seen more of Sybs than you have."

"I'm starting to think," he said ruefully, "that everybody's seen more of everything than I have."

"That's the inevitable result of a condition known as youth. But time has a remedy for it. When you get back, you'll have seen more of everything than anyone in Norgreen – except for Mr Jagger. And you'll still be a young man."

Why was it that every adult must go on about his youth? He said, "How did you know I was going to go ahead without Taylor?"

"I'm not your aunt for nothing. Are you ready?"

Even as she spoke, a knock sounded at the door. Not Daisy's light tapping, but a stout double rap. Racky Jagger stood there. He wasn't in travelling clothes, nor was he kitted out for a journey.

"What's this," Racky demanded, "that I hear about Taylor Flood? Is it true he's sick?"

"He's got the sweats," replied Thorn. "And it's a pretty bad bout."

"So . . . we shan't be setting off today after all. And I was looking forward to it." Racky grinned at Thorn.

"That's where you're wrong," said Thorn. "I'll be ready to leave when you are."

"Is that so . . . Right then, I'll go fetch my gear. I'll call back for you." And he was off without more ado.

When Thorn went to say farewell to his uncle, Taylor was sleeping. He touched the sick man on the cheek. "Goodbye, Taylor," he murmured. "Get well." He thought for a moment, then added, "I hope to make you proud of me."

Then he went out of the room.

In the living room, Thorn and Morry faced one another.

"Thorn, you will take care now, and come safely back to us?"

"Of course, Morry. And Haw will be with me when I come."

"Oh, I hope so with all my heart."

There were tears on his aunt's cheeks.

"Goodbye, Thorn."

"Goodbye, Aunt."

She embraced and kissed him.

"Remember, Thorn, we love you."

"I know. I love you too."

Two sharp raps came on the door. Thorn swung his pack up onto his back. Strapped to the pack was a quiver of arrows. He picked up his bow, opened the door and went out.

Similarly armed, and carrying a battered but well-filled rucksack, Racky was waiting there. He nodded to Morry as she came out. And he and Thorn set off.

"These yellow-feathered men," said Thorn. "How are we going to find them?"

They were clear of the settlement now. It was time to pose the question that was foremost in his mind.

Racky replied: "There's an inn in the wood at Judy Bridge – the Punch and Judy Inn. I know the landlord there, and *he* knows or sees everybody who passes through. We'll make for the inn and enquire there."

"What if the landlord *doesn't* know them?"

"*Then*, lad, we'll have to think again – won't we?"

6

MASKS AND MIRRORS

A hand was on her shoulder, gently shaking her.

"Come on, girl," said Elliott. "Time to get moving."

She glanced across at his sleeping bag. He'd slept in it – but for how long?

He was in a good mood this morning. Clouds were scattered across the sky, but weather prospects looked good. As they ate a quick breakfast, he neglected to ask about her experiences of the previous evening, instead rattling on about his hopes for the day – little different though they were from his hopes for earlier days in similar places.

"I've decided on our pitch," he said. "You go and collect Smoky."

The rat jumped up when she saw her mistress. Jewel hugged her and the animal licked the girl's ear with her tongue. It tickled. Soon Smoky was between the shafts of the wagon and they were off.

Elliott had picked out a spot on the far side of the fairground, on the edge of the approach road from Shelf settlement. "Catch them early, catch them fresh," was his simple philosophy. He positioned the wagon with its rear door facing the road, leaving just sufficient space to set up his display, and released Smoky from her harness so the rat could curl up comfortably on the ground. Then he and Jewel set to work to erect his stall and stock it.

Soon other carts arrived, and before long an avenue of stalls had blossomed into being. On one side was a vendor of pots and pans, on the other a woman who sold hand-carved animals and birds. Opposite them, a man with a glowing brazier was cooking slabs of meat and offering sizzling, steaming pieces of it impaled on wooden skewers. From one point of view, this was a nuisance, as smoke was sometimes wafted in their direction along with the smell. From another, it wasn't unwelcome, for people who bought from him would often linger to eat their purchases, and many were happy to cast an eye over what Ranson and Daughter were selling.

Elliott had invested heavily in his present stock. Roughly half of it was priced reasonably, and was what people were used to. The other half was of a quality and stylishness which he rarely came across, and comparatively expensive. Here were frocks and skirts, shirts and blouses, and stockings and scarves made of unusually fine materials, in eye-catching greens, blues, purples and reds. He'd taken a gamble on this stuff, telling himself that if it went well he'd clean up; nothing ventured, nothing gained. Anyway, there it was, laid smartly out on his table or hanging from a cross-pole, a riot of brilliance. Scouting out the rest of the stalls, he saw that only one other was offering women's clothing; but it was drab, old-fashioned stuff: no competition *there*.

People soon began to appear. Elliott, his spiel polished by years of practice, embarked on his routines while Jewel held up items of merchandise and smiled fetchingly. It was too cold to model them – as she often did in summer – apart from the scarves, which she would stretch out across the back of her neck, sometimes twirling round on her toes.

Trade was slow at first. But then the Snaffles appeared, with Rona Futtock and Dunk Stott. Jewel could see that Maddy and Rona were captivated. They held up garment after garment of the new, expensive stock, exclaiming with wonder and surprise at everything. The style! The colours! They'd never seen the like. They wanted this item and that – they wanted a wardrobe between them! Impossible, of course. They didn't have that kind of money. They settled for two items each. Cannily, Elliott let them go for less than he normally would. He tapped the side of his nose. "Don't let your friends know what you paid," he told them. "But please *do* recommend me." "Oh, we *shall*," was the response. Tom and Dunk paid up, perhaps reasoning that it might have been a whole lot worse. And they had two happy women: that surely was worth it.

Maddy and Rona proved as good as their word. A steady stream of Shelf women arrived at the stall, eager to look at the kinds of things their friends had already purchased. Seizing his opportunity, Elliott pushed his prices up. The inevitable round of bargaining reduced them, of course, but he was still coining it. Midday came and went. If things continued like this, he'd have made more money by closing time than he'd ever seen before. Jewel was as busy as she could ever remember being. She might be a little cynical about her father sometimes, but this was business, this was their livelihood. She was just as tough as he was and, an appealing girl to boot, got away with things more easily. She only had to smile at husbands and boyfriends to disarm them.

The quality stuff, she noticed, was going exceptionally well, and pulling the cheaper along with it. Sometimes a customer would buy an expensive item and a cheaper one, as if to balance things out. Copper and silver – and even, from a couple of exceptionally rich customers, pieces of gold – flowed in, rattling the money-bags strapped around father and daughter's waists. The day seemed to zip by. The cart was empty; all that remained unsold was out on display. In a brief lull, Jewel seized the chance to cast her eyes about –

– and saw, twenty paces away, the man with flame-red hair. He was lounging by the food stall. As she watched him, he bit off a piece of meat with white, perfect teeth and started to masticate it. She turned away, but some impulse compelled her to turn back. He was looking directly at her. As their eyes met, he spat something from the corner of his mouth – a piece of gristle? – and grinned at her. There was something feral in his grin. She turned quickly back to the stall, and busied herself straightening things. When at length she looked again, he was still there, still looking at her. As she stared, unable, it seemed, to unglue her gaze from him, he bit off a final chunk of meat, tossed the stick over his shoulder, turned, and swaggered away.

If her father's mood of the morning had been good, that of the evening was irrepressible in its ebullience. As the wagon trundled back to the inn, he simply couldn't stop talking. Never had he known a day of trading like today's. Shelf Fair was a silver mine. Four-fifths of his stock had gone, their money-bags were full to bursting. Grandiose schemes tumbled from him. She'd heard them all before, but never expressed so forcibly. She wanted to calm him, but couldn't find the words.

They dined again at the Dewdrop. Again the place was busy, but tonight there was no sign of the Snaffles and their friends. Elliott ate and drank with gusto, but, with other traders present, buttoned his tongue about their triumphs of the day.

"Last night," he told Jewel, "I'm afraid I neglected you. But tonight I'll make up for it. We'll go to the Fair together, have a wonderful time."

Jewel protested she'd seen everything, didn't need to go again. "Nonsense!" said her father. You couldn't have too much of a good thing, in his opinion. Besides, she deserved it. If she hadn't pressed him to cross the Barrens, they wouldn't be here now. Their success was entirely of her making. She demurred; what she'd done was very nearly get them killed. "Rubbish!" he declared. They'd never been in the slightest danger. He'd always had the situation totally under control. (Was she really hearing this? Had he forgotten what had happened? Could it be that he'd already revised the contents of his memory?) They must celebrate, he said. She protested – she was tired – she'd rather have an early night. He wouldn't hear of it. He'd treat her to this and that, then she'd know how much he loved her.

"But I know how much you love me!"

"Well, you were short-changed last night. Tonight you shall have whatever you want, and more besides. Get your glad-rags on!"

She gave up. In this mood, he was simply incorrigible. The best she could hope for was not too late a night.

The fairground was crowded again, but its sparkle had dulled for her. She trudged along beside Elliott, trying to smile when he glanced at her or pressed things upon her, to pretend she was enjoying herself, while all the time wishing she were elsewhere. What on earth was wrong with her? Well, a good night's sleep tonight . . . she would feel much better tomorrow.

Booths and amusements passed in a vague, continuous blur. They sampled this, then that. At least, if *she* wasn't enjoying herself, her father was. He was like a kid on a birthday treat. She drifted along in a sort of dream.

They were passing through a quieter area when he said to her, "Must just nip down here . . ." indicating an unlit alley between a couple of tents which led off towards open country. Call of nature, she supposed. She stood yawning on the corner. When he got back, perhaps she could persuade him to call it a day.

Time passed, and he didn't return. This is odd, she thought, he should be back by now. She peered along the alley, but saw only darkness at the end. Then a dreadful thought struck her: what if he'd been attacked, and was lying on the ground, injured, unconscious perhaps, unable to call for help? Like her, he was wearing his money-belt: it would tempt any thief. She looked about her. No one was near at hand. What if it was all in her mind? What if she dragged some stranger down there, and her father turned out to be perfectly all right? What a fool she'd look then.

She began to walk down the alley, then broke into a run. As she ran, her apprehension grew, as if the very act of running were augmenting her fears. It was very dark here. She slowed to turn the corner –

– and ran slap bang into someone coming the other way. Strong arms gripped her shoulders—

"No!" she cried out before she could help herself.

"It's me, Jewel, me!" came the sound of a well-known voice.

Panting for breath, though she hadn't run far, she gasped: "Father, thank God. I was so worried about you. I thought you'd been waylaid . . ."

"Silly girl!" Elliott was laughing. "I was on my way back."

"But you were such a long time . . ."

"I'm here now. Come on. This way."

She'd had enough. She wanted to leave the Fair *now*.

"All right," he said indulgently, "we'll go. But you're worrying about nothing. I've told you: today's *our* day. Nothing can spoil it now."

They made their way through the gaily-coloured makeshift streets. Laughing, animated people thronged the most popular amusements. Things would bubble on for a good while yet. Well, thought Jewel, they can bubble without me. I've had more than enough of it.

They were moving along one of the quieter avenues when Elliott came to a halt.

"Well, there's a thing!" he exclaimed. "I haven't seen one of these for years."

An illustrated board stood at the entrance to a marquee. It showed a man in front of huge mirror, but curiously distorted. The man himself was as thin as a rake, but in the mirror he bulged in the middle, as if his stomach had been inflated. He goggled with saucerlike eyes. As they examined the illustration, a barker came out of the entrance and, spotting them, went into his spiel.

"Roll up, folks, roll up. Two marvels for the price of one. Here in this very tent is the original mirror maze: wander slowly through astonishing, twisting corridors of glass, and as you go, watch your selves watching you. Yes: not one self, not two, not even three selves or four: but a whole host of selves, amazing you on every side. Yes, a-*mazing* you!" He paused briefly, to enjoy his own wit. "But no, that's not all. I said *two* marvels for the price of one. In the centre of this maze – if of course you can find it! – is the world's greatest gallery of distorting mirrors. See yourself as you've never ever seen yourself before: stretched and squeezed into the most impossible shapes. And laugh at yourself – laugh, yes – as you've never laughed before!"

He paused for breath.

"Come on, Jewel," said Elliott. "*This* we must see."

"Oh, Father," she complained: "you said we were going."

"But we *are* going – just as soon as we've been round this exhibit. Do you know, Jewel, I haven't see a mirror maze for years. They're so rare – and so difficult to transport. Wonder how they do it . . ."

"Oh, we don't transport it, sir," said the barker, who'd been listening. "At least, not far. The panels for this maze are kept permanently at Shelf. We put them up every Fair day. In fact," he added, as if sharing privileged knowledge with an especially favoured client, "the maze was designed and constructed by a master glass-maker who came to live at Shelf – a remarkable man. This show is his masterpiece. Extremely popular, is the maze."

"Very interesting," said Elliott. And to Jewel: "Well, there you are, my dear. We may never get the chance to see it again. Oh, come on, it won't take long. Then we'll go. I promise you, this is absolutely the last thing we're going to do tonight."

"Oh very well," she sighed, "if you promise. Come on then."

They paid their money and went inside. A few paces, and they were standing in a glassy corridor, duplicates of themselves suspended in front and on either side. Lamps dangled from the ceiling, and these, with their many reflections, filled the space with brilliance. Jewel had never seen anything like the effect all this produced, and was intrigued despite herself. When she moved, several versions of herself moved with her. When she turned the first corner, the other Jewels turned too – though not all in the same direction. Some went this way, some that, and some in no direction at all – slipping sideways into the upright wooden partitions between the panes. She advanced; they advanced. She stepped backwards; they stepped backwards. She stuck an arm out – fast – but it was impossible to take the many Jewels by surprise: so, immediately, did they. They knew her mind as well as she. If she waved, so did they. If she smiled, so did they. Whatever she did, they did. She went on a little further, turning this corner and that. No, she then thought, I'm wrong. They can't know my mind as well as me. How can they? They've no minds of their own . . . How thin is a reflection? Much too thin to harbour a mind. She was an amiable tyrant commanding a mindless multitude. And now, in this particular spot, she realised something strange – or stranger, she thought, than anything else up to this point: not only did the mirrors reflect her, they reflected one another. Mirrors reflecting mirrors. A recession of her selves stared in puzzlement back at her, their manifestations diminishing into remote distances. She poked the glass with a fingertip; and touched the finger poking back. What a funny place it was . . .

Her father came up behind her. "Told you it would be good. Haven't you learnt your lesson yet? Old Father Elliott's always right."

A little further, and they stood in the distorting gallery. Here the mirrors were arranged in a long double row. In the first, the slimmest Jewel there'd ever been grinned back at her. In the next posed the fattest: a disgusting slob. The third squashed her down to a mere inch in height. In the fourth, her body zigzagged from side to side. In the fifth her waist contracted to the breadth of a hand, while her legs turned to treetrunks and her head to a giant ball. She squinted hideously at herself from weirdly stretched-out eyes, opened and closed a wide, fish-like mouth. Chuckling, she bent her knees and, as she descended, her body wobbled its way through a sequence of contortions. In the next mirror, her head disappeared into her neck, but, as if to compensate, her feet became enormous – great lumpy clod-hoppers that looked too heavy to lift. But she could lift them easily. Up and down they went, like gigantic cobbles of lead. Laughing aloud now, she walked backwards through the sequence, letting her father go on ahead. She wanted to see it all again.

She was contemplating her fat self with equanimity when a gigantic hand on a knife-thin arm clamped itself over her mouth. Another arm went round her waist, pinning her arms to her bulbous sides. She struggled, but her assailant was much too strong for her. In the mirror, two pudding-like entities wobbled back and forth, ineptly parodying a passionate embrace. Her attacker was wearing a black skin-tight covering over his face and head. Only his eyes and lips were visible through snipped-out holes. Dressed entirely in black, he was a piece of night sculpted into pseudo-human form.

Her father had seen them now. "Hey, you there!" he shouted. But a figure rushed past her, even as her father started towards them. The two met halfway and closed, silently grappling together. The second assailant was also hooded and clad in black. In the opposing rows of mirrors, a rabble of fantastic beings lurched and staggered drunkenly, seemingly inseparable, changing shape with a frequency and ease that boggled the mind. Heads, bodies, legs, feet – nothing kept the same shape for more than a moment. Grunts and curses made their escape from these wildly unstable masses. As the Jewels watched, horrified, along with their iron captors, the second man and his many reflections drew back a selection of arms, no two identical, and at their ends flashing extensions, and jabbed at the merchant – once, twice, a third time, a fourth: a salvo of strikes. Then the two moved apart, and all her fathers fell to the ground.

Now for helpless Jewel the madness mercifully simplified. The black figure stooped, swiftly unbuttoned her father's coat and tugged at something near his waist. His money-bag. He had it now. Her father was groaning. The masked man jabbed him again, silencing him. The man straightened and came over to her. She kicked out at him and heard an answering yelp of pain, half-smothered behind the mask, as the toe of her boot struck his shin.

The man pressed up against her so she couldn't kick him again. Now she was sandwiched between the two. The rancid stink of their exertions filled her nose. Her father's attacker's mask was identical to that of the man who held her. His eyes locked on hers: ice-blue, she would never forget them.

"You vicious little mouse!"

His lips were voluptuous: they seemed made more for kissing than for uttering cruel words.

There was a brief pause in the action while the three held the tableau. Then –

"How about it, bro – think a facial tattoo would improve her pouty looks?"

"Definitely, bro. But it needs the touch of an artist."

Her head was pulled to one side.

Suddenly, from behind them, came the sound of a voice, "The mirror room is just through here."

"Time to scarper, little bro," said the man gripping her arms.

Jewel was flung to one side. The two men fled down the gallery. Glittering mirrors sucked them in.

As she sprawled there, shaking, unable to get her body in motion, people appeared around the corner. There were three men and a woman. They took in the scene with astonishment.

"We've been attacked!" Jewel gasped. "My father's hurt."

"Attacked?" – from one of the men.

"Two men in masks – they went through there." She waved a hand at the other exit. The three men exchanged rapid looks, then were off in pursuit, their movements perfectly synchronised. In rapid triple sequence, they vanished into the panes of glass.

The woman knelt beside Elliott and took hold of his wrist.

"Help him," wailed Jewel. "Please, tell me he's all right."

A long moment passed. When the woman turned back, Jewel recognised her face. It was the juggler she'd assisted.

"I'm truly sorry," said the woman, "but no one can help your father now."

7

MANNINGHAM SPARKS

Thorn and Racky made camp that night a few hundred paces from Judy Wood. The light was fading, but the Wood was a darker thing than the sky. Silent and forbidding, a massive natural palisade, it rose up blackly above them.

"So, lad, what d'you think of it?"

Racky was studying him intently.

"It's – it's – like *a wall*," Thorn finally managed.

"A wall . . ." said Racky musingly. "Ay, I know what you mean." For once his words were devoid of irony. "Yes, a barrier: that's what it is. I've known men who got this close but could go no further. The Wood got into their heads, see? Like a big green worm, burrowing in, eating their courage away. Fear it was – fear of the unknown that got to them." He looked thoughtfully at Thorn. "Got to you, has it, lad? Is this as far as you'll dare to go?"

The corner of his mouth curled. Thorn knew that mouth by now.

"Anything *you* can do, *I* can," he said. But he didn't feel the man his brag made him out to be.

"That's the spirit, lad." Racky spat on the stony track. "I'll hold you to that boast."

Tucked in under the Wood's skirts was a ruin from the Dark

Time. Its roof was agape with holes and its windows goggled like square eyes. Ivy and other growths had rampaged over its stonework, clothing it in vegetation.

Ever since, as a small child, he'd first heard the word *giant*, Thorn had been curious about the past. What had happened to the giants? What had caused the Barrens to form? Had there been a time when humans and giants lived side by side? Some people – albeit a minority – maintained that the giants were figments of myth and that the Barrens had always existed. Such folk followed the teachings of the True Believers, a self-dubbed Ranter sect which held that God had created the scattered remains and the wastelands. Why? Precisely in order to tempt people into the sinful belief that another and far more advanced civilisation had once ruled the world. But most people were quite content to believe in giants. Stories – mostly comic – of interactions between giants and humans were the inheritance of every child. These now struck Thorn as fantastic, but he was firmly persuaded that the giants had existed. Human memory was short. It stretched back three, at most four generations. Beyond that lay obscurity. Hence the name the Dark Time. Most people assumed that life went on as life had always done, but to Thorn things seemed more mysterious than that. There were, quite simply, too many unanswered – too many *unanswerable* – questions about the world. As for the God of the True Believers, he was far too tricky a customer to command Thorn's allegiance.

Next day they entered the Wood. Thorn had been in woods before, but nothing on this scale. Not only did the size of this

Wood beggar imagination, the trees grew big here: beech, birch and oak he recognised, sycamore and horse chestnut. But there were other varieties whose names he didn't know. Their trunks shot up to alarming heights and lost themselves overhead. Now that the trees were richly in leaf, tossing out canopies and sprays, light had a job to penetrate. Only here and there, where they thinned or for some reason didn't grow, did light break in.

Then there was the silence. Since leaving Norgreen the travellers had not been out of earshot of birds. But here in the wood, where you might have expected plenty of them, there was barely a sound but for that made by the contact of boots with earth, or the creak of a backpack. Thorn was to try, over the coming days, to find the right words to describe the quality of this silence, but they always eluded him.

How tiny, how insignificant he was down here! He was well aware, of course, of the general bigness of the world: how things outreached him, overtopped him, made him small to himself. Animals and birds were his size, or a little larger or a little smaller: he was accustomed to them. But the natural realm in which they lived . . . it was built on so vast a scale. Harvesting vegetables or fruits from the settlement's garden-plot, he'd been conscious from the first of their size compared with his own; what an effort it took, for example, to dig up root vegetables; how many men were required to unearth a carrot or an onion, then lift it, using block and tackle, onto a rat-cart and convey it to a storeroom. Then there was the effort required to cut the thing up. A single vegetable could feed many families. Then there was the business of reaping crops. He remembered clearly the first time he'd attempted to use a scythe in a stand of wheat: uncomfortably aware of how far above his head the kernels of grain reared, he kept botching the angle of the cut, so that the stalks, rather than sideways, fell back upon his head. Just as well they were so light!

Racky was a dour companion. He said little, and that little was almost always functional. If Thorn asked him a question, the brevity of Racky's reply discouraged further talk. Thorn began to wonder if Racky had ever had a friend – someone with whom to share his hopes, his joys and disappointments. It hardly seemed likely.

Thorn was young and fit, but Racky, at more than twice his age, never seemed to tire – nor even to overextend himself. He maintained the steady pace of the experienced traveller, calling breaks at regular intervals for rest and refreshment. Thorn was keen to forge on, but Racky's regime was sensible. They had a long way to go; what was the point of exhausting themselves?

And the Wood? Far from living up to the lurid tales Thorn had heard of it, it seemed a dull place, and deserted. By mid-afternoon, he was entertaining a sense of anticlimax. He'd anticipated incidents, excitement aplenty, but nothing at all had happened.

But then something did.

They were sitting side by side with their backs against a tree stump, when Racky touched Thorn's arm.

"We have company," he whispered. "Do as I do."

When Racky got to his feet, Thorn did likewise. When Racky drew his pack close so his quiver was near at hand, Thorn followed his lead. When Racky nocked an arrow, raised the weapon to eye level and sighted on a dense patch of nearby undergrowth, Thorn copied him. Then the two stood and waited.

Company? wondered Thorn. What kind of company?

Racky's hearing must be sharp indeed, for Thorn could hear nothing. Or perhaps Racky's ears were just more practised than his own. Time passed. Then Thorn heard it – a light scuffling. Silence again. Then the creak of a twig.

"There are two of them at least," said Racky quietly.

"Two of what?"

"Wait and see."

What a time to choose to be mysterious, thought Thorn.

Now there was movement under a bush. A furry white head appeared, a pair of button-black eyes. Then, beside it, a second head. They don't look particularly dangerous, thought Thorn. Then one of the creatures snarled, revealing a row of wicked teeth.

"They'll come at us fast," whispered Racky. "Take the one to the left."

"And if there are more than two?"

"Use your initiative, lad. Let's hope it doesn't come down to knives."

He sighted afresh. Thorn did the same.

The animals moved with such speed that Thorn was taken by surprise. Sinuous shapes were leaping towards them. One, two, three, four . . . there was no time to think. Racky's bow twanged; one of the creatures went down; Racky reached for a second arrow. Thorn fired belatedly. His aim was adequate: his shaft thocked solidly into the target he'd picked out. Still two animals came on – they could be no more now than a couple of feet away. But instinct had taken over in Thorn. Those bared jaws, those wild eyes . . . So quick was he with his second arrow that it left his bow only a fraction of time after Racky's. A malevolent scream. Then it was over.

The pair lowered their bows. Three animals lay dead or dying, the nearest only inches away; the fourth, an arrow in its flank, had turned tail and fled.

"You did well, Thorn Jack. Couldn't have done better myself."

So surprised was Thorn to hear praise from Racky's mouth that it didn't strike him till later that, for once, his companion had addressed him not as "lad", but by his name.

"Let's have a look at them. But be careful – don't get too close until we're sure they're dead."

The nearest animal could hardly be other than dead. Thorn's second arrow protruded from its brain. Yet still it glared savagely: as if, even in death, its blood lust remained unsatisfied. Racky poked its furry muzzle with the tip of his bow, then cut out Thorn's arrow with his knife and gave it to him.

"Vicious thing, eh?" His eyes sparkled with humour, as if death was a joke to him.

Thorn nodded, then wiped his arrow on the grass.

The creature he'd killed was long-bodied but short in the leg. It measured perhaps ten inches in length; its fur was white but flecked red-brown. It had a jutting snout and a pair of neat, semi-circular ears.

"Is it a weasel?" asked Thorn. He'd sometimes seen weasels in the country around Norgreen.

"No," said Racky. "This here's a stoat. You can tell by the white fur. But its coat's already changing: in the summer it'll be reddish-brown — yellowy-white underneath. Stoats'll attack anything, including a rat. They're devils when they hunt in packs."

They examined the other animals. One was dead, the other too badly injured to stand. It lay on its side, eyes glittering. It growled and pawed feebly at them, hooked claws extended. Thorn put a shaft between its eyes. The beast stared back unseeingly.

"Mister Mercy, eh?" grinned Racky. "Can't myself say as I mind seeing these devils suffering." He tapped the animal on its snout. "A set of teeth like these once fastened in my leg. No joke, I can tell you. The stoat had it in mind to make me Racky One-leg. I cut its throat double-quick and prised its jaws apart with a stick. That was in this wood, too. Took me a long time to heal. If it hadn't been hunting alone, I wouldn't be here now." He turned to Thorn. "And that can be the difference, young man, between life and death. Pure chance. But people make their own luck: you shot pretty well today. Bit slow to get going, but that's understandable. And you more than made up for it." He turned back to the stoat. "We'll have no more trouble from this direction, I'm thinking." He pulled his knife from its sheath. "But every cloud has a silver lining. Fresh meat! We'll eat well tonight."

He began to skin the animal with dextrous strokes of his knife.

"Well, come on, don't just stand there, lend a hand. Take what you can comfortably carry, I'll do the same. Pity we have to waste so much — but we didn't choose to kill them."

The two carved slabs of meat from the animal's flanks. Then

Racky took a couple of cloth bags from his pack and put the pieces inside. "It pays to be prepared," he said. One bag he gave to Thorn; the other he slung over his shoulder. Then they resumed their journey.

The track wound on ahead. The light began to fail. They came to a fork in the path, but Racky knew which route to choose. On his own Thorn would long since have been lost. But after the battle against the stoats and the praise he'd won for his part in it, he felt more comfortable with Racky. They were more like comrades now.

Still Racky pushed on. Thorn was feeling weary and hungry, he was more than ready to stop. Nevertheless, he said nothing: calling halts was Racky's job.

When Racky stopped, so did Thorn.

"Can you smell it?" asked his guide.

Thorn sniffed the air. "Wood-smoke," he said.

They rounded the next bend. To one side of the trail, a bulky figure knelt on the ground, warming his hands at a fire. Racky laid his hand on Thorn's arm, and lifted a finger to his lips. Motioning Thorn to stay where he was, he tiptoed up behind the man. What on earth was he up to? Thorn's puzzlement turned to apprehension when Racky unsheathed his knife and, stooping over the figure, clamped a hand over his mouth and whipped the knife round under his throat.

"Where's your money?" he demanded, then took his hand from the man's mouth.

"M – Money? I have no money . . . I serve G – God," the man spluttered.

Racky re-sheathed his knife. "G – God or D – Devil, it's all the same to me," he said.

The man turned to face his assailant.

"God in heaven!" he exclaimed. "You'll be the death of me, Racky Jagger!"

"I very much doubt it," replied Racky. "There's a lot worse than me to be found in this Wood." He turned and gestured to Thorn. "Come and meet our fellow traveller."

Thorn went forward to meet the man, who by this time was on his feet.

"Thorn Jack," said Racky, "meet the Reverend – the *very* Reverend – Manningham Sparks." Then, turning to the Ranter: "My young companion here – a dab hand with bow and arrow, as he proved not long since – is Thorn Jack of Norgreen."

"Pleased to meet you, Thorn Jack of Norgreen," said the Ranter. Then added, "Are you of the true faith?"

"Now then, no proselytising," said Racky before Thorn could reply. "Leave my companion be."

"Pleased to meet you too," returned Thorn.

Manningham Sparks was a tall, stocky man in his forties. His belly pressed roundly against his coat, yet he didn't seem fat. He had a fleshy face and full lips, a jutting bony nose, and stern grey eyes that didn't look as though they missed much. His iron-grey hair was swept back and gathered into a tuft by a black ribbon tied in a bow.

Thorn, of course, had identified the man's calling by his clothes. Sparks wore a black knee-length coat over knee-breeches of the same colour. Black stockings encased his sturdy calves. His shoes, black again, sported square metal buckles. His hat (black – what else?), which had a broad brim and a high, flat-topped crown, sat on the ground – in case, of course, it fell off his head and landed in the fire.

"You're a Ranter," said Thorn.

"That I am, young man, and that I shall stay till the day I die. Mr Jagger and I, as you must already have guessed, are old acquaintances – though you wouldn't have thought it from the way the devil crept up on me. It's a good thing I boast a strong heart."

"And if memory serves me right, a strong stomach too," said Racky. "Can I take it, Manningham, you've no objection to roasted stoat? The meat couldn't be any fresher."

"None whatsoever, Racky. Who am I to reject what the Good Lord provides?"

"First time anyone's ever called me the Good Lord."

Sparks laughed. "The Good Lord has many disguises. He can conceal himself in the most unlikely vehicles."

"First time anyone's ever called me a vehicle, too."

"Well, what are you two doing in Judy Wood?"

"All in good time, Reverend. Stomach first, soul after. Let's get this fire going properly and the meat on the spit. You can chatter till you're blue in the face once our stomachs are fed."

"Such a heathen, your friend," said Sparks to Thorn good-humouredly. "If my past experience of him is anything to go by, it's stomach first with him, stomach second and stomach third."

Racky was right about Manningham Sparks's appetite. When at length the food was ready, the Ranter ate as if he hadn't eaten for days. Roasted stoat disappeared inside him as into a bottomless pit.

"Delicious," he pronounced, giving his jaws a rest at last. "But tell me how you came by this beast. One doesn't eat stoat often."

They were sitting around the fire, using the fallen branches of trees as props to support their backs.

"You tell him, lad," said Racky.

So Thorn proceeded to tell the story of how they'd fought off the stoats. While he did this, Sparks poked shreds of meat out of the gaps between his teeth with a sharpened twig.

When he'd finished, "My goodness – I was lucky, then," said Sparks, tossing his twig into the fire, "for I myself travelled that way today. If they'd chosen *me* as their victim – well, I wouldn't be here now . . . Instead of me dining on stoat, stoats would have dined upon me." He paused, then added, "But they didn't, gentlemen, did they?" Looking upwards (to Heaven, Thorn presumed, though in the surrounding dark even the foliage above them was no more than a shadowy presence), he pronounced reverentially, "The Good Lord sees and protects his faithful servants." He then performed the weaving motion with his right hand that Thorn had seen from Ranters before.

Noticing Thorn watching him, Manningham Sparks said, "So, Thorn Jack, are *you* a member of the faith?"

"Erm, not really," replied Thorn. "My guardians don't attend services, and I never myself got into the habit."

"I see. So in your case, perhaps, your pagan nature is due to negligence, not to ungodliness?"

"I suppose you could say that," said Thorn.

"Then let me ask you this." Sparks gestured vaguely in the air. "Do you think this bountiful world you see – or would, if it wasn't dark – came into being of its own accord?"

Thorn stared at him.

"Imagine nothingness," said the Ranter. "Emptiness. Non-existence. Suddenly there's the earth, complete with trees, people, stoats. Do you think these things could simply have *wished* themselves into being?"

"Well, I suppose not," said Thorn. "Something caused them to exist."

"Exactly. Well, we call that something God. What but the supreme Mind would have the vision to conjure up a thing as intricate as creation?"

"I don't know," said Thorn.

"Don't you? Consider how perfectly every thing fulfils its nature and purpose. The sun gives light, the clouds bring rain, these trees furnish shade, this fire keeps us warm, this stoat fills our bellies."

"Not so long since," retorted Thorn, "this stoat was trying to kill me."

"Naturally. Stoats are designed to hunt and kill. But *you* killed the stoat, being designed to defend yourself."

"I suppose I did," agreed Thorn.

The Ranter turned to Racky Jagger. "What a great one for supposing our young friend is," he said.

"Well, Manningham," said Racky, "if *I* were a stoat I wouldn't dare attack *you*."

"And why would that be, Racky?"

"Because you'd debate me to death before I could make a meal of you."

The two men laughed, and Thorn joined in.

"Take note of this, Thorn Jack," said Racky: "Reverend Sparks can laugh at himself. Now in my experience, that's rare among Ranters. Most of them are so serious, with faces as stiff as skittles, that they would rather cut their own throats than bestow a smile on you."

"How kind of you to praise my sense of humour, Racky," observed the Ranter. "But I fear that you traduce my fellow servants of the Divinity. Few are such joyless die-hards as you paint them."

"Not in my experience. But don't trouble to pursue the point, for I refuse to argue with you." He glanced at Thorn. "The Reverend and I know one another's views of old."

Later, Thorn lay in his sleeping bag, thinking over the Ranter's words. The idea that everything was designed for a purpose was powerful. Yet, although he could see the purpose or purposes of a stoat, the proposition that trees existed to provide shade for humans seemed less than convincing. What then *were* trees for? To grow, to put forth leaves and blossom and propagate their kind? Closer to home loomed the question of his own purpose in life. Well, I know what that is, he thought: to rescue Haw from her kidnappers. But if God had created Thorn for this purpose, it followed that he must have created the kidnappers for the purpose of kidnapping Haw. What a strange god he must be . . .

From somewhere out in the night, a sound carried to Thorn's ear: the hoot of an owl – another hunter. So much of existence seemed to be killing and eating. By human beings as well as animals. Humans enjoyed it, too. Were they then also animals?

Racky Jagger and the Ranter were humped shapes around the fire. Thorn snuggled deeper into his sleeping bag. His sleeping bag . . . Now wasn't *that* perfectly designed for sleeping in? But God hadn't designed it, had He? Some human was responsible, somebody who'd wanted to keep warm when sleeping out under the stars or under the trees. Had God designed men to be designers in their turn? If so, were men little gods? Thorn suspected Manningham Sparks wouldn't approve of that idea. Well, these were deep matters, and more than Thorn could puzzle through. He turned on his side, and fell asleep.

8

RAINY GILL

Four men were lowering Elliott Ranson into the grave. In accordance with pedlar tradition he was dressed in ordinary clothes. In some places, Jewel knew, the dead, wrapped in winding sheets, were buried in wooden boxes. Her father had always regarded that practice as barbaric. Much better to be buried with the earth close about you. Nature could then begin its business without let or hindrance, taking you back with all speed into its womb. This was how, five long years before, Jewel's mother was buried. Now husband had joined wife. If not in the same place, at least in the same dark substance.

Abruptly, the girl's pent-up emotions overwhelmed her. She grasped Maddy Snaffle's hand and the dam burst. Shuddering sobs shook her body, tears blinded her vision. But an arm went round her and, immediately, she clutched the woman tightly, grateful for a comforting body to anchor her.

"There, there," said Maddy soothingly, "I know." And, "Go on, love, cry – it's the best thing to do."

It was the only thing to do. It seemed an age before the tempest passed, and Jewel could look up again into Maddy's kindly face. She smiled through her tears. Somebody now was holding out a handkerchief to her – it was Tom. She said, "Thank you," and dabbed at her eyes.

Once again she became aware of the people around the grave – far more than she'd expected. As well as Maddy and Tom, there were Dunk and Rona and the rest of the crowd from that night in the Dewdrop. Behind them stood the innkeeper and his wife, the ratman too. Quite a number of other people from Shelf were present – people who'd bought clothes from Ranson and Daughter two days before. Many of the other merchants had stayed over for the funeral, out of respect perhaps for a fellow-trader, conscious perhaps that the dead man might have been one of them. Then there was a contingent from the Fair. As well as the juggler, whose name Jewel now knew to be Rainy Gill, there were the three men who'd been with her in the mirror maze – the three tumblers. The fire-eater and glass-eater also were there, as was the barker from the maze. Then there were others she didn't recognise.

She stood still, holding Maddy's hand, while Ranter Larkin said some words over the grave. It was fortunate, she thought, that he was resident in Shelf. True, her father hadn't exactly been a religious man, but she didn't want his funeral to pass without some sort of ceremony. She'd asked the Ranter, if he would, not to go on about Heaven and Hell, and he followed her wishes. But, to be honest, she wasn't listening. She was thinking about her father and her behaviour towards him: had she been a good daughter? Had she done all she might to make him proud of her? He'd loved her and she him, despite his faults. But she must have faults too, for didn't everyone?

Slowly, she became aware that Ranter Larkin had fallen silent and that everyone was waiting for something to happen. The Ranter, at the head of the grave, made a discreet sign to her.

"*Earth*, love," Maddy whispered, "throw some earth into the grave."

"Earth?" she said. "Yes . . ."

She stepped forward, stooped and picked up a handful. It was cool and moist in her hand, and black. Oh, so very black . . . For a moment she was reluctant to let it go, for more would quickly follow and her father would be entombed. She couldn't bear to look at his face. Then her hand jerked and the earth dropped into the grave, striking his chest with the faintest of thuds. She stepped back. Maddy followed her, and Tom, then everyone else, one by one. Some did it quickly, picking up soil and tossing it in in a single movement; others took theirs to the lip of the hole and looked down at the man they were commemorating before they dropped the earth in.

People came up to offer condolences. Many were awkward, as if they didn't know quite what to say. It didn't matter – she felt awkward too. She thanked them for coming, they drifted away. Ranter Larkin approached her and gravely shook her hand. "If you should wish to speak with me," he said, "you know where I am. Just knock on the door." She thanked him too, but could find nothing else to say.

Last in the line of mourners was a man she half-recognised.

"Didn't you have a clothing stall at the Fair?" she asked bluntly.

"Yes," he said, surprised. Then added, "Stuff not half as good as yours, though, I have to say."

"Are you interested in buying the rest of my father's stock – I'll give you a good deal?"

He seemed taken aback. "Well, yes," he replied, "but—"

"Good. Come and see me at midday," she said. "The yard behind the Dewdrop. You can't miss the wagon."

He nodded. "I'll be there." And moved away.

To break with the only life she'd known now seemed inevitable to Jewel. The more she'd thought about what to do since grasping the fact of her father's death, the more impossible it seemed for her to go on as before. It was Elliott who'd connected her to the merchant's life. Now, in his going, he'd taken her pleasure in that life along with him. What's more, it was an encumbrance: she saw no way to reconcile it with what she now had to do.

The only people who now remained were Maddy and Tom, Rainy Gill (watching a short distance away) and two men with spades.

"Would you like to come back with us, love?" asked Maddy solicitously.

"You're very kind," replied Jewel, "but I'd like to be alone for a bit."

"Well, you know where to find us. And think on what we've told you."

"Yes," said Jewel, "I shall. I'm very grateful. But . . ." She lapsed into silence.

"But you need to think things out. That's only natural." Maddy turned away. "Come on, husband. Time we went."

Tom gave Jewel a sad little smile; then the two of them walked away.

What Maddy had told her was that she, Jewel, was welcome to stay with herself and Tom for as long as she liked. By now, Jewel knew that the Snaffles were childless. They seemed genuinely fond of her. But she could never live in a settlement, never get used to settlement life – not even with people who cared for her. The life of the road was too much in her blood. She must have movement, and change. Still, that was only part of it. When, two nights before, she'd finally grasped the brutal fact that her father was dead, a simple notion had lodged itself in her mind: his killers must pay for what they'd done. By this time, the three tumblers who'd chased the masked men had returned to report that the killers had vanished into the night. By this time, too, Shelf's Headman had been informed. He came straight to the maze. The fairground fell under his jurisdiction; he arranged for the dead man to be removed to the building that was used for such purposes. He tried Jewel with a couple of gentle questions, but the girl was too shocked to speak to him coherently. He left her with Rainy Gill who, refusing to quit her side, had spontaneously assumed responsibility for her welfare. Rainy took the girl off to her own tent on the edge of the fairground, made her a hot beverage with some sleep-inducing herbs, and put her to bed.

Jewel slept soundly and rose late the following morning. Rainy offered her breakfast, but she couldn't eat anything. After a while the Headman reappeared. The killers, he said, had got into the mirror maze by forcing the lock on a rear door, and had made their escape by the same route. None of the fairground people had seen them. He questioned her about her attackers, but she could remember little: they were masked, they were dressed in black, they'd stolen her father's money-bag.

"But not yours?" prompted the Headman, noting the bulge at her waist.

"No ... I think – well, maybe they were going to, maybe they didn't see it . . . I don't know. Father was carrying most of yesterday's takings anyway, three-quarters perhaps . . ."

"And you've no clue as to their identity? Did they use each other's names?"

"I can't remember," she said. "My mind's a blank . . ."

"Best leave the girl be," said Rainy Gill. "Perhaps she'll remember something later."

Jewel set off along one of the paths that led away from the graveyard. She didn't care what direction she took: she simply wanted to be on the move. The graveyard lay a short distance from the settlement on the opposite side of Shelf to its garden-plot and fields. Criss-crossed with pathways, the area must be used by the locals for exercise. When she looked back, the men with spades were busily at work. She sniffed, and blew her nose. It was time to focus her mind. She must try to remember: to picture in her mind the men who'd attacked herself and her father. What they'd looked like, what they'd said.

They were masked, and dressed in black . . . but she needed more than that. She closed her eyes and concentrated: the mirror-glass of memory, it was there she must look. For a time there was nothing, but then something welled up and she saw the figure who'd seized her. But "masked" was only half of it: he was hooded too . . . What did that mean? That he wanted to hide the top of his head as well as his face? The hood was close-fitting, would have been harder than a mask for an opponent to tear off . . . The man had been tall and athletic, very quick on his feet. So had the second assailant, the one who'd murdered her father. The two were so alike . . . The first figure dissolved, to be replaced by the second. She saw again his mouth, with its full, vermilion lips . . . his eyes of coldest blue that had looked at her as if she was barely human, something disposable, an insect you might crush beneath your foot unthinkingly . . . The men had called each other *bro*—

Bro. She'd forgotten that. *Bro* . . . a strange word. What could it mean? They could hardly have the same name . . . But *bro* wasn't a name. Bro . . . *brother*! She'd heard the term before: an intimate form of address. They were brothers, they had to be. Not only that, *twin* brothers.

Instantly she knew with certainty who they were. Not their names, no, but *who they were*, what they looked like. The man with red hair, who'd watched her from the cook stall . . . who'd fought in the boxing match and bitten off Dan Block's ear: Red the Ruthless. He was one of them. The other was the blond man who'd acted as his second. They were identical, except for hair colour. The hoods they'd worn . . . yes, of course, to cover up their hair, which would have given them away! No other two men resembled them.

Whom to tell? The Headman, of course. But first, Rainy Gill. She got about, she might even know the men's names.

Jewel hurried away. The greater part of the Fair had already been disassembled. It made for a melancholy sight. As she passed

121

through what remained, a nearby marquee subsided airily with a long sigh. Rainy was outside her tent, juggling ferociously.

"Rainy! I know who they are!"

One by one, Rainy's clubs dropped to the ground.

"What, the men who killed your father?"

"Yes!"

"Calm yourself, Jewel. Tell me their names."

"I don't know – but I know who they were! We must call the Headman."

"How can you know who they are if you don't know their names?"

"It's the man with red hair, Red the Ruthless, and his brother. I've just remembered – they called each other *bro*!"

"Hold on: Red the Ruthless?"

"The one who beat the Champion of Champions – bit his ear!"

"Right . . . What about *bro*?"

"That what's they called each other in the maze. Don't you see? *Bro* for *brother*! They're identical twins! That's why they're so alike! Now all we need are their names!"

"Oh, I know their names."

"You do? Wonderful! We'll tell the Headman, and he'll go and bring them in."

But Rainy, it seemed, didn't share her enthusiasm. She looked thoughtfully at her dropped clubs.

"What's wrong?" asked Jewel.

"You didn't see their faces . . . Nobody saw their faces . . . All you know is that they called each other *bro* – but any brothers might, identical twins or not."

"But I know it's them!"

"I believe you. But don't you see how flimsy all this is? Say the Headman goes and confronts them: all they have to do is deny it was them; say they were somewhere else at the time. They'll laugh in his face. But I very much doubt the Headman would even bother to go near them."

"But why not, if they're guilty?"

"Because I've heard of these men, what they're like, and so has he."

"What do you mean?"

"Jewel – these aren't ordinary men you're talking about. They're rich and powerful. They do what they like. They're a law unto themselves. You saw what the redhead did to Dan Block's ear. He didn't care. He knew the Headman wouldn't take any action against him."

"But if they're rich, why do they steal?"

"Who knows? Because it amuses them, perhaps? Because they can? I've told you: they do just what they like. They're the sort that steal just for kicks."

"And kill for kicks, too?"

"I fear so."

There was a silence. Jewel was staring at Rainy, despondency etched into her face.

"Another thing," said her friend. "They live a good way from here – up on the ridge above Judy Wood. They live in a house called Roydsal. It was built by the giants. They have men working for them – men prepared to do whatever's asked of them, even down to killing. Or so the rumour goes. I'm afraid it's hopeless,

Jewel: no Headman would approach them on the evidence you have."

Even as she said this, Rainy hated herself. She might just as well, she knew, have slashed the girl's arm with a knife. But these things had to be said: Jewel had to face the truth. And Rainy believed in being truthful, even if the truth hurt the one to whom it was told. But now, as she looked at Jewel, the girl's face – before so soft, so full of expression, so attractive in its euphoria – seemed to cool, to petrify. This gemlike Jewel said, "If nobody else will avenge my father, I'll do it myself. Tell me please, Rainy Gill: what are the names of these men?"

She means it, thought Rainy.

"The red-haired one is Lanner Spetch. The blond is Zak Spetch. As you guessed, they're identical twins."

"Thank you. Please excuse me. I've got something to do." She half-turned on her heel, then looked back at Rainy. "Thank you for looking after me. I'm all right now. Goodbye."

"Goodbye, then," said Rainy.

Jewel turned away again, and Rainy watched as she marched away.

When the girl was out of sight, Rainy picked up her clubs. But she couldn't juggle now. That cold goodbye . . . to part like that, without even speaking one another's name . . . She moistened her lips. The taste of dust was in her mouth. Things, the day itself, seemed brutally broken-off. What would the girl do now? What *could* the girl do now? Rainy felt guilty: Red the Ruthless . . . But wasn't she Rainy the Ruthless, with her blunt truth-speaking? There's more than one way, she thought, of biting off someone's ear. Still, she'd had to say what she'd said, hadn't she? No one could touch the Spetches, of that she was convinced. If Jewel confronted the brothers, they'd laugh in her face . . . or do something worse. One thing was certain, she couldn't let Jewel go like that, ignorant, alone . . . A purpose formed in her mind, and she moved towards her tent.

Jewel knocked on the Snaffles' door.

"I've come to say goodbye," she said.

"Goodbye?" repeated Maddy. "But where are you going, Jewel?"

Unwilling to speak of her intentions, Jewel said, "I don't know."

"You don't know?" echoed Tom.

"Please don't worry about me. I'm used to life on the road. Look . . ." She searched for the right words. "You're lovely people, and if I thought I could settle down, it would be here with you. But – I can't. You see, travelling's all I've known. It's in my blood, and there it is." This, of course, was less than the whole truth, but it certainly wasn't untrue.

"We understand, love," said Maddy. "Well, may God go with you, child."

"Yes, may God go with you," echoed Tom.

"Goodbye, then, Jewel Ranson," said Maddy. She threw her arms around Jewel and gave her a great hug, which Jewel returned.

"Goodbye, Maddy," said Jewel.

She embraced Tom, and they too said goodbye.

When she got back to the Dewdrop, the trader she'd spoken to at the funeral was waiting in one of the snugs, a pot of beer in front of him. They shook hands, he downed his ale, and they went through into the yard. There she showed him the goods that remained unsold.

He examined them, then said, "How much do you want?"

Jewel had already done her sums, and named a figure double what her father had paid the makers for the clothes. "You'll get twice, three times that, when you sell them," she told him.

"Umm . . ." The man pondered, then offered her a sum somewhat less than the one she'd specified.

"Let's split the difference," said Jewel.

"It's a deal," said the man. They shook hands.

Then the man said, "Do you want to sell the wagon?"

"Yes." She steeled herself and said, "Do you want to buy my rat? She's called Smoky – she's a superior animal."

"I know, I've seen her. I'm tempted – my own rat is getting on. But it would have to be part-exchange. And you don't want a rat yourself now, do you? Look, the landlord of the Dewdrop will give you a fair price. Sell her to him, then I'll take a look at her."

"Right. The wagon, then."

They haggled briefly, and agreed a sum. Again they shook hands. The man counted out the money from his waist-bag, and handed it over. Jewel removed her own and Elliot's personal effects from the wagon. Then, together, she and the trader put the garments she'd sold him back in the wagon.

The man said, "Have to get this little beauty repainted."

"You will." She could say no more.

He nodded to her, and went off to get his rat.

Jewel contemplated the wagon. Farewell, RANSON AND

DAUGHTER, she thought. But though these visible signs of her old life would soon be gone, she felt little sense of freedom. Till I settle with the Spetches I shall never be truly free . . .

She went into the tent and squatted down on her sleeping bag: here was all her father's gear. Not to mention a good deal of her own which she couldn't possibly squeeze into her rucksack. What to do with it? I'll give it all to the landlord, she thought – let him distribute it to needy people, if it's worth distributing. Only one thing of her father's would she keep. She took it out of her pocket and laid it on her palm: his gold ring. As she looked at it, tears pricked her eyes, and she had to wipe them away. But she'd done her crying. The ring was too big to wear on her finger, but somewhere there'd be a goldsmith who'd re-size it for her. In the meantime . . . she threaded the ring on a strong piece of twine and hung it around her neck.

She sat for a while, then got up and went to look for the landlord. Yes, he'd be perfectly happy to get rid of whatever she didn't want. There were families he knew who'd be glad of the clothes. And the rat: well, he was certainly interested in her, but he'd have to consult his ratman.

Selling Smoky was almost more than Jewel could bear. As she stood outside the stall with the landlord and the ratman, dispassionately discussing the finer points of the animal before them (her sleek fur, bright eyes, small ears – erect and wide-spaced – and straight, whippy tail), Jewel felt truly awful. Guilt washed in upon her. Smoky watched them as they talked, and the girl didn't need the ratman to tell her the rat was intelligent. Smoky knew perfectly well what was happening. She lay with her head on her forepaws in a posture bespeaking her powerlessness, gazing up at Jewel with mute reproach in her eyes.

When a price had been agreed and the money added to Jewel's stock, she asked if the landlord would grant her a little time alone with his new purchase. Of course, he answered.

As for the last time Jewel stroked Smoky under the jaw and the rat nuzzled affectionately into her chest, it seemed impossible to the girl that she had done what she had. Who was she, *what* was she to behave with such detachment, such single-mindedness? If I don't know, I'm going to find out, she told herself.

She kissed Smoky on her muzzle, feeling her coldness on her lips, murmured "Goodbye, goodbye", turned away and left the rattery without looking back.

She was tying the tent onto her rucksack when a voice spoke behind her.

"Hello, Jewel."

She turned. Rainy Gill.

"I didn't get to tell you, but I'm going your way. I was wondering if you'd like to have a travelling companion."

Jewel smiled. "I'd like nothing better," she said.

One last thing had to be done before Jewel took leave of Shelf. Rainy accompanied her. Elliot's grave, filled in now, was a painful mound of fresh-turned earth. Rainy stayed back as Jewel unshouldered her pack, approached the grave and knelt down beside it. After a time, she put out a hand and grasped a handful of loam. It was cool and gritty. Her lips moved in a solemn vow, then she let the soil trickle back onto the grave. It was done.

For some time they walked in silence. Ahead of them and

behind them, other people were on the move. Some drove wagons, others were pushing or pulling handcarts. But Jewel was too preoccupied to pay much attention to what was outside her. When at last she did begin to take note of the country through which they were travelling, she saw that its contours were softening, patches of moorland with rocky outcrops giving way to stretches of grassland dotted with clumps of trees and bushes.

"This road," she said, "where does it go?"

"The nearest settlement's called Butshaw, but we're not going that way. I live in a place called Harrypark. Lowmoor lies beyond it. But the road you want's the Wyke road. We'll reach the turn-off around midday tomorrow."

"What kind of place is Harrypark?"

"A place like no other."

"Do you live alone?"

"I live with my father. He's blind."

"How sad . . . And your mother?"

Rainy hesitated, then said, "She died two years ago, in an outbreak of the sweats."

"I'm sorry . . . My mother died five years ago. She got a fever. The Syb couldn't save her."

"Sybs can only do so much, can't they? Even the cleverest . . ."

They walked on, conscious of a mutual sympathy.

"Are you away from home a lot?"

"Yes, quite a bit," said Rainy. "It comes with doing what I do. I go round all the Fairs and perform at festivities. It's an enjoyable life. Not that I make a lot – just enough for us to live on. We don't need much."

"And your father – he copes all right when you're away?"

"Oh yes. He moves around the house quite easily. We have neighbours who visit, help out with food – that sort of thing."

"Was he always blind?"

"No, it was an accident a good few years ago – when my mother was still alive. He was exploring the ruined ironworks on the far side of Lowmoor. He knew it was dangerous, but he's always been headstrong. He had a lamp in this dark building. There must have been something in the air, for there was a flash and his eyes were seared. He never got his sight back. But he's cheerful by nature. He's glad to be alive, when so many people aren't." She paused. "Why don't you come and stay for a day or two? I have a friend who knows the Spetches. He could tell you something about them."

Jewel considered this. "It's nice of you to ask, but I feel I have to get on. I can't think of anything but these brothers and what they did."

"But what will you do when you get to Roydsal and see them?"

"I'll think of something."

The truth was that Jewel had no idea what to do. How could *she*, a girl of fifteen, kill two grown men? She couldn't even fire a bow.

Rainy was thinking the same thing. But what could she say?

As afternoon wore on, the ramparts of a great wood became visible to the west. Through the evening it grew in size, greenly buttressing the sky. Its name was Judy Wood, said Rainy, children hereabouts were raised on tales of the horrors that lurked within. Sensible folk kept their distance. Though she and Rainy were the travellers, it seemed to Jewel that the trees too were in motion, stealthily creeping towards them.

The road skirted its northernmost part, and they made camp that night in its lee. Sharing a tent with another female was a new experience for Jewel, but it proved a pleasant one. The pair had fallen into an easy comradeship. What a pity that tomorrow Jewel would have to bid Rainy goodbye.

Next morning, the atmosphere between them had changed. Both women seemed constrained by the awareness that they must part, and Jewel walk away into an uncertain future. Rainy did her best to hide her worry about her friend, but without much success. Conversation limped along, broken by awkward silences.

The road followed the curve of the wood then began to drop away, leaving the treeline marching south-west along the brow of the hill.

"Here's the fork," said Rainy.

The Harrypark road ran away westwards.

Just then a rumble of wheels became audible to their rear. A rat-cart was approaching.

Jewel and Rainy halted.

"Rainy—" began the girl.

But Jewel got no further. A savage pain had erupted at the front of her skull. She cried out, put a hand to her forehead and dropped to her knees.

"What is it, Jewel?" asked Rainy, anxiety in her voice.

But Jewel was prostrate, clutching her head with both hands, and could say nothing.

9

THE CRAYFISH HUNT

"So," said Racky Jagger, "where are you making for, Manningham?"

They were at breakfast the following morning. The Ranter, his taste for stoat not yet exhausted, was washing down cold cuts with mugs of herbal tea. Racky and Thorn contented themselves with oatcakes and dried fruit.

"God willing, my way lies westwards, Racky. First call Shibbin, then over the top to Hallax. But to tell you the truth . . ."

His voice tailed away.

"Tell me what?" prompted Racky.

"I've got a horrible feeling that I've taken the wrong turning."

"You *could* have taken the last left. You can turn round and go back. But there's another track on the far side of Judy Stream. Well-marked and direct, too. Once you're on that you can't go wrong."

"You don't know me. Fine. I'll stick with you until we get there. And where are you making for?"

"Us? We have business at the Punch and Judy Inn."

"What! You're taking this young man to that godforsaken place?"

"That's what I said, Manningham."

132

It was clear that the Ranter disapproved of their destination. Thorn's curiosity was aroused.

"What's wrong with the inn?" he asked.

"Don't you know?" exclaimed Sparks.

"Well, no," replied Thorn.

"Don't you tell this young man *anything*?" said the Ranter to Racky. Racky grinned and shrugged. The Ranter turned back to Thorn. "If the inn was merely an inn, I'd have no objection to the place. It's what's *at* the inn that's the problem."

He fell silent again. Another prod struck Thorn as necessary. "What's that, Reverend Sparks?"

The Ranter levelled his gaze at Thorn. "The Judymen, that's what."

"Judymen?" echoed Thorn.

"Yes, the Judymen. Pagans – idolaters – self-styled enemies of God."

"Can't you convert them?" asked Thorn.

The Ranter laughed. "You might as well try to teach a jackdaw table-manners. Some have tried, but the Judymen are far gone in godlessness. Now, ignorance of the Divinity is one thing, young man, but heathen rituals such as they practise – well, our comfort must be that they will be damned eternally in the eyes of God for what they do."

"Surely," said Racky mildly, "you exaggerate, Manningham. They may be odd, but they're harmless."

"Harmless!" The scandalised Ranter all but exploded. Shreds of half-masticated stoat shot out of his mouth. "Harmless? How can they be?"

133

"Well, I've never heard of them hurting or killing anyone – which is more than you can say for the Woodmen. Now *there's* a dangerous lot. Capable of anything. Dabbled in blood, they are."

Judymen – Woodmen – strange names were coming thick and fast.

"Can't say I've ever bumped into the Woodmen," said the Ranter.

"And you don't want to neither. But the route you'll be travelling goes nowhere near their patch. As long as you stick to it, of course."

"Don't worry: I mean to."

"I'm not the worrying type."

Thorn found none of this exactly reassuring. But it was time to put to the Ranter the big question he'd saved up.

"Reverend Sparks—" he began.

"Yes, young man?"

"Can I ask you something?"

"Of course."

Reaching into a pocket inside his jacket, Thorn pulled out the yellow feather and passed it to the Ranter.

"Have you ever seen the like of this before?"

Sparks examined the feather, then handed it back to Thorn.

"I'm afraid not." Seeing the disappointment on his questioner's face, he added: "I can see this is a matter of some importance to you. Would you like to tell me why?"

"My sister was kidnapped. I found this at the place where it happened. It looks like an emblem. But we don't know whose. That's why we're going to the inn – to ask the landlord there."

"I see . . . Just the two of you?"

Thorn nodded.

"That's a tall order. I'll pray for your success – and for your sister to have the strength to cope with her adversity."

Thorn wasn't sure what help praying might be, but he wasn't going to say so to the Ranter. He muttered his thanks.

"Well, Reverend," said Racky. "Time to move. Shake your legs."

They packed up their gear, stamped out the fire and were on their way.

The ground began to rise. Soon they were really climbing. Racky and Thorn were fit and nimble, but in front of Thorn the Ranter began to huff and puff.

"Racky – Racky!" he panted. "Must stop for a rest."

Racky stopped and looked back. "Finding the going tough, eh?"

"Just a tad," gasped the red-faced Reverend.

"Stick around. It gets tougher."

"What do you mean?" exclaimed Sparks.

"Brokenbanks is what I mean. The place is well-named. You'll see why when we get there."

The Ranter did, too – not only *see*, but gape in dismay. Between steeply sloping banks of yellowy clay, pitted with rocks, the earth dropped away. At the bottom of the ravine the Judy Stream gushed along, too boisterous to ford or swim. To complete the cleric's misery, anchored to stakes on either side, a rudimentary rope bridge hung across the chasm. It was made of close-set planks attached to a double row of cables. Along the left-hand side of the walkway, connected to the base at intervals by vertical cords, ran a hand-rope.

"Surely," said Manningham Sparks, "this isn't the only way across."

"Oh, but it is," said Racky. "Still, what's a bit of a bridge to a man of your calibre?"

"A 'bit of a bridge' is exactly what it is," came the reply. "Why didn't you warn me about this?"

"Warn a Ranter? A man who can always pray to God for a helping hand?"

The Ranter was indignant. "God helps those who help themselves."

"You don't say?" said Racky dryly. "Well, you can always go back."

The Ranter thought for a moment. Then, unexpectedly, he laughed and declared: "Why should I worry? I'm in the hands of God. He creates and He destroys. If my time has come, so be it. Lead on, Racky Jagger."

Gripping the rope, Racky stepped onto the walkway. It trembled as he did so, but he advanced confidently, sliding his fist along the handrope. Soon he was halfway across. The bridge had been tightly stretched, and there was barely a breeze today. Even so, the walkway swayed.

Gaining the far bank, Racky turned and waved at them. "Nothing to it!" he called. "You next, Reverend!"

Manningham Sparks advanced to the bridge, performed his ritual hand-movement and stepped onto the walkway. At first he tried to cross as Racky had done, but had taken no more than a dozen increasingly faltering steps when he stopped, held his position for a moment, then twisted his body round so that he faced the handrope and was looking down the ravine as opposed to across it. Gripping the rope with both hands, he edged sideways along the walkway. He'd got a little over halfway across when the trouble began. The bridge began to wobble, the wobble turned into a pendulum movement. When the Ranter tried to correct the yaw by leaning backwards, the planking swung up and away from him like the platform of a swing on which a child is standing. It looked, for a moment, as if the minister would fall backwards into the stream. But somehow he managed to keep his feet in contact with the planks. He clung there, his boots almost level with his head, his body bent in a comical arc, his broad bottom sticking out. Thanks to its chinstrap, his hat stayed on his head. Yet all the time his backpack and his weight were dragging him downwards, towards the roiling waters.

His position was undignified and absurd. But perilous too. It was obvious that he couldn't help himself. As Thorn watched, Sparks pulled on the rope with both hands, trying to shift his weight and re-level the walkway: but the effort failed, and he was left in the same position as before. Racky, meanwhile, lounged at the far end of the bridge, content – it seemed – to do nothing. Was there even the ghost of a smile on his face?

Now the Ranter shut his eyes. His lips began to move. Could it be that he was praying?

There was nothing else for it. Quickly unhooking his pack, Thorn stepped out onto the bridge. He edged sideways along the bridge as the Ranter had done, leaning on the handrope so that his weight angled the walkway in the opposite direction to that caused by the hanging man. But the nearer he got to the Ranter, the more the planks resisted him. The Ranter was heavier than he was. Should he have kept his pack on? But then he'd have forfeited manoeuvrability.

He called out to Manningham Sparks. "Come on, Reverend: try again to level the bridge, but steadily, now."

The Ranter made no reply, but again he hauled on the rope, trying to raise his body and bring the planking back beneath him. Again the manoeuvre defeated him. This is crazy, thought Thorn. I'm supposed to be here for Haw, not this clumsy lump of a Ranter. Below, furious water churned along the narrow gorge. If Thorn let go, he'd drop like a shot bird into the foam. And that would be that.

He held his position for a moment, furiously thinking: what else could he do? Only one thing, perhaps. Turning his body so that he faced in the opposite direction to the Ranter, he gripped the rope with both hands, let his body sag back and forced the planking away from him. Then he edged along towards the centre. Between himself and Manningham Sparks, the walkway was violently twisted.

"Now, when I give the word, try again. Slowly, mind you. Are you ready, Reverend?"

The Ranter nodded, as if too exhausted to speak.

"All right. Now!" called Thorn.

The two of them strained on the rope, striving to bring their feet back beneath their bodies. The bridge wobbled as the two men moved towards the point of balance; then, with a convulsion that nearly threw Thorn into the river, the walkway untwisted, shivered, and re-levelled itself.

Carefully, Thorn manoeuvred himself back under the rope till he faced along the bridge.

"You now, Reverend," he called.

The Ranter edged along the walkway. As the bridge swayed, Thorn held still, steadying it. It seemed to take an age, but at last the Ranter was across. He collapsed, heaving and gasping, on the grass at Racky's feet.

"My goodness, Manningham, you made a meal of that," said Racky. "I thought you were going to stop for a swim."

"A swim?" managed the Ranter. "A drowning, more like. Thank you so much for your help."

"It seemed a shame to interfere. I was waiting to see what your God would do for you. Funny thing is, He didn't seem to lift a divine finger to help you out."

"That's where you're wrong," said the Ranter. He gestured back across the gorge at Thorn, who had returned for his backpack. "Haven't I told you before? God works in roundabout ways. He sent help, all right – but in human form."

Racky laughed. "You zealots!" he said. "Got an answer for everything."

"Not so," said the Ranter, fast regaining his equilibrium. "Only God has an answer for everything. But that's not something *you're* ever likely to understand."

They watched Thorn as he came back across the bridge. He moved slowly and carefully.

"That young man's one in a thousand," said the Ranter.

"Then you were lucky," said Racky, "that he wasn't one of the other nine hundred and ninety-nine."

They drank from their bottles. When the Ranter declared himself ready, they moved on again.

Soon Brokenbanks was behind them and – to celebrate their triumph? – the sun made an appearance. Thorn felt his spirits expand. Men with yellow feathers? He'd show them!

The pathway here was broad enough for two to travel abreast, and Manningham Sparks fell back and kept pace with Thorn. For a time, neither spoke. Racky had moved some way ahead.

Then Manningham said, "I thank God, Thorn Jack, that the good Lord has touched your soul – unlike that heathen there." He indicated their leader. "If any man was ever bound for Hell, he's the one."

Thorn pondered for a moment. Racky might be untrustworthy, but he had no evidence he was wicked. And he was definitely brave. "What exactly *is* Hell?" he asked.

"Well, I have to admit that opinions among the sects differ somewhat about Hell. The most common belief is that Hell is a fiery place under the earth, full of ugly, malevolent devils who inflict monstrous torments upon sinners. A few of us, however, hold a different view. For myself, I'm more inclined to think that if Heaven is the place where God *is*, Hell must be the place where He is *not*."

"Where He is *not*?" Thorn was puzzled.

"Yes. I think of Hell as a place much like the Barrens – void and featureless, with nothing to nourish and sustain body and soul. Imagine being condemned to wander in such a place for ever, never to escape from it, seeing nothing but the whiteness under your feet, no other person, and raging with thirst. And day after day, to feel nothing but despair, utter despair . . ."

Thorn, who had fallen under the spell of the man's words, shuddered despite the sun's heat: for a moment he was in the Barrens, trudging across the white earth, his tongue parched in his mouth, light dancing in his eyes.

"What are you saying to the lad?" said a sharp voice.

Shaking himself out of his reverie, Thorn saw that Racky Jagger had stopped, and was staring at them. He and Manningham Sparks stopped too.

"Oh, just this and that," said the Ranter nonchalantly.

"This and that be damned. You've been filling his head with nonsense, putting the fear of God into him."

Now the Ranter was indignant. "I've been doing no such thing – have I, young man?"

"Er, no . . ." offered Thorn.

"I'll bet," said Racky. "The lad saves your life and you stuff him with flap-doodle. Well, there'll be no more of that. Come on, lad, walk with me."

And so, their party reconfigured, the three set off again.

They broke for a longer rest and a bite to eat just after noon. Still smarting, perhaps, from Racky's unexpected rebuke, the Ranter said nothing, contenting himself with getting something into his stomach. Racky seemed sunk in thought. It was Thorn who broke the silence.

"Ranter Sparks," he began, "you seem to have thought deeply about the nature of the world . . ."

The Ranter glanced at Racky, saw his attention was elsewhere, and raised an encouraging eyebrow.

Thorn went on, "Well . . . I was wondering about the giants, those who lived in the Dark Time. What do you think happened to them?"

"That's a very good question, Thorn, and we men of the cloth don't all subscribe to the same answer. There are those who believe the giants caused themselves to disappear – even destroyed themselves. But, powerful though they were, I don't myself believe the giants were powerful enough to manage that."

"So someone else made them disappear?" suggested Thorn.

"Very good. But who?"

"God?"

"Exactly. God alone has that kind of power."

"So they're in Heaven or in Hell?"

"Yes, but which? Now, setting aside such sects as The True Believers, we Ranters divide pretty evenly on those who think the giants are in Heaven and those who think they're in Hell. Myself, young man, I go for Heaven, and I'll tell you why. When I look at the structures the giants left behind – even though most are in ruins now – I'm convinced their makers were a superior race. Having perfected themselves and proved themselves in the eyes of their Creator, they were lifted up and away to enjoy their eternal reward. As we ourselves might be lifted up, if we could perfect our own natures. But alas –" and here the Ranter looked glum "– I fear we are a long way from that at present."

This rather downbeat comment brought the exchange to an end. After a pause, Racky said dryly, "You're right about that,

Manningham, if about nothing else. But that will be the last that we shall hear from you today – for very soon now we'll hit the parting of our ways."

He spoke the truth. They had not gone much further when the track divided.

"Well, Manningham," said Racky, "this is where we part. Stick to this path and you'll come out on the forest road."

"I'm in your debt," said the Ranter.

"Nonsense. Your company was as stimulating as ever."

"Yours too," said the Ranter wryly. "Had it been any more so, I'd have been stimulated to death. Goodbye, you old rogue." He turned to Thorn. "And you, young man, take care. And so, farewell."

"Goodbye, Manningham Sparks," rejoined Thorn, "and go well."

And he watched the Ranter stride off down the path. Where it twisted, Sparks turned round, waved once, then was gone.

"So much for religion," said Racky, and on the two of them went.

Once more, they were in the thick of the wood. So dense was the leaf-canopy, only occasional shafts of sunlight succeeded in breaking through. The forest floor was a black mulch of rotting twigs and leaves up through which, here and there, a brave sprig poked where a beech seed or acorn had germinated.

The afternoon wore on. They passed a group of three pedlars coming the other way, who acknowledged them with wary nods. One of the pedlars was pushing a cart; the others carried heavy packs. With them was a young lad, three or four years younger than Thorn, limping along a little behind them. He looked exhausted.

At last they came to a stream – a very different proposition from the torrent back in the ravine. Four feet wide at its broadest point, it meandered pleasantly past, lit where the sun struck through. The ground was firm on either bank and sloped gently down to the water. In places it was no more than a couple of inches deep. And here was a line of stepping-stones.

They went across, pausing halfway to replenish their water bottles. On the far side, however, Racky surprised Thorn. Instead of carrying on down the track, he threw out a curt "This way!" and set off along the watercourse.

They hadn't gone far when the stream emptied itself into a broad pool. Around its margins, under the shade, the water's barely moving surface appeared almost black. Further out, the sun burnished it to a golden gloss. Haw, thought Thorn, would have loved this place.

Racky Jagger unhooked his pack. Thorn followed suit.

"Wait here," said Racky, climbed the bank and disappeared into the greenery.

Thorn studied the play of the light on the skin of the pool. Out in the middle, a fish jumped – probably a brook trout. The air was heated here, like an early summer day. It would have been easy to lie back and fall asleep.

But he didn't. After a time, Racky returned. In his hands were two straight staves. They were eight inches long and had been sharpened at one end.

"We need a change from stoat," he said. "Also something to

trade at the Punch and Judy Inn. Can you swim underwater?"

"Of course," replied Thorn. He'd been taught to swim by Taylor at the age of six in a pool near Norgreen. He and Haw loved to swim.

"Have you ever hunted crayfish?" was Racky's next question.

"Crayfish? What are they?"

Racky grinned. "You'll find out – if we catch one. But first a warning: they'll look like nothing you've seen before – so don't waste time being surprised: that's a luxury you can't afford. They have pairs of claws with vicious nippers you've got to avoid. Also, they're covered in shell-like plates a stave can't penetrate. Ugly creatures but great to eat. You have to attack them where the plates join. Best of all, go for the mouth. That's under the head. Got it?"

Thorn was not at all sure that he had, but he nodded.

"Right," said Racky. "Strip off. It's warm here, but the water will be cold."

He began to undress. Thorn followed suit. When they were both down to the short pants they wore under their trews, Racky strapped his belt and knife-sheath back around his waist. Thorn copied him.

Then Racky handed one of the staves to Thorn. "Good hunting, lad. And remember – keep away from those pincers." He waded into the pool and disappeared beneath its surface.

Is he crazy? thought Thorn. If he is, so am I.

The water was chill against his flesh. Taking a deep breath, he ducked down and pushed out after Racky.

His stave wanted to return to the surface, which gave him a

problem. He solved it by tucking the weapon underneath his body. Keeping a hand on its shaft meant he could use only one arm for swimming, but it would do. He liked being underwater, and knew he could stay down for quite a time. In any case, the pool wasn't deep – no more than eighteen inches, perhaps, at its deepest point. The water was very clear, especially where the sun struck. He swam over a gravelly bottom, steering clear of the rocks that here and there jutted up. Feathery streamers of weed wavered, reaching up towards the sun. A shoal of minnows, silver darts each the length of his arm, shot away as he approached. Ahead of him, Racky swam with powerful kicks of his legs.

After a time Racky surfaced. Thorn knew he could have stayed down longer, but there was no point in overstretching himself. He did likewise.

"Cold enough for you?" asked Racky.

"Just how I like it," replied Thorn.

"Right – down we go again. Stay close, and don't poke me with that stick!"

They re-submerged. A brown trout, hovering over a rock, spotted Thorn with a glaucous eye and, with a flick of its powerful tail, was away across the pool.

But it was the only thing of any size he saw. They surfaced and dived three times more.

"Could be we're out of luck," gasped Racky, treading water. "We've covered the best places. One more try, and we'll call it a day."

Down they went again.

This time, they hadn't been long underwater when Racky

touched Thorn on the shoulder. Thorn followed his pointing arm and saw the crayfish on a stone. It might have been an inch or two shorter than he was. Its back and sides, encased in tough-looking armour-plates, were a dull green. Later he'd observe that it had a yellowish underside. It had a fanlike tail and numerous pairs of what looked like jointed legs. Its head was almost flattened at the end. On top, set on moveable stalks, were its eyes. From underneath protruded two long feelers and several shorter ones. Here too was its mouth, which as Thorn drew nearer dropped open, disclosing jaws that looked designed to bite. Its pincers were powerful enough to crush your limbs. It looked a formidable foe.

Racky motioned Thorn to move a little away from him; then they moved in together, slowly.

But not slowly enough. The crayfish had seen or sensed them, and with a swish of its tail was a foot away, landing on another stone. Again the swimmers came towards it –

– and again it jumped away. Like an underwater grasshopper, only bigger, thought Thorn. This time it came to rest on a patch of gravel, barely disturbing the fine grains. At this rate they'd never catch it. They returned to the surface for air, then dived again.

Remembering Racky's advice, Thorn came in low, swimming as close to the surface of the gravel as he could. Browny grains brushed his knee. This time, for some reason, the crayfish didn't move. Propelled by growing excitement, Thorn was slightly to the fore. Pulling his legs in underneath him, he stood upright on the pool's bed. Then, finding himself solidly based, he reached out with his stave, and jabbed at the creature's head. But he'd misjudged his lunge: the point of the stave struck an armoured plate and glanced off to the side. Before he could recover, the crayfish had seized the stave in a pincer, and wrenched it away from him. Its jaws gaped and it swiped at him with its free claw. As Thorn kicked himself up and away, Racky stabbed at the monster's mouth. His aim was good: the point slid home and the creature jerked backwards. But now, with a wave of its other pincer, it had snapped the stave in two. The broken portions floated upwards.

Still the animal was alive. Thorn now grabbed hold of the end of his stave. For long moments, he tried to wrestle it from the animal in the slow motion of underwater. Then the crayfish shook its claw, and Thorn lost his grip. But so had the creature. As the stave twirled lazily away from the pair of them, Racky caught hold of it, kicked downwards and lunged at its jaws again. The point drove into the creature's throat. It convulsed, and swung a claw. Its pincers scored Racky's shoulder. Scarlet threads of blood spiralled up through the water, but the man hung onto the stave. Thorn now grasped it too and together the pair drove it deeper still. The crayfish leapt upwards, carrying the pair with it, then its body went slack. Its claws drooped loosely, and it drifted down to the gravel. Racky pointed upwards, and he and Thorn kicked up to the surface.

Now what? wondered Thorn as he thirstily sucked in air. The answer came soon enough. Racky looped a rope around the unresisting body; with the help of the water's buoyancy, they dragged the crayfish into the shallows. Then, with Thorn following his companion's instructions, they went to work with their knives. As they sawed and hacked, the warm sun dried their skins, and Thorn felt the chill leaving his body, bit by bit.

Racky made light of his wound. "It's a scratch," he said, "no more."

He took some ointment from his pack and smeared it on the cuts. Then, using flint and tinder, he built a fire on the edge of the pool, and they roasted joints of crayfish in the shell, to protect the meat from charring. A pungent fish-flesh aroma scented the air. Handling the scorched shells with care, they cracked them open with stones and picked the hot flesh out with their fingers. Thorn had never eaten anything quite so wonderful. The delicate, savoury flesh melted on his tongue.

Racky, tucking in with just as much gusto as Thorn, was, as usual, silent during the meal. He'd made no comment at all on what had happened underwater. It was as if the incident was a thing of no consequence, an everyday occurrence. What a strange man this was, thought Thorn. Twice, now, they'd shared situations that might have ended in either or both of their deaths. He ought, surely, to feel closer to this man than any other he'd ever known – and that included Taylor. Yet Racky was as distant now as he'd been when he'd rapped on the door on the morning of their departure. What was it the Ranter had said of him – that he was a puzzle? – that he was as changeable and as unpredictable as the weather? It was true: Thorn could make nothing of the man. Did he trust him? Well, hadn't he just done so – trusted Racky with his life?

His one regret, as he settled down to sleep in the flickering, kindly light of the fire, was that Haw was not there to eat crayfish by his side.

10
LINDEN'S BABY

Turquoise water. The mesh of fish closed, swirling around Jewel like a flock of wingless birds. But she kicked out and the net broke and went spiralling away from her, silver on emerald.

Sunlight struck down through the water. Above lay a flat, silken membrane – the surface. She arrowed her fingers towards it, broke through and opened her eyes.

There was a room, flowery-painted. There was a window, flowery-curtained. There was a bed, flowery-quilted. And in the bed, herself.

Her headache, she realised, had gone. On a cupboard beside the bed stood a mug and a jug of water. She drew her body up into a sitting position and the curtained window in her line of vision lurched. *Whoops* . . . She sat still, and the window in her head settled gradually down to align itself with the window in the wall. That was better. She reached out for the jug, carefully now, and poured out some of the water. She lifted the mug to her lips and drank. Ah, that was good.

Her memories, like that shoal of fish, were a whirl of fragments. Lying in an open cart . . . feverish, delirious, her head throbbing with pain . . . cold, moist cloths against her forehead . . . later – much later? – an impression of green avenues . . . two

150

men carrying her . . . voices . . . Rainy's anxious face bending above her . . . sleep . . .

She must have fallen ill on the journey and Rainy had brought her to Harrypark. She hadn't intended coming here, but here she was all the same.

The curtains were closed, but from the light that came through them (even the flowers, red and blue) she could tell it was day outside. Morning or afternoon? There was no way of knowing. But it didn't matter since she didn't feel like getting up and in fact was going to, quite soon, award herself a nap. She just had time to notice that she was wearing some sort of nightgown (flowered, of course) which wasn't hers but which suited her, before her eyes drooped and she fell asleep.

When she opened her eyes a second time it still was daylight outside. This time, when she raised herself in the bed, her head stayed clear. Now she pulled back the bedclothes and drew her legs up. The nightgown extended to her ankles. As she swung her legs to the floor, a wave of giddiness hit her. She let it pass, got down on the floor and peered underneath the bed. Was there . . .? Yes! She pulled the pot out, squatted, peed, then pushed it under again and got back beneath the sheets.

Altogether better. She poured more water into the mug and, while she sipped it, contemplated the room. It was a very nice room. Was it Rainy's? A spare for guests? It had a dresser, a large cupboard, a chair – on which sat her backpack. From the things on top of the dresser, it looked inhabited rather than rarely used. Yes. She would plump for Rainy's room.

At which point the door opened and Rainy herself came in.

"Jewel, you're awake!" Rainy smiled. "How do you feel?"

"Not bad. I woke up, but fell asleep again. Just now I got out of bed – but I felt a bit dizzy."

"I'm not surprised. You need to build up your strength. Stay in bed for the rest of today. Tomorrow, you can sit in the sitting room. Then my father can bend your ear."

"I shall look forward to that. But Rainy, I've only the vaguest notion how I got here."

"We were lucky. That carter we saw just before you collapsed was on his way to Lowmoor. A lovely man – he brought us right to the house, and some friends carried you in. That was yesterday afternoon. You've mostly slept since then."

"So I've lost all of two days . . . But what was wrong with me?"

"Some sort of fever. It's not surprising. You had a terrible shock, Jewel. You had to cope with your father's death. Had to make quick decisions. Then off you went from Shelf. I should have tried to stop you . . ."

"It wouldn't have made any difference. I wouldn't have listened to you."

"Maybe not . . . Well, you're looking a whole lot better. I predict a full recovery. Are you hungry?"

"Ravenous!"

"That's a good sign."

Rainy went out and came back bearing a tray. There was fish stew, barley cakes, and a pot of blackcurrant tea.

"Shall I stay while you eat?" Rainy asked.

"Please – if you've nothing else to do."

"Not for the moment, I haven't."

Rainy put Jewel's pack on the floor, pulled up the chair and sat down.

"Mmm . . . this stew is delicious. Did you cook it?"

"No, my father did."

"It's got herbs in it . . . Rosemary? Parsley?"

"Yes. And some others. We're very keen on herbs. We have a little herb garden."

"Where did the fish come from?"

"Jugdam."

"Jugdam? What a funny name."

"There are two lakes in Harrypark. Jugdam is the smaller one. It's in the shape of a jug, complete with a spout in the top corner. Then there's Harrylake, which is huge. People fish in both of them. My father's a keen angler and Jugdam isn't far away."

"But how does he manage if he's blind?"

"You'd be surprised. Since he can't watch the float, he keeps his fingers on the slender end of the rod. If it twitches, he strikes. He doesn't get them all, but he gets enough. We eat a lot of fish."

"My mother used to say that fish make brains."

"Then I ought to be very brainy. But I think my cleverness is in my hands."

"Well, perhaps fingers can have brains . . ." Jewel munched on a barley-cake. Then she said, "Have I pinched your room?"

Rainy smiled. "I wouldn't say 'pinched', exactly."

"So I have. Where are you sleeping?"

"I made up a bed in the sitting room. I'm quite comfortable. You shall sleep in this room as long as you stay. You would have

153

done even if you hadn't happened to be ill. Visitor's privilege."

"Are they all as nice as you in Harrypark?"

"I'm not sure I'm all that nice . . . But setting that aside, your question's still not easy to answer. There are some nice people, sure, particularly in the little group of cottages this is one of. But elsewhere in the area . . . well, there's Rotten Pavilion . . ."

"Rotten Pavilion? What's that?"

"It's a building on an island in Harrylake – Lake Island. It's from the Dark Time. It calls itself a Pavilion, but it's really a gambling den. You get all sorts there, from well-heeled high-rollers to card-sharps and chancers on the lookout for a killing. Once upon a time, it would have been just a one-storey building. Very small, in giant terms. But it's been converted inside. There's the gaming room, of course, but also a dining room and rooms you can stay in – as the high-rollers do. I've been inside a couple – they're luxurious." She stopped.

"Go on," said Jewel. "It sounds interesting."

"Well, it's the sort of place that attracts people like the Spetches."

"*Like* the Spetches?"

"I've seen them there myself. There's a little stage where performers like me entertain the clients. But you should talk to Harry the Wag, the master of Rotten Pavilion. He knows everyone who goes there."

"Harry the Wag? What's a *wag*?"

"A joker – life and soul of the party, loves to pull your leg. But in Harry's case it's a joke name. Harry is the dourest man around."

"But he can tell me about the Spetches?"

"If he's in the mood. You never know, with Harry. Sometimes he doesn't speak to anyone for days. Stays in his private room, knocking back barley wine – disgusting stuff. Now you're here you may as well go and talk to him. Luckily – or should I say *un*luckily – he's got a soft spot for me."

"Fancies you, does he?"

"He first asked me to marry him a couple of years ago. Every now and then, he repeats the question. He's around ten years older than me. Rich, of course, but he'd drive me round the bend with his black moods."

Rotten Pavilion . . . High-rollers . . . Harry the Wag . . . Harrypark got more interesting the more she heard about it.

"This island," said Jewel, "do you take a boat to get there?"

"No, it's near the shore. There's a pontoon bridge. You can just walk across."

"Is Harrypark called after Harry the Wag?"

"No – it's always been Harrypark. Maybe Harry took his name from Harrypark. Nobody knows his surname – if he has one – or where he came from. But that goes for a lot of the people who've fetched up in Harrypark. They're the sort who don't fit into settlement life."

"Like me and you?" asked Jewel.

"Yes, like me and you."

Rainy got up from the chair and took the tray from the bed.

"Enough questioning for now, you inquisitive girl." She smiled. "Get some rest, Jewel."

"Resting's all I'm doing."

"What about eating? You made short work of the fish stew."

"Yes – thank your father for me. He's a very good cook."

Rainy took her departure and Jewel settled back down in the bed. Being ill had its compensations, she thought. Particularly when you were confined in such a pleasant room. She studied the patterns of the flowers on the curtains and the quilt. She remembered a couple of occasions when she'd been ill as a child, and her mother had nursed her back to health. She would sit by the bed and tell Jewel sentimental stories. She couldn't remember the details – a fact that told its own story. Her mother, for all her virtues, didn't have much imagination and they were never very exciting. Rotten Pavilion, now . . . that was much more promising . . . And the Spetches gambled there . . .

She slipped into a drowsy sleep.

Jewel got up next morning after breakfasting in bed. There was no dizziness this time. She washed her hair in a bowl of water Rainy had heated on the fire. She towelled her hair, but, being longish, it would take a while to dry. On top of the dresser were a comb, a brush and a mirror. She sleeked out her hair, looking critically at herself. She didn't look *hugely* tired, but there were still dark areas below her eyes. She dressed, preferring trews as usual, a shirt and jumper. She slid her feet into rabbit-fur slippers: no boots today, she wouldn't be going out.

Rainy's room occupied a corner of the house, and had a window in either wall – one to the front, one to the side. The one at the front looked out towards three other houses. They formed a rough semicircle. Beyond them, off in the distance, grew an enormous high bank of dark green plants – a kind she didn't recall seeing before and which she couldn't name. The window at the side showed the bank stretching away, seemingly endlessly; above the plants rose the leafy crowns of trees.

The three houses must be inhabited, for smoke rose from their chimneys. The two flanking ones appeared ordinary enough, and of similar design: wooden, single-storey and pitch-roofed. But the third was an oddity. For one thing, it was circular. For a second, its base was raised well above ground level. Accessed by a little flight of steps, it had a verandah that looked as though it might run right round the outside. Its conical roof rose to a central chimney and was thatched with some sort of broad-leafed grass – reeds perhaps. Jewel had only ever seen one thatched house before. Who lived here?

But now she was due to meet Rainy's father. She pulled herself away from the window, feeling a little apprehensive. She would like him, she was sure. But would *he* like *her*? She very much wanted him to.

She entered the sitting room and there he was, in a chair by the fire. And here was Rainy too, saying: "Here she is, Dad."

Rainy's father rose from his chair. Rainy made the introductions: "Jewel Ranson – Luke Gill; Luke Gill – Jewel Ranson."

Luke put out his right hand and, as Jewel clasped it with hers, his left hand came up and covered it. His grip was firm and warm, and as leathery as mousehide.

"Jewel Ranson, I'm pleased to meet you. Rainy has told me all about you."

"Mr Gill, I'm so happy to meet you. But I must apologise for arriving—"

"Don't apologise," Luke interrupted, kindly but firmly. "You were ill. You got here – that's the important thing. And please, call me Luke. *Mister*'s too formal."

"I wouldn't have got here, Mr – *Luke* – if it hadn't been for Rainy."

"Well, now we've been introduced, let's sit down, shall we?"

Rainy said to Jewel, "Sit down by the fire and dry your hair."

When Jewel hesitated, Rainy smiled, "Go on, Jewel – no need to feel self-conscious. Dad can't see you anyway."

"More's the pity," said Luke. "*That*'s the worst thing of all about being blind: you can't see pretty girls. Rainy has described you. She's my eyes now, you know."

It was on the tip of Jewel's tongue to deny that she was pretty, but then it occurred to her that Mr Gill was being gallant. She sat on the edge of the hearth and spread her hair to let the heat get in.

Then she said, "I'm told you manage very well on your own. Cooking, fishing . . ."

"Told you about the fishing, did she? I never go alone. It takes two or three to land a big fish – roach or perch or trout. Hook a monster – tench or pike – and you can say goodbye to your rod. Who's got a yen to end up in the stomach of a pike?"

Luke was a sturdy, raw-boned man, but not tall: shorter than Rainy in fact. A shock of grey hair crowned his craggy, angular features. Deep creases in his cheeks and sprays of wrinkles around his eyes suggested he laughed a lot. Like Rainy's, his eyes were brown, and they looked quite normal. But where the eyes of most of the blind people Jewel had seen tended not to move much while you were talking to them, his roamed restlessly in their sockets, as if striving against possibility to catch a glimpse of the outside world. How awful it must be not to see things, she thought: things like flowers, trees, water, the rocks on the moors . . .

But Luke was speaking to her, "So – do *you* fish, Jewel?"

"No, I never have. I like *eating* fish, yes, but I'm not sure I could kill one. Of course, I don't object to other people killing them – they're for eating, after all. I mean, we have to kill things, we have to eat, don't we . . ."

Luke said, "I met a Ranter once who said we shouldn't kill animals, even to eat. They had souls, he said. I asked him if he'd ever looked closely at a gudgeon. A gudgeon, he said, what's that? It's a fish, I said to him – not that anyone would want to eat one, though they're easy enough to catch. Well, I defy you, I went on, to look a gudgeon in its fishy eye and maintain it's got a soul. You'll be telling me next, I said, that woodlice and worms have got souls. So they have, he said: just like us. We agreed to differ. But to be fair to the man, he lived his beliefs: I never heard he'd been seen eating fish, flesh or fowl."

The Gills' parlour was spotlessly clean and – like the bedroom – ruled by flowers. Flowery curtains and chair-covers; also, attached to the walls, hangings embroidered with flowers. Jewel wondered who'd done the latter. Somehow, Rainy didn't seem the sort of person to sit and do embroidery. She'd prefer twirling fiery brands. Perhaps her mother had done them . . . But there were real flowers too – pansies she thought – tucked into big pots standing on the floor, and surely Rainy had cut and arranged them. Real flowers had never featured much in Jewel's own life, lived as it had been on the move, but then an odd memory surfaced in her mind: of walking beside her mother once, and struggling to carry a crimson rose with a blossom as big as her body – and grimacing as the thorns pricked her hands . . .

"But that's enough about fish," said Luke. "At least till tonight, when you'll get to eat some more. That fish stew's still going strong."

A knock came on the door. Rainy answered it. "It's Linden and Jay," she announced. "Come to enquire about the patient."

"Let's have them in," said Luke.

Now there were more introductions. Husband and wife, Jay and Linden Sweet were physically much alike: short, plump and fresh-faced, with blue eyes, snub noses and full lips; both had light brown, curly hair. But Linden was the plumper by some distance: she must be pregnant, thought Jewel.

When Linden was settled in a chair, Jewel said, "I believe I have to thank you, Mr Sweet, for helping to carry me into the house."

"Jay, please. It was nothing. Only too glad to be of assistance, as you might say."

"Well, it was very good of you."

"It was very good of you to be ill, for if you hadn't I shouldn't have had the pleasure of carrying you."

Jewel wasn't quite sure what to make of this.

Linden said, "And how are we now? Better, I hope?"

"Much better, thank you. But my nurse is very strict. She's not allowing me out until tomorrow."

"Quite right too. We mustn't do too much too soon now, must we?"

"No we mustn't," agreed Jewel, slipping into Linden's odd way of talking, and smiling. "But I'm very much looking forward to seeing Harrypark. Everything I hear about it whets the appetite."

"What else are appetites for, except to be whetted?" This was Jay. "Whet your appetite, slake your thirst, feed your boots. That's how the world works."

"My husband's a great studier of the world," said Linden Sweet. "There's no greater in Harrypark. Always studying, he is."

"Studying," said Luke, "was what got me into trouble. I've told you that before, Jay."

"But what can we do?" said Jay. "Man is born to be curious, to stick his nose deep into things."

"And what are you studying at the moment?" asked Jewel.

"This here dumpling," he answered proudly, indicating his wife's swollen belly. "And when the lad's born—"

"Girl," interrupted Linden. "It's going to be a girl."

"Never in a month of Sundays," declared Jay. "All the signs indicate a boy. I can't be wrong."

"Well, we shall see," said Linden shortly. "But it's *our* belly, and *we* know."

Jay smiled, his composure not in the least disturbed, but he said nothing.

"Ooh!" exclaimed Linden.

"What is it?" asked Jay quickly.

"She kicked."

"Kicked? Ah . . ."

Linden turned to Jewel. "Here, feel," she said.

"Should I?"

"Of course."

She took Jewel's hand and placed it palm-flat on her stomach. Jewel waited for a while, then felt a bump from within as if a tiny foot had thumped on the womb-wall. At the same time, with utter certainty, she knew that Linden was right: the baby would be a girl.

"That's wonderful," said Jewel. Something else clicked in her. "I've been admiring your house," she said. "It's most unusual."

"How kind of you to say so," said Jay. "A house is its inhabitants, don't you think?"

"I've never thought about it, to be honest. My father and I — we were travellers, so I've never lived in a house — I mean, had a house of my own."

"Built that house with my own hands," said Jay. "Every plank, every nail, every last tuft of thatch. It's me, is that house. Of course, it's Linden as well now. And in due course, it'll be baby too."

"You must come and visit us," said Linden.

"I'd very much like to."

"Pop over this afternoon, if nurse will let you come. It's no distance, is it? It's hardly going out at all."

"I think we might manage that," said Rainy with a smile.

Shortly after this, the Sweets said their goodbyes. "Must get on, mustn't we?" said Linden.

"Yes, must get on," agreed Jay. "Come any time." Then they were gone.

"What a nice couple," said Jewel.

"So they are," said Luke. "We couldn't wish for better neighbours. They keep us amused, as you can imagine."

Later, when Luke was out of the room, Rainy said: "Tell me something, Jewel. How did you know which of the houses the Sweets live in? *I* didn't tell you. And Dad didn't either."

"I don't know," said Jewel. "I didn't really think about it. But all of a sudden, I knew. And I'll tell you something else."

"What's that?"

"Linden's right. The baby's a girl."

Rainy looked at her strangely. "And this came to you when your hand was on her stomach?"

"Yes."

Jewel fully expected Rainy to pooh-pooh her claim, but the juggler did not. Instead she said, "Back at Shelf you were equally sure that the Spetches killed your father. Are you in the habit of having openings like these?"

Openings? thought Jewel. The word was new to her.

"What's an 'opening'?" she asked.

"When you suddenly 'see' something – see with your mind, not with your eyes."

"Like a Syb, you mean?"

"Maybe."

Jewel laughed lightly. "Rainy, I really can't believe I'm anything like a Syb."

But Rainy did not laugh with her, and appeared preoccupied for some time after this exchange.

That afternoon, they called on the Sweets.

Jay was showing them round the outside, when Jewel saw that someone was digging in the garden of the house next door. It was a very big garden, and meticulously arranged.

"Hey, Parker," called Jay. "Come and say hello to Jewel Ranson."

The man stuck his spade in the ground, vaulted his low wall with an athletic leap, and walked over to the edge of the Sweets' verandah.

"Jewel Ranson, meet Parker Catt," said Jay.

"Charmed I'm sure," said Parker Catt. "Excuse me if I don't shake hands – they're somewhat grimy from gardening."

"Delighted to meet you," said Jewel.

Parker Catt was a tall man. Under his shirt, his shoulders were broad and muscular. He was older than Jay, but younger than Luke: between thirty and thirty-five. He had jet-black hair and eyebrows, deep-set eyes, a nose that had been broken without spoiling his good looks, and a firm mouth. He was handsome, Jewel thought. Feeling him sizing her up with his sharp, intelligent eyes, she wilted a little.

"Parker's a great gardener," said Rainy. "It doesn't matter what the weather's like, he's out here growing things."

"The earth does the growing," said Parker. "I just give it a bit of a nudge."

"A hell of a push, if you ask me," said Jay.

Parker grinned and said, "We have an excellent arrangement here. Luke and Jasper catch fish and snare rabbits, I grow crops and vegetables. And Jay there – Jay brews the ale and keeps us amused."

"The ale amuses you as much as I do," Jay corrected him. "Especially when you've had a few pots."

"It's very good ale," said Parker. "Jay sells it to Harry the Wag."

"Harry knows a good thing when he sees it," said Jay.

"He also knows a bad thing when he sees it," said Rainy.

"How else would he make his money?" said Parker. "Know your customer, that's Harry's motto."

"Rainy's going to take me to see Harry," said Jewel.

"Is that so?" said Parker. "Well, tread carefully in the Pavilion. I got this there." He indicated his nose.

"The other two guys got worse," said Jay.

"They started it," said Parker. "Then I hit back and they obligingly fell over. But it's not something I'm proud of. Anyway, I've kept out of there since. Gambling's best avoided: it brings out the worst in people."

"Ah, but you'll never stop people gambling," said Jay. "It offers people their dreams: win and you'll be rich, and the world will be at your feet."

"But they never win, do they? Or if they do, it's never enough."

"You want people to be rational, Parker, but they aren't. Offer someone a choice of reality and fantasy, and he'll always opt for fantasy."

"That's why I stick to growing things." Parker dug his heel into the soil. "The earth: that's what's real. Treat it right, it'll never let you down."

Shortly after that, Parker returned to his spade and they completed their circuit of the house. Jewel noted that there were windows at regular intervals in the walls, and a total of four doors

– to west, south, east and north. A little away from the house was a second and smaller circular building that had been hidden from the window of Rainy's bedroom. This, Jay explained, was his brewhouse.

"Now," said Jay, "you must come inside. Linden's lying down. She tends to get tired in the afternoons. Perhaps she'll appear. But you can see most of the house."

"Well, if it's not inconvenient . . ."

"Not at all. It's convenient for me and the house isn't going to complain. It knows the people it doesn't want inside, and you're not one. Welcome to my humble abode, as you might say."

Not so humble, thought Jewel, when she got inside. The room she stood in cut a thick slice through the middle of the building. Thus, it was rectangular, except that the narrow ends curved outwards. At each end stood a door with, either side of it, a window. Thus light entered at both ends. The near end was for sitting in, the far for dining in. A metal chimney rose up one wall and disappeared through the flat ceiling. There were two doors in each of the walls. So much for the architecture. Along the walls, and spread over the floor, were brightly-coloured tapestries and rugs. Then, everywhere you looked, there were plants in pots, climbing the high walls. They'd been carefully selected for size, of course, but even then many of them reached the ceiling and curved over, their fronds, and here and there blossoms, hanging down. Jewel was lost for words.

"What do you think?" prompted Jay.

"I'm bowled over," she confessed. "It's, well – amazing – and beautiful."

"Those words will do just fine," said Jay. "But you should be here in high summer when more of the plants are in bloom. It's a hothouse then! Please sit down. Would you like a drink?"

"I think two glasses of your best ale," said Rainy. "Not too much, mind."

"An excellent choice," beamed Jay. "Kitchen," he said, pointing at a door. Then he went through it.

Jewel and Rainy disposed themselves in comfortable chairs.

The ale, dark and sweet, lived up to the brewer's name. It would be easy to fall in love with Harrypark, thought Jewel, feeling stronger all the time.

11

THE ONE AND THE TWELVE

It was mid-afternoon when the sound registered on Thorn's ear: a low rhythmical thrumming, like the drone of distant bees. But as it came nearer, he realised it was a drum – or more than one.

Racky cocked an eye at him. "Hear it, lad?"

Thorn nodded.

"We'll see the Judymen sooner than I thought," said Racky. "They must be on walkabout."

"Walkabout?"

"Sometimes, when the weather's fine, they parade through the wood. Or, not so much *parade* as *dance* – if you can call it dancing."

The fabled Judymen . . . the men abhorred by Manningham Sparks!

The drums were hammering loudly now, a drubbing tattoo, barbaric, brutal, punishing the drumskins.

Alien colours flickered through the undergrowth – yellow, red, blue, black – and a figure pranced into view. It was outlandish, grotesque. And coming straight at Thorn and Racky. Other figures, little less bizarre, came bouncing after.

Racky drew Thorn off the track.

The figure that capered in front was scarlet-faced and hook-nosed. He had huge ugly ears and a jutting chin. The whites of his eyes were large and round, their irises black and inhuman. His lips, drawn back in a leer, revealed gleaming, predatory teeth. His stare was the essence of the malign. It's only a painted headpiece, Thorn had to tell himself. Around his neck the Judyman wore a broad white wheel of some frilled material. His jerkin and trews were striped in black, scarlet and gold, as was his cap, which curled up and over, the golden bell on its tip tapping against his forehead. He flourished a red pole.

"That's Mr Punch," said Racky.

Bells jangling, the figure cavorted off the track and leapt towards them, raising his stick. Thorn flinched, expecting a blow. Mr Punch chuckled malevolently, swiped the air above Thorn and swung away in a gust of sweat.

And here came his followers, one by one in single file, moving with little, skipping steps, in perfect time with one another and the rhythm of the drums.

In the wake of Mr Punch danced a figure with similar features, if a smaller head. She wore a voluminous dress, secured around the waist by a yellow belt, from which dangled a fat red heart and a pair of silver scissors.

"That's Judy," said Racky as she passed: "Mrs Punch. Then come Baby and Mr and Mrs Clown. The next three are Judge, Policeman and Hangman."

From head to foot, Hangman was dressed in black. His hood had eyeholes cut from it so that he could see through.

The next figure had pointed ears, a shaggy beard and a forked

169

tail. From his forehead jutted a pair of horns; wings sprouted from his shoulders. He carried a vicious-looking whip, which he cracked at intervals. He leered at Thorn and Racky, but made no move to approach them.

"The Devil, of course," said Racky. "Hard on his heels comes Death. Last of all is Dog Toby."

Death wore a long black cloak that swirled as he danced along. A pointed hood covered his head, but as he turned towards Thorn and Racky they glimpsed what it concealed: a painted skull.

Two drummers brought up the rear. They wore green and red costumes and hats stuck round with feathers. Their big drums hung down from their necks and stuck out in front of their chests, so both surfaces might be beaten. The men were stiff with self-importance.

The procession moved away.

"Let's give them a lead before we follow," said Racky. "That drumming makes my head ring."

Thorn, whose ears were also humming with the noise, was happy to comply.

"Judymen," he said thoughtfully, "Judy Wood, Judy Bridge . . . Are they all called after Judy?"

"Who knows?" answered Racky.

"Why not *Punch*men, *Punch* Wood?"

"Good question. I don't know."

"I thought you knew everything."

"Well, I don't," said Racky Jagger.

"Are we far from Judy Bridge?"

"Can't be far. The Judymen stay close to home. So, who impressed you most?"

"Mr Punch, I suppose. He looks insane, a maniac. But they're all pretty weird."

"*Weird*'s a good word. *Unique*'s a better one."

"Dog Toby . . ." prompted Thorn. "What sort of animal is a dog?"

"Mythical, they tell you. Sacred to the giants. You won't find one in our world." Racky took a swig from his water bottle. "Manningham has a theory about it, though."

"What's that?"

"Well, 'dog' is 'god' backwards. So Dog Toby's an insult to our Maker. Manningham's not very keen on the Devil, either, or Death. But Mr Punch bothers him more than any of them. He's the one who leads them, he's the master. The others dance to his rhythm – even the Devil and Death. That makes Mr Punch, to Manningham, a sort of pagan god, a squeaking lump of blasphemy. But before you make your mind up about the Judymen, watch them perform. Which they will tonight, as it's Saturday."

"I hope they don't bang on those drums throughout the performance."

"No – just now and then. One more thing. Did you think of *counting* them?"

"No, but –" Thorn made a quick calculation "– there are thirteen, including the two drummers."

"That's right. But you'll never hear the Judymen use the number thirteen. They always refer to themselves as the One and

171

the Twelve. Don't ask me why. Maybe it's to do with the fact that thirteen's an unlucky number. There are always thirteen of them – never fourteen or twelve."

The Judymen were long since out of sight, and the drumbeat was receding, but Thorn and Racky lingered. He seems talkative, thought Thorn, time to get some questions in . . .

"Racky, how well do you know this wood?" he asked.

"Better than some, worse than others."

"That doesn't tell me much."

Racky grinned. "Let's say I know enough about the wood to know where not to go, and who and what to avoid."

"We didn't avoid the stoats."

"Stoats, Thorn Jack, are not a factor you can calculate."

"When did you begin travelling?" asked Thorn.

"I was just a couple of years older than you," he said shortly.

"Don't you like settlement life?"

"It's all right in its way. But it's limited, too routine. Routine bores me. I like the unexpected."

"Even when it's dangerous?"

"Yes – especially then. Didn't you feel more alive when we fought the stoats, tackled the crayfish – didn't your blood kick through your veins, didn't it hammer in your heart?"

Thorn had never heard Racky use such passionate words before. Did they offer a clue to the man? "Yes," he said, "it did."

"Then maybe that's why we're alive – not just to till fields, cobble boots, cook rabbit stew."

"Somebody has to do those things."

"Sure – and somebody does. But – apart from cooking stew, in which I've a certain expertise – it isn't going to be *me*. And –" he looked sharply at Thorn "– I suspect it's not going to be *you* either, lad. You've started something now, and you'll have to finish it. If, of course, it's *ever* finished . . ."

"What do you mean, *if it's ever finished?*"

"Only that life has a way of surprising us. We think it's one thing, chase its tail, but all of sudden we realise it's turned into something else."

Thorn was mystified. "But—" he began.

"Peace, lad. You ask too many questions. Seek out your own answers. That's the only way to live. Come on, time we were moving."

The sound of the drums had faded away. They got to their feet, hoisted their packs onto their backs and set off again.

Not long after that the track they were following came out onto a broad stony thoroughfare that was clearly the work of the giants.

"This is the forest road," said Racky, and pointed away westwards. "That way lie Shibbin and Hallax."

The forest road took them downwards. Soon they could hear running water again: so much more pleasing a sound than the Judymen's crude drums. The track steepened, bending left – and suddenly, there below them, were river and bridge. The bridge looked ancient, as old as any Thorn had glimpsed from the Dark Time. A single archway of time-blackened stone, it spanned the water picturesquely, weed-tufted and moss-hung. Oaks and beeches sprang from the water's edge, throwing parts of it into shade. High parapets lined it, but these, unlike the underside of the arch, had suffered from the years. Stones had got dislodged, some of them dropping into the river. The biggest collapse affected the middle portion of the bridge, where on one side the parapet had broken away almost to the level of the bridge road. And here someone had shown exceptional cunning – or imagination: it was on the remaining stones that the Punch and Judy Inn had been built.

Thorn and Racky paused at a convenient vantage-point, and Thorn took in the hostelry – or what he could see of it from this angle. Bigger than any structure in Norgreen, it had two storeys, the lower constructed from stones and cement, the upper from wood. Each floor was equipped with a continuous wooden balcony. Around a table on the lower of the two, a group of men sat talking and drinking. A couple leant on the balustrade, looking down at the river. Directly below, the water ran out from under the arch of the bridge, its surface wrinkled in a number of places – presumably by the fallen stones that lay beneath its surface. The river, Thorn thought, might be twelve feet across at its broadest point. What a pretty spot it was! If only Haw . . . But as soon as that thought began to form in his mind, another usurped it. Had her abductors brought her this way? Could she have seen what he was seeing?

"When shall we ask the landlord about the feather?" he asked keenly.

"When he's alone," said Racky. "Leave it to me."

Thorn followed Racky onto the bridge, and they made their way to the centre. The roadway, roughly finished with packed rocks and dirt, had been colonised by weeds and coarse grasses.

Hawthorn and elder bushes sprang from the base of each parapet, but only served to increase its charm.

Outside the inn, a colourful sign depicting Punch hung from a post. A little beyond it, at ground level, was a separate structure – a rattery. A flight of wooden steps led up to the inn's first floor, then doubled back upon itself to reach the second. Tied to the upper and lower balustrades of the balcony, fronting the roadway, were eleven pieces of cloth, each depicting a Judyman. The drummers went unpictured.

"They put those out," said Racky, "on performance days."

"Where do they perform?" asked Thorn.

"Inside the inn. You'll see."

You'll see. Racky's favourite phrase.

Just as they were about to set foot on the staircase, a distant rattling drew their attention to the opposite end of the bridge from which they themselves had come. A rat-drawn cart was approaching, its wheels bumping over the stony surface. It was the first such cart that Thorn had seen in the wood.

They climbed the wooden staircase, their feet thumping on the springy planks, and entered the inn. First came a lobby with three doors. Racky chose the one on the right. It led to a bar-room. Drinkers, mainly men, turned to study the newcomers. Behind the bar, drying a pot with a cloth, was a large, red-faced man with a double chin, heavy jowls, small, deep-set eyes and erratic tufts of wiry brown hair.

"Racky Jagger!" the man exclaimed. "Here's a sight for sore eyes! It's a while since you were here."

"Hello, Jonas," said Racky.

175

"And what've you been up? Nothing good, I expect."

"You know me, Jonas. Or rather, you don't."

"Who's this young fellow?" said the barman, eyeing Thorn. "I don't believe we've met before."

"Nor have you," replied Racky. "This is Tip Little. Tip, meet Jonas Legg, landlord of the Punch and Judy. Tip's come to see the Judymen."

"Pleased to meet you, Tip Little . . ." Jonas nodded at Thorn, who nodded back. "The Judymen, eh? You've got a treat in store. The first time's always the best." He turned back to Racky. "You'll be wanting beds, then?"

"Have you any?"

"Might be able to squeeze you in. As you can see, we're busy today."

"Perhaps we can discuss the matter in private," suggested Racky.

Jonas eyed the bags the two carried over their shoulders. "Come through, then," he said.

He lifted up part of the bar-top and they went through to a private room.

"So," said Jonas. "What have you got to offer me this time?"

Racky and Thorn produced the crayfish joints. Jonas examined them with evident satisfaction and the two entered a quick negotiation from which Jonas emerged with the crayfish and Racky with a free room for himself and Thorn, with dinner thrown in. This seemed generous on the part of the landlord, and got Thorn wondering what the relationship between the men might be. They obviously went back some way.

176

"Right," said Jonas finally. "Room nine. You know where it is." He dug around inside one of his capacious pockets. "Here's the key. Must get this fish to Jinny. She'll cook it tonight."

He turned away.

"Wait a moment!" cried Thorn.

"What is it, lad?" asked Jonas.

Thorn fumbled in his jacket pocket and pulled out the yellow feather.

"Have you ever seen a man wearing one of these?" he asked, the words tumbling out of his mouth.

The landlord's eyes narrowed. "Never seen anything like it," he said, and almost hurried out of the room.

Thorn was stunned with disappointment. Glancing at Racky, he found his guide regarding him with the sternest displeasure.

"I told you to leave it to me," said Racky.

"Yes, but—" began Thorn.

"Yes but nothing," declared Racky. "Jonas knows something, and now you've frightened him off."

"Can *you* talk to him?" pleaded Thorn.

Racky looked thoughtful. "I can try . . . Tomorrow morning, perhaps."

"Not before then?"

"Not before then."

Thorn followed Racky back through the bar and outside again. Up they went to the next floor. Their room was on the side of the inn, and had no river view. Still, there was the balcony.

Thoroughly depressed, Thorn wandered out and leant on the rail. The river meandered under the bridge, its liquid voice seductive and low. A little way upriver was a small landing-stage. Two rowing boats, each big enough for four passengers, were tied up there. How agreeable it would be to hop in a boat and row away, to travel upstream or down, taking a picnic basket along . . . He shook the fantasy out of his head. There could be none of that for him till Haw was safe.

Racky had shed his jacket and his boots. He lay on his bed, relaxed, his hands clasped beneath his head.

"Why did you introduce me as Tip Little?" asked Thorn.

"I wanted," said Racky, "to keep your identity under wraps – at least until we left the inn. But if Jonas knows the kidnappers, he'll now realise who you are."

"I can't see that one night makes much difference," said Thorn.

"It probably won't – as far as our stay here is concerned. But if Jonas takes it into his head to get a message to the kidnappers, things could get tricky for us sooner rather than later."

"I don't care," said Thorn. "Things can get tricky just as soon as they like."

"Ah!" Racky exclaimed. "The blind confidence of youth! If you were my age, lad, you wouldn't be so cocksure."

"Just as well I'm not your age then, isn't it?" said Thorn.

He lay down on his bed.

"How will we know when the Judymen are ready to perform?"

"How do you think?"

"The drums?"

"That's right. Performance first, dinner after. That's the order of things here. Sensible, too. But first, a nap."

He closed his eyes.

Thorn's mattress was luxurious after the nights he'd spent on the ground. He lay thinking for quite a time about what Racky had said. Then he fell into a drowse.

To be awakened almost immediately, it seemed, by the drums. Their rhythmic thrum was shaking walls and floor.

Racky was standing by the window. "Time to move," he said.

It was early evening. The drummers stood one on each side of the inn door. They beat, as before, in perfect time and ignored Thorn and Racky as they passed by. They crossed a bar-room and went through a second door, which was ajar.

This inner room was big and high-ceilinged and lit by many lamps. In the foreground, their backs to the door, were half a dozen rows of chairs, a good number already occupied. Several heads turned to take in the new arrivals, and a couple of people nodded at them. Racky and Thorn took seats in the third row from the front.

A large, box-like structure faced them, slightly higher than it was wide. It sat on a raised wooden platform that extended to front and sides. Its façade had a colourful frame. A red curtain bordered with yellow tassels hung inside it.

"What's this?" whispered Thorn.

"A theatre," Racky replied.

"A *theatre*? What's that?" Thorn had never heard the term before.

"An artificial arena specially designed for a performance. A kind of framework for an action. It separates players and audience, them and us. It's like a world within a world."

Not for the first time, Thorn was both fascinated and piqued by Racky's store of knowledge. What else did he know that Thorn didn't? Just about everything, it seemed . . .

The drums fell silent, and shortly after that the drummers made their entry through the door by which the audience had entered. To left and right, in perfect step, they marched round to the front of the room and took up positions on the platform to either side of the theatre. There they stood, faces impassive, staring out as if the people facing them didn't exist.

The room was silent but for the muted voice of the river beneath the bridge. There was a palpable sense of expectancy in the room.

Out from behind the back of the theatre came the Judyman called Dog Toby. In one hand – or paw – he held a white cloth bag. Thorn watched as he walked to the rearmost row and handed the bag to the nearest person. The man put a coin in the bag and Dog Toby nodded approval. The bag travelled along the row, and for a time there was only the sound of coins clinking as more dropped into the bag. When it reached Racky, Thorn noted the amount his companion put in and added the same. When the bag had made its journey to the front, Dog Toby retrieved it and took it behind the theatre.

Soon came a roll on the drums. The curtain rose, dividing as it went, till it tucked into the upper corners of the frame.

There came a second roll on the drums, and the performance

commenced. Mr Punch was first to appear. He came to the centre of the theatre and bowed mockingly.

Punch bullied Judy and terrorised Mr and Mrs Clown. Then he strangled the bawling Baby. When Judy tried to hit him, Punch wrested her stick from her and beat her to death. Arrested by Policeman, Punch was brought before Judge, who donned his square of black cloth and mimed his verdict – the death sentence.

The next scene featured a gibbet and Hangman. Punch, however, seemed incapable of understanding what Hangman wanted him to do – which was, of course, to insert his head in the loop. When stupid Hangman stuck his own head in the loop as a demonstration, Punch gleefully seized the end of the rope and strangled him.

Punch held the audience mesmerised. Incorrigible, endlessly resourceful, he seemed godlike, untouchable. Only the Devil and Death were yet to appear, and maybe neither of them would have the cunning to outwit him.

It was then that some twitch of an obscure sense made Thorn look round. A few latecomers were standing at the back of the room. The eyes of all but one were fixed on the theatre; those of the odd man out were scanning the audience. And now, even as Thorn's gaze fixed, in thrilled surprise, at the yellow and black feather the stranger wore pinned to his hat, the man's eyes met his. Recognition passed between them, and next moment the stranger had swung on his heel and disappeared through the door.

Thorn jumped up from his chair, almost knocking it over, and grasped Racky by the arm.

"A man – with a yellow feather," he hissed.

"Where?"

"There – at the back of the room. He saw me. He's gone."

Racky leapt up and followed Thorn, who was pushing his way past the other people in the row, treading carelessly on their feet and prompting a volley of protests. He shot down the side of the room and along the back, barging past those who were standing there. Just before he made his exit, he glanced back at the theatre. The Devil had joined Mr Punch, but the two had suspended their business. Instead they were staring keenly out at the action in the room beyond, their eyes – like those of the rest of the startled audience – locked on the figures abandoning one scene for another. Only Dog Toby, like some huge stuffed animal, was looking a different way, as if spellbound by some apparition that nobody else could see.

The bar-room was empty, but the far door stood open. With Racky close behind him, Thorn careered between the tables and out onto the balcony. But the man was neither on the stairs below nor down on the bridge. Then a sound came from above them.

"Upstairs!" prompted Racky. "You go right – I'll go left. And be careful. Shout if you see him."

Thorn sprang up the stairs, his youth and fitness lending him winged heels. Racky clattered up behind. Go right, Racky had told him. This way led past their room, but as Thorn rushed towards it, he saw that the door was ajar. The lock had been forced. He skidded to a halt, but as he reached out to push the door open it swung back of its own accord and a man jumped out. The two of them went sprawling. Thorn was thrown against the balustrade, jarring a shoulder.

"Racky!" he shouted. "Racky!"

After the first man came a second. Seeing one route blocked by fallen bodies, he instinctively went the other way – which would take him round to the river and straight into Racky's arms. But the first man – the man from the theatre room – was on his feet again. As Thorn scrambled to his feet, the man ran back the way Thorn had come. The two of them skidded around the corner. Further along was the stairway. As the man slowed and turned to go down, Thorn threw himself forward and flung out an arm. He meant to grab hold of a leg, but succeeded only in tapping an ankle. The man took off like an ungainly bird and dived out of sight. Thorn slid the last few inches on his chest and came to a stop with neck and shoulders overhanging the top step. He was just in time to see and hear the sickening sound the man made as, arms flailing helplessly, he crash-landed heavily halfway down the staircase. His impetus carried him rattling down till his head slammed into an upright. He lay still, his neck skewed at a grotesque angle to his shoulders.

Racky! thought Thorn. He got to his feet and set off at a run. Turning the second corner to the stretch overlooking the river, he saw Racky and the second man grappling halfway along. As he neared them, the two men lurched violently against the balcony rail. It snapped, the fighters parted, and the unknown man skidded over the edge. As he fell, he made a grab at Racky. His hand caught the pocket of Racky's jacket, pulling Racky towards the edge. As Racky teetered over the drop, throwing his arms out in a desperate effort to regain his balance, the jacket tore. Clutching a ragged square of cloth, the stranger dropped from view. Thorn seized Racky's nearer hand and jerked him to safety.

A splash sounded from below.

Thorn and Racky peered down through the wreckage of the railings. Several lamps hung to light the balcony below, and their glow just reached the water. Circles were spreading on the dark surface. There was no sign of the fallen man. Soon the ripples would vanish, the river be just as it was before.

12

BLACK PEARLS

The night after her visit to the Sweets, Jewel slept soundly. When she rubbed the sleep from her eyes, climbed out of bed and drew the curtains, the sun was shining brightly. They could be in for a lovely day. The strong light sharpened the contrast between the blue of the sky and the deep green of the plantation that lay beyond the Gills' house. Out in the front yard, Rainy was at her juggling routines. Silver clubs flashed in the sun.

Jewel dressed and went through to the parlour. Two men sat at a table that bore an array of breakfast things, chatting and drinking tea. One was Luke, but the other was as yet unknown to Jewel.

Luke might not have seen the girl come in, but he'd heard her.

"Come and meet Jasper, Jewel," he said. And, as Jewel and Jasper shook hands, added, "Jewel Ranson – Jasper Tallow. Jasper is my fishing partner. We're off to Jugdam after breakfast."

Jasper had stood to shake hands, and he and Jewel now sat down. He was much the same height as Luke, but leaner and older. His long head was hairless but a grizzle around his ears matched the thin growth on his chin. His skin was wrinkled and reddened by weather, his eyes a contrasting pale blue. Rolled-back sleeves revealed sinewy, black-haired forearms, tanned like his face. He looked to possess a wiry strength.

"Pleased to meet you," said Jasper, shaking hands. "And looking so much better than you did when I last saw you."

Jewel looked puzzled at this.

"I helped to carry you into the house," Jasper explained with a smile.

"Ah!" said Jewel. "Well, thank you for that."

"Oh, I'm always somewhere about." Jasper nodded towards his companion. "Luke's been telling me about you. I'm sorry to hear about your father. Losing a parent's a painful thing."

"Yes," said Jewel. "Thank you . . ."

There was a short pause.

"Luke tells me you believe the Spetch brothers murdered him."

"I'm certain of it," said Jewel. "I shan't rest till they're brought to justice."

"Justice, I'm afraid, isn't easy to come by in this world."

"So I've discovered. It looks as though I'm going to have to kill them myself."

Some strangers, thought Jewel, might have laughed to hear a girl of fifteen make such a statement. But Jasper Tallow did not laugh.

"You're a determined young woman. I hope you succeed."

Just then Rainy came in. Dumping her clubs in a corner, she came over and sat down.

"Ah, breakfast!" she exclaimed. "There's nothing like a work-out for putting an edge on your appetite."

"I'm glad you've joined us, Rainy," said Jasper. "I was on the point of telling your friend that, as it happens, I know something of the Spetches." He turned to Jewel. "I'll tell you the story, if you like."

"Yes, please, Mr Tallow," she said. "The more I know about them, the better."

"Good. But before I begin, you'd better pour yourselves some tea. It's not the shortest of stories."

When Jewel and Rainy had filled their cups and taken their first sips, Jasper Tallow began.

"Well, as I think you know," he said, "the Spetch brothers are masters of Roydsal – a mansion built by the giants on the ridge above Judy Wood. Why anyone would choose to live up there is beyond me. They must rattle around in the place. Well, they weren't always its masters. Before them came Gummer Wrench. Gummer was very rich, arrogant and self-centred, and he paid men to protect him. They, of course, were no better or worse than they should be. Now, Gummer had a weakness that amounted to an obsession. He was crazy about pearls. He had a big collection of necklaces and bracelets and brooches and earrings – all from the Dark Time – and he'd sit and gloat over them for ages, like a miser. He counted them over and over, so that if even one went missing he'd know about it."

"Did he wear them?" asked Jewel.

"Only one – on a thin gold chain around his neck. A big rose pearl it was, his absolute favourite. I believe he even wore it in bed."

"Sorry to interrupt," said Jewel. "Please go on."

"Well, if Gummer heard that anyone owned any pearls, he immediately wanted them. He'd do anything to acquire them, and he usually got what he wanted. Or he did until the Spetches came – and he got their pearls too, in a strange sort of way." Jasper paused for a moment, then resumed. "It happened like this. Word came to Gummer that this pair of brothers, the Spetches, owned a string of black pearls – tiny but very fine, and most rare. Nobody knew anything much about the Spetches then. If people had, matters might have turned out differently. The Spetches were new in the area, staying at an inn on the Wyke road. All anyone knew was that they didn't seem short of gold. They rode a matched pair of saddle-rats – jet-black, haughty beasts. Anyway, Gummer dispatched a man to find out how much the Spetches would sell their pearls for. When he returned, it was to tell Gummer that the Spetches weren't sure they wanted to sell them, but they were willing to come and see him and talk the matter over. Well, Gummer wasn't a man much given to entertaining, but he immediately sent the man back with an invitation: the Spetches were welcome at Roydsal any time.

"The Spetches kept Gummer waiting, but in the end they sent word that they'd come on such and such a day if Gummer would be at home. He would indeed, and they came. Gummer allotted them beds in one of Roydsal's grandest rooms – or should I say what had *once* been one of Roydsal's grandest rooms – and ordered his servants to prepare a feast. Oh, he was confident he'd persuade them to part with the pearls. He was Gummer Wrench, wasn't he? Didn't he always get what he wanted?

"So there they were, Zak and Lanner Spetch, the blond and the redhead, pouching Gummer's food and drinking Gummer's drink and oozing good-humour and charm."

"*Charm!?*" Jewel couldn't help herself.

"Yes, charm. The Spetches can be quite charming when they want to be. They have a reputation as lady-killers, among other things."

"Among the other sorts of killers they are?" said Rainy acidly.

Jasper shrugged and went on with his story.

"Gummer had a good appetite, but he was so excited that he ate less than usual and drank more than usual – he was a bit the worse for wear by the time the meal ended. Not a good idea if you're about to do business. He was nervous too. You could always tell when Gummer's nerves were getting to him, because he'd lift up his rose pearl, pop it into his mouth and suck it. And who knows, it might have been this very habit that gave the Spetches their diabolical idea. Anyway, Gummer waited until they'd eaten their fill, then asked if he could see the necklace. Zak had it in a bag on the floor at his feet. He motioned to one of Gummer's men (Gummer never allowed himself to be alone with anybody he didn't own), and the man carried it round to Gummer. Gummer opened the bag and drew out this string of pearls. They were indeed very small, but they were beauties too, because Gummer's eyes went as round as saucers and filled up with *cupidity* – that truly delightful combination of greed and desire.

"'How much do you want for them?' he asked.

"The Spetches, who were sitting next to one another, put their heads together and whispered for a time.

"Then: 'You can keep as many as you can eat,' said Lanner.

"'As many as I can *eat*! Is this a joke?' exclaimed Gummer.

"'No joke,' stated Lanner, as cool as you like. 'You can take them off the string: we wouldn't want you to choke, would we? And if you can eat them all, you'll get a bonus.'

"'A bonus?'

"From pockets inside their jackets, Lanner and Zak each drew an object and placed it on the table. There sat a matched pair of earrings, gleaming handsomely. Black pearls again, needless to say.

"'Pretty, aren't they?' grinned Zak.

"Gummer said nothing. He was staring as if he couldn't believe his luck.

"'Put some salt on the pearls, if you like,' said Lanner. 'You know – make them tastier.' Was that a wicked glint in his eye?

"Well, Gummer didn't know whether to stare harder at his guests or at the stones. Then his fingers moved along the string: he was counting the pearls.

"'There are thirteen,' he said after a time.

"'That's right,' agreed Zak. 'I trust you're not superstitious, Mr Wrench.'

"'Of course not,' said Gummer a little too quickly. 'Only idiots are superstitious.'

"'No problem then,' said Zak. 'Nobody would take *you* for an idiot, Mr Wrench.'

"Gummer looked hard at Zak, but his guest's face was expressionless. Then he turned back to the pearls, and thought for a time.

"'Well, they're not the biggest string of pearls I've ever seen . . .

But they *are* very fine . . .' He looked hard at the Spetches. 'And you want nothing in exchange?'

"'Not right now,' said Zak. 'But in the future, yes.'

"'What do you mean?' asked Gummer.

"'We have a fancy to be your heirs. Give us your word that we'll become masters of Roydsal when you're dead. But only if you happen to have no blood-born heir. If you produce a son or daughter, our claim disappears.'

"Now, Gummer was in his late thirties, rich and in good health, so he could expect to live for many years yet. He also had plenty of time to acquire a wife and children, though he'd never shown much interest up to now in doing so. So I don't suppose it cost him any effort to agree. He gave his word and, at the Spetches' request, made his men witnesses to the agreement. Then he took the pearls off the string and started to swallow them, one by one.

"It went pretty well at the start. By dint of drinking plenty of water with them (he didn't bother with salt), he swallowed the first six or seven without too much trouble. After that, each stone took more and more of an effort. Soon he was gasping and striving not to vomit after each one went down. Nevertheless they stayed down – and now there was only one to go. 'Nearly there!' He grinned. 'Nothing to it!' and popped the pearl into his mouth. There was a loud gulp, his Adam's apple jerked, and the pearl disappeared. Or did it? Gummer went purple in the face. His mouth flopped open and grim, half-strangled noises began to emerge from it. His eyes were wild and he was pointing at his mouth. He was choking.

191

"The Spetches looked at one another for a moment. Then Zak shrugged, got languidly up out of his chair, walked round behind Gummer and gave him a tremendous thump on the back. The last pearl flew out of Gummer's mouth, bounced across the table top like a pebble across a pool, just missing the dishes there, skittered across the wooden floor and disappeared under a great lumbering piece of furniture – a couch made by the giants, ancient and full of dust.

"When Gummer had recovered enough to speak, he said: 'Right, that's it then. The earrings are mine.'

"The Spetch brothers looked at one another. Then Lanner said, 'I think not. We're most impressed, Mr Wrench. But the agreement stipulated that you eat *all* the pearls off the string. One still remains.'

"'Yes,' said Zak. 'It clearly got no further than your throat. You're going to have to find it. Otherwise, no bonus.'

"Gummer stood up and stared at the spot where the pearl had disappeared. The couch cleared the ground by a couple of inches, so there was just about room to crawl underneath. He then glanced at the Spetches. They were lounging in their chairs. On their faces were identical, lightly amused smiles.

"'You lot.' Gummer waved his hands at his men. 'Get under there and find it. A piece of silver for the man who succeeds.'

"There were three of Gummer's hirelings in the room – two bodyguards and a servant. The bodyguards were proud, hard-bitten men. But in a moment all three of them had obeyed his orders.

"Time passed. It must have been grim under the couch,

because volleys of coughs and sneezes came from there. But nothing else emerged. Gummer was walking up and down, rubbing his painfully bloated belly. He kept eyeing the earrings, still on the table in front of his guests.

"'Have you got it yet?' he shouted.

"Three dusty voices answered No. Time passed. Gummer might have been all right if he'd stayed in his chair and taken it easy. But impatience got the better of him.

"'What are you doing, you stupid oafs?' he shouted. 'Find it! Bring it here to me. A *gold* piece for the finder!'

"But nobody, it seemed, could lay his hands on the last pearl. Unable to contain himself, Gummer jumped up from his chair and crawled beneath the couch. Now, Gummer was a plump, well-built man with a big round belly, which partly explains why he'd been able to accommodate so many pearls inside himself. But the human body can only take so much. Swallowing a string of pearls is one thing. Slithering about under ancient, dusty furniture with them bulking out your gut is something else. It proved too much for Gummer. There was an explosion of coughing, then a muffled cry for help, then some dry retching, then a croak, then silence. When in due course Gummer's men dragged his body out, his tongue hung out of his mouth with his teeth embedded in it, his eyes were wide open in horrified surprise, and he was as dead as a doornail.

"And that's the story of how Lanner and Zak Spetch became masters of Roydsal. Quite how they knew the pearls would do for Gummer I don't know. Perhaps they didn't. Perhaps the game with the pearls was merely devised to amuse them, or to get them in with Gummer. Perhaps they had plans to finish him off later, before he sired any children. A rumour went round that the pearls had been coated with poison. But then it would, wouldn't it? The Spetches are the sort of men around whom rumours tend to multiply like rabbits. In fact it didn't look as though Gummer had been poisoned – it looked as though he'd had some sort of fit, and choked. Anyway, who cared? Not Gummer's men and servants, because the Spetches simply kept them on, and paid them even better than Gummer did."

Jasper's story was followed by silence. It was Jewel who broke it.

"You were there, weren't you?" said Jewel. "You were one of Gummer's men when this happened."

Jasper smiled wryly. "Yes. Clever of you to spot it. How else would I know what happened in such detail? In fact I was one of the crawlers who scrabbled around under the furniture for the missing pearl – then pulled the dead man out. I fancied those silver and gold pieces. Oh, I was young and foolish then. I thought I knew everything."

"But you didn't stay on, did you?"

"No. I had nothing against the Spetches, personally speaking. But you know the phrase 'stinking rich'? Somehow the Spetches stank, and I couldn't live with the odour. I suppose Gummer had stunk too, but then I'd been infatuated with his wealth and power. Up until that night, that is, when I saw him stuff those pearls down his throat and kill himself. Then I saw exactly what wealth was worth, how it corrupts. As for his successors – double

Gummer Wrench, add a touch of style and lot of ruthlessness, and you've got Lanner and Zak Spetch. Or so I thought at the time. Anyway, I left after less than a fortnight."

"There's something else, isn't there?" prompted Jewel.

"Something else?"

"Something else – one more thing to tell."

"Now, how do you know that?"

Jewel shrugged.

"Well, you're right." Jasper reached into one of the pockets of his jacket. "Hold out your hand," he said to Jewel.

The girl did as she was bade. Onto her palm dropped a round stone.

"The pearl!" she gasped. "But it isn't black!"

"No. Black pearls are really grey. But this is the last one. Do you know where I found it?"

"Where?"

"It rolled from Gummer's hand as we were dragging him into the open. He must have found it just before he had his seizure. Maybe it was even the thrill of finding it that killed him. I never let on that I'd got it, and nobody in any case seemed to care. When Luke told me yesterday how your father met his death, I thought I'd bring this with me today. I often look at it. It serves to remind me of the futility of greed."

Jewel and Rainy gazed at the opaquely gleaming sphere.

Jasper said, "Gummer was buried with twelve pearls still inside him. Maybe some bright spark dug him up and cut them out. People are capable of any enormity, don't you think?" He paused, then added, "You wouldn't think, would you, to look at it on your hand, that that mild, insignificant stone had done a man to death?"

That afternoon, Rainy took Jewel out for a walk. By now the girl was aware that the little community of houses lay halfway along an avenue five times as long as it was broad. Down each side of this corridor ran thick, high banks of dark-leaved bushes. These, said Rainy, were rhododendrons, and they grew in dense plantations all over Harrypark.

They went down the avenue. The grass sprang thickly on either side, but feet and cartwheels had marked out a track of sorts. At its end the avenue made a right angle, so that now it went south-west.

This stretch took them past the ends of two more avenues parallel to the one from which they'd set out. Every so often Rainy asked Jewel if she was tired and Jewel said no, so they kept going.

At last, Rainy stopped. "Let's sit down for a bit," she said.

They sat down.

"Actually," said Rainy, "I brought you here for a purpose, Jewel. I'd like to try an experiment."

"An experiment?" said the girl.

"Yes. How about it?"

"What must I do?"

"Shut your eyes. Empty your mind. Open yourself up. Then tell me something about Harrypark you couldn't possibly know."

Jewel looked askance at her. "But that's impossible!"

"Is it? Are you sure?"

Jewel smiled. But Rainy, she saw, was perfectly serious.

I'll humour her, she thought. What have I got to lose?

She shut her eyes and tried to empty her mind. It wasn't easy. Wisps of ideas kept floating in, distracting her. After a time she thought: This is silly, and opened her eyes again.

"There's nothing there," she declared.

Rainy seemed undaunted. "Give it another try," she urged. "I'll tell you what, *this* time, put your hands on the ground: feel the earth. Concentrate on that sensation."

Jewel shrugged. But she closed her eyes again and put her hands flat on the grass. Now that she had something to touch, to focus on, it seemed easier to let her mind go slack. The grass-stalks felt cord-like, strong and springy against her palms. Below the roots of the grass, the soil was rich and busy with minute life. As she sank into self-abeyance, each grain pressed in on her. There came an abrupt squirming motion: an earthworm was slithering by. But her concentration held. There was nothing unpleasant here: she was earthy, and the worm belonged to the earth just as she did.

Soon, somewhere near, she sensed something else: a pipe. Inside the pipe, water ran. The pipe was stone-like, resistant, but her consciousness pierced it; and she was snatched and carried off in the liquid rush.

The water ran happily along, straight and true in the sloping chute; till, all of a sudden, it burst out into daylight. It rollicked down a waterway, swung sharply left, shot over the brink of a fall, smashed and reunited itself, tumbled underground, then rolled down a declivity into a pool bright with sunlight. As the water expanded in all directions, Jewel sensed fish moving past with whippy tails. How tiny they were.

Jewel opened her eyes. Rainy sat watching her.

"Right . . ." said the juggler eagerly. "Tell me: what did you see?"

Jewel opened her mouth but couldn't trust herself to speak. She felt caught between two worlds. Time passed before she answered.

"There was a worm . . . Then I found a pipe beneath the earth. Water runs through it, then, when it comes out, goes over a fall and into a pool, a circular pool . . . There are fish there . . ." She paused. "This is impossible," she added. "I was dreaming, wasn't I?"

"Were you?" Rainy got to her feet. "Let's find out, shall we?"

Some time later they stood on the edge of what for the giants must have been no more than an ornamental channel, but was to them a small ravine. Some two feet deep and perhaps three feet across, its steep banks had been shored up by rocks. Ferns and mosses grew abundantly. Down the channel, water tinkled in a stream.

They set off again. Further along, the channel veered sharply left, taking the flow of water south. They turned with the ravine, and went on until they stood above a waterfall. Jewel thought it pretty, with its rocky sides, mossy ledge, and slow pour of clear liquid. The stream bubbled from the base of the fall and disappeared under a rocky overhang. Reappearing, it trickled down the cracked, sloping rim of a circular pool. Another artificial construction. Right in the middle, some sort of decorative feature thrust up; but it had crumbled into unrecognisability, leaving no more than a roundish shelf with an eroded stub at its centre.

"This is the Round Pond," said Rainy. "The pipe you discovered carries the outflow from Jugdam. It runs all the way down here; then the Pond feeds in turn into Harrylake."

Jewel was still trying to take everything in. Ravine, fall, pond were all as she remembered them – except that her earlier point of view had been, to say the least, different . . .

"I don't understand . . ." she said slowly. "What happened to me?"

"I don't know. But I know someone who might."

"What do you mean?"

"Well, remember me telling you that all sorts of odd people fetch up in Harrypark?"

"Yes . . ."

"What if tomorrow, on the way to Harrylake, we drop in on one? Her name is Elphin Loach."

"Elphin Loach? What a strange name."

"She's no ordinary person."

"Oh? What sort of person is she?"

"Why don't you see for yourself?"

13
WHISPERING OAK

Thorn sat on a pebble beside the bank of Judy River. The water flowed past, its wrinkled surface lightly silvered. The moon soared above, bathing the earth in pale beams. It was almost at full. Away to his right, high on the bridge, the Punch and Judy Inn was in darkness. Is everyone asleep tonight but me? he wondered.

When he'd left the room they shared, Racky, flat on his back, was sleeping the sleep of the just; snoring gently, his mouth open. How could he sleep so soundly after the evening's events? Had the man he'd fought drowned? Although Jonas Legg had mounted a search and scoured both banks of the stream, and although a couple of men in boats had poked about with long poles in the water beneath the bridge, no body had come to light. Perhaps the man had swum ashore, and got away.

No such doubt surrounded the fate of the man who'd fallen down the stairs. His neck was broken. I killed him, thought Thorn guiltily. All I did was tap his ankle, but it did for him as surely as if I'd shot an arrow from point-blank range smack into his heart. Had the man deserved to die? Nothing, it turned out, was missing from the room – perhaps the man had just gone in. Well, he shouldn't have been there, shouldn't have worn a yellow feather, like the men who abducted Haw. Perhaps this was one of the very men who'd taken his sister. In which case, he *did* deserve to die. So Thorn kept telling himself, but then back into his mind came a picture of the man as he lay crumpled at the bottom of the steps, his neck grotesquely askew . . .

Two yellow-feathered men . . . one dead, one fate uncertain. Thorn's mind went back to what he'd told Racky the previous evening when they were up in their room: *Things can get tricky just as soon as they like.* Well, how quickly things had! Was it down to the fact that he'd shown the feather to Jonas Legg? Not necessarily: the landlord might or might not be in league with the men. It was possible that the men had just happened to be at the inn, and had spotted Racky and himself. It was also possible that the men were expecting them.

Who were these men working for? Racky had promised to speak to the landlord at breakfast-time. Perhaps he'd now be able to get Jonas to loosen his jaws. Or perhaps Jonas's jaws would be more tightly clamped than ever . . .

The yellow-feathered men had chosen to set their mark on Thorn. Now he'd set his mark on them. Let the rest beware, he thought. I'll find them, whoever they are – wherever they may be.

He picked up a piece of gravel and tossed it into the river. *Plop!* Circles travelled outwards from the point of disturbance, their rims bright with moonlight. A river – one stone – many circles . . . That's all it takes.

Thorn came slowly to wakefulness and opened his eyes. He was back in his room. The curtains had been parted, and through the narrow gap this left a diagonal shaft of light struck. In its radiance, motes of dust rose and fell indolently.

Racky was not in his bed. His pack lay on top of it, strapped up and ready to go. He must have gone out. How late had Thorn slept?

He climbed out of bed. He felt a touch bleary, but otherwise fine. After all, he'd slept for only half the night. He stripped off his shirt, doused his head with water in a bowl on the chest of drawers, and towelled his hair. That was better.

He pulled on his clothes and went out to the balcony. A stream of puffy white clouds was drifting across the sky. It might be pretty warm later. A couple of people were walking away up the bridge. The world was serene: no body hunched at the foot of the stairs. For a moment his mind tilted, and he wondered if he might have dreamed the events of the previous evening. No. It happened all right. I killed a man.

He went slowly down. There, at the base of a stout upright, was a small, reddened patch where the fleeing man had bled after ramming into the wood. And somewhere in the inn lay his body, still and anonymous. Jonas Legg would see it buried.

Racky sat at a table, the only person in the room. Before him was a plate, on the plate the scraps of a meal.

"Ah, the conqueror comes at last. You slept late, neck-breaker Jack."

"That's because I couldn't sleep. I went down to the river. There was a moon."

"Couldn't sleep, eh? Ah, the tender conscience of youth."

Racky smiled knowingly. "It does that to you, doesn't it – killing a man? Or should I say, killing your *first* man? No matter how much he deserves it."

"How many men have *you* killed, Racky?"

"More than I might have, less than I should have. But one thing I know: you'll get over it." He gestured at a table against the wall on which lay bowls and platters of cold food. "Help yourself to some breakfast. Everyone else has been and gone."

"I'm not sure I'm hungry."

"Feed your belly, not your appetite." Racky got up from his chair. "I'm going to have a word with our host about men with yellow feathers. And *this* time I'm *not* going to take silence for an answer."

Thorn jumped up. "I'll come with you."

"No you won't." Racky spoke firmly. "Let me do this my way."

Seeing the glint in Racky's eyes, Thorn sat down again and watched him walk out of the room.

Thorn picked at the food before him, tense with anticipation. Time dragged on. What was taking Racky so long? Then he came back into the room.

"What did he say?" demanded Thorn.

Racky closed both doors, then sat down and spoke quietly.

"He said nothing – to start with. I had to use all my powers of persuasion on him." Racky's mouth curled in an unsavoury half-smile. "Even then he wouldn't say much. Jonas is afraid of these yellow-feathered men – more afraid of them than he's afraid of

203

me. I'm pretty sure they've used this place, pretty sure they're paying him, but he wouldn't admit that. All he'd say was, 'Ask up at Roydsal – they may be able to help you. But for godsake, Racky, don't tell them I sent you.'"

"*Roydsal?* What's that – a settlement?" asked Thorn.

"It's a mansion the giants built at the top of the wood."

"The giants?" Thorn failed to understand.

"That's what I said. Roydsal goes back to The Dark Time. I've seen it from a distance and it looked fairly intact. By the sound of it, humans have taken up residence there."

"Humans? That's weird."

"Some humans *are* weird, lad. Haven't you noticed?"

"So the kidnappers are from Roydsal, and they're holding Haw there?"

"Jonas didn't say that: he only said to *ask* there. But it's a possibility. We'll have to tread carefully."

"How do we get there?"

"If your sister *is* there, and we go trotting up to the front door, knock and introduce ourselves, how far do you think we'll get? What's more, we forfeit the advantage of surprise. We don't know how many men they have – whoever 'they' may be. We've got to be cleverer than that. So here's what I propose. In order to give the slip to anyone who's inclined to follow us, we'll take a boat upriver, then cut through the wood and approach Roydsal from the west – not the east, as the road does – in case they're watching it."

"Then what? Break into the house?"

Racky grinned slyly. "The idea had crossed my mind."

Thorn jumped to his feet. Things were moving at last, the search for Haw had a focus.

"Let's get going," he said.

"Can you row?" Racky asked.

They stood at the landing-stage.

"After a fashion," Thorn replied. "I've gone boating a few times on pools and streams near Norgreen."

"Good." He gestured to one of the boats. "Get in – and don't capsize her! Sit in the stern – I'll take the first stint. You are now a privileged user of Legg's Ferry-Yourself Service. Jonas didn't really want to lend me a boat, but I asked him so nicely he couldn't resist giving way."

Thorn clambered aboard and took the seat in the stern. The boat was narrow enough to be manned by a single rower, but not so narrow that two people, at a pinch, couldn't have sat side by side and each taken an oar. As Thorn and Haw had sometimes done, giggling as the boat rocked from their clumsy early efforts to propel it along . . .

Racky had cast off before he came aboard, and, by the time he'd inserted the oars into the rowlocks, the boat had drifted away from the bank, but he quickly took control, and soon the craft was moving upstream.

The arch of the bridge closed over them. Mosses grew here on the walls a little above the waterline. Higher up, and overhead, tufts of wiry grass sprang from fissures between stones.

Out of shadow into sunlight. On account of the recent rains, the water level was fairly high. Trees grew down to the water's edge and even out of the flow itself, bending over the water as if to listen to its voice. As the boat passed through the drooping curtain of a willow, its foliage rustled, lifting and dropping its green fingers. Underneath, they were encircled by the fall of a leafy fountain.

Racky had found an easy rhythm and was exerting just enough effort to keep the boat in steady motion. The current might not look strong, but Thorn knew that he himself couldn't row as well as this. No matter, he'd do his best when his turn came.

And now the idyllic setting and sense of being indulged joined forces with his lack of sleep, and his eyelids began to droop –

– when something shot by overhead, overshadowing the boat with the stretch of its wings, and he jerked awake in time to catch a blur of bluey-purple streaking away above the river.

"What was that?" he exclaimed.

"A kingfisher," said Racky. "You see them here from time to time. The fastest thing on two wings."

Silence descended again – though you couldn't really call it silence, given the rhythmic slap of the oars, the ripple of the river and the twitter and gossip of birds from bush and tree. Thorn closed his eyes. As the boat moved in and out of sunlight, the quality of the darkness inside his eyelids altered. He slipped into a drowse . . .

. . . till something nudged his leg.

"Your turn to row," said Racky.

Thorn yawned. "Fine."

The boat rocked as they changed places. Thorn dipped the oar-blades into the water. The boat had slipped out of alignment with the banks, but a couple of touches brought it to heel. He rowed steadily. If he couldn't match Racky for style, he could copy his approach. There was no knowing how long he would have to keep going.

"I've seen worse," said Racky after watching him for a time. "Practice makes perfect, lad – or so they say. Keep to the middle of the channel."

The river took on a different aspect now that he was rowing. Trees, bushes and rocky or grassy banks slid into view from behind his shoulders and then receded, the trees seeming to nod as the boat went by. Racky seemed disinclined to drowse or fall into a reverie. He either watched Thorn in silence, or scanned the banks as they passed by – though what he expected to see, Thorn didn't know.

After a time, Thorn said, "Since I met Manningham Sparks, I've thought a fair bit about the things he said to me . . . you know, about God and Heaven and Hell. But it's obvious you don't have much time for his views, Racky. Will you tell me why?"

Racky had been looking at the river when Thorn began, and he was still looking at the river when Thorn posed his question. For a time, it seemed to Thorn that he wouldn't receive any reply.

Then, turning his head and fixing Thorn with a cool stare, Racky said, "Manningham's an agreeable fellow, and I have a soft spot for him, but his beliefs are codswallop – fit only for infants and other deluded souls like him. God's not a benign figure, and his actions aren't shaped by my and your best interests. He's conniving and merciless, a law unto himself. He created this world to be a world of suffering, and he doesn't care what agonies humans have to go through. If you want to imagine God, imagine someone gleefully driving a nail through your head. It's not love that rules the universe, as Manningham likes to think. It's pain – *pain,* lad. Anyone who tells you otherwise is a fool."

Racky turned his face away and gazed moodily at the river. Only now did Thorn realise that at some point in the man's speech he, Thorn, had ceased to row. He looked down at his oars and the hands that gripped them, stunned both by what Racky had said and the passionate way he'd said it. It was as if, for a brief moment, Racky had peeled back his skin so Thorn might glimpse what lay beneath – red-raw and pulsating.

He began to row again, stroke chasing mechanical stroke. After a while, pulling back on the oars and glancing along the boat, he saw Mr Punch's gloating features superimposed on Racky's – that hooked nose, those insane eyes, that savagely grinning mouth. Startled, but in the rhythmic grip of the process of rowing, he leant forward into the following stroke, and when next his body rose with the lift of the oars, the disturbing vision had gone. Plain Racky Jagger sat opposite him.

On the following upstroke, one of the oars slipped from his grasp, and he had to break stroke in order to re-establish his rhythm. If Racky noticed this, he gave no sign of it. Still he stared into the water, as if to penetrate its dark mirror and see what was down there, gazing back at him.

By the time they changed places again, Thorn had discovered muscles he'd never known he had. His back was the worst, it protested with an array of aches as he slumped gratefully onto the stern thwart. Racky's idea had seemed a good one at the time, but like many ideas it seemed less attractive when you discovered the consequences.

The river ran on against them to its remote destination. For a time it would run straight, then angle left or right in recognition of some rocky point whose planes its busy waters endlessly worked to wear away.

Rounding one such bend, oak-hung and sunlit, Thorn caught a movement on a stretch of stones that out-topped the flow by no more than a few inches.

"There's a man up ahead, fishing."

"Is that so?" replied Racky. But he didn't look round.

When the boat drew level with the man – now no more than eight feet away – Thorn could see his features clearly. Beneath short, sandy hair, his lean, prominently boned face was impassive. A ragged scar ran from the corner of one eye towards his chin, narrowly missing the corner of his mouth. His jacket and trews were green, but patched with brown.

"Hello, there!" called Thorn.

The man did not reply. His eyes were on Thorn, but his face was expressionless.

Then the boat was past him. Thorn watched Racky as he pulled away, but his companion kept his eyes riveted on the boat's wake. He must have glimpsed the stranger, but gave no sign of doing so. His face was as blank as the angler's. The rhythmic splash of the oars seemed to reverberate in the river-space. The atmosphere above the river seemed charged, as if the conspiratorial silence of oarsman and angler had strained the air's delicate nerves.

The tension was all too much for Thorn. "Do you know him?" he asked.

Racky took his time to answer. "Oh, I know him all right." His face was unyielding as a stone's.

"Who is he then?"

But Racky did not reply.

The boat moved on towards another bend. Just before they reached it, Thorn twisted in his seat and looked back. The man had gone.

Thorn did a second stint at the oars, but it proved shorter than the first. As he rowed, the banks of the river became narrower and increasingly stony, the surface more disturbed. Had he been alone, Thorn would have had to keep glancing round to make sure his position was sound, but Racky took to issuing curt instructions, and he was able to carry on without continually looking round.

At last Racky said, "Right, there's a landing-stage coming up on your left. Pull in there."

Thorn looked round and saw it: a platform of planks raised on piles just above the river-surface. He manoeuvred the boat in and Racky stepped ashore. Thorn tossed the painter to him, and Racky tied up. As soon as they'd disembarked their packs and bows, Racky said, "Time for a spot of refreshment, I think," and they sat down on the grassy slope above the landing-stage and took out food and water.

They ate in silence. Racky's air was morose; he cast occasional glances back down the river, almost as if he expected another boat to materialise.

It's the man with the scar, thought Thorn. Was the man dangerous? Why had he disappeared as soon as they'd gone by? What was between him and Racky? The man had been on the opposite bank to the one on which they'd landed, so he'd have to cross the river if he was minded to follow them. But why should he do that?

"Let's get going," said Racky brusquely.

Soon they were moving again.

The track wound up and away from the river through sprays of hawthorn, elder and alder. Soon the sound of water, which had been with them all morning, was relegated to a memory. They were in deep forest again, dwarfed by beech and oak. The sun had gone into hiding – or rather he and Racky had, labouring along down here at ground level. Perched on a twist of exposed root, a grey squirrel glanced down at him with black, enquiring eyes, an old beech-nut clutched in its paws. Much bigger than Thorn, it was utterly unafraid – unlike the squirrels he'd seen near Norgreen, which would be away into the branches, tails flying behind them, before you could draw a bead on them. He'd not eaten squirrel for ages, but to shoot the animal would be a sad waste.

The morning wore on. Thorn plodded after Racky, who seemed now to be following no marked track, but some undefined route existing only in his head. He seemed more withdrawn than ever. Their shared battles with the stoats and crayfish, and even the yellow-feathered men at the inn, seemed a lifetime away.

A gulf had opened between them, although they were only inches apart.

But even as Thorn was thinking this, Racky halted, turned to him and said, "We'll pass Whispering Oak soon. We'll take a break there. Some people claim it's the biggest and oldest tree in the world, but that's nonsense, of course. What do *we* know of the world? We're ants crawling on its skin."

"Why do they call it Whispering Oak?"

But Racky was moving off again. His answering words came over his shoulder, "You'll see, Thorn Jack. Or, rather, you'll *hear*."

They pushed on, boots crunching on the rotting forest floor. On one decaying stump, astonishing fans of reddish fungus billowed like raw meat.

When suddenly Racky halted, Thorn all but bumped into him.

"Whispering Oak," his guide announced.

Directly ahead rose a colossus. The girth of its trunk seemed twice that of any other oak Thorn had seen. Its branches jutted far out from its trunk, greedy for space. As if in deference to its magnitude, the surrounding trees had fallen back to give it room, and there it stood, arrogantly holding the wood at bay. Even so, all was not well with it. Some of its branches were stripped of bark and bare of leaves: sooner or later, winds would snap these limbs and bring them crashing down. Several already lay on the forest floor. Its trunk, and some of its lower limbs, were twisted and deformed as if by some inner agony. It was pocked with great holes – three, four that Thorn could see.

Inside, there must be hollow regions where insects, birds or animals were even now at work to extend their domain.

They advanced to within a couple of feet of the trunk. Exposed roots writhed like a nest of maddened snakes, curling out from the trunk before plunging into the ground. Here and there were gaps and holes, easily big enough for a man to go through without needing to crawl. Thorn leant back, following the trunk upward to where the tree thrust a massive arm out over his head.

"See what I mean?" said Racky. "Ants on the skin of the universe, that's what we are. Here we stand beside one of the great ones of the world, old beyond imagination. But, as you can see, even this oak's days are numbered."

Did Racky derive a perverse satisfaction from such thoughts? He'd spoken with a thrilled eloquence.

"Listen!"

At first Thorn could hear nothing. Then that nothing became something, a kind of light murmur, as if a voice was in the tree.

"Do you hear it?"

"Yes," said Thorn. "But where does it come from? There's no wind that I can feel."

"Well may you ask. Some people say it's the breeze, others that it's insects gnawing away, others that it's just the creaking of wood in its old age. You can take your pick. But for me it's the sound time makes when it's trapped. The sound of time . . . Melancholy, don't you think?"

The sound didn't strike Thorn that way, but he didn't say so.

In fact, it didn't strike him as anything in particular. It seemed a neutral sort of noise.

Racky said, "We're making good time. Fancy taking a look inside?"

Thorn was reluctant to delay, but he felt tired and the tree was undeniably intriguing.

"All right," he agreed. "What about our packs?"

"We'll take them with us. There may be people prowling about."

Racky was being overly suspicious, thought Thorn, but perhaps he was still thinking about that man by the river.

Racky moved in closer and ducked under a woody arch. Thorn followed. They turned and twisted through serpentine galleries. When they halted, Thorn saw – thanks to shafts of light that cut through from above – that they stood in a sort of tree-cavern created – over what must have been hundreds of years – by the erosion of the oak's root-system. The smell of dry oakwood was in his nostrils.

"This way," said Racky. "And be careful – there's something I want to show you."

He led Thorn through a triangular entry into a further chamber and they climbed onto a broad horizontal root that was part-sunk into the earth. Still light penetrated, and Thorn saw that the ground fell sharply away into a pit, most of whose sides were formed from tree-roots. Directly in front of them, a rope-ladder was nailed to the wood and dropped into the hole.

"This is the Echo Hole," said Racky. "You can't truly appreciate Whispering Oak unless you've been down there. It's only a couple of feet deep. The light's as good today as it gets. Are you up for it?"

Was this another of Racky's tests? There was no way Thorn could refuse without seeming a coward.

"All right," he said, "lead the way."

"Wait till I call. Then come down."

Racky dropped his bow in the hole and set off down the ladder. Before his head disappeared, he glanced up at Thorn and winked.

After a time, his voice floated up, "I'm down. Your turn." But it was not one voice, it was two – three – four, as his utterance was taken up by the tree and multiplied.

"Watch out for my bow!" Thorn called, and dropped it down the hole. Then, carefully, he too began to descend. The ladder fell loosely into the hole: it wasn't attached to the root wall, which made for awkward going.

The rope was coarse and chafed his hands, but he was down. He stood on a sloping earth floor at the bottom of a well maybe two feet in width. The light here was dim, but all about him were roots, some tight against each other, others with gaps in between; at least two of the gaps looked wide enough to allow a man upright passage through. Racky's pack and the two bows were propped against a wall. But the man himself was invisible. A fantastic idea jumped into the young man's head: had his companion been devoured by the tree?

"Racky!" called Thorn. The word reverberated away from him, tormented and diminished by the spirit of the place.

"Here – through the biggest crack!" came the muffled reply.

Thorn unhooked his pack and set it down beside his bow. Then he squeezed into the crevice.

The fissure ended, and he stepped carefully forwards, but again found earth beneath his boots. He was in a root-walled chamber so dark that he could do no more than sense the vague, knotted shapes of ancient growth all about him. The smell had changed now: mixed with the dry odour of oak roots was that of loam, musty and dank.

"A proper labyrinth, isn't it?" came a voice – as if the tree itself had spoken. The sounds had no sooner reached him than they collapsed into fragments, into wisps and curlicues that slipped away through the alleys and chimneys of the tree.

"Where are you?" said Thorn.

"Everywhere," replied the many tongues of the tree. "All about you."

Racky was playing a game with him. As his eyes grew accustomed to the gloom, Thorn was just able to make out further cracks and openings between the tree's subterranean limbs. Racky must have gone through one of them. But he wouldn't be drawn into following. He'd wait here till the man reappeared. In the meantime, he tried an experiment.

He spoke, "I am Thorn Jack."

The sounds fractured, dissipated.

"I am Thorn Jack, Thorn Jack."

Sound bounced around the chamber, vibrating in his ears, draining away into the darkness. *Thor-Ja, Kor-Ja.* Whispering Oak stole your words and mangled them into unmeaning. What had Racky said – that human beings were ants on the skin of the universe? Was that what he'd brought Thorn down here to understand?

He waited in the silence, but Racky did not appear. Where is he? wondered Thorn. All right: if he's not coming out, I'm going back.

He squeezed back through the fissure. But here a shock was in store for him. Racky's pack and bow were gone. Gone too was the rope-ladder. It must have been pulled up from above. He tilted his head back, searching the space above. What was Racky up to – playing another game with him?

"Racky!" he called. "Are you up there?" His voice and its echoes swirled upwards.

"What do you want?" came the booming reply.

What do I want? What sort of an answer was that?

"Drop the ladder. I want to come up."

"I expect you do, Thorn Jack. But I'm not ready for you yet."

Not *ready* for me yet?

"Come on, Racky. This isn't a game."

"You're wrong, lad. A game is what it is. Here are the rules. *You* want something from *me* – out of the nasty hole you're in. But *I* want something from *you*. Not much – just the answer to a simple question. Tell me what I want to know, and I'll let the ladder down. Then you can come up. How does that sound?"

It sounds like betrayal, thought Thorn. He said: "Why didn't you ask me before?"

"Because you wouldn't have told me what it is I want to know."

"How can you know that?"

"Because I know you, Thorn Jack – better than your own mother."

My mother? *My mother?*

There was a pause. Thorn examined the smooth, sheer sides of the hole. There was no way he could climb up without the ladder. Racky had him over a barrel.

He said, "What is it you want to know?"

"Now you're talking. You brought something back from Wyke. Then you hid it. Where?"

Thorn's mind whirled. Racky wanted the crystal. All this way through the wood . . . the mutual dangers they'd shared . . . and now, suddenly, *this*? He said: "You know what I brought back from Wyke – a diamond ring."

Racky's laughter echoed in the well, a bunch of madmen braying together.

"Don't pretend to be simple-minded, lad. I know very well you're not. Where did you hide the crystal? It's not in the Floods' house and it isn't in your pack."

Thorn was stunned. It would have been easy enough for Racky to search his pack, but the house, his room . . . When had he done that? While Thorn was off hiding the crystal? Had this been Racky's purpose all along – not to help him get Haw back, but to take the crystal from him? Why did he want the crystal? What was so special about it? But he could ask none of these questions, since to do so would confirm that he had what Racky wanted.

He thought rapidly, then said, "A crystal? What crystal? I know nothing about a crystal. I stole a diamond ring, that's all.

It's in Norgreen Treasury. Come on, Racky, let me up. This isn't funny any more."

"Don't take me for a fool. Where did you hide it? *Where?*"

Thoughts went tumbling through Thorn's mind. He ought to have heeded the Syb's warning. But he and Racky had shared dangers, grown into comrades of a sort, and Thorn had relaxed his guard. Now the damage was done. Say he did tell Racky where the crystal was hidden, what guarantee did he have that the ladder would be dropped?

No – there was no way back from this. The two of them could never coexist as they'd done before. Racky would leave him in this hole whether he told him or whether he didn't.

He called, "There is no crystal. You've had your joke. Let me up."

"I'm starting to find your obstinacy irritating, lad. I'm going to leave you for a time, let you think about things. You'd better have an answer ready for me when I come back. If you haven't, you'll rot down there. Then you'll be rich pickings for rats."

"Racky!" shouted Thorn when the resultant clamour ceased. "Racky! Racky!"

Racky Jagger did not reply. His name came bouncing off the tree to ring in Thorn's abused ears like some mad and mocking bell.

14

ELPHIN LOACH

The house of Elphin Loach was sited in a sun-dappled arbour at the top of a grassy slope. The south-west corner of Harrylake could be glimpsed through the vegetation, sunlight riding its blue surface.

The house was a mishmash of colours and materials. To the left of its front door (painted emerald green) was a single large square window; to the door's right were two smaller circular ones. The planks that composed its frontage were nailed together at all angles. Some of its roofing tiles were red, others black, others green. Its tubular metal chimney went straight up, then horizontally, then straight up once more till it finished in a conical cowl. Smoke drifted up from it.

Primroses grew profusely in a number of rockeries, prompting Rainy to remark that these were Elphin's favourite flower.

"And of course they have the advantage that they look after themselves. She's fond of violets too – but they come later in the year."

A brass bell hung by the door. Rainy stepped up and rang it. The door was opened by the most startling woman Jewel had ever seen. Hair cascaded onto her shoulders and down her back, russet and tangled, partly obscuring her face. Above carmine lips and a bold nose, a pair of green eyes, outlined in black, assailed her visitors. Elphin wore a long black dress and a crimson shawl.

"Well now," she exclaimed, "look what the winds have blown to my door! Rainy Gill, if I ever saw her. And who might *you* be, I wonder?"

"This is my friend Jewel Ranson," said Rainy.

"Jewel Ranson," repeated Elphin. "There's a name to conjure with. Do you glitter in the night, Jewel?"

"I – er – no," said Jewel, embarrassed. "It's just a name."

"Just a name? Nonsense, girl! Names are things and things are names. Nothing happens by chance in this world. Well, come in and have some wine."

She turned, skirt aswirl, and they followed her into the house. The room was crammed with cupboards. They stood or leant against the walls, some with knobs, some with handles; they came in all shapes and sizes and were gaily painted with flowers. The floor was strewn with rugs, and they were all shapes and sizes too.

A fire crackled in the hearth. Elphin indicated two chairs.

"Well, sit down, sit down. Do you like gooseberry wine, Jewel?"

"I, erm, I don't believe I've ever tasted any."

"Never had gooseberry wine? Then you must – you shall! Gooseberry wine is the nectar the fortunate sip in paradise."

She visited two cupboards in turn, taking from one a pottery keg and from another three cups. The liquid she poured was yellowy-green, and it sparkled in the light lancing in through the windows.

She handed Jewel a cup.

221

"Tell me what you think of that."

Jewel held the wine on her tongue, and her mouth flushed with savour: the wine was deliciously acid.

She said, "It's wonderful, but hard to describe. If you could taste the colour green – the palest green . . ." She came to a halt, and blushed.

Elphin nodded appreciatively, then said sharply. "Did you have fish to eat last night?"

"Erm, yes," replied Jewel.

"I thought so. From Jugdam, of course."

"Yes, that's right."

"If I've told Rainy once not to eat fish from there, I've told her a hundred times."

Rainy said to Jewel, "Elphin, I'm afraid, doesn't approve of Jugdam – or anything to do with it."

"Never liked the place," said Elphin. "There's too much darkness in the water. That dam reeks of death."

"Elphin is convinced people have drowned there," Rainy explained.

"What – recently?" asked Jewel.

"Throughout time," said Elphin. "Drowned themselves or been drowned, willing and unwilling. My knuckles ache if I go there – that's a sure sign."

Jewel glanced at her own knuckles. Could they, perhaps, tell her things . . .?

"Are you a Syb?" she asked.

Elphin laughed. A night bird's croaking, it seemed.

"Something more and something less," she said at last. "Not all

Sybs are the same. Some are good at healing, some at potions, some at seeing. Very few do all three equally well. Healing has never held much interest for me. Most Sybs concern themselves with the white arts, of course, but what excites me is the darkness in people. Now you, Jewel Ranson . . ."

"Me?" Jewel exclaimed.

"Such a sweet girl, to look at you . . . But looks can deceive . . ."

"What do you mean?" demanded Jewel.

Elphin smiled. "Don't take offence. May I hold your hands, Jewel?"

Jewel looked at Rainy, who nodded encouragingly. Elphin moved her chair closer. Jewel set her cup down and stretched out her arms. Elphin took the girl's hands in her own. Despite the warmth of the room, Elphin's double clasp felt cold. First, she closed her eyes and sat unmoving. Then, after a time, she opened them again and, lifting Jewel's hands to her face, held them flat against her cheeks. As she did so, she fixed Jewel with a piercing stare. To the girl it felt as if the woman had suddenly slipped inside her through the corners of her eyes, and was reaching into her brain. She wanted to pull her gaze away, her hands too, and run away, but no: she could not.

After what seemed an age, Elphin relinquished Jewel's hands. Jewel examined them. They now seemed anyone's but her own. She ordered a finger to twitch. It did. They *were* her hands . . . She put them in her lap.

There was a silence; then Elphin spoke.

"I'm sorry, Jewel Ranson, for the sorrow that's in your life, but no one can change the past. The future is another thing. I'm not one of those who think our fates are fixed from the day we're born. Our lives are made by chance and necessity, as humans clash and collaborate in the dance of light and dark." She paused. "You, Jewel, are more than you know. You'll see and do astonishing things – things perhaps that people in this world have never done. But what most strongly I feel in you is the force of your will. And will is a dangerous thing: you should be wary of its promptings."

She fell silent. Jewel was looking at the shadows in the corners of the room, beneath the ceiling. How they flexed their boundaries, shifted a little, never seemed to be still.

Rainy said: "Tell us: is Jewel a Magian, Elphin, as you seem to imply?"

Elphin laughed. "That's a word I haven't heard in many a moon, Rainy."

"What's a Magian?" asked Jewel. "Is it like a Syb?"

Here they were discussing her, and she was already lost.

"No," said Elphin. "Magians are to Sybs as Sybs are to ordinary folk. No two Magians are the same. They are rare – very rare. I myself have known only one."

"Yesterday we tried an experiment," said Rainy. "Jewel put her hands on the ground and cleared her mind. She sensed an earthworm, then a water pipe she followed to the Round Pond – yet no one had mentioned it to her." Then Rainy described the openings that had first alerted her to Jewel's exceptional nature.

"Excellent. But her powers are as yet young in her."

"I'm confused," said Jewel. "I didn't know I had any powers."

"Sometimes it takes a severe shock to awaken them."

"A shock? My father died recently . . . or rather, he was murdered."

Elphin nodded sagely. "For some the death of a parent is like a knife stuck in the soul. It leaves a scar that never fades; it changes you – for ever. Have you been ill recently – had bad headaches, perhaps a fever?"

"Yes, both. But I thought—"

"That it was an ordinary illness? I doubt that it was. And I think you'll find, for some time to come, that exerting your powers will take a certain toll on you."

Jewel pondered this. "But what *is* a Magian?" she asked. "What does a Magian *do*?"

"For you, that remains to be known. That you can *see*, that you can project yourself: so much we can assume. But the mass of your powers will still be asleep. You must awaken them, nurture them. For a Magian to know herself fully is the work of many years – perhaps a lifetime."

"This Magian you say you knew . . . What was her name?"

"I do not like to speak it, but I'll tell you, for she lives yet. Her name is Querne Rasp."

"Querne Rasp . . ." repeated Jewel. The sounds were harsh and dry in her mouth. She shivered. "How did you come to know her?"

"You are inquisitive, Jewel, but it is proper that you should know. Here then is the story. We grew up together in Lowmoor settlement, close friends when we were small. But Querne was always competitive, and when it became apparent we were both gifted with powers, her competitiveness increased. She couldn't

225

bear to be second best. As it happened, her powers were much greater than mine, and when she saw this she began to look down on me as a lesser being. Then, when we were a couple of years older than you are now, we fell in love with the same young man. Sadly for him, he preferred me. Querne drew apart from me. Then, mysteriously, my admirer fell ill. Our Syb could do nothing, skilled healer though she was. The sickness was beyond her – she'd never seen its like before. It was, she said, *unnatural . . .*"

Elphin lapsed into silence. She seemed engulfed in memories.

"What happened?" prompted Rainy.

"He died, of course," said Elphin. "Querne came to his funeral, and when I walked by her, I saw on her face a smile of triumph, and felt her joy in my pain. I understood then that somehow she'd caused what had happened and that, henceforth, she would use her powers for evil, not for good. That's why I developed the special interests that I have: in a way, Querne shaped me. And this is why I warn you against yourself, Jewel Ranson. Power is temptation by another name: the greater the power, the greater the temptation to misuse it."

"Why should I wish to misuse it?"

"Because you are human, and wicked deeds are as easily done as good."

"You don't know me, Elphin Loach."

"I don't need to know you. It's enough to know you are human. You're too young to know yourself."

Jewel's response was forthright. "I don't believe I am."

Elphin smiled crookedly. "Let's hope that you are right."

*

They hadn't got far from the house when Jewel burst out, "Who does she think she is – patronising me like that?"

"It's just her way," replied Rainy. "Don't think badly of her."

"What does she know of murdered fathers?"

"More than you might think." Rainy paused, then said, "She told me once that every person she touches – as she touched you – leaves a certain deposit in her. It might be hatred or anger, it might be pain or fear. And those feelings she's condemned to carry for the rest of her life."

"I didn't ask her to carry mine."

"No . . . but I did. Blame me if you're going to blame anyone."

"Rainy, I could never blame you for anything. You're all goodness."

"Am I? Good intentions are one thing . . ."

"Look, I'm sorry. Perhaps I overreacted. I know she was trying to help."

"Do you know what I think?"

"What's that?"

"That you and she are rather alike – though she's more than twice your age."

Jewel looked hard at her friend. "Sometimes, Rainy," she said, "you puzzle me. Wait till I start blackening my eyes, curling my hair and talking in riddles. *Then* you can tell me she and I have something in common."

They looked at one another and, at exactly the same time, burst into laughter.

Elphin Loach's house was close to Harrypark's eastern boundary. To reach it that morning, Rainy and Jewel had come down past the Round Pond and crossed Harrypark's central avenue. This ran from side to side and carried the through-route to Lowmoor. Harrypark was a huge rectangle. Tidy, high walls of stone had once bounded most of it, but these were much the worse for wear, while the massive iron gates that had stood sentinel at each end of the central avenue had long since collapsed to lie rusting in grass. It was the general belief that Harrypark had been a pleasure-ground. There people could walk, lounge, picnic, angle, play games, go boating. That Jugdam and Harrylake were both artificial creations was obvious from their shapes and the materials of their construction. Harrypark also boasted some unusual structures and today, Rainy had promised, Jewel would see a couple of them.

Now, having retraced their steps to the central avenue, they came on the first of these. A four-sided pillar of stone perhaps three feet in length, it lay where it had fallen, its chipped and eroded base jutting into the air. Its capital had sunk a little way into the earth and was half-obscured by sprays of purple campion. Inset into its flat top was a square metal plate on which a pattern of lines and symbols could still be discerned. They meant nothing to Jewel. Sticking sharply out from this plate was a metal triangle.

"What is it?" asked Jewel.

"Nobody really knows. Opinions vary. Some people think it was purely ornamental, like the feature at the centre of Round Pond. Others think it conveyed information about Harrypark, or what was in it. Others think it's some sort of religious symbol. That's my guess, for what it's worth."

228

Moved by a sudden urge, Jewel stepped up to the metal plate, placed her palms flat against it and closed her eyes. She stayed like that for some little time, as if caught in a dream. A robin flew down with a whirr of wings and perched on the upthrust base of the pillar, from where he regarded Rainy like a schoolmaster a pupil. Still Jewel did not move. At last she opened her eyes, looked straight at Rainy and smiled.

"You're all wrong," she said. "It's a device to tell the time of day."

"The time of day? What do you mean?"

She pointed to the metal plate. "It seems the giants divided the day up into segments of time. When the pillar was upright, the sun would strike this metal triangle, casting a shadow on these lines. From the position of the shadow, anybody passing could easily tell the time of day."

Rainy almost said, "How could you possibly know *that* . . .?" But she knew how Jewel knew. Jewel had exercised her powers, the first time she'd done so consciously at her own prompting.

"Tell me," said Rainy, "what did you see when you closed your eyes?"

"Nothing, for quite a time," said Jewel. "Then a picture came into my mind. It was two people, a boy and a girl. They were looking down at the pillar. The boy was tracing the shadow with a finger, and the girl said, 'I should have been home by now!' They both laughed. And I knew straight away what the thing was for . . ."

"Looking *down* at the pillar . . . But that means . . ."

"That they were giants? Yes. Their clothes were different from ours, but they were human just like us."

Rainy was stunned. What was Jewel capable of? She stole a glance at her friend.

The central avenue was well-marked by the wheels of rat-carts. Jewel and Rainy hadn't been tracking its rutted surface for very long when, from behind them, a noise came to their ears. The crunch of wheels, undoubtedly.

They didn't have long to wait before a vehicle pulled by a matching pair of rats swung into view. It was moving briskly, and it was coming straight towards them.

They hurried out of the way, then turned to watch as it passed by.

The rats were a matched pair of bucks, and as sleek and powerful as any coupling Jewel had seen. They had snow-white fur, pinkish ears and ruby-red eyes. Smartly harnessed in black, they scampered along, whiskers twitching, and sniffed at the women as they passed. After them came an open carriage fronted by a box on which the driver sat in an elevated position, his back to his passengers. Jewel had thought her father tall, but the driver of the carriage looked considerably taller. Or so she supposed, for of course he was sitting down. What's more, he was amazingly thin, as if the effort of growing that had driven his body upwards had left nothing to fill it out. His knees in their narrow black trews jutted bonily out from the box; his long arms ended in slim, knuckly hands. One held the reins, the other gripped a carriage whip. As the vehicle passed, he glanced at them and cracked his whip. Half a dozen rooks erupted from the nearest tree and

230

flapped away, cawing wildly. The man grinned ghoulishly, his face all ridges and hollows, his nose as sharp as a knife.

The woman passenger was the first whose face was clearly visible, as she occupied the seat at the back of the carriage and faced the way that it was going. She was achingly beautiful, with a shock of glossy black hair and full, purple-painted lips. Yet she lolled in her seat listlessly, one arm dangling outside the conveyance as if forgotten. Her head was turned in their direction, but if she saw Jewel and Rainy she gave no sign of it. For all she was concerned, they might have been a couple of round stones on the wayside.

Only when the carriage drew level did Jewel see that the occupant of the backwards-facing seat was a man with a chubby face. His demeanour was exactly the reverse of his companion's. As soon as he spotted them he doffed his hat, which was white with a black band, beamed amiably down at them and said gracefully, "Good afternoon, ladies! A beautiful day, don't you think?" But before they could reply (if a reply was needed, for his words didn't demand one) the carriage was past them, leaving puffs of dust in its wake.

"Red-eyed whites!" exclaimed Jewel as the carriage rumbled away. "What gorgeous rats! I didn't believe they existed."

"Oh, they exist all right. But they cost so much, only the richest can afford them."

"Do you know those people?"

"Yes. I've seen the carriage before."

"So who are they? Have you met them?"

Rainy laughed. "Met them? Me? Not likely. They're the

231

poshest of the posh. I know who *they* are, sure, but they don't know *me*. You and I – or any of my neighbours, for that matter – don't belong in their world. We appear at the edges, as tradespeople or entertainers or servants or gardeners or cooks. But it's we who make their pampered lives possible. They'd die without us."

Jewel had never heard Rainy speak like this before. Resentment rang through her words. Jewel said, "You sound as though you've got a grudge against them."

"Well, against Deacon Brace – that's the driver. He insulted my father once, simply because he got in his way and was blind. Not that he knew who Dad was – and that's my point: the Deacon Braces of this world don't want to know."

"But he's driving a carriage: isn't he a servant too?"

"In a way. But Brace is much more than a servant. He does his master's dirty work, and very dirty it is too, if you believe the rumours. Everyone's afraid of him, including the Spetch brothers. But he figures in the story Harry the Wag tells about them, and he must tell you it, for he was there; I wasn't."

"Who are the man and woman?"

"The man's Crane Rockett. He's master of Minral How, a house built by the giants on the other side of the Barrens, and he's reputedly the richest man in the region. Charming, generous even, when he wants to be. But it's all a front. He's a snake underneath. The woman is Briar Spurr. Men go weak at the knees when they look at her – I've seen them – and men who should know better too, but they can't seem to help themselves. Whatever it is that makes a man grovel with adulation, she's got it and to spare. And the odd thing is, she couldn't care less. I don't know what she sees in Rockett, because he's hollow, and I don't believe for a moment that she's stupid. But he's rich, and that seems enough for her."

"She seemed bored," said Jewel. "She looked straight through me, as if I wasn't there."

"That's how she is most of the time. But suddenly she'll come alive, and then she's devastating. She makes absolute fools of men, but they seem to love it. Anything so long as she doesn't simply ignore them. But she's got a vicious streak. I'm not sure she isn't more dangerous than Crane: he'll do anything for her."

"Anything?"

"Anything. And, as Deacon Brace will do anything for Crane . . . By the look of it, the three of them are bound for Rotten Pavilion. We may well see them there. Keep out of their way – they're trouble."

"Don't worry," said Jewel. "I will."

15

UNDERWORLD

Enough of this, thought Thorn: sitting, waiting for tomorrow. Tomorrow's not going to come.

He got to his feet, picked up his pack and bow and went over to the fissure he'd gone through before. With his bow in his right hand, he squeezed sideways between the root-walls; then, with his left hand, pulled the pack in behind him. Halfway through, the pack seemed to stick, but he gave it a good tug and, buckles scraping, it came free. Now he was in the further chamber.

Squatting in the almost-dark, he unstrapped the pack; then began to empty it, setting the items carefully aside. The bag the Syb had given him lay at the bottom. He dug around in it and extracted the items he wanted. Now to test the first of Minny's gifts. Sliding one of the lucifers from its box, he dragged its bulbous end against the striking surface. A spark jumped through the darkness, momentarily illuminating his hand, but the object did not light. He tried again, and was pleasantly startled as it flared up, releasing an acrid tang. He put the lucifer to the head of the – what had Minny called it . . . link? – and the brand immediately ignited, lighting the chamber with its brilliance. It burned with a halo of blue fire, not the yellow flames of commonplace brands. He blew out the lucifer and stuck the link into the soft earth. A dozen beetles with metallic green bodies made themselves scarce. A scarlet centipede was inspecting his pack, but he grabbed it with both hands, hauled it back and watched it squirm away. Then he repacked his gear.

His predicament might be pretty dire, but all was far from lost. If now wasn't the time to use these gifts, when could that be? Had the Syb *seen* him here – trapped, desperate? If she had, surely there would be another way out. True, Racky believed him trapped, but it seemed unlikely his erstwhile guide – or anyone, come to that – had fully explored these galleries.

Thorn surveyed the chamber. There was a choice of two fissures besides the one he'd come through. Selecting the nearest, he held the link up just inside its entry, but was immediately able to see that the shaft soon narrowed: he'd never get through it. The other looked promising. Holding bow and torch in his right hand, he moved into it, again pulling his pack in after him. As he moved onwards, the fissure widened, then narrowed. Would his luck hold to the other side? It did. Here was another chamber, earth-floored again but smaller than the last, and it offered only one avenue of progress. This time the fissure slanted steeply downwards, and pushing in, he had to lean back against the root-wall in order not to fall forwards. The link coloured the fibrous muscle of the great oak orange. The deep shadows were mauve. Scandalised by the light, more insects fled away from him. Again fortune was kind, he was through.

The third chamber was larger than the previous two, and on the floor were scraps of fur and bone. The remains of rabbits, by the look of it . . . With them came a faint, slightly sour animal scent. Gaping darkly in the chamber's far wall, a tunnel led down into the earth. Could this be part of a warren? If so, he could be in luck, for unless the tunnel had collapsed up ahead, and these were old excavations, there must surely be, somewhere, a way out in that direction . . .

He listened, but could hear nothing – not even now, he realised, the whisper of the tree. Hefting the pack onto his back, he entered the tunnel, stooping slightly, holding the torch up before him to light the way. The passageway ran downwards at a slight angle, and he soon saw why: the ceiling was plaited with roots. The animals that had made the tunnel must have had to dip down beneath them to make progress. As soon as he got past this rooty region, the tunnel began to rise again. But he hadn't gone far when a new problem confronted him: the tunnel forked.

The two new galleries looked identical. There was nothing to be gained by pondering the matter, so he set off down the one to his right. It twisted and turned, passing around and under stones. Insects skittered away from the light. After a time, he found himself in a stretch where soil had fallen from the ceiling. This wasn't a good sign. He clambered over the mounds, his boots sinking into the softness. Soon they were caked in muck. Then he rounded a stone and stopped: the passage was blocked – a ceiling collapse.

He tramped back to the fork. The left-hand tunnel proved equally stony. As he clambered over one obstacle, something fluttered into his face. Only a moth – but, jerking back, he banged an elbow on the stone, lost his grip on the link and slid to the earth floor, grazing his arm as he went. Damn . . . But the link stayed alight. He rubbed his elbow.

Time passed. The tunnel snaked along, now high-ceilinged, now low. At length the link's radiance started to dim, darkness to close in. But the Syb's gift had long outlived an ordinary brand. He lit a second link from the first. Moments later, the first went out. He cast it aside and went on.

The tunnel bent again – and suddenly two green eyes were staring at him, inches away. A startled rabbit. For a moment it crouched transfixed; then it swung round and hopped away, kicking the earth up as it went. Quickly the gloom sucked it in.

He grinned in the bluish light. Where there were rabbits, there must be rabbit holes. He'd soon be out of this. He felt strong, resilient, master of his own destiny. Before, he'd been subservient to the decisions of his guide. Now he was on his own, and dependent on himself. He thought back to Wyke: I passed that test, didn't I? Well, I'll come through this one too and go on to Roydsal alone.

He came to a second fork. He chose a passage at random. It led uphill to another labyrinth, the second of the day. A maze of roots, a maze of tunnels . . . Which way to go? If only he had the instinct of a rabbit or a mole. No chance of that: he was a creature of light not darkness, of the upper world, not this earthy dungeon.

He chose and went on. Time passed. He paused to scrape off the sticky, thick soil that gummed his boots. His trews and hands were filthy. The tunnel turned, descended, ascended, turned, descended again. His legs were getting heavy, he was starting to tire.

He came to another roof-fall. He would have to retrace his steps.

All at once dispirited, he trudged back along the tunnel. Up, down, up, around . . . Where was his luck? Had it left him? He'd long since lost any sense of direction. Even if he got out into the open air, he wouldn't have the slightest idea where he was.

Must keep going, he told himself: somewhere there's a way out. Here at last was the labyrinth. Which passage now? This one . . .?

As he plodded on, Manningham Sparks's picture of Hell came into his mind: not the torment of devils but a sort of nothingness, the sinner condemned eternally to wandering in a Barrens. Well, the Reverend should try this – scuffling like some human mole in subterranean warrens: muck, roots, stones, insects, silence. If you fell asleep here, slept for ever without dreaming: might death be like that? He shuddered, and tried to shake the dark thoughts out of his head.

I'm hungry, he realised. But could he afford to stop and eat? He had only this link, and one more after that. But could he afford *not* to eat? He had to keep his strength up. Right, he'd forfeit time.

He halted, stuck his brand into the ground, propped his bow against the tunnel-wall, unshouldered his pack and brought out some food. Then, his back against a stone, he began to eat. Did the food smell of must and taste of earth, or was he imagining it? He ate it anyway.

How weary he was. His arms ached from holding the link, his neck from continual stooping. He felt filthy from head to foot.

Oh, for the clean waters of the pool where he'd hunted the crayfish . . . When he'd eaten his fill, he rested his head against the stone. His eyelids felt heavy, he could barely hold them open. They closed. He was asleep.

Thorn jerked awake to blackness. Something was crawling across his cheek. He brushed it away. The link had died. From somewhere near came a scratching sound. He listened, night-senses alert. Claws on stone? An invisible animal. Another rabbit? If so, no problem. But since when did rabbits have claws . . .?

The scratching noise came again, closer now. Fire would repel any animal – had he time to light a link? He reached for his pack, but even as his hand closed by chance on the lip of the quiver strapped to its side, there came a snuffling sound, and he was assailed by a stench. Reacting without thinking, he pulled an arrow from the quiver, seized his bow, nocked it, and fired from his sitting position – blind into the darkness.

The twang of the string was followed by a *thock!* and a high-pitched squeal. A second arrow chased after the first. A second *thock!* was followed by silence. The stench seemed to fill the tunnel. He waited . . . Nothing. He laid aside his weapons, groped for the Syb's bag and, with stupidly shaking hands, lit his last link.

No more than six inches away was the body of a brown rat. Its fierce little eyes stared directly into his face. His first arrow was in its flank. His second stuck out from the inner corner of its left eyeball. As he watched, a ruby tear dribbled down the creature's muzzle.

That's one arrow I shan't bother to retrieve, he told himself.

The stench was easily explained. To one side of the creature was a rag of raw flesh and fur. The rat had dragged its half-eaten booty down the passage. If he hadn't awakened when he had, thanks to that curious insect . . . Never say your luck's deserted you, he told himself.

He got going again. At least the sleep had refreshed him. He was moving with more vigour now, more purpose. First the rabbit, now the rat; that, too, had come from *somewhere*. But where there was one rat, there could be more . . . He would have to stay on his toes.

The tunnel forked again. Left – right: which had been the eye of the rat he'd hit? The left. Left then; he plunged on. Soon the tunnel forked again. This time he went right. He didn't fancy going in a circle, to find himself revisiting some point he'd passed before. The tunnel rose, then dipped, then came out into a chamber. With a muddy toe he poked at some remains – a severed ear, a paw, some gnawed bones. A baby rabbit. Now, a single passageway offered itself to him.

He laboured on. Just how long, he wondered, will this final link burn? At length he came to another chamber, smaller than the last. Here were more fragments of fur and, this time, a choice of two openings. He chose the left-hand option. The tunnel plunged on, seeming to drag interminably. Would he ever get out into light again, see grass, trees, water, rain, sun, and hear birdsong?

The link was dimming now. He ploughed on, as fast as he could. The tunnel made a left ahead. But the halo contracted to tiny tongues of blue flame; darkness was gathering its forces against him. Soon he was in the almost-night. A moment later, pitch blackness. He flung the brand down with a curse. Taking the box of lucifers from his pack, he struck one. Then, holding its tiny fire before him, walked on. But it didn't last long. He struck a second. In this way, he made good ground before the box was exhausted.

But exhausted it was. He sank to the ground. All at once, he felt the weight of the earth above his head. It seemed to press down on him, a black, monstrous load that sought to crush the life from him. I'm going to die here, he thought, and rats will gnaw the flesh from my bones . . . His head sank onto his chest and he stayed like that for some time, his mind empty of thought.

Till a picture formed there, an image of Haw by their secret pool, laughing and splashing him . . . Haw, lost and stolen away . . .

Hauling himself to his feet, he felt for the tunnel wall and began to grope forward.

Till he almost tripped. His right foot had hit a stone. No – it was more a kind of step: for here it seemed the earth floor gave way to one of stone. Pressing forward now, he soon felt stone under his hand. So: was this a corridor? He reached blindly upwards but could feel nothing above him. This might be a cavern, then. But what size was it, what shape? What if there were pits beneath his feet, and he slipped into one? Out of the frying-pan into the fire . . . Equally, this could be the way out at last.

The stone floor sloped upwards. First gently, then not so gently. Before long, he was down on all fours, scrabbling up the stone, his bow gripped awkwardly in one hand. He mustn't lose that, whatever happened. Twice already it had saved his life . . .

The floor levelled again. His outstretched hand felt something yielding. An animal, perhaps? Gingerly, he explored its surface. No: it was some coarse fabric. Fabric meant humans . . . He began to explore the extent of the thing, first with one hand, then with both. It was some kind of a drape, surely. It stretched across in front of him. From wall to wall, from ceiling to floor, it was held tautly there. At the under-edge, he encountered a cord . . . and here, another. It went from a hole near the edge of the drape to a pin or a nail in a wooden frame. A wooden plank had been jammed in place across the base of the opening. To this the drape was fixed, closing off the shaft in the rock . . .

Humans had done this. Where could he be?

He listened, but could hear nothing. What period of day – or night – was it? Impossible to tell. He'd long since lost all sense of time.

The cords were well knotted. He slipped his knife from its sheath and cut first one tie, then the other. Shuffling sideways on his knees, he found a third and cut that . . . a fourth . . . then a fifth. Surely now there'd be space enough to squeeze underneath . . .

He raised the drape. Darkness still. And, wedded to it, silence. He crept forward, the material rustling, ever so slightly, against his pack. But he was through. He got to his feet and rubbed his knees. So far so good. He moved slowly forward, testing ahead for solid ground before he committed himself to each step, keeping his fingers in touch with the wall. The rocky floor was a little uneven, but manageable. He took perhaps twenty steps, then his foot struck something. It was loose, and as it shifted it made a scraping sound.

Thorn stopped dead. Carefully he poked the invisible object with his foot. It rocked away. Bending, he touched it. It was hard, dry and tubular. He felt along it. It ended in a sort of knob.

He jerked his hand away with a quiver of horror and disgust. It was a bone, a human bone – a leg bone or an arm bone. But stripped and clean, as if boiled in a pot and greedily scraped with a knife.

He straightened up and stepped over the bone. Now he began to inch forward, testing the blackness ahead with his boots. When his left foot made contact with a second object, he didn't touch it. He moved gingerly forward, desperate not to betray his presence. His foot touched another bone, then another and then another. Soon he lost count of their number. The rock floor was a boneyard. The Woodmen! he thought. The stories about their gruesome taste for human flesh were true. This must be the place where they dumped the remains . . . He stayed by the wall, stepping with the delicacy of a long-legged water-fly, grateful for the simplicity and honesty of rock.

At last he was past the bones. The wall began to curve to the left, bending away from him. As he followed its curvature, the darkness grew less intense. He glimpsed the wall ahead, its planes, outjutments and angles, then the floor on which he trod. As the light strengthened, the opposite wall came into view, and last of all the ceiling. He was moving along a rocky corridor, perhaps a foot in width, but more than two feet high at its lowest point. As he began to walk more confidently, the wall ahead seemed to move: faint shadows were playing on the stone.

The light grew steadily stronger; the corridor widened. Now he saw shapes ahead of him – bundles and boxes, items of furniture, a variety of objects. The light came from oil-lamps attached to the walls.

Oh my god, he thought with a pulverizing sense of despair – I'm deep inside a Woodman's cave!

16

SIX THROWS OF THE DICE

"We call it the Obelisk," said Rainy. "Most people think it's a religious monument."

Many times the size of the time-telling device she'd seen earlier in the day, the Obelisk stood erect and proud, dominating the avenue. Set on a stepped hexagonal plinth, it boasted an elegant square-edged spire set on a more massive lower trunk.

Around the plinth moved tiny people. Short flights of stairs on the giant steps allowed them to climb to the top of the plinth. Others sprawled nearby in the sunshine, picnicking. Some, said Rainy, were residents of Harrypark; others were up from Lowmoor and even further afield – many, no doubt, for a night at the tables in the Pavilion.

As they passed the Obelisk, Jewel saw that its mottled stone was marked with symbols or illustrations as well as columns of words. Time had done little to erase them, but, unlettered as she was, they meant nothing to her. Though tempted, she thought it better not to draw attention to herself by repeating yesterday's experiment with the time-telling device. In each of the monument's four faces, at a height of around three feet, objects that looked like metal bowls were mounted below a sort of spout and, as she idly considered the nearest of these odd embellishments, an image flashed into her mind of water spurting from the spout and a giant child bending to drink.

Leaving the central avenue, Rainy and Jewel turned down a track towards the lake. It dipped and curved around a rocky promontory, piercing the inevitable banks of rhododendrons.

At the lake's edge were boatmen's huts, each with its own yard. In one, the partly-built upturned shell of a dinghy rested on trestles. A number of craft bobbed at the quay: modest vessels, mainly, for rowing or fishing trips, but also a couple of larger boats for more high profile excursions. Out from the bank, its planking lifted above the rippling water by stoppered cylinders, stretched the pontoon bridge. Boldly it rode the waves, lifting and falling with their motion as they slapped against it. Along either side a rope rail was strung, but the bridge was wide enough to accommodate a cart with room to spare.

At its further end, no more than fifteen yards from the shore, lay a sizeable island. Thickly planted, it ran parallel to the shore, so that eastwards a channel stretched away between island and mainland.

"Lake Island," announced Rainy, as if reading Jewel's thoughts. "But you can't see Rotten Pavilion. It's hidden among the trees."

The island's plant-life seemed no less dense than the mainland's.

From here only the eastern half of the lake was visible, but Jewel knew from Rainy's description that it was almost square in shape, its banks in most places constructed – though not here – from bricks and dressed stones. The lake's southern extremity seemed a long way off: one hundred and fifty yards – two hundred? Jewel couldn't tell.

As they approached the bridge, a white-bearded old man wearing a broad-brimmed blue cap got up from his chair beside one of the huts and, with the aid of a stick, hobbled towards them.

"Good day, Miss Rainy and Miss Unknown," he greeted them, affably doffing his cap.

"Hello, Sam," said Rainy. "How are the knees?"

"Crocked, lass, but I can still row."

Rainy gestured to her companion. "Sam, this is Jewel Ranson; Jewel, Sam Dyker. Nobody knows Harrylake's waters better than him."

"I ought to; I've been doused in them often enough."

They laughed.

"So, Miss Jewel Ranson," continued Sam. "And what brings you to Harrypark?"

"Just passing through," replied Jewel vaguely. "It's a fascinating place."

"That it is. The only place in the world to live, if you ask me."

"Is that where you live?" asked Jewel, indicating the hut.

"It is. I have a roof for my old head, sun and rain, a lake with fish in, friends – what else could any man need?"

"But men don't always live by what they need, do they?" said Rainy. "Some live by what they want." She glanced over at the island and the hidden walls of Rotten Pavilion. "Which tends to complicate things."

247

"More's the pity," observed Sam dryly, following her gaze. "Going to the Pavilion, are you?"

"We are."

"Hmm . . ." Sam looked at Jewel. "That's a bad place, lass. Lock up your money, if you go there."

Jewel smiled, but said nothing.

"Doesn't say much, does she?" observed Sam to Rainy. Then, to Jewel: "Deep waters, eh, little miss?"

"Oh, pretty shallow, I think," said Jewel.

Sam Dyker grinned, as if to say: so *you* say, but *I* know what I know.

"Well, don't let me keep you from your business," he said.

As they approached the bridge, a small cart appeared out of the greenery on the island and, without pausing, rolled onto the bridge. Its wheels clattered loudly on the boards, but the bridge took its weight easily. The rat was obviously used to the crossing, and soon regained solid ground. As he passed them, the carter tipped his cap.

"Morning, Miss Rainy," he called.

"Morning, Jemmy," replied Rainy.

"Pavilion's busy this week. Good crowd in." The last words were thrown over the carter's shoulder.

"One of Harry's suppliers. Comes up from Lowmoor," Rainy explained.

They stepped out onto the bridge. The planks felt buoyant underfoot. This is like walking on air, thought Jewel. From the underside of the planking came the muted splosh of water.

Reaching the island, they set off down a broad, shady track.

Rhododendrons were fewer here, and amongst the variety of trees Jewel saw lilac and laburnum. Lake Island, it seemed, was popular with birds, for above them and from both sides sounded a host of twitterings. Here and there were arbours with seats in which people could sit and dream.

She said, "How peaceful it is here."

"Yes," said Rainy. "But for every visitor who appreciates the quiet of the island, twenty prefer the excitements of Harry's gaming room. Funny old world, isn't it?"

Rainy, it struck Jewel, was in an odd mood today: harmless remarks seemed to provoke her.

The roofline of Rotten Pavilion became visible through the trees.

They turned a corner. Coming their way was an odd couple. The man appeared assembled from assorted rolls of flesh. His face was a pinkish pudding, his features inserted as afterthoughts. Bushy sideburns grew to his chin. His fat arms terminated in clusters of sausagey fingers. His check suit was brown and orange. He hummed as he rolled along.

The woman was stick-thin and could have been packed into the man's skin at least three times over. Her black dress was so tight she could take only the tiniest steps, and this turned her progress into a parody of walking. Her hair was piled on top of her head and held with clips and a comb. When she spotted Rainy and Jewel, her angular face took on the haughtiest of expressions, as if to say: How dare you walk the same path as me?

Unabashed, Rainy favoured her with her sweetest smile. "Hello, Gilda. Fine day for a stroll."

The woman hoicked her nose up and didn't deign to reply. Her consort gave them a look of puzzlement, but also said nothing.

Tottering past, the woman stumbled, and had her arm not been entwined with the man's, would surely have toppled over like a freshly felled sapling.

"Ow!" exclaimed her companion, whose leg she'd jabbed with her heel.

"Damn!" said the woman, and stopped to fiddle with a shoe.

Rainy and Jewel exchanged glances and burst out laughing. The woman looked up at them with murder in her eyes. But Rainy and Jewel continued on, and soon the path twisted, taking the couple out of sight.

"Who were *they*?" asked Jewel.

"The woman's Gilda Buckle, good-time girl and the biggest leech in Harrypark. She's attracted to money like a wasp to jam. The man's Tarry Ramsbottom. A Lowmoor businessman and a real high-roller. He comes here a lot. Sometimes wins, sometimes loses. Looks fatter each time I see him. Loves Ned's cooking – that's Harry's chief kitchenman. Tarry's all right actually, from what I've seen of him, but *Gilda* . . ." Rainy snorted.

"You two know each other?"

"Gilda and I go way back. She was born in Lowmoor, brought up in Harrypark. We were friends when we were kids. But we fell out over something and nothing, and it's beneath her dignity now to acknowledge a mere entertainer. Though what *she* does apart from entertain men is hard to see . . ."

Another turn of the path delivered them to a courtyard. On its far side were a carriage-house and a rattery. The carriage-house door stood open, and inside a number of vehicles were drawn up in a row. Framed in the doorway, a couple of men were engaged in conversation.

Seeing the women's approach, one lifted an arm in salute. Rainy waved back.

"You seem to know everybody," observed Jewel wistfully.

"That's the advantage of a small world. But it has its drawbacks. It's nice sometimes to be where no one knows you at all."

Crossing the courtyard, they began to climb a flight of stone steps. Above them soared the walls of Rotten Pavilion, ivy-clad. But, as giant-built structures went, the Pavilion was small – too small, probably, to ever have functioned as a dwelling. Perhaps it had been a storeroom. At the top of the steps, an ancient stone-flagged path ran along the foot of the wall. Straight ahead, framed between the side of the building and the vegetation that fringed the path, appeared a vertical slice of the lake. Halfway along the wall, what had once been a giant doorway had been transformed by a clever builder and featured a human-sized door and a series of small windows. The door was open, but Rainy led Jewel past it and around the next corner.

Here was a paved rectangular terrace twice as long as it was broad. At each end were rockeries crammed with flowering plants. A metal railing ran along the lakeside edge. On the terrace were tables and chairs, some presently occupied by people drinking and talking or simply drowsing in the sun. Inevitably, the human scene was dwarfed by the Pavilion, whose lake-facing wall also contained a converted window.

251

They crossed to the railing and Jewel leant against it, looking down. A couple of yards below, water lapped at the dark rocks that fringed the shoreline, protecting the soil of the island from being washed away. The lake spread itself before them, the crests of its wavelets sparkling as they caught the light. Its southern shore seemed far away. A few pleasure-craft moved or drifted on its waters, the smaller boats hugging the island. From the stern of a fishing craft an angler, strapped into a chair bolted down to the deck, cast his line afresh, then slotted his rod into the socket designed for it. A girl waved at them from the prow of a passing dinghy, and Jewel and Rainy waved back. To their right, a flight of steps led down to a small landing-stage where a few boats were tied up.

"Why do they call it Rotten Pavilion? It's lovely," said Jewel.

"According to Harry, because of the state of the building when he came here. It was derelict and filthy, full of fungi and spiders. But he saw its possibilities, and now it's transformed. Took a big investment, but it's paid off nicely. It's unique, and people come from a long way off. Shall we sit a little?"

"Yes, let's."

They chose a corner table by the far rockery, and no sooner had they sat down than a thin, freckled youth with short-cropped ginger hair and wearing a waiter's apron materialised at their side.

"Hello, Miss Rainy," said the youth. "Are you wanting a drink?"

"Hello, Nog," she replied. "A glass of Jay's best, I think."

"And you, miss?" said Nog, turning to Jewel.

"Apple tea for me, please."

252

Jewel gazed about her while they waited for their drinks. To the Pavilion, along with ivy, clung a second adventurous plant. Thickly clustered, its mauve blossoms seemed to concentrate the light.

"What's that plant?" Jewel asked.

"Wisteria," answered Rainy. "Jay calls it *hysteria*. Last spring when we were here he climbed it and sat with his head sticking up out of the flowers – all to amuse Linden. She shouted for him to come down – or *she*'d be hysterical."

Soon Nog arrived, with their drinks on a wooden tray. Jewel reached into her pocket for money but the waiter waved away payment.

"On the house." He turned to go.

Rainy said, "Nog – could you check to see if Harry's available? We'd like a private chat. But no rush. We'll be here through the evening. I'm down to perform tonight."

"I know," replied the youth. "I'll enquire."

"So, Jewel," said Rainy after a time, "you've seen a fair bit of my stamping-ground. What do you think of it?"

"It's lovely," said Jewel. "Sort of enchanted, as if the rules that apply to the rest of the world have been suspended here."

Rainy looked thoughtful. "If only that were true," she said. "Still, I know what you mean. I sometimes feel the same way. Especially when the sun's out, and I'm alone in some pleasant nook. But then something happens that reveals a different reality. So far you've seen the best of it. Or, to put it another way, you've seen the surface of things. But there's another Harrypark, a darker one. Like the lake itself, which some say is incredibly deep in the middle. There's a legend, according to Sam Dyker, that the giants tried to tunnel here to the centre of the world, but it was beyond even their skill. When they gave up, they filled the huge shaft they'd made with all this water to hide their failure."

"How did they manage that?"

"Search me. It's a legend, and you're not supposed to question such stories. Perhaps they diverted a river. Who can guess what was possible for those who lived in the Dark Time?"

"Do you believe the story?"

"I think it's a story, that and no more. But it's suggestive, don't you think? The beautiful surface of things, the deep pit underneath it born of human frustration, full of who knows what . . ."

Or just water? thought Jewel.

She said: "How gloomy you are, Rainy. And it's such a lovely day! Look at the water – look at the sun! The trees, the flowers!"

"You're right, Jewel, I'm sorry. It must be the prospect of talking to Harry. I know exactly what he's going to say – oh, not about the Spetch brothers, but about him and me. We go round and round in circles, never getting anywhere. It gets a little wearing."

"That one, Tarry!" said a shrill voice.

Gilda Buckle had arrived. In a scraping of chair legs, she and Tarry seated themselves at a distant table. But no sooner had Gilda settled than she was up on her feet again, demanding Tarry change places with her. Uncomplainingly, he complied.

Nog materialised beside them. Did they want a drink?

"Elderflower champagne!" declared Gilda in a loud voice. "Tall glasses, not those stubby ones. And make sure they're clean."

"Right away, madam." Nog's face was expressionless.

Everyone present was watching the couple, but Gilda, busily engaged in smoothing down her dress, seemed oblivious of the attention she was drawing. Rainy raised an ironic eyebrow and winked at Jewel. Gilda hadn't cast a single glance in their direction.

The waiter reappeared with a bottle and showed the label to Tarry. "Fine. On my bill, Nog." The youth popped the stopper, which shot out over the railing and vanished into the lake.

Tarry lifted his foaming glass. "Here's shine for your eye-teeth, darling."

"Here's to your *luck*, my love," Gilda pronounced, with more than a hint of sternness. "Tonight," she added, "tonight."

"I'll drink to that," said Tarry.

They clinked glasses and drank. As she set hers down again, Gilda turned in Rainy's direction and smirked at her, as if to say: No champagne for *you* today, you miserable juggler!

And no Tarry for me either, thought Rainy. For which, kind fate, much thanks.

But here came Nog again.

"Harry can see you now, Miss Rainy. In his room, if you'd like to go up."

"Thank you, Nog."

Never before had Jewel set foot inside a giant structure. To *live* in one, as the Spetches apparently did, was one thing. To *convert* one for human use – that was something else. From a high-ceilinged hallway, they turned up a flight of stairs. At the top was a vast room divided part way down its length by a tall, trellised screen. The first section constituted a bar and sitting room. In one corner beneath the heavy pink florets of a rambler rose, a couple was talking intimately. Other plants rooted in pots had colonised the screen, and the air was scented with perfume. Rainy led Jewel through a gap in the screen into a large dining area. Light flooded in through panes of glass cunningly carpentered into the lower half of the original window-space. Beyond danced the lake's greeny-blue, light-tipped waters. The upper tier of panes she'd seen from outside must light the guest-rooms on the Pavilion's second floor. Tall curtains, crimson and emerald, hung at each end of the windows.

Jewel turned and looked around. At the rear of the room was a small stage. That must be where Rainy would perform tonight. Lamps, unlit as yet, hung from slim, arching standards, or were attached to the side walls.

On the far side of the dining area were a second partition-wall and more pots of flowers. Rainy opened its only door and ushered Jewel into the gaming room. Possessed of a single windowpane, it was more discreetly lit, and struck Jewel as enclosed. Tables of various sizes were set up for cards, dice and other amusements. There was a large wheel whose rim was divided into squares displaying various multiples and, beside it, a cloth that duplicated them – some game of chance, she supposed. Over against the far wall was another bar, and small tables where gamblers could take a break.

The women's feet made no sound on the matting as they threaded their way to a side door. Rainy tapped on it with her knuckles and Jewel preceded her in, treading the shaft of light that fell through the door until it disappeared as her companion clicked the door shut behind them.

"Ah, my favourite juggler!" said a man's voice from the shadows.

"Hello, Harry," said Rainy Gill.

After the previous rooms, this one was so small and so dim that it was some time before Jewel's eyes accustomed themselves to it. Here were no windows: the only source of illumination was a pair of lamps on one wall, and their wicks were turned low. Against the wall were a desk and chair. In addition to them, the room contained a couch, a table and four chairs that had seen better days, a battered dresser and wardrobe that did not match one another, and a rumpled cot in one corner. After the luxury of the previous rooms, the shabbiness of this one came almost as a shock.

Not waiting to be invited, Rainy crossed to the wall-lamps and turned them up.

"Oh, make yourself at home," said Harry the Wag rudely.

The master of Rotten Pavilion lay on the couch with his feet up, stocking-clad but unshod, his back propped against cushions. At his elbow was a table, on the table a bottle and a half-filled – or half-empty – glass of amber liquid. The infamous barley wine? Rainy and Jewel pulled chairs up to the couch and sat down.

"Harry, this is Jewel Ranson."

Harry looked at his guest, but, as he offered no greeting, neither did Jewel. The silence lengthened.

Harry the Wag looked ill. Under a disorderly thatch of greying hair, his eyes were veined and sunken. Dark bags lurked beneath them. Even in the gloom Harry's skin had a pallid sheen, as if it hadn't seen sun in years.

Rainy said, "Harry, you're not looking after yourself."

Harry grinned blearily. "There she goes. Nurse Rainy."

"Your nurse is the last thing I'd be. You're going to kill yourself, Harry, if you go on like this."

"So what, my sweet? We're all going to die."

"You don't have to help the process along."

"Why not? There's only one thing I want, and as you know I can't have it. How long do I have to wait for you to save me from myself?"

"I can't save you, Harry. You've got to save yourself." Rainy paused. "But we've had this conversation before. It led nowhere then and it will lead nowhere now."

Harry grunted. "That's life, my love."

"*Your* life, Harry. And one reason why I won't marry you."

"If you married me I'd be different. I'd emerge from this cocoon; I'd spread my wings, fly away. What a time we'd have."

"I'd like to believe that . . ."

"Why won't you? People can believe anything – all they have to do is to say 'I believe . . .'"

"Well, I don't."

"Give me a chance, Rainy. You'll be rich. You'll want for nothing."

"I want for nothing now."

"That's because you've *got* nothing."

"It's *you* that's got nothing. I've got a home in a beautiful place, a loving father, friends, a craft . . . That sounds to me like everything."

Harry stared at Rainy for a time, then turned to Jewel. "Are we boring you, little girl, with our futile adult wrangles? Are we embarrassing you?"

Jewel thought for a moment, then said, "We've just been sitting in the sun, looking at the lake. It's all so beautiful . . ." She paused, then went on, "I don't understand why you sit here in this darkness . . ." Her voice trailed away, as if defeated by the gloom that seemed to emanate from this man.

"You speak your mind, don't you? What's your name again, little girl?"

"Jewel Ranson, Mr Harry. But I'm not a little girl."

"Hmm . . . perhaps not. But you're young in the ways of the world, Jewel Ranson."

"Am I? I'm here because my father was murdered."

"Are you now? I'm sorry for that. But *I* didn't kill him. What's it to do with me?"

"Nothing – nothing at all. But he was killed by the Spetch brothers. Rainy says you can tell me about them."

"Does she now? Well, I can tell you they're bad news. Stay out of their way, unless you fancy joining your father."

"If they're bad news, Mr Harry, why do you let them into this place?"

Harry grinned. "If I excluded people on the grounds of undesirability, I'd have next to no clients. Gamblers are a single-minded bunch; they live their passion. They sometimes get overexcited. You have to give them a bit of rope. All I ask is that they behave themselves while they're here. Anyway, the Spetches haven't come for quite some time."

"So they're not here at the moment?" This was Rainy.

"No," said Harry.

"Good."

"Why do you say that?"

"We saw Crane Rockett, Briar Spurr and Deacon Brace on their way here."

"I see what you mean . . ."

"Rainy says," resumed Jewel, "that Deacon Brace is the only man who scares the brothers."

"They're not the only ones he scares. Anybody who takes Brace lightly is a fool – or Rockett for that matter, though he's rarely without a smile." He considered Jewel for a moment. "Very well, I'll tell you the story." He knocked back the last of his wine. "But my throat needs oiling." He pointed at the cupboard. "You'll find more bottles in there – bottom shelf – glasses too, if you fancy a drink. Will you get it for me?"

The request was addressed to Jewel, so she got up and fetched the bottle. Harry pulled out the stopper and filled his glass. But neither Jewel nor Rainy accepted a drink.

"So then," said Harry. "This happened last summer. I remember the night quite clearly, as anyone would who'd been there. We had a number of high-rollers in. I was down in the gaming room, keeping an eye on things. Big money was changing hands, but the bank was doing all right, so *I* had no worries. As time went on, a crowd gathered round one of the tables. A dice table, it was. The Spetch brothers were there, and so were Crane and Briar. Brace sat on a stool at the bar, slowly sipping a drink. Something non-alcoholic – I've never seen him touch booze. The five of them had never been here before at the same time. The twins had drunk a fair bit and were betting big, as was Briar. Crane was taking a back seat. He's more of a watcher than a doer. Anyway, Briar was making the running – piling chips on the table as if there were no tomorrow, but in that careless way of hers that suggests she doesn't give a damn whether she wins or loses. Well, Jewel Ranson, unless you've seen Briar Spurr in the flesh—"

"I have," said Jewel.

"Then you won't need me to tell you why men get a little flustered when she's around. Zak Spetch, who fancies himself a bit, had already come onto her in a small way. She'd ignored him of course, but he was still trying to impress her by playing with that blond mane of his, striking poses and betting big. But as Crane took no notice of him, Deacon kept his distance. It's Deacon's job to protect Briar, though if ever a woman could look after herself, she's the one: Briar by name, Briar by nature. But Zak can't stand to be ignored and he got hot under the collar. In the end, he turned on Crane.

" 'You there,' he said, 'Bucket or whatever your name is, why don't you bet instead of hiding behind your woman?'

"Crane just smiled at him, and said: 'I don't know what *your* name is, but your manners leave something to be desired. My name is Rockett – *Mr* to you.'

"He's a suave talker, is Crane Rockett.

"Zak, who isn't, said, 'So, Rockett, who gives a toss about manners? Why don't you answer my question?'

261

" 'Very well,' said Crane. 'Since "my woman", as you vulgarly call Miss Spurr, is doing very well without my help – while you, by comparison, seem to be doing rather badly – I see no reason to get involved.'

"Zak stared at Crane for a moment, then said, 'I think it's time you *did* get involved. Are you a man or a mouse? How about a side-bet?'

"At this point I noticed Brace get up from his stool, but Crane gives a little shake of the head in his direction, and he sits down again.

" 'What's your proposal?' asks Crane.

" 'Five gold pieces on the next roll. Highest takes all.'

"Crane sighs. 'Very well, if it will satisfy you – and if, on behalf of the house, Mr Harry is agreeable.'

" 'I have no objection, Mr Rockett,' I says. 'May I offer myself as stake-holder?'

"Zak and Crane agree to this, so there I am with ten gold pieces in my pocket. It's by some distance the biggest single bet the room has ever seen. Well, as you can imagine, action elsewhere is completely suspended, and there is a crowd around the dice table. The only person keeping his distance is Deacon Brace. I toss a coin for order of throws, and Zak wins, rather rudely inviting Crane to throw first. So Crane takes the dice, and throws a pair of twos. Four! You can see Zak thinks he's home and dry. He takes the dice and rattles them in his fists. Then he throws. Three! A two and a one!

" 'Four beats three,' I say. 'The stake to Mr Rockett.' And I hand him his winnings.

"Well, Crane gives Zak a neutral look and says, 'I trust that satisfies you as to my manhood, Mr . . .'

"'Spetch,' says Zak, 'Zak Spetch.'

"'. . . Mr Spetch.'

"'No, it doesn't,' says Zak. 'Let's double the stake.'

"'Double it? Is that wise?'

"'What's *wise* got to do with it? Will you double or won't you?'

"'If that's what you want,' says Crane a little wearily. 'But win or lose, it won't prove anything.'

"So there I am now, with *twenty* gold pieces in my pockets. Things are hotting up.

"'Your turn to throw first, Mr Spetch,' says Crane.

"So Zak picks up the dice and goes into his ritual of shaking them in his hands and whispering to them – the sort of nonsense some gamblers go in for – and throws ten: a six and a four. He's pleased with that. Pretty good, says the look on his face: beat that if you can. But Crane takes the dice and tosses them straight down – no messing: and would you believe it, he throws a pair of sixes.

"There's hullabaloo around the table. Zak's beginning to look a fool, and that's something he can't abide.

"Crane says, easy as you please, 'Satisfied, Mr Spetch?'

"'No,' says Zak, who's on the point of bursting like a balloon. 'One last cast.'

"'For what stake?' asks Crane.

"'The most precious single thing you possess.'

"That stops Crane in his tracks – and everybody else too.

"'What – my house?' he says incredulously. 'You're joking. Not in a million years.'

"'Not your house,' says Zak insolently. 'Her.' And points at Briar.

"For the first time in the proceedings, Crane Rockett looks ruffled. But he gathers himself together, and says firmly, 'Impossible. Miss Spurr is not my – or anyone else's – possession.'

"Now Briar Spurr has been lolling in her chair, seemingly bored by the whole thing – though it's hard to be sure with her. But Zak's talk of precious things has visibly perked her up, and now, for the first time, she takes a hand, 'And what is the most precious thing *you* own, Mr Spetch?'

"Zak puts his hand inside his jacket and tosses an object onto the table where it lands with a thump. It's a brass key – giant-made, maybe an inch long. At this, Lanner Spetch, who up to now has contented himself with watching, says, 'No, Zak, you can't wager that.'

"Zak looks at Lanner and says, 'I can, bro, and I do. It was me that acquired it.'

"'It's not a good idea,' says Lanner.

"'Indulge me, bro,' says Zak, laying his hand on his brother's arm.

"'Very well, if you must, but this is crazy,' mutters Lanner. You can see he hates arguing with his twin brother in public. But Briar finds their exchange very much to her liking.

"'So it *is* a precious thing . . .' she murmurs, half to herself. 'Or the key to a precious thing . . .'

"Zak opens his mouth to speak, but Briar gets in first: 'No, don't you dare say out loud what it opens. Whisper it in my ear.'

"So Zak comes round the table to Briar, leans in close and whispers to her.

"'Fascinating . . .' she murmurs. Then she turns to Rockett. 'Do it!' she tells him.

"'What?' says Crane, as surprised as everyone else in the room. 'Briar, are you out of your mind?'

"'Do it!' she says again.

"'But . . .' says Crane. That's all he says. His voice just dies away.

"For he's seen what everyone else can see. There's a flame in Briar's eyes, as if life has flared up in her where there was no life before, as if she's burning deep inside. She's twice as beautiful now, and for a moment it's as if the room, the Pavilion, the whole of Harrypark itself has gathered around her and she's the centre of everything. I know it sounds absurd, but if you'd been there you'd have known it just as I did, and everyone else present.

"So then there was this silence. Everyone's looking at Crane: it's his move. And how does he look? He looks shrunken, deflated.

"'Very well,' he says at last.

"Briar now reaches out and pulls the key across the table so that it lies in front of her. Zak and Lanner observe this, but say nothing. And there she sits, with this smile on her face: but it's a smile for no one else – just herself, if you see what I mean. An inward smile, as if she knows something no one else could know.

"'Right then,' I say. 'Shall I toss for first cast?'

"'You call,' says Crane to Zak, as if he's no longer interested.

"Zak calls and calls it right. 'You throw first,' he tells Crane.

265

"Crane picks up the dice, hesitates, then throws: a two and a five – a total of seven. Not wonderful. Crane looks distinctly unhappy. And here we are now: a dice-throw for a woman. All eyes are locked on Zak as he rattles the dice and whispers to them. Then he throws: double threes! The poor fool has lost his key.

"Crane says smartly, 'I win. The lady *and* the key.' You've got to hand it to him, he's got his poise back already.

"But now listen what happens. Zak bangs on the table and shouts 'No!' Everyone stares at him. 'You cheated,' he says to Crane. 'The dice are loaded. The key's mine.'

"But Briar has scooped up the key.

"'Give it back!' demands Zak.

"Briar smiles sweetly at him. She has no intention of giving it back.

"Zak starts to push his way round the table. Crane gives him a look that would freeze a fish, then lifts a hand and clicks his fingers. Deacon Brace comes fast through the crowd. He gets between Zak and Briar and – well now, it's hard to say exactly *what* he does. According to some, he simply lays a hand on Zak's shoulder – but one or two people say his fingers were on Zak's neck. He leans forward so his bony face is almost touching Zak's and says something under his breath. Only Zak hears what he says. Now, I've seen fear once or twice on a man's face, but never anything like the fear on Zak Spetch's at that moment. He might have been looking death in the eye. He's so pale, you'd have thought Brace had sucked the blood from his body. In the meantime, Lanner has begun to move towards his brother, but Brace holds a finger up and Lanner just stops dead.

"Then Zak says, in a half-strangled voice that belongs to someone else, 'My apologies to Mr Rockett. The throw was good. The key is Miss Spurr's. I'll arrange to have the article I mentioned sent to you.'

"'Keep it,' says Briar Spurr. 'The key's enough for me.'

"Zak and Lanner are astonished.

"'But,' Lanner says, 'the thing's useless without the key!'

"'Naturally,' says Briar. 'That's why I'm letting you keep it. It will remind you of me – something else you haven't got.'"

Harry paused. Then he grinned.

"Diabolical, isn't she? Imagine possessing something precious that's utterly useless to you. As for what the key was for . . . Tantalising, eh?"

Yes, thought Jewel, it is. But the story intrigued her more for what it told her about the twins. They *could* be frightened, they *could* be cowed; even, they could be beaten. If Briar Spurr could stand up to them, why couldn't she? If provoked, they might act rashly, commit themselves to silly risks. Perhaps, at some future date, she could use this knowledge against them.

17
THE TREE-HOUSE

A sound fell on Thorn's ear. Someone was snoring up ahead!

It had to be night-time. In an instant his despair was transformed into hope. *Perhaps I can slip through the sleepers . . .*

Here was what looked like a family: on one pallet, two children; on another, two adults. The woman made no sound. The man grunted as if something was stuck up his nose. The hair of all four was long, greasy and wild. And their skin was green – stained by some plant-derived dye?

Beyond these pallets were many others. Adults and children packed together. There would be no privacy here. All told, Thorn reckoned, there must be upwards of sixty people. And the foetor of the unwashed: perfumes of sweat and urine mingled with that of roasted meat.

One wrong step and he'd never leave – except in a host of gurgling stomachs. He moved among the pallets as quietly as a drifting seed, slipping by one and then another, overstepping heaps of belongings – for these were tumbled together much as the bodies of their owners.

Further down the cave he came to living and working spaces. He passed collections of tools and weapons and piles of animal skins and furs. There were cooking utensils and pots and flagons for storage. There were chairs and long tables, rudely made but serviceable. Then he caught sight of a shelf set against the rock wall. On it was a row of skulls: white, eyeless and broken-toothed. As light and shadow flickered over them, they grinned intimately: Let us whisper in your ear; we'll tell you the secrets of the dead . . .

A fire smouldered in a stone hearth against the wall. A whiff of wood-smoke entered his nostrils . . . Somewhere above there must be a flue to take the fumes out and away.

Beyond, two coarse sheets of fabric covered the cave entrance – no doubt to minimise draughts. They overlapped in the centre and were secured there by cords. Their hems trailed on the cavern floor, weighted down by stones.

Did the Woodmen mount guards? Perhaps they didn't need to. Well, he could take no chances. He unfastened two of the cords, pulled the drapes slightly apart, and peered through the gap. Below the cave, rocky ground dropped away into trees. The space seemed scoured by silvery light. The moon must be at full. It also showed him a guard. Slumped on a rocky ledge by the entrance, he was asleep.

Thorn untied more of the cords and stepped through the gap. It would be impossible to retie all of them from the outside. Best to vanish: let the Woodmen puzzle the matter out come morning.

At the bottom of the slope, a number of well-trodden trails led away into the forest. He'd travel faster if he took one, be harder to track.

But which? He looked up and scrutinised the clusters of stars.

The Rat, the Belt, the Archer, the Plough, the Tree – he knew them all. He'd been taught a couple of years back how to navigate by them. As long they stayed visible . . . Selecting a trail, he set off north-west.

The night forest was a realm of strange sounds and secret doings. From time to time he caught the distant cry of a night-bird, the scuffling of some animal hunting in the undergrowth. Nocking an arrow to his bow, he carried it loosely at waist level, the arrow pointing earthwards. He could aim and fire in a fraction of time.

But nothing came to threaten him. His progress was quiet if not soundless. Another night-walker would need sharp ears to hear him.

Even so, after a while a sense of unease grew in him. He stopped and listened. Nothing but night sounds . . . He moved off again.

Yet he hadn't gone far when he stopped a second time and peered back along the trail. It wound away into shadows. Nothing seemed to be moving there. He set off once more.

To halt for a third time by a spur of shadowy rocks. Was it a mind thing, this unprompted anxiety? Was the wood haunting him? Some night-floating spirit, some ghost of the trees? Well, he'd lay this ghost. He slipped behind the rocky spur.

He didn't have long to wait. Whoever else was on the trail was moving as quietly as he had, but existed all right. A single pair of feet, he thought. Bad in one way, good in another. But if this was no mass pursuit, what was it then?

As he crouched, bow poised, a figure moved into view. A small figure, the size of a child of twelve or thirteen. Dressed in baggy clothes and hooded, sex indeterminable. A small bow and a quiver of arrows were slung over its shoulder. But when the figure drew level with the rock it came to a halt, sniffed the air like an animal and turned in his direction.

"You – boy-man, behind the rock. I smell you. Come out and speak."

The accent was outlandish – as if the words had emerged from lips of earth-mould. Yet the voice was a girl's.

Thorn stepped out onto the track. The figure gestured at his bow.

"Won't need that."

"Why should I trust you?"

"Won't need that. If I wanted you dead, Woodmen take you by now."

She had a point. He unnocked the arrow and put it back in his quiver.

"Let me see your face," he said.

The girl lifted both hands to her hood and threw it back. A matted web of hair framed her green-tinged cheeks. Between forehead and mouth, her face seemed oddly flattened – as if, when she'd been born, a hand had pressed down on it, squashing the prow of her nose. Her eyes squinted up at him – dark and glinting in the moonlight. She was far from pretty, yet she was not ugly either – just different, he thought.

"Who are you?" he asked. "Why are you following me?"

She regarded him levelly. "Woodmen will wake, see your marks and they will come. You must hide. I know a place."

271

"Why should I trust you?"

The girl's face remained neutral. "Trust me or trust Woodmen, boy-man. Choose."

She spoke with cool authority. She might be a child in years, but she was old in experience.

"What's your name?" enquired Thorn.

"I am Emmy," said the girl.

"Well then, Emmy, my name is Thorn."

She considered this gravely, then delivered her verdict. "Thorn. That is a good name. Come with me now, Thorn."

Something in the girl's blunt manner persuaded him.

"All right, Emmy. Lead on."

She turned and set off down the trail. He followed. They walked in silence. After a time they came to a region of low, humped stones. This she began to cross, jumping – sometimes clambering – from one to another. Encumbered by his pack, it was all he could do to stay not too far behind.

At last the stones came to an end. Still her pace did not slacken. She moved unerringly, as if she knew each bush and tree. The moonlight was filtered here, but there was quite enough for her. From time to time, she glanced back to check that he was still there. He was. As for that spirit of the wood he'd imagined earlier, here it was now, flitting before him like some lightless will-o'-the-wisp.

Why is she helping me? he wondered. Going against her own tribe . . .

On they went, past sprigs of oak or beech that might, one distant day, mature into trees. Things, he thought resignedly, are no worse than they were: I was lost when I came out of the cave, and I'm lost now. Maybe Emmy is my best chance of escaping from this place . . .

The moonlight seemed to intensify. Hereabouts grew only oaks. In the spaces between them, bluebells began to appear – first thinly, then more densely, the first that Thorn had seen in the wood, though it was late in the year for these flowers to be in bloom. The blossoms swayed to and fro at head height or higher, creating a miniature forest all of their own.

Soon they came to a cairn of stones. Motioning him to follow, Emmy began to climb up it. From the top there was a view across the glade.

The girl said: "This is my place. The flowers, they grow for me. Everywhere else, they are gone. Look, Thorn. Listen."

Thorn looked and listened. All around, the flowers turned the earth's surface blue. A slight breeze wafted across them, stirring their blossoms in watery ripples. It seemed to Thorn they rang with soundless notes in the pale light.

"Do you hear them?" she asked. "The blue flowers of the moon?"

"I hear them," he said. "It's magical here."

He smiled. Lost in moonlit forest, half-soaked with dew and given over into the hands of a strange girl of doubtful intentions, here he was claiming to hear the midnight language of bluebells . . .

They climbed down from the cairn and pushed their way through the flowers. At last, at the foot of a low-growing oak thickly twined about with ivy, Emmy stopped. She reached into the ivy and pulled out a knotted rope. Its upper end disappeared among the branches above their heads.

"This is my tree," announced the girl. "I go first. When I whistle, you follow."

Wrapping her legs about the rope, she began skilfully to climb and was soon lost to sight. Thorn waited. A night-bird called – Emmy, signalling him.

Grasping the rope, he started to shin up. But this wasn't a skill he possessed and he progressed slowly. Higher and higher he went. Now, if he fell, he was sure to break his neck, even though the ground was cushioned by the leaf-rot of years. A couple of times his boot soles slipped off the knots, but he was holding on tight and got them back in place again.

At last he came to the lowest branch. Here he was able to step off the rope and take a breather. But he hadn't been there long when his night-bird called again. This girl was a hard taskmistress . . . Once more he began to climb, a shadow moving among shadows.

He found the girl on the next branch, leaning against the tree-trunk, one hand resting on a stubby protuberance. The rope disappeared above. Turning, she unpeeled (or so it seemed) a section of bark from the tree to reveal a black, egg-shaped opening, five inches high and four across.

"Hold that," she commanded, offering him the edge of the bark drape, "and wait there." She stepped inside the tree.

Soon there came the sound of a striking flint, and after a time a light shone from inside the hole. Emmy's head reappeared, haloed in a yellowy glow.

"My house is your house," she announced, and beckoned him in.

Thorn awoke and opened his eyes. Close at hand, a lamp burned, dimly lighting the tree-room. Emmy was kneeling by his side. How long had she been there? His lips parted to speak but she slipped a hand over his mouth.

"Quiet!" she hissed. "Woodmen below!"

He nodded. She took her hand away. She rose to her feet, drew back the drape and stood intently listening. It was daylight outside. Warm under his coverings, Thorn traced the curve of her neck and the whorl of an ear. She was human all right, yet seemed half animal. He strained to catch the sounds of men moving somewhere below, the noises of the hunt. The hunt for a human quarry. But nothing came to his ear. If Emmy could hear something, her hearing must be acute.

Emmy's refuge was a scooped-out hole, a bulbous almost-sphere with a sloping floor. It contained little of note: a few utensils on a rough shelf, three boxes with close-fitting lids (from one of which Emmy had extracted the bed-covers), the lamp, two straw mattresses. He wasn't the first person to share the secret of the tree-room. Near the entrance was a stone hearth where a fire might be lit, cooking perhaps be done. A fire in a tree? Why not, if kept contained. The smoke, he supposed, could be persuaded to doff its hat and leave by the entrance-hole.

Half a dozen woodcarvings hung on the walls. Of the four he could see most clearly, two were grotesque masks, the third a bird of some kind, the fourth an animal – a vole or shrew.

Was Emmy a woodcarver? Somehow he couldn't see her in that role.

Time passed. Still Thorn heard nothing. At length, Emmy turned to him.

"Woodmen gone," she announced. "We must wait a little. While we wait we will eat."

They shared food. Emmy's contribution was an assortment of chopped nuts and dried fruits – not unpleasant, he thought.

"Will they come back?" he asked.

"When a scent is in their noses, Woodmen follow it. Your settlement scent draws them."

"My *settlement* scent?"

"I smell it too. I smelt you in the cave before I saw you. So I followed."

"But if their noses are that good, why don't they know I'm up this tree?"

"It is difficult for them to think a thought like that. Woodmen do not climb trees. Trees are sacred to them."

"But surely they burn timber."

"Dead branches. Windfalls."

"But you're a Woodman . . . *Woodgirl*," he corrected. "You climb trees."

"I am of them, but not of them. My father was a Woodman, my mother from a settlement. They met by a stream at the wood's edge. She loved his green skin, his body like a birch, his hands like leaves. Two days after he came for her and she went with him. It is rare, but not unknown."

"Where are they now?"

"They went on."

She means *dead*, he thought. "But you stay here?"

"Where should I go? To a settlement? What should I do there?"

"But you're only half-Woodman . . ."

"I belong to the wood."

"Yet trees can't be sacred to you, or you wouldn't be here now."

"When I am with Woodmen, I worship as they do. When I am not, I do as I wish. I come and go, I do not stay all nights in the cave. They do not mind because I am different. But they know nothing of my house in this tree. If they found me here—"

She made a swift cutting motion across her neck with the blade of her hand.

"Then they will drain my blood, pour it on the trunk of this tree. To beg the tree's forgiveness."

Thorn marvelled at the matter-of-factness with which she spoke. It was as if she were speaking of the death of someone else.

"Yet knowing this, you still come here, take this risk?"

"Woodmen do what Woodmen do, I do what is me. I will not change." She paused, and to Thorn now it seemed that she looked piercingly at him. "Until something, someone comes and changes me."

Until you're taken away like your mother was taken? wondered Thorn. Is that what you're waiting for? You look like a child, but you don't behave like one.

He said, "I have a sister. She might be your age."

"How old is she?" asked the girl.

"Thirteen."

"That is my age."

"In the settlement I come from you're a child if you're thirteen."

"I am not a child. I bring forth blood in the moon-time. Woodwomen mate at thirteen, fourteen, have children soon."

Do they now? he thought.

"You carry a bow," she stated. "Are you a hunter, Thorn?"

"Yes," he said.

"My mother says a hunter is a fine thing to be."

"*Says?*" he countered. "But she's dead, isn't she?"

"Dead? Flesh dies, but spirit does not. She often comes and speaks to me. My father too, but not so much." She regarded him intently. "She came in the night to look at you."

Weirder and weirder, thought Thorn.

"And what did she make of me?"

"I shall not say."

Won't you now? he thought. Then why tell me she came?

He said: "Look – I'm grateful to you for helping me, but I can't stay here in the wood. My sister was kidnapped, taken away against her will. I've got to get to a house called Roydsal, up at the top of the wood. It's a mansion built by the giants. Do you know the place?"

"Roydsal?" Emmy repeated. "No, I do not. Is your sister there?"

"Perhaps . . . I don't know. She was kidnapped from my settlement by men who wore black feathers painted with yellow bands. Have you seen such men in the wood?"

"No, I have not. Tell me something, Thorn Jack. Are you a shaman?" she asked.

"A shaman? What's that?"

"One who knows wood magic."

"No, I'm not a shaman."

"Then how were you in our cave?"

"I walked underground and came up there."

"Underground? That is impossible. There will be rats in the darkness."

"There was. I killed it."

The girl looked suitably awed. "You are truly a hunter, Thorn. But still I do not understand. Where did you come from?"

But he'd had enough of her questions. "Look, it's a long story, Emmy. I've got to get going. Can you take me to the forest road that goes to the top of the wood?"

She pondered for a while.

"Perhaps your sister is dead."

The bluntness with which these words were delivered took him aback.

"I don't believe that," he replied. "I'll go on looking till I find her – and nothing will stop me."

"That is good," she said. "If I had a brother and he was stolen, I would seek him as you do."

I bet you would, too, he thought.

"Fine. Then can we get going?"

"Soon, I hope. I will listen."

She slipped out through the drape. In the lull, he found himself looking at the carving of the bird. It had been caught in flight. Below was a sprig of oak leaves, as if the bird had outsoared the woodland and above it was only sky . . .

Emmy came in again, a look of concern on her face.

"Woodmen are back below. This is not good," she whispered. "Perhaps they realise where you are . . ."

"If they do, I'm done for. Is there anything we can do?"

She considered this notion. "Something *I* can do, perhaps . . ."

"What's that?"

"Draw them away."

"Won't that be dangerous?"

"Stay here," she said. "Don't move. I will come back when I can."

And with that, she was gone.

He got up and followed her out, but already she'd disappeared. The climbing rope dropped past the branch. He touched it. It was taut. Emmy was on her way down.

He listened, but not a sound came to his ears. He sat cross-legged on the branch, his back against the trunk. Time passed, and more time. Where could she be? What was she doing?

An insidious idea now took root in his mind. What if she's gone to betray me? No matter how hard he struggled against this idea, it grew on him.

She protected me last night, said one half of his mind.

Did she? said the other. *She decoyed you to her tree-house. Now she's gone to betray you.*

But Woodmen don't climb trees.

How do you know? She told you that.

She's a young girl. She doesn't look in the least like a liar.

What do liars look like? Have you seen a single emotion in her face since you met her?

I trust her.

I *don't.*

Time passed. For the life of him, he could hear nothing below. Right, he told himself, I'm off.

Collecting his bow and pack, Thorn began to descend the rope. Climbing down was a damn sight easier than climbing up.

The forest floor was deserted. She lied to me, he thought. She's gone to fetch the Woodmen. He struck off through the trees.

But the sky above the forest canopy was covered with cloud. It was impossible to know in what direction he was going. When he'd put some distance between himself and the oak, he stopped to think.

I can keep moving, he thought, or I can stop where I am. If I move I may blunder into a party of Woodmen. Equally, if I stay here, the Woodmen may track me down. The sky may clear, he thought; then I shall be able to see the sun. Equally, the weather might not improve for days.

The two sides of the argument cancelled each other out. He decided to move. At least that gave his legs something to do. I *might* get lucky and find my way out of this place . . .

As he walked, it started to rain. Nevertheless he kept going. When he started to feel hungry, he stopped to eat, then set off again.

Water dripped down from above. The air smelt musty. Everything was brown or grey; green had leached from the leaves. This was dreary, dreary. He was heartily sick of trees. And of the forest floor – soft, damp, perpetually rotting.

He heard no one, saw no one. Perhaps, he thought, I'm walking in circles, crossing paths I've already trod.

As the shades thickened about him, his sense of futility grew. Rescuing Haw now seemed to him a whole world away, a fantasy some simple-minded self had entertained.

Then a new idea struck him: what if the Woodmen had never set out to track him down at all? If they had done, surely they'd have caught him by now? He'd only Emmy's word for it that they were in pursuit. What if Emmy had been playing some silly game with him . . . But you get bored with games, he thought, and then you break off. Was that what had happened? Had she got bored and gone home? I'd have been no worse off than I am now if we'd never met . . .

He halted beneath a beech tree. The damp air had chilled him through. Despondent, careless of Woodmen now, he gathered some dampish twigs, improvised a circle of stones and managed to get a fire going. A mug of herb tea warmed him, but what wouldn't he have given for one of Morry's hot stews!

He unrolled his sleeping bag, slid inside and settled to sleep.

18
TARRY'S THUMBS

Rainy was juggling blindfold – her final act. Her three clubs moved in precise arcs, departing from and returning to her hands in perfect rhythm.

"How on earth do you do that?" Jewel had asked, when she'd seen the juggler practising this trick.

"The man who taught me said blindfold juggling was the best sort of practice. Blank your mind out, he'd say; feel the clubs as extensions of your body, live the rhythm."

She caught the clubs, pulled the blindfold away with a theatrical gesture, then held the clubs up above her head triumphantly. Jewel, sitting at a table at the side of the dining room, clapped enthusiastically. Polite applause sounded from the majority of the tables. Tarry Ramsbottom, she noticed, had begun to clap with vigour, but a disapproving look from Gilda silenced him. Gilda's hands stayed attached to her knife and fork. But little food seemed to find its way to her mouth. Tarry, by contrast, was devouring enough for three people; he'd already polished off most of Gilda's previous course. Still, if Gilda was reluctant to eat, she wasn't averse to drinking. She knocked back just as much wine as Tarry, and the pair had broached their second bottle.

Sweeping one of the clubs in an arc that almost touched the floor, Rainy made her final bow, then turned and disappeared behind a curtain at the back of the stage. There, Jewel knew, a door gave access to changing rooms. Rainy would join her shortly. Then they would eat, modestly, at a besotted Harry's expense. The master of Rotten Pavilion would have joined them, but had work to do.

A conjuror took to the stage. With slick fingers and an ingratiating smile, he began to perform devious actions with colourful handkerchiefs.

The dining room was busy, but a number of tables remained unoccupied. The conjuror abandoned his handkerchiefs in favour of white balls, which he rolled between his fingers. After a certain amount of this he began, with ostentatious motions and much exaggerated goggling, to swallow them one by one.

Till the arrival of three diners diverted all eyes elsewhere.

The head waiter was a short but self-important individual. The look he'd given Jewel as he'd ushered her to the table told her she should have been aproned in the kitchen, washing dishes. Rainy said to ignore him. "He's a pipsqueak," she declared. Now here he came again, showing Briar and Crane to their table with obsequious flourishes. When they were seated, he retraced his steps to the edge of the room to fetch Deacon Brace, who'd entered a fraction after his master and mistress. Brace towered over the flunkey. Jewel watched as the pipsqueak led him to the table next to her own. He'll never get his legs under there, she thought, but somehow Brace managed to tuck his bony poles away. The head waiter then returned to Crane and Briar and reeled off the menu, while Nog, his patient underling, did the same for the gaunt man.

Crane gave this process his full attention; but Briar stared round the room until her gaze came to rest on the indefatigable conjuror. He, with a complacent leer at his distracted audience, now tapped a red box with a black and white wand before placing it on a stand and whisking a yellow cloth over it. Crane said something to the flunkey, after which the two men waited for Briar to add her order. Meanwhile, the conjuror snatched the cloth away to reveal that the red box had magically altered its colour to green. The yellow cloth went over again, and still Briar remained silent; till at last Crane said something to her. She waved a negligent hand and spoke a few syllables. They might have been: "Oh, anything." Or again, they might not. The head waiter looked enquiringly at Crane, who gave him further instructions. Then the man was off. Ignoring the raised hand of a less important diner, he steered speedily between the tables and pushed through a swing-door at the rear.

Jewel transferred her attention back to Gilda. The woman was staring at Briar's table, her knife and fork becalmed before her. Tarry, however, had emptied his own plate and was now eyeing his companion's with the same degree of relish with which a spider regards a fly that has flown smack into its web. He nudged her elbow and pointed with his knife-blade at her food. With a languorous waft of the hand, Gilda ceded her plate to him: a faithful copy, Jewel would have sworn, of Briar's recent gesture. Taking lessons, was she? Well, she wouldn't find a better tutor.

So focused was she on these goings-on, that Jewel was unaware that Rainy had come back into the room. But here was her friend, pulling out her chair and sitting down. Jewel had no sooner congratulated her on her immaculate display, than Nog came smartly up to them and asked if he could interest them in something to eat.

"What are you recommending tonight?" prompted Rainy.

"Cook's special pigeon pie."

They both settled for that, with Jay's best to wash it down, and Nog took himself off.

Jewel now launched into a detailed description of what she'd observed while Rainy was out of the room. As she did this, Rainy cast surreptitious glances at the two couples.

"Poor Gilda," Rainy observed when Jewel had ended her account, "she hasn't an ounce of imagination. She used to copy me when we were kids. She had to wear what I wore, do what I did, say what I said. It became tedious. But she hated childhood. To her way of thinking, being a kid was a waste of time. She couldn't wait to grow up: chiefly so she could start to exercise power over men. She had a tarty attractiveness even at thirteen, and she knew it. There was one boy in Harrypark she treated like a slave. It didn't matter that he was pimply and fat as a barrel. She got him to do the most abject and disgusting things just to show she could. Once, when the three of us were together, she got him to eat a worm in exchange for a kiss. It was only when he'd eaten the worm that she realised what she'd be kissing, and made him go and wash his mouth out. Then she gave him the meanest, most perfunctory of pecks. She was practising for adulthood. Now she's got her hooks into Tarry Ramsbottom, the poor slob hasn't a clue what he's in for. But he'll find out soon enough."

Their pigeon pies arrived, piping hot, and with the food their conversation lapsed. Soon, diners began to finish their meals and drift away to the gaming room. Jewel and Rainy had just ordered a sweet when Tarry and Gilda got up and left. Gilda tottered along on her companion's arm. She had changed her dress, of course, but this evening's was as tight as this afternoon's, if not tighter. And Gilda herself was a little tight too. Was that a hiccup drifting in her wake?

The sweet – a headily-light fruit concoction, flavoured with raspberry wine – turned out to be just as delicious as Nog had promised. Now, besides the two of them, there was no more than a handful of diners in the room. Among them was the trio of late arrivals. Deacon Brace paid as much attention to his master and mistress as to the food on his plate (which he ate to the last mouthful). But though people cast frequent, envious glances in their direction, no one so much as approached Mr Rockett and Miss Spurr. Among the rich they were the richest, and even among the rich, thought Jewel, there's a pecking order. But Briar Spurr: now *there's* a woman who'll never stoop to any pecking. She probably doesn't even know the meaning of the word . . .

Crane and Briar rose from their chairs and moved towards the gaming room. With them went the head waiter, clucking inanities. He remained unacknowledged till the last moment, when Crane pressed something into his hand. This, with a self-satisfied smile and a bow, the man pocketed. Deacon Brace was no more than a few steps behind, but when the flunkey tried to ingratiate himself with Brace in turn, the tall man frowned and brushed him away as you would a midge. Then Brace, too, was gone.

Rainy, who like Jewel had been observing their departure, turned to her friend.

"So, Jewel, what do you fancy doing on your last evening in Harrypark? Do you want to go home – or stay on for a while and watch people with too much money unloading generous portions of it into Harry's grateful hands? We can walk home later. There's a lovely moon tonight."

"I'd like to stay," answered Jewel. "It's my last night in Harrypark, and I'd very much like to see the gaming room in action." She patted the money-bag at her waist. "I may even have a bet."

Empty of people, the gaming room had been inert; now it had come alive. All the tables were in action, each with its band of devotees. Nothing so crude as money disfigured their colourful surfaces: instead, people bet with rectangular wooden plaques. These came in various colours, sizes and values, and could be obtained at a booth in exchange for cash.

Crane and Briar had joined some sort of a card game on the far side of the room. Deacon Brace lurked nearby, a watchful non-participant. Tarry and Gilda were at one of the dice tables, so Jewel and Rainy decided to wander over in that direction. Tarry had hoisted his bulk onto a stool, which he overflowed. Surely he must be uncomfortable up there, thought Jewel. His role seemed to consist in feeding betting plaques to Gilda. Her willowy body in its glittering sheath pressed against the raised lip of the table as she took the dice, lifted them up to her ear and listened intently as they rattled in her fist. Was this a good or a bad sound? Did it indicate success or failure? At last, leaning forward, she cast them onto the table with a practised flick of the wrist. Gaily they leapt along it, struck the far side with a double rap, bounced back and came to rest. As the table-man called out their total number, Gilda turned to Tarry with a look of triumph.

"Two on the trot," she said. "Some luck at last."

"Not before time," returned Tarry.

But Gilda had spoken too soon. She lost on her next nine throws, and the last of Tarry's plaques were gone.

Undeterred, "Let's change some more money," she urged her consort.

"Let's sit out for a bit," he replied. "I need a drink."

This time he got his way. As they moved off to the bar, Gilda shot Rainy a baleful look to which the juggler did not respond.

"Not betting tonight, ladies?" said a voice from behind Jewel.

She and Rainy turned. There stood Harry the Wag. He had spruced himself up. He wore a crimson jacket and trews and had combed his hair and shaved. But he still looked the worse for wear.

"What?" retorted Rainy. "On the amount you pay me?"

"And there's me thinking I'm overgenerous towards you." Harry sounded a touch hurt. "And didn't I throw in dinner for two?"

"Harry, I'm only joking. And we're grateful for the dinner, which was delicious. But you should know me by now. I've got no interest in gambling." Rainy nodded towards Jewel. "But I can't speak for my friend. She says she may have a crack."

"Is that right? Well, good luck to you, Jewel – though I shouldn't say that, should I, since anyone who wins is taking the bread out of my mouth."

"That'll be the day," said Rainy.

Harry grinned. "See you both later. Things to do."

"Right," said Jewel when he'd gone. "Time to try my luck, I think."

They crossed to the booth, and Jewel exchanged some of her money for plaques. She'd spent little since Shelf Fair and, given the amount she'd retained from Ranson and Daughter's successful day of trading, plus what she'd raised on her sale of the cart, the goods and Smoky, now had more cash than she'd ever seen in her life.

The plaques felt solid in her hands. Now: what game to play? Not the dice table, she thought: that seemed contaminated by Gilda. Nor the card tables, either: she didn't understand the games. The table with the wheel, then? Roll-a-ball, it was called. Rainy had explained it. It seemed straightforward enough. You could bet on a number (one to thirty) – the longest odds, but the biggest payout – or on a colour (red or black), or on odd or even numbers: which, if you were successful, paid much less. So, Roll-a-ball.

For a time they stood by the table, observing the play. Then a man sitting in front of them picked up what remained of his plaques and, with an air of disgust, got up and wandered away. Rainy motioned Jewel to take his seat and stood behind her.

Jewel stared at the apparatus: its black trim, its glittering circle of numbers, its conical centre, rising to an ornate silvery point.

When the table-man next retrieved the ball, and called "Place your bets, please!" she closed her eyes and concentrated. When she opened them, she placed half her plaques on the red square of the betting cloth.

The table-man spun the wheel and set the metal ball a-roll, counter to the direction of the whole mechanism. Winding its way down to the row of coloured pockets, it rattled against their ridges and jumped back, then descended again. For a moment it seemed to have settled in one of the black pockets, but at the last moment it slipped lethargically over into the red square next to it. The table-man raked in the lost plaques and placed some of the bank's with those bets that had won, Jewel's among them.

Jewel closed her eyes again. This time when she opened them she invested her winnings on black. Again the wheel spun; again she won. Four times more she bet on colours; four times more she won. People were starting to look at her now. At the seventh time of asking, she placed all her winnings to date on a number: seventeen. This was the real test: guessing the colour six times running might well be luck, but there were thirty numbers . . .

The wheel was slowing. The ball pinged its smooth black rim, bounced into a black pocket and stayed there: seventeen. A murmur went up from the table. The table-man pushed a stack of plaques across the cloth to Jewel. All eyes were on the girl as preparations were made to bet.

The number of people around the table had suddenly swelled. Rainy noticed that Gilda and Tarry had arrived. Gilda was staring – as if mesmerised – at the wheel; as if by sheer force of will she could extract its secret from it. Harry was there too, looking thoughtful; and maybe a touch apprehensive. And there, to the rear, most surprising of all, was Briar Spurr. Her eyes, dark and animated now, were not on the table but on Jewel, as the girl sat with her eyes closed, as if in another world.

At the last moment, she opened them and transferred her stake and winnings to number twenty. Immediately, several other people dropped plaques on that square. The table-man spun the wheel.

The ball seemed to circle the shining cone in slow motion. Lazily it rebounded from the ridge between two pockets, did it a second time, then a third. It seemed to be putting on an elaborate performance, deliberately toying with the numbers. Only when the wheel had almost halted did it settle: box number twenty. There was an intake of breath from the crowd. The table-man, who was starting to look punch-drunk, dreamily added what seemed an immense stack of plaques to Jewel's pile. Harry was rubbing his chin – an action that Rainy knew signified consternation.

"Amazing!" commented the woman on Jewel's left. "How do you do it?"

Jewel said nothing. This time she did not close her eyes, nor did she shift her stake, which remained on number twenty. A number of players hurried to invest on the same number. Among them was Gilda. But Briar Spurr contented herself with watching. On her face was a quiet smile, as if she'd tapped into some quiet, personal source of amusement. Crane Rockett, meanwhile, remained on the other side of the room, one of the few with no interest in the happenings at the wheel.

Once more the wheel spun and the metal ball rolled, drawing every eye with its random acrobatics. An object so tiny, yet so significant. At last, it came to a stop.

A groan of disappointment greeted the result. The ball had lodged in number nine. Those who'd bet on the same number as Jewel reacted with disbelief. If looks could kill, Gilda's eyes would have knifed the girl to the heart. In her anguish, she raised a fist in front of her chest, clenching and unclenching it as if squeezing some small creature to death. Briar Spurr's smile had broadened. She gave a curious little self-communing nod, as if acknowledging the just outcome of a wager with herself, and then, with a brusque toss of her hair, turned on her heel and walked away.

"Bad luck, my dear," said the woman next to Jewel. "I was just beginning to think you couldn't lose."

Jewel smiled. "It seems I can."

"That's life, my dear!" said the woman.

Jewel collected her remaining plaques and got up from her chair. Rainy accompanied her to the booth, where she converted wood back into money.

"How about a drink?" said Jewel.

"Very well," said Rainy.

They chose a quiet table at the edge of the room. When they were settled, Rainy fixed Jewel with a thoughtful stare, and said, "You deliberately lost on that last bet, didn't you?"

"Now why would I do that?"

"Because winning's too easy for you? Because you'd attracted too much attention? Because you felt you were cheating; which, in a way, you were? You took away from that table no more than you brought to it."

Jewel smiled, but said nothing.

"So tell me, how did you do it?"

"I don't know, Rainy. All I can tell you is, that if I concentrated on the idea of colours I saw a colour, or if on the idea of numbers I saw a number. I bet on them; they came up."

"You could have broken the bank, couldn't you? Then bought the place, and employed Harry to skivvy in his own kitchen."

"Who knows? I might have guessed wrong."

"I very much doubt it."

Jewel smiled again.

"But it's just as well you lost," continued her friend. "Now people will put your wins down to a simple run of luck; not what *we* know it is."

They sat sipping their drinks, ignoring the rest of the room, chatting easily to one another. Some time later, Harry the Wag strolled over and sat down. Once more the suave man of affairs.

"You went exceptionally well there for a time, Miss Jewel."

"*Miss* Jewel," repeated Rainy. "There's deference for you."

But Harry wasn't to be deflected. "You were starting to look invincible."

"No one's that," said Jewel.

"Very true. Let me give you a tip. Never play the same number twice running at the wheel. The chances of it coming up again are very small."

"Nobody told *me* that." Jewel spoke with mock indignation.

"Tell me, Mr Harry, do you make a habit of advising your clients on how *not* to lose their money?"

"No. But they *all* lose their money sooner or later – it's only a matter of when. So, no more gambling for you tonight, then, Miss Jewel?"

"I think not, Mr Harry."

"Just dipping your toes in, eh? True gamblers never know when to stop. Take our friend Gilda, there." He indicated one of the card tables with a movement of his head.

"What's she up to?" asked Rainy.

"Sorely trying Mr Ramsbottom's patience, by the look of it. Even *his* pockets aren't bottomless. Take a look – it may amuse you."

"Perhaps we will."

"Bye for now then, girls."

When Harry had gone, Jewel said, "He seems to have cheered up."

"Probably because you lost in the end. But that's how he is. He's on an upswing tonight. He'll be down again tomorrow. Probably won't be prised out of his room with a crowbar."

"Poor Harry . . ."

"Don't start feeling sorry for him. Well, shall we do as he suggests, and have a look at Gilda and Tarry?"

"Why not? After that I think it will be time to go."

They found the odd pair at a card table. Nine people were seated around the table, among them Crane Rockett and Briar Spurr. Deacon Brace was sitting a little distance away, attentive as usual. When Jewel and Rainy arrived, to hover in the background, Gilda shot the two of them a venomous glance. But Tarry seized her arm. His urgently whispered words to her were audible to Jewel.

"It's time to pull out, Gilda. I've lost more than I can afford."

"Cold feet, Tarry? Chin up, now. Time to show some spirit, love. Change some money. Our luck will change, it's got to."

"It *has*n't got to. Look, Gilda, it's not our night. Accept it."

"No. *You* look, Tarry – look at yourself. Show some guts."

Tarry, thought Jewel, was showing plenty of guts. There was more in this vein from Gilda. If you can't get what you want by persuasion, get it by brow-beating. And it worked. Under Gilda's scorn, poor Tarry wilted visibly. He got up from his chair and shambled off to the booth.

"What are they playing?" Jewel asked.

"Twenty-one," her friend replied and explained that you had to get as near to a total of twenty-one as possible. Go over, and you went bust. Masters, mistresses and knaves counted ten; aces eleven or one; all other cards their pip values. An ace paired with a master, mistress or knave was a "natural" and beat all other hands. Any five cards totalling twenty-one or less beat any hand except a natural. The banker dealt one card face-down to each player, and the players bet on that. Then a second card was dealt and all hands were shown. Players could call for extra cards until they decided to stick, or went bust. Each player was pitted against the bank, which on this table meant the last player to have a natural.

"It's not *too* complicated," Rainy finished, though the game sounded it.

"I *think* I've got it," said Jewel.

Tarry arrived with more plaques and grumpily dumped his weight into his chair, which squeaked in protest. The game resumed. Like Tarry and Gilda, Crane and Briar were playing as a pair. The bank-holder was a pasty-faced individual with large ears. In their fleshy lobes were diamond studs that winked in the light of the wall-lamps. Gilda bet enthusiastically on her first card, which turned out to be a mistress. Her second was a four. The bank had a ten and a nine. Gilda asked for another card: it was an eight, so she'd lost. She glared around the table, radiating anger, as if the cards had taken it upon themselves to insult her publicly. The bank collected her stake. He won everyone else's too. Briar had a knave and a seven. She turned over an ace, which gave her eighteen – still losing. Then a six – too many. Her face betrayed no emotion.

The bank dealt again, and Gilda advanced double the basic stake. This time she was triumphant: she had a natural, an ace and a mistress. The bank had seventeen, which proved good enough to beat everybody else. The bank paid triple Gilda's stake and surrendered the pack to her.

Gilda's first deal didn't go well. She had a master and a five: not enough to stand on, and dangerous to add to. She dealt herself a third card: an eight. She had to pay all but one of the players. Briar, with a knave and a nine, had bet high, and made a killing.

Gilda dealt again. This time she had two sevens – another horrible combination. Her third card – a knave – took her past twenty-one. Again she had to pay every player except one. But no one had a natural, so the bank remained with her. Tarry's new store of plaques had already been reduced, and worry was palpable on his face. He and Gilda whispered together.

"We're *bound* to get lucky this time," Gilda told him. "Stop worrying, Tarry."

"But I've got no more money. What if we can't cover the bets?"

"We'll be all right – believe me."

She dealt again. Tarry looked on aghast as five of the six players ranged against them – Briar included – staked the table maximum.

"This looks bad," he whispered to Gilda.

"It's only one card, Tarry," she hissed back. "Anything can happen. Trust me: we'll be fine."

The next voice that spoke was Crane Rockett's. "But what if you're not, as the lady says, *fine*, Mr Ramsbottom? By my calculations you easily could fall a long way short of being able to meet your obligations. What then?"

"Don't answer him," said Gilda.

But Tarry took no notice of her. His next words were blurted out, stiff with desperation. "Perhaps, umm, Mr Rockett, as a fellow-player, you'd agree to cover any shortfall. I'd give you an IOU, of course."

Crane laughed. "Would you, now? Unfortunately for you, Mr Ramsbottom, I don't recognise 'fellow-players', only opponents. That is what you are. And in my experience IOUs are worthless." He paused. "Still – there might be terms under which I'd agree to settle your debts . . ."

"Might there? What would *they* be?"

Crane turned to Briar.

"What would we want for settling Mr Ramsbottom's debts, Briar?"

Her answer was instantaneous, as if it had been prepared. "How about his thumbs, Crane? Such nice, plump thumbs."

Crane considered this. "They'd make a handsome conversation piece, mounted and framed."

"There you are!" said Briar. "I knew the idea would appeal."

"My thumbs?" said Tarry, appalled. "You can't be serious."

"Miss Spurr never jokes about gambling matters," said Crane. "Very well, then: your thumbs. And I'll tell you what, as I'm feeling particularly generous tonight, I'll also pay your room bill – win or lose."

Deacon Brace now made his move. He came up behind Tarry's chair and looked down at the fat man. Tarry twisted round and looked up into his face. Brace's features, chiselled and chalk-white, radiated menace.

Tarry turned back and stared at the table. Perspiration beaded his forehead. He lifted a hand to his mouth and gnawed nervously on a knuckle – something, Jewel thought, you could imagine Brace doing if he got hold of Tarry's thumbs.

"Take the deal, Tarry," Gilda urged in a loud whisper. "They're only joking. You'll be all right."

"I can't, it's madness," he hissed.

"Yes you can. Trust me. Our luck is about to change."

By now word had spread about what was happening here. Abandoning their own games, people crowded to the table. Among them was Harry the Wag, who made no move to intervene. All eyes were on the agonised man, all ears pricked to hear him. The silence stretched itself out.

"I – I agree," stammered Tarry. Seemingly drained by the decision, he sagged in his chair like a sack of assorted pebbles.

"Excellent," said Crane. "So, play the deal out."

Gilda swung into action. She dealt the second round of cards, then turned over her own pair. She had an ace and a five – a total of six or sixteen. But sixteen wasn't good enough. Briar held a natural – an ace and a master. She'd have to be paid anyway. Another player had twenty, another nineteen, and two eighteen. The fifth had twelve, and asked for a third card. It was a nine, making twenty-one. Now Gilda needed something spectacular. Her third card was a three, which made nine. She took a fourth. It was a seven, which made sixteen. Still she was losing to everyone, ruinously. There was only one thing for it. Tarry covered his eyes as she visibly clenched her teeth and unpeeled a fifth card. A six or less would save the day, apart from Briar's natural, which Tarry could cover . . .

A collective intake of breath greeted the card. It was a nine.

Crane Rockett's amused voice broke the tingling silence. "Mr Ramsbottom, you owe me a pair of thumbs."

Gilda was the first to react. "Don't be ridiculous. You can't mean that."

"Why can't I?" said Crane.

"Because it's inhuman!"

"Nonsense!" said Crane. "Mr Ramsbottom agreed – at your prompting, I seem to remember. Avarice: now, what could be more human than that?"

Gilda turned on Briar Spurr. "It's you," she said accusingly. "You're the source of the evil."

But Briar was coolness personified. She sat easily in her chair, smiling slightly, saying nothing.

Gilda wasn't finished. "What are you?" she spat out. "Not a woman, not flesh and blood, but a monster, a witch!"

"I may be a witch," said Briar, stung, "but you're a fool. Your man wouldn't have bet but for your stupidity. Perhaps I should have gone for *your* thumbs, not his."

This was too much for Gilda. She jumped up from her chair and, pushing aside a couple of bystanders, flung herself at Briar. But Deacon Brace was too quick for her. Even as Gilda clawed for the seated woman's hair, he reached out, grasped her arm and pulled her back. Gilda squirmed, trying to wriggle free of his grip; but, failing to dislodge him, she swung round and lunged at him with her free hand. He swayed back, but not far enough: her long nails raked him from eye to mouth. Blood welled in the weals. Frowning, Brace slapped Gilda smartly across both cheeks with his free hand. The double *clap!* was loud in the room.

Tarry had risen to his feet. Before Brace had time to duck, the fat man punched him on the side of the head, putting his considerable weight into the blow. Most men would have gone down, but Brace merely blinked. He pushed Gilda away, but before he could retaliate or Tarry could swing again, Harry the Wag shouldered between them.

"That's enough! Enough!" he called out.

But it was Crane Rockett's words that deterred the tall man. "Let him be, Deacon," he ordered.

301

Calm was gradually restored. Harry prevailed on Gilda and Tarry to sit down again. Deacon Brace stepped back and, taking a handkerchief from his pocket, dabbed at his scratches. But there was poison, Jewel saw, in the looks he was giving Tarry. By contrast, Briar Spurr seemed entertained by what had happened.

When all was calm, Harry the Wag said, "Now then, where were we?"

This was Crane Rockett's cue. He said, "Mr Ramsbottom gambled and lost. Simple as that. I insist he settles his debt to me. *Now. Immediately.*"

Harry the Wag looked at Tarry. "I'm afraid he's within his rights, Mr Ramsbottom," he said.

Tarry's face was ashen. His momentary triumph over Brace was history. Gilda watched with horror as, slowly, he held his hands up in front of his face as if to commit to memory the image of them whole, then placed them, palms down, on the table top, offering them up for sacrifice.

Crane motioned to Deacon Brace. "Mr Brace, I'd be grateful if you'd collect what's owing to me."

"With pleasure, Mr Rockett."

Deacon Brace was smiling now. His blanched face with its livid stripes was that of a predatory ghoul. A knife appeared in his hand as if it had slid down out of his sleeve. It shone in the lamplight. Stepping back to the table, he put one hand on Tarry's left wrist to hold it steady. But as he positioned his knife for a downward chop—

"Wait!" said an urgent voice.

Brace swivelled towards the speaker: Jewel Ranson.

302

"Carry on," ordered Crane.

"No, Deacon," said Briar Spurr. "I want to hear what the girl has to say."

"Very well," said Crane.

Jewel was on the opposite side of the table to Briar and Crane. "I want to buy out Mr Ramsbottom's debt," she announced.

Briar smiled wickedly. "Do you now . . . Fancy his fat thumbs all for yourself, do you, sweetie? What will you do with them? Pickle them and hang them on a chain around your neck?"

"Is that what *you*'d do? No. If I buy his debt, Mr Ramsbottom can keep them."

"How boring." Briar thought for a moment. "I'm sorry to have to tell you that the value of Mr Ramsbottom's thumbs has just doubled. Can a little girl like you afford such a sum?"

"Let *me* worry about that," Jewel replied curtly. "*And*, Mistress Briar Spurr, I'm *not* 'a little girl'."

"That remains to be seen," murmured Briar. She leant over and whispered in Crane's ear. He whispered back. What they said couldn't be heard.

Briar turned back to Jewel.

"What's your name, girl?"

"Jewel Ranson."

"All right, Jewel Ranson. I'll *play* you for the thumbs. A single deal of the cards. If you win, the thumbs are yours. I'll waive the debt to us, and you can settle what's owed to the other players. If you lose, you pay us double what Mr Ramsbottom owes us – and Mr Brace gets his cut." She grinned at Jewel – beautiful, playful and malign.

303

"I agree," said Jewel, "on one condition."

"A condition, eh? And what would that be?"

"That Mr Harry deals the cards." She gestured at the owner of Rotten Pavilion. Briar lifted a well-plucked eyebrow. "Mr Harry?"

"Fine by me," said Harry the Wag.

"Then let's play," said Briar Spurr.

Deacon Brace let go of Tarry and straightened up. Thoughtfully, he rubbed the flat of his blade across his lips. Gilda linked arms with Tarry, and smiled encouragingly. Around the table, people nudged and shuffled to procure a clear view.

The pack was cut for precedence and Jewel won. "You go first," she told Briar. Two cards were dealt; then two more. Briar had two mistresses – of spades and clubs.

She said, "Now those are what I call cards. Beat twenty if you can, Jewel Ranson."

Jewel surveyed her cards. She had a two and a five.

"Another card, Mr Harry," she said.

He dealt her one: a nine. Now her total was sixteen.

"Another, please," she said.

It was a four.

"Twenty," announced Harry. "Miss Briar will win unless Miss Jewel can draw an ace."

Briar smiled complacently. But everyone's eyes were fixed on Jewel. Everyone's, that is, except for humiliated Tarry, who gazed into his lap as if unable to bear the proceedings.

Jewel put her hands on the edge of the table, closed her eyes and emptied her mind until all she perceived was the wood. How hard it was; but as her senses explored it, it seemed to melt and flow, and she ran with its grain to the stack of cards at its centre. Up through the layers she went, till she came to the topmost one. Now, in her mind, she caused an image to form: an ace of hearts – pristine, blood red, a saviour.

Her eyes still shut, she said, "Another card, please."

"As you wish, Miss Jewel." Harry turned up a fifth card.

Exclamations burst from the crowd, then a spontaneous outbreak of cheers. Crane looked miffed. He shifted about in his chair, as if suddenly uncomfortable. Gilda shot Jewel a look of awe – but then her face hardened, as if the thought of deliverance from such a quarter was too much to bear.

Deacon Brace closed the blade of his knife with a snap. His face would have frozen water. When he turned away, the crowd parted to let him through as if fearful of touching him. Without a word, he moved back to his chair. Tarry was blinking, like a mouse an owl has carelessly dropped – too dazed even to scuttle off down its hole.

Briar Spurr smiled. Lifting her hands, she began to clap lightly, too lightly to make a sound, as if damning with faint praise some flashy conjuror's sleight of hand.

Rainy tugged at Jewel's arm. "Jewel, Jewel!" she said.

At last the girl opened her eyes and looked at the card on the table. Then she nodded and, detaching her purse from her belt, gave it to Harry.

"Please settle Mr Ramsbottom's debts, Mr Harry."

Harry had long since calculated exactly what Tarry owed. Adding a sum from the purse to what Tarry had left on the table, he paid the fat man's creditors. Then he leant towards Gilda and Tarry.

"I think you should call it a day," he said.

"Yes, of course," mumbled Tarry. Pulling himself together, he said to Jewel, "Miss – Miss Ranson, isn't it? I can't thank you enough. I don't know why you did what you did. I'm a fool: I don't deserve your help. But I'll always be grateful. I'll repay you as soon as I can. And if there's ever anything I can do for you . . ."

Jewel nodded vaguely. It seemed to her she'd been standing in one single spot for an age. A huge weariness seized her, enveloping her flesh in a crushing, suffocating blanket. She opened her mouth to speak to Rainy, then swayed and fell sideways into Harry the Wag's arms.

19

THE MAN WITH THE SCAR

One moment Thorn was dreaming, the next he was tumbling out of his sleeping bag onto his head.

Shadowy forms moved above him. Strong hands gripped his neck, hauling his shoulders up from the ground. Half-choking, arms flailing, he lunged with his feet. But he'd taken off his boots, and pain stabbed through his toes as he made contact with something hard. He was flung back and punched in the cheek; a kick to the hip-bone followed. He squirmed away from the blow but now others came sailing in: to his shoulders, flanks, thighs. He curled up and covered his face. There were more kicks to his back. Then the blows ceased.

Gruff voices broke out in a rapid-fire exchange. Voices like Emmy's, but masculine, and speaking an alien tongue.

The exchange ended. A toe poked him low in the spine.

"Get up, boy," said a voice. *Boy* emerged as *bo-eee*, the last sound elongated, as if twisted by the neck.

Experimentally, he shifted one arm from his head. Three green faces were staring at him. Like Emmy, they had squashed-in faces and flattened noses, also wide mouths, stubbled cheeks and chins, and the tangled, greasy hair of the snoring man he'd seen in the cave. They wore knee-length trews and jerkins of tanned rabbit hide.

The toe poked him a second time. Then the world turned bizarre. There was a *zing!* in the air and a thud. The Woodman who'd addressed him staggered a single pace forward. Puzzlement washed through his features. Then, like a stalk of wheat clean-cut by the scythe, he toppled to the earth. An arrow protruded from his back.

The other Woodmen reacted slowly, but even they now got the message. They swung round, suspicious of the dense undergrowth.

Thorn's reaction was quicker. Whipping his knife out of its sheath, he jabbed it into the bare, muscular calf of the nearest man. The Woodman let out a yell and hopped away on one leg. The second man glanced wildly around, then broke into a run. But he hadn't gone more than half a dozen steps when there came a second *zing!* and an arrow buried itself in his shoulder. He lurched sideways, but somehow managed to stay on his feet.

Meanwhile, the man whom Thorn had hurt in the leg had swung back to face him. A scowl was on his face, a knife clutched in his hand. He hobbled back towards Thorn and stabbed down at him. Thorn twisted sideways; the knife narrowly missed him. Then, even as the Woodman drew back his arm for another lunge, Thorn swung his torso upwards and plunged his knife into the man's heart. Life-force drained from the Woodman's body. His arms dropped to his sides and he fell forward across Thorn, pinning him to the ground, inert as a sack.

Thorn struggled to shift the body, and it was some little time before he contrived to half-roll it aside and squirm from under it. Only then did he see that the Woodman who'd tried to run away was lying on the ground. A second arrow was deep in his chest. He muttered in his dialect and raised a vague hand. But the hand fell away and, in a long-drawn exhalation, his spirit abandoned him.

Thorn rose to his feet, wincing at the pains this simple action discovered. The Woodman's blood red-dewed his shoulder. He flexed his limbs and poked himself gingerly with a finger. His assailants had merely bruised him; it could have been worse. It *would* have been worse if they'd taken him off with them.

He looked down at the man he'd killed, but could feel nothing for him. I never sought to do him harm, but he tried to kill me. I acted in self-defence. I'm alive: that's all that matters.

He scanned the perimeter of the glade for a sight of whoever had rescued him. Nothing moved – not a fern, a tuft of grass, a spray of green. Emmy? Surely no thirteen-year-old could shoot like that. Racky Jagger, then? He was handy enough with the weapon. But if it was Racky, Thorn was in trouble . . .

"Who's there?" he called.

The vegetation made no answer.

"Who are you?" he called again.

Moments passed. Then a figure stepped into the open. There was a bow in his left hand, a quiver of arrows on his back. A knapsack hung at his waist. His jacket and trews were green, but patched with brown. He had short, sandy hair and a long, livid scar where once a blade had sliced the tender flesh of his cheek. He walked to the Woodman whose body sported two of his arrows, knelt beside him, unsheathed a knife and cut the shafts from the man's flesh.

"You have strange friends," he said, without looking at Thorn.

"These are no friends of mine."

Now the man turned to Thorn. "I don't mean these three. Woodmen don't have friends. What Woodmen have is kin, blood of their blood. Make an enemy of one, you make an enemy of them all. But if you don't kill them first, they'll kill you anyway. So no choice."

"That's what I was told."

"You were told true. By that strange friend of yours?"

"Racky Jagger?"

"Who else? He was with you on the river."

"*I* was with *him*. Now I'm not."

"Does that mean you're no longer friends?"

"We were never friends. We might have been comrades. Not any more. He betrayed me."

"Did he, now? He's good at that. He betrayed me too, once. That's when I got this." The man indicated his scar. "I was lucky to escape with my life. If I ever get the chance, I'll kill him for it." He spoke with perfect equanimity, as if what he was stating was a simple fact of life, a truth he lived with day to day. "Where is he now?"

"I don't know. He trapped me in Whispering Oak – the Echo Hole – but I escaped. I haven't seen him since."

"You escaped the Echo Hole? How?"

"I went underground, through tunnels."

The man's scrutiny of Thorn seemed to deepen. He said, "See in the dark, can you, son?"

"No, but I had something with me that could."

"It seems there's more to you than meets the eye." He held out his hand. "My name's Burner May."

"Thorn Jack."

Gripping Burner May's hand, Thorn felt its sinewy strength.

"So: where are you from, Thorn Jack?"

"Norgreen settlement."

"Norgreen? You're a long way from home."

"I'm also lost."

"Lost? Looks to me –" Burner May gestured at the nearest Woodman "– as if you'd just been found."

Thorn smiled. "I'm sorry, Burner May. I haven't thanked you, have I? I owe you my life."

Burner May grunted, as if to say: Think nothing of it.

Thorn said: "So you live here in the wood?"

"Here and there. The wood suits me. I'm not fit for civilised society. I prefer trees to men. Trees you can depend on."

Thorn thought of Emmy's oak trees. "I know what you mean."

Burner May glanced round the glade. "Let's get out of here, leave these carrion to their kind."

"I'm all for that. But they woke me up. I've had nothing to eat."

"No problem. We'll put a little distance between ourselves and this place, then stop."

As Thorn got his gear together, he said: "It was lucky for me you turned up when you did."

"There was no luck involved. I'd been tracking those three for some time. They were looking for someone, and I wanted to

311

know who. Something told me it might be Racky and his unknown companion."

"Just me," said Thorn. He didn't want to mention Emmy. "The tunnel I was following came out into the Woodmen's cave. It was night-time. They were all asleep. But I must have left some tracks."

Burner nodded. "Where are you making for?"

"The top of the wood. Roydsal – a mansion the giants built."

"I know the place. But you're lost, you say. Like some help to get you there?"

"I would."

"Then you have it."

"I'm grateful. But aren't I taking you out of your way?"

"All ways are my ways here. I'll take you to the wood's edge, put you on the forest road."

"Are we far from the wood's edge?"

"No. Less than a day's travel."

They left the Woodmen where they'd fallen. Insects buzzed about them, drawn by the scent of fresh blood. Birds and animals would follow. Unless their kin quickly found them, there'd be nothing on the grass but a strew of bones and clothing scraps.

These images stayed with Thorn as he walked beside his new guide.

He said, "You don't think much of Woodmen, do you, Burner May?"

"Got no reason to. They'd kill me, if they could."

"Why are they like that?"

"Who knows? They just are. There are people in the world,

Thorn Jack, who recognise only the right of their own kind to life. Other kinds are fair game. But the Woodmen stay within their own territory, for the most part. Eastwards, they rarely venture further than Whispering Oak. And they shun the Oak itself; they think a demon inhabits it."

"But I thought they worshipped trees."

"So they do. But what's the difference between a god and a demon? A demon's only a god who happens not to be on your side. Fear is the other face of worship; the same face, sometimes."

"It sounds as though you don't have much time for either of them."

"Gods and demons? I believe in what I can touch and see. Trees are wonderful things, but they're trees, not gods or spirits. Same with rocks. Same with rivers."

Soon after that Burner declared himself satisfied with their progress. They found a dry spot and settled down. Burner remained silent while Thorn ate, but spoke at last, "May I ask why you're making for Roydsal?"

Can you refuse to answer the question of a man who's saved your life?

When Thorn had got through a heavily edited version of his story, Burner said, "These men with yellow feathers . . . Racky claimed not to know where they were from?"

"That's right."

"A gold piece to a penny he was lying to you. Racky tells the truth when it serves his purpose, not otherwise."

"Well, he's out of my hair now."

"Don't count on it. He has a habit of turning up when you

least expect him to. He's the burr that sticks to your jacket." He paused. "But let me tell you something that you *will* be glad to hear. The men with yellow feathers definitely come from Roydsal. I think it's highly likely that you'll find your sister there."

"Do you *know* these men?" asked Thorn quickly, excitement in his voice.

"Not personally. But I've seen them at the Punch and Judy Inn – an unsavoury bunch. They work for the masters of Roydsal, a pair of identical twins whose names are Zak and Lanner Spetch."

Thorn was puzzled. "I've never heard of them. Why should they kidnap my sister?"

"I can't tell you that. But you can be sure they'll have a reason."

Thorn pondered for a time, then tried another question.

"What are they like, these Spetch brothers?"

"From what I've gathered, the sort who are never satisfied. Not with power, money, possessions. They'll go hungry into the grave. And I'll tell you something else."

Burner May leant towards him, as if imparting a great secret.

"They think money will make them free. But it won't, it's a kind of bondage. The freest man has nothing, for he's got nothing to lose."

Thorn had never heard anyone speak like this – not even Taylor, whom he'd always considered wise.

"Look at these trees," continued Burner, "and ask yourself what they need."

Thorn hesitated, then opened his mouth to reply, but Burner, it seemed, was more than ready to answer his own question.

"I'll tell you: rain, nourishment from the ground, birds or wind to spread their seeds. That's all a tree needs."

Thorn considered this, then said: "But human beings aren't trees. Surely we need more than trees do. A tree doesn't need another tree – but human beings need one another."

"Only to give them birth, a start in life. After that . . ."

After that, what? thought Thorn. And the answer came: solitude. He's talking about himself: alone in the wood, self-sufficient, distrustful of men. Well, that life might work for him, but it won't for all men. Won't for most men. And certainly not for me. Thorn couldn't imagine himself going through life all on his own. Live without family and friends, without love? Impossible.

He was half-inclined to keep his thoughts to himself, but curiosity got the better of him. He said, "Don't you think you might be missing something, alone in the wood?"

"What would I be missing?"

"Companionship. Love."

"Love?" Burner May chuckled dryly. "How can you miss what you've never had?"

"Quite easily, I'd have thought."

"I don't agree. You can only miss things that have been taken away from you. Like your sister, Thorn. You love her, you want her back. I can understand that."

"But you never had a sister?"

"No – as far as I know. Nor a brother either."

"You must have had a mother and father."

315

"No doubt I did. But I never knew them. I was found crying, wrapped in a bundle, by a stream on the edge of the wood. An old wood-hermit found me. Some people might have ignored me, but he was deeply religious, and thought it a sign from God. He took me in and brought me up, taught me how to survive in the wood."

"But didn't you love him?"

"No. Why should I? He didn't love me. He saw it as his duty to look after me, but no more. He never gave me love – if he was capable of human love, which I very much doubt. He loved God, I think, but that was as much as he could manage. He'd no love left for any person, any other thing."

To Thorn, this sounded strange. Racky Jagger, Manningham Sparks, Emmy Wood, Burner May . . . how different they were. Each had his own way of living, a different set of values. It was confusing.

Burner May said, "Right, let's get moving. Talking passes the time, but it doesn't get you anywhere. Only feet do that. Hence the superiority of toes over tongues."

Soon they were moving again.

The rest of the morning passed uneventfully. There was no sign of further pursuit. Burner stayed under the great trees, where there was little undergrowth, and the going was manageable. Despite the absence of the sun, he navigated with certainty. Occasional showers pattered down. The branches dripped above them.

Thorn walked with a new sense of purpose, a fresh vigour. He'd be out of the wood soon. And he was well-nigh certain – at last – where Haw was to be found.

316

They stopped to eat by a stream at what they judged was midday. Brisk water ran over gravel and rushes clustered along the banks, shooting spikily above their heads.

As they replenished their water bottles, Burner May asked, "How much food do you have, Thorn?"

"Not a lot," he admitted.

"Then you must take some of mine."

"I can't do that."

"You can't do otherwise. I've time aplenty to get more. But your time is precious."

The lean man pressed on him dried meat wrapped in cloth. Thorn thanked him, and packed it away.

In mid-afternoon they emerged from the forest. Along the edge of the trees ran a broad stony thoroughfare: the forest road again. The rain had done little to soften its surface. The walls on either side had long since fallen into ruin.

Thorn did a quick calculation. Today was the twelfth of May. He'd spent five nights and the best part of six days in the wood. But it seemed to him he'd lived a whole life in that time. In one sense, he was unchanged; in another, he was different. He'd gone in as one person and come out as another. The new Thorn would do things the old Thorn couldn't conceive.

Burner gestured up the highway. "Follow the road till you come to a fork. Take the left-hand turning. Roydsal lies that way."

Above them, the road climbed away and turned a bend. Below them, it curved into the forest and out of sight.

Thorn turned to his new friend. "So this is goodbye?" he said.

"Yes. Goodbye. And good luck."

Thorn grasped Burner's hand. "Once more, I can't thank you enough," he said.

"No thanks are necessary."

"I think they are."

Burner grinned, still gripping Thorn's hand. But in that momentary silence, as they stood there, there came a noise from down the road: a human cough.

Burner pulled Thorn off the road and stationed him behind a stone. "Stay out of sight," he whispered. "Probably it's a harmless traveller, but you never know . . . Nock your bow, but leave the first move to me. I'm going to work my way forward."

He moved quickly away. Thorn fitted an arrow to his bow. His heart was a red drum, but the weapon in his hands was as steady as the stone.

Boot heels crunched on the road. There was more coughing, and a male voice gave vent to a stream of colourful curses. When he judged the man well past, Thorn peered round the stone. A hunched figure was moving slowly away from him. He wore a jerkin with the hood down, a hip-pack, a bandolier to which a quiver of arrows was strapped, and he carried a bow. Pinned to the quiver was a black feather with a yellow band. But the man hadn't gone much further when Burner May stepped out from behind a thick tuft of grass, his bow drawn at eye level.

"Stop right there!" he commanded. "Move, and I'll put an arrow in you."

But the man twisted his head round, as if assessing his chances to make a dash for it.

"Don't even think of it," said Burner. "My friend's behind you there."

Thorn moved out into view, his bow too aimed at the man.

"Step off the road. Lie on your stomach with your arms out," said Burner.

The man did as he was told. Face-down in the grass, he looked a pathetic sight.

"What do you want?" he asked hoarsely. "I've some money – take that."

Burner spoke to Thorn. "I'm going to tie his hands. If he tries anything, put an arrow in his leg."

"Hey – there's no need for that. I won't run," the man assured them.

"No more than fish will swim and birds fly, I suppose," said Burner.

Laying down his bow, he extracted a length of twine from his knapsack and tied the man's wrists behind his back.

"On your feet," he commanded. "Let's walk a little. And remember: run, and you're the world's newest cripple."

The man embarked on a coughing bout – as if to suggest that running was way beyond him right now.

Soon, with the man a few steps in front, they were in the wood.

"That's a nasty cough you've got there," said Thorn. "How did you get it?"

"What's it to you?" replied the man.

Burner kicked him behind the knee. The man yelped and fell down.

Burner poked him with his boot. "Answer my friend's question," he said.

"Hurt me," said the man, "and my friends will come after you."

"I'll say this for you," said Burner, "you're a man with a sense of humour. Let's consider *your* options, shall we? One, you could answer our questions and appeal to our better natures. Two, you could lie or say nothing. We then consider *our* options. Option one: we shoot you, bury you, and no one's any the wiser. Option two: I take you into the woods and leave you tied to a tree by one of the Woodmen's trails. That would give you time to reflect on the error of your ways."

Horror came into the man's face. He began to cough again. "The Woodmen," he spluttered, "not them, please . . . Kill me if you like, but don't leave me for them . . ."

"Answer our questions and you'll live. It's up to you."

"What is it you want to know?"

"Let's start with your name."

"Denny Sweat."

"Right, Denny. Now answer my friend's question. How did you come by your cough?"

"I got wet and caught a cold."

"Fell in a river, didn't you?" This was Thorn, his voice harsh.

The man stared at him.

Thorn said, "Where have you been since you fell in? No, let me guess: you've been hiding in the Punch and Judy Inn, haven't you – care of Jonas Legg?"

There was a brief pause.

"Who are you?" asked Denny Sweat.

"I think you know," answered Thorn. "Well, am I right?"

"Yes. You were with Racky Jagger, you're the girl's—"

Denny shut up, but the damage was done. Anger flared in Thorn. He kicked Denny in the side, and the man curled up in an attempt to reduce the size of the target he made. But Thorn set his boot on Denny's cheek, pressing his face into the earth. Strangled noises came from his throat. Starved of air, his body convulsed.

"Easy, Thorn." Burner laid a restraining hand on the young man's arm.

Thorn took his boot away and the Roydsal man jerked backwards, coughing and choking, his face filthy with leaf-rot.

"My sister," Thorn said grimly, "I hope for your sake she's alive."

"Yes, yes," the man gasped. He spat out bark. "Safe at Roydsal."

"Were you one of her kidnappers?"

"No, not me. That was Rafter, Blacky and Leech. It was Blacky got killed at the inn."

"Why do the Spetches want my sister?"

"I don't know . . ."

Burner thrust the tip of his bow into Denny's cheek. "Have you forgotten option two?"

"No, no! Cross my heart, I don't know why they want her. They don't give reasons – just orders."

"That rings true," said Burner to Thorn. "The Spetches aren't the kind who explain themselves to hirelings."

"How are you treating my sister?" asked Thorn. "Well, I hope, for your sake."

"She's fine," said Denny hurriedly. "In the pink. We were ordered not to harm her."

"So – where's she being held?"

"In this lock-up in the old hall."

"Where's the key to the lock-up?"

"No key. Just bolts on the door."

"All right. So how do I get into the house?"

"Get into it? You can't. I mean, they'll never let you in."

"It has a door, hasn't it?"

"A converted ventilation point. Down the side, opposite the rattery. But it's always locked. And there's always a guard inside."

"How many men have the Spetches got?"

"Five. Four, now Blacky's gone."

"And without you, three," observed Burner. "A tall order . . ."

Thorn said, "Let's try again, Denny. How do *you* get into the house?"

"Me?" Denny looked surprised. "Well, they know me. Of course, I still have to give a password to get in."

"A password? Why's that?"

"Well, if it's dark or the weather's bad, it's a kind of insurance. You give your password and in you go. Each man has his own."

"What's *yours* then, Denny?"

Just for a moment, the man hesitated. Then he said, "*Toad*."

Burner kicked Denny again. "You're the toad, Denny. Did you know Woodmen eat toads? They spit them and roast them – like they do their enemies. They'd make short work of you."

Denny Sweat was living up to his name. A rank odour rose from him. He began to cough again.

"It's *devil*. DEVIL," he spluttered. "That's God's truth, I swear."

"You wouldn't know God's truth if it hit you," said Burner. "*Devil*, eh? You flatter yourself. *Toad* was closer to the mark." He glanced at Thorn, who was deep in thought. "You all right?"

"I'm fine," answered Thorn. "I've got an idea how I might get in. With a bit of luck . . ." He looked down at the sweating man. "But I need more information . . ."

"Ask away," said Burner. "You're our man, aren't you, Denny?"

Denny was. When Thorn finally ran out of questions, he said to Burner, "So: what do we do with him?"

"He can be my guest for a while – a few days, let's say."

"Will you kill him? He's been helpful."

"Had no choice, had he? But no – I don't kill people without a reason. This morning I had a reason – as did you." He looked down at Denny. "Now, my pathetic friend, is there anything you haven't told us yet that we ought to know?"

"The doormen," said Denny hurriedly. "They go in strict rotation. It'll be Lippy Dimmock tonight."

"Lippy?" said Burner. "Talkative sort, is he?"

"Just the opposite."

"So – another charmer like you?"

"Got a reputation, has Lippy."

"What for?"

"Letting his fists do his talking."

"So, another deep thinker. Hear that, Thorn?"

"I hear it," said Thorn. "I can't wait to meet him."

20

THE BODY IN THE LAKE

Jewel sat up in the bed.

"Let's get going," she said brightly.

Her long, deep sleep had served fully to restore her, and she felt fit and alert.

Beside her, Rainy yawned. She'd passed a troubled night. "All right," she agreed.

The night before, Harry had graciously offered them this bed. The room was little more than a cupboard, but Jewel was in no sort of shape to walk home, so here they'd slept.

Jewel asked, "Ought we to say goodbye to Harry?"

"Probably, but he never gets up before midday, and he wouldn't thank us to wake him."

As they came down through the Pavilion, they encountered none of the other guests. Lapped in luxurious sheets, they were sleeping off the previous evening's overdose of thrills.

The sky was pale, undecided how to comport itself. Jewel and Rainy set off across the island towards the pontoon bridge.

But were arrested by the sight of a lone figure on a bench. Head bent, she was sobbing.

"Gilda?" said Rainy. "What on earth is the matter?"

Gilda lifted tear-streaked cheeks to the new arrivals.

"It's Tarry," she said hesitantly. "He's disappeared."

"Disappeared? How can he have disappeared?"

Gilda looked away for a moment, as if calculating the damage confession would do to her self-esteem. Then she sniffed and said: "It was last night, in our room. We had a terrible argument. Tarry went off to get some air. I went to bed and fell asleep. I slept like a log. But when I woke a short time ago, Tarry wasn't there. I don't believe he ever came back to the room."

"Perhaps," suggested Rainy, "he slept somewhere else."

"I've looked in all the public rooms. None of the staff have seen him . . . And he's not in the seats overlooking the lake."

"Then he must be out here somewhere . . ."

"Doing what? He's no walker."

"Did he take a coat with him?"

"A coat? I think so. Oh, it's all my fault. If something's happened to him, I shall never forgive myself."

Rainy doubted that Gilda's capacity for self-blame was quite so developed.

Jewel exchanged a look with Rainy. After last night's events, the girl felt obscurely connected to Tarry – almost to the point of nurturing a sense of responsibility towards the missing man.

"Why don't we take a look around the grounds?" she suggested.

"All right," agreed Gilda, and got up from her chair. She seemed glad to have someone to tell her what to do.

The three women set off. Gilda trotted nervously along at Rainy's side, her hands never still. She was wearing a sensible dress, so they made reasonable progress. The birds were singing even more lustily than they'd done the previous day, but the other seats in the arbours were deserted. They passed no one, and Gilda's frequent calls of "Tarry!" went unanswered.

At last they came to the bridge.

"There's Sam," exclaimed Rainy.

The old boatman was working on a dinghy in his yard. As they came over the pontoon, he lifted an arm in salute.

"Something the matter?" he enquired, seeing the serious looks they wore.

"We're looking for Tarry Ramsbottom," said Rainy. "He's gone missing."

"A big man," said Gilda. "Bushy sideburns. You'd remember him if you'd seen him."

"Afraid I haven't," said Sam, "and I've been here since sun-up. If you can call it sun-up . . . Searched the island, have you?"

"Only the paths. We couldn't find any sign of him."

"Hmm . . ." Sam pondered. "What if I sailed you back round to the Pavilion? We might spot something from the lake you'd miss from land."

"Yes please," said Gilda quickly.

They went to the quay and embarked. Jewel and Gilda sat in the bow. Rainy had crewed for Sam before. He cast off, then took the tiller. Rainy hoisted the sail. The breeze filled its white triangle, and the boat moved out from shore.

Jewel scanned the banks of the island. They were constructed from rocks that rose above the waterline. But here and there the rocks had collapsed, and the lake water lapped gravel. Bushes and trees crowded the shore, their lowest branches brushing the water. In many places, blossom sprayed in white or pink showers.

They failed to brighten Jewel's mood. A sense of foreboding was growing inside her.

No one spoke. Gilda's eyes were fixed on the shoreline. She called out Tarry's name, but no voice answered. And here was Rotten Pavilion, with its landing-stage and boats.

"Do you want me to pull in?"

Gilda would have answered Sam's question in the affirmative, but it was Jewel who spoke first.

"Can we go a little farther?"

"Sure," said Sam.

Gilda made no objection. As the boat followed the curve of the island round, the lake's north-western corner came into view.

"Over there," said Jewel, pointing. "Is that an inlet, Sam?"

On the lake's northern shore, near the entry into the channel that divided island from mainland, its waters ducked into a tree-shadowed recess.

"That's Bugsarbor," replied Sam. "But bugs are all you'll find there. It's a mucky hole – nothing but a home for flotsam."

"I think we should go there. Can you sail us in?"

"No problem," said Sam. He'd sail through the eye of a needle if it were needed.

But this was too much for Gilda.

"Bugsarbor?" she cried. "Why waste time going there?"

Rainy spoke quietly, "Gilda, if Jewel says we should, that's what we ought to do."

"But why?" Gilda protested again – weakly, and no one answered.

The boat moved towards the shore.

In the mouth of the inlet, three ancient metal posts stuck up out of the water. Once, perhaps, they'd barred the entry to giant-sized vessels. Sam bisected two of them and, on flat water, the boat drifted in beneath the overarching branches. Jewel peered into the shadows. Here the giants had for once neglected to shore up the bank. Bare, black earth sloped down into the water. In one corner, a stream trickled out of a culvert's maw: the overflow from Round Pond – ultimately the excess from distant Jugdam. The long vein connecting the higher lake to the lower one.

In the air was a tang of putridity. Gilda took out a handkerchief and held it to her nose. Jewel scrutinised the tangle of snapped branches, broken reeds, dead fish, scum and mixed detritus crowding one corner of the inlet.

The sailing boat was becalmed.

Jewel pointed. "Sam, can you take us in closer?"

He nodded, took up a long pole and gently propelled the boat towards the clot's periphery. Ripples ran into the rubbish, which rose and subsided.

"There!" she cried. "What's that?"

A dark mass bulked near the clot's outer edge.

As the boat nudged into the flotsam, Sam positioned himself with the pole. Jewel looked on impassively, but Gilda's face was strained. Rainy could scarcely bear to look. Sam prodded the dark mass, which wallowed in the water. He poked more forcefully, and as the thing lifted, a human head with a staring eye broke from the surface.

Gilda screamed; then started to weep.

*

Sam sailed back to Rotten Pavilion and tied up at the landing-stage. Rainy sat with Gilda while Jewel sought out Harry the Wag. Still in bed, he wasn't pleased to be roused. But, quickly grasping the seriousness of the situation, he took charge. As master, he had the authority of a settlement headman. He and one of his men sailed back to Bugsarbor with Sam, got a rope around the body and towed it back.

By the time the boat returned, word had got around of this latest twist in the tale, and most of the guests had gathered on or above the landing-stage. Gilda was there with Rainy and Jewel, looking pinched and nervy.

Poor Gilda, thought Rainy guiltily. Can I have misjudged her? I took her for a weasel with Tarry's wallet in her claws. Perhaps she *was* fond of him . . .

After the body had been manhandled onto land – no easy task, given its bulk and the weight of water soaking its clothes – the crowd watched in silence as the three women went towards it. Gilda held tightly to Rainy's arm as Harry, Sam and another man struggled to roll the corpse onto its back. Lake water dribbled from it, forming pools on the quay. And its identity? That could scarcely be in doubt. A body of such dimensions could belong only to one person.

Tarry's face was puffy and moon-white. His eyes were wide open, his face expressive of nothing. Gilda dissolved in fresh tears and buried her head in Rainy's shoulder.

The juggler drew Gilda away, back up the steps and through the crowd. Jewel remained behind, reluctant to tear herself away. Less than half a day before she'd saved Tarry's thumbs, but death had emphasised its dominion and claimed all of him. Was fate mocking her paltry human attempt to intervene?

Harry too seemed deep in thought. At length, rousing himself, he said, "You shouldn't be here, Miss Jewel. This is really no place for you."

"It's too late to say that. Death and I are well acquainted. It was death that brought me here."

Harry could make no answer to this.

In a softer voice Jewel said, "Could it have been an accident?"

"More likely suicide. He was pretty down last night. Humiliation at the tables, then his argument with Gilda. Look at his face – it's unmarked."

He closed the gambler's eyes.

But how earnestly Tarry promised to repay me, thought Jewel. Why should he kill himself?

Kneeling, she placed her right hand on his chest. He was wearing his coat, and under her fingers the material felt cold as well as damp. She closed her eyes and sought to blank out conscious thought, to let come in – from wherever it might – some impulse or perception . . .

Harry stared down at her. This was a strange girl. He'd seen what she'd achieved the night before at Twenty-one. Chance? A confirmed fan of chance, Harry was not superstitious. But this girl . . . He stood quietly watching, content to let her finish whatever it was she might be doing.

Abruptly, she stood up.

"Turn him over," she commanded.

Harry motioned to Sam and his other helper, and the three rolled Tarry back onto his stomach.

"Phew!" exclaimed Sam. "I'm too old for this."

"The back of his head," said Jewel simply.

The lake had slicked down Tarry's hair, turning its mouse-brown to black. Harry squatted and touched the clotted strands with fastidious fingertips; then, with some reluctance, pushed in to explore the firm curve of the skull.

Abruptly he pulled back. His fingers were tinged with red.

"Is it blood?" asked Sam.

"Yes, he has a lump there."

"He must have hit his head falling . . ."

"Impossible," said Harry. "If the damage were on the *front* of his head, yes. But who commits suicide by throwing himself *backwards*?"

"I see what you mean," said Sam. "You think he was struck from behind . . . But why? Attempted robbery?"

"He was broke – as everyone knew. No, he was killed for some other reason . . . I think he was struck on the back of the head and fell or was rolled into the lake. Probably with a stone that ended up in the water too."

Harry stood up and looked at Jewel. "You know who did it, don't you?"

"Don't you?" she fired back.

Harry looked thoughtful. "It's one thing to have one's suspicions, another to have proof. We have nothing. I shall talk to my guests. Perhaps someone saw something . . ."

"And if they didn't?"

"If they didn't, there's no evidence, and if the killer doesn't confess –"

"Some chance of that!"

"– there won't be anything I can do."

"Can I accompany you? I'd like to hear what people say."

"I don't see why not. I'd value your insight. But first I've got to do something with this poor fellow."

Later, while Rainy stayed with Gilda (now sleeping fitfully after downing a calmative), Jewel accompanied Harry on his rounds of the guests. His questions drew a blank. No one admitted to leaving their rooms during the night – never mind to witnessing murder.

Harry left the Minral How contingent to last. It was late in the morning by the time he caught up with Briar and Crane. They were lounging in the gardens. Brace, for once, was elsewhere.

"I suppose you've heard," said Harry, "about Tarry Ramsbottom."

"I hear he fell in the lake and drowned. Which just shows," said Crane, "no matter how bad your luck is, it can still get worse."

"Luck had nothing to do with it."

"You mean he committed suicide? Well, he wouldn't be the first to do that here, would he?"

A high-roller called Lester Fortune had slit his wrists after a disastrous night at the wheel some years before.

"It was murder," said Harry. "He was hit on the back of the head."

"Well, there's a thing. You can't credit the evil in the world, can you, Harry? And such a harmless fellow. Why would anyone want to kill him?"

"Why indeed?" said Harry dryly. "You'll appreciate, Mr Rockett, that I must ask you some questions."

"Of course, Harry. And you'll want to be thorough. No stone unturned, eh?"

"I appreciate your co-operation, Mr Rockett. Now, there was a certain degree of ill-feeling between yourself and Miss Spurr and Mr Ramsbottom and Miss Buckle in the gaming room last night."

"Ill-feeling? I wouldn't say that. I offered to help him out of a hole, as I remember."

"Yes – at a price. His thumbs, you may recall."

"Come on, Harry: gambling involves risk, as well you know. The two go together like fish and water. All *I* did was add a dash of spice to the transaction."

"Some people might feel," said Jewel, "that making someone gamble his thumbs isn't particularly spicy."

Crane grinned indulgently. "One person's spice is another's stomach upset."

"Some of those present last night," said Harry, "thought you weren't too pleased when Miss Ranson's intervention got Tarry off the hook."

"Nobody likes losing, as I'm sure you're well aware. But win some, lose some – such is life, Harry."

Briar Spurr spoke for the first time. "Surely, Harry, the logic of your argument would point to Miss Ranson being the object of any displeasure, not Mr Ramsbottom. Yet here she is, alive and well, and impertinent to boot."

Briar smiled mockingly. Jewel said nothing.

"So, Mr Rockett," said Harry after a pause, "would you mind telling me where you went after you left the gaming room."

"We retired to our room and slept the sleep of the just."

"You didn't go out."

Crane Rockett shook his head.

"And you confirm that, Miss Spurr?"

Briar said, "Surely you can't imagine I go prowling round in the dark, looking for overweight men to bash on the head?"

Harry smiled tightly. "Thank you both."

Deacon Brace was outside the carriage-house, seeing to some minor repairs to Crane's carriage. Today he looked even more alarming than usual. One eye was almost closed; Gilda's scratches burned on his cheek.

"How are you feeling this morning?" enquired Harry.

"Wonderful," replied Brace.

"You don't look too good."

"I don't get paid for looking good."

"What *do* you get paid for?"

Brace grinned lopsidedly. "This and that," he replied.

"Tarry Ramsbottom is dead, as I'm sure you know. We believe he was murdered. How do you feel about that?"

"I don't feel anything about it."

"I see . . . How do you account for his death?"

"I don't account for it."

"Perhaps he upset someone. *You*, perhaps, Mr Brace?"

"I don't take kindly to people who punch me. Do you, Mr Harry?"

There was a pause. Then Harry said, "Tarry was struck on the back of the head – probably with a stone. He wasn't a small man. It would have taken someone tall to deliver the blow."

"So?"

"You're a tall man, Mr Brace."

"So are you, Mr Harry. Did *you* kill him, by any chance?"

"I had no quarrel with Mr Ramsbottom. *You*, however, did."

"If I said he was my favourite human being, you wouldn't believe me. So I won't."

"Was he unfavourite enough for you to kill him, Mr Brace?"

Deacon Brace said nothing.

Harry tried another tack, "Tell me, do you have a favourite human being?"

"Doesn't everyone?"

"Imagine I'm that person. Imagine you want to unburden yourself to me. Did you kill Tarry Ramsbottom, Mr Brace?"

"When they doled imagination out, they passed right over me."

"Just answer the question. *Did* you kill him?"

"If I did, you'd hardly expect me to confess."

"*Did* you?" persisted Harry.

Brace's good eye went small. "You're beginning to bore me, Mr Harry. Go and pester someone else."

"I wasn't aware I was pestering you, Brace."

Brace said nothing.

Harry went on, "Last night, after you left the gaming room, what did you do?"

"What did I do? Escorted Mr Crane and Miss Briar to their room. Escorted myself to my own. Admired my handsome face in the mirror. Went to bed."

"So you didn't go outside, see Mr Ramsbottom, follow him, and strike him on the head?"

Brace's lip curled. "How could I, when I was fast asleep, dreaming of the fairies?"

"Thank you, Mr Brace," said Harry. "I think that's everything."

Brace glowered at them both, and turned away.

Harry and Jewel mounted the steps towards the Pavilion.

"Brace killed Tarry," said Jewel.

"That seems more than likely. But there's no evidence against him, no chance of getting any, and he's not going to confess."

"So he just gets to walk away?"

"Ride away, in his case, merrily cracking his whip."

"He's killed men before, you can see it in his eyes."

"He'll make a mistake, sooner or later."

"You think so? He doesn't look to me much like the type who makes mistakes."

"Everyone makes mistakes. Brace will make one some day."

"I wish I had your confidence."

"You're taking this very personally. I wonder why, Jewel?"

"I don't know, Harry. I suppose I feel responsible."

"You've taken on more than enough responsibility. Let this one go. And if you and Rainy have any sense, you'll get away from Gilda as soon as possible. She's poison, that woman, and she infects other people. She got Tarry into this mess."

He's right, of course, thought Jewel. Why am I tangled up

with these people? Tarry and Gilda, Brace, Crane Rockett and Briar Spurr – they're passing figures in my life. I've a more pressing score to settle with the Spetch brothers . . .

But there was to be no departure from Harrypark for her that day. Rainy couldn't yet leave Gilda, she said, and in any case there was Tarry to bury. Reminded of that melancholy fact, Jewel saw that she too must remain for the time being. So they hung on at Rotten Pavilion, keeping Gilda company through dinner. Their glum-faced companion said almost nothing and picked at her food. Gaming, of course, was out of the question. But, as they could hear from where they sat in the dining room, Tarry's death had failed to dampen enthusiasm for the tables. The Wag paid them a brief visit to report that things were going with an even greater swing than usual. It was as if the very violence of the fat man's demise had whetted every punter's appetite for excitement. People were throwing their money about as if tomorrow would never come. Crane, Briar and Deacon Brace were all there, with a sparkling Briar (tonight at the dice table) on a winning streak.

Harry communicated these facts with little pleasure. He was clearly depressed, and his presence in addition to Gilda's made for a double downer. Jewel was relieved when he finally said goodnight. Shortly after that, Gilda declared herself exhausted, and ready to turn in. So all three of them went to bed.

The following morning saw the interment of Tarry's body. The island's burial plot was packed. Crane and Briar stood on the brink of the assembly, faces impassive. Deacon Brace was not to be seen. As the body was let down into the ground, Jewel thought of her father. How long ago and far away his funeral seemed. Yet it was almost yesterday . . . When tears came from her eyes, she couldn't have said whether they fell for Elliott, for Tarry, or her own bereft self.

Arm in arm with Rainy, as pale as a wraith, Gilda stood morosely through the brief ceremony – conducted by a pompous Ranter up from Lowmoor who spoke rather too pointedly of the wages of sin. Gilda seemed too dazed to offer a show of emotion. In a brief speech, Harry spoke of the vagaries of fate known to all gamblers, and recalled anecdotes of happier times for Tarry in the Pavilion. But if they'd been designed to lighten the proceedings, they failed. Afterwards, as people lined up to offer condolences to Gilda – all, that is, but Crane and Briar, who left directly the rite was over – she virtually ignored them.

But, as soon as the crowd had dispersed, her mood changed.

"I'm going to the Pavilion to pack," she announced briskly. "Then I'm leaving for Lowmoor."

Rainy's offer of assistance was met with a crisp rejection.

"No, I'm perfectly capable of looking after myself. It's time to put all this behind me."

"But what will you do?" asked Rainy.

"Don't concern yourself about that. Goodbye to you both now."

Barely pausing to acknowledge their farewells, she was off. Jewel and Rainy watched her go with astonishment.

"She's more upset than I thought," said Jewel.

"Is she?" replied Rainy.

The women looked at one another.

Then Rainy said: "Come on. Let's say goodbye to Harry, and go home."

Harry had stayed while people left. Now he came up to them.

"What's with Gilda?" he asked.

"She's leaving," said Rainy. "Going back to Lowmoor."

Harry produced a cynical smile. "Always did possess a quick recovery factor, our Gilda. She'll be back in a week or two, talons honed to sink into some other poor mutt. Poor as in unfortunate, of course, not impoverished."

"We're leaving too," said Rainy. "So we'll say goodbye now."

Harry grimaced. "Are you? Well, I suppose you've stayed longer than you intended, so I can't complain. Rainy – you'll be back, I know. For work, if nothing else. But you, Jewel: will you?"

"Who knows, Harry?" said the girl. She stretched up and kissed him on the cheek. "Goodbye," she said. "I shan't forget these last few days."

"Nor me," said Harry. "I suppose I ought to wish you luck. But somehow *luck*, it strikes me, isn't something you've much need of."

"I wouldn't say that."

"Go carefully now, both of you. And remember, there's always a welcome for you here."

On the road to the pontoon bridge, Jewel told Rainy she meant to get away that day – as soon as she'd said goodbye to Luke and got her gear together.

Rainy studied her friend. "Well," she said at last, "you *do* seem fully recovered. Actually, there's something—"

She never finished the sentence. A tall, familiar figure had stepped out in front of them.

Deacon Brace favoured them with a cadaverous grin. "Fancy seeing *you* again so soon," he said to Jewel.

She looked him straight in the eye. "You don't fool me, Brace. It was *you* who murdered Tarry Ramsbottom. In cold blood."

The grin faded from Brace's face. "Did no one ever tell you to mind your mouth, girl?"

Jewel took a couple of paces, making to walk around him, but he stepped in front of her. She halted, and the two stared coldly at one another.

"Are you going to kill me too?" said the girl defiantly.

Brace did not reply.

Rainy stepped forward. "Let us by," she demanded.

Brace ignored her. "Nobody calls me a murderer," he said sharply to Jewel.

"But that's what you are, Deacon Brace. You disgust me. You're a rat without a tail."

The man's lip curled. "You're a foolish little girl. It's time someone taught you a lesson."

Shooting out a long arm, he grabbed her by her jacket front and lifted her into the air. Jewel gasped and thrashed about.

Rainy flung herself at Brace, but he swung his free arm and caught the side of her head with his fist, knocking her to the ground. She lay stunned; blood ran from her nose.

Unable to reach Brace with her fists, Jewel kicked out. Her right boot connected with his knee. He retaliated with a vicious double slap to her face. Then, holding the shocked and unresisting girl high in the air, he strode to the edge of the path and plunged into the undergrowth.

Jewel, half-choking, her eyes blinded by tears, was swung like a limp puppet through blurred greenery. Plant-stalks and grass stems swirled by in the gloom.

There was a sudden sense of expanse. She could hear the slop of water.

She coughed, struggling for breath, and tried to blink away the tears. Brace's eyes, close up now, burnt into hers.

"Say your prayers, girl," he sneered, smacked her again across the face and tossed her away like a rag doll.

She was falling. There was a splash. The cold waters of Harrylake closed over her head.

21

BOLTS AND HINGES

Just the place, thought Thorn.

Unshouldering backpack and quiver, he pushed them into the crevice in the dilapidated wall. After them went his bow. Now that he was able to don Denny's bandolier and quiver, he felt less encumbered. He'd swapped his own jacket for Denny's hooded jerkin, and he wore Denny's hip-pack and carried his bow.

It was pretty dark now, but he didn't believe that even in daylight a passer-by would spot his cache. He counted the number of paces to a nearby blackthorn tree: thirty-six.

Thirty-six, he said to himself as he walked on. Remember that. Remember too the shape of the tree. Beaten and bent by the wind into a premature old age, it was one of only three on this final stretch of road.

Judy Wood lay below and behind him. The trees appeared to have called off their attempt to climb the hill. Well, trees and men had different priorities; I'm nearly there, he thought . . .

Roydsal loomed in the twilight, its chimney stacks black and stubby against the darkening sky. Roydsal . . . And his sister, shut in a small, wooden room. He strode on, determination quickening his steps.

A pair of mighty gateposts marked the entry into the Spetch

brothers' domain. From each of their capstones, eight feet above Thorn's head, a hook-beaked bird glared fiercely down at him. The birds had been cast in metal and seemed barely touched by the years. Had such creatures existed outside their creator's imagination? Beyond them, a double rank of trees had once stood, soft-shading the approach to the house, but now only a few remained. Most lay rotting on the ground where savage winds had uprooted them. Next came a few outbuildings, ruins all. Even where walls were still standing, roofs had fallen in. Over everything lay an air of desolation.

Who would choose to live up here? No one in his right mind. But maybe the Spetch brothers weren't in their right minds . . .

Halfway along a high wall, its red bricks raddled and crumbling, was an archway overhung with tendrils of ivy and other plants. Inside was what might once have been an ornamental garden, but was now a wilderness. Over long years, plants had overflowed their appointed boundaries, obliterating pathways and battling for survival. Beyond this chaos of vegetation stood Thorn's destination.

Roydsal was a two-storey house, graciously designed with mullioned windows and built to last. Yet it looked deserted. Its front door was cracked and weathered, but still stoutly held its place. Had Thorn been a giant, he could have mounted the short flight of steps and rapped on the wood with his fist. At the corner of the house, a second archway gave access to a path to side and rear.

Halfway along this path, absurdly small and out of place, was a brick-built rattery. The Spetches must be rich indeed if they thought nothing of the cost of hauling the raw materials to this windswept hilltop, then setting builders to work. Here, as Denny had promised, was the entry-point to the house, once a ventilation duct. In the days of the giants, vermin might have squirmed in here. Now humans used it. What did that say of Thorn and his kind? That, in comparison with the giants, they were a piddling infestation?

He pulled the hood up over his head, then checked that his knife was in its sheath. He didn't want to use it, but if he had to . . . Then he took a deep breath and knocked on the door. He waited. Nothing happened. He knocked again, longer this time.

The door was equipped with a glass spyhole. Now, behind this, a cover slid to one side, revealing a circle of light in which a human eye appeared. Thorn bent forward so that the hood obscured his face.

"Password," a voice commanded from behind the door.

Thorn began to cough. "Devil. That you, Lippy?" he said hoarsely.

"Denny? You ill, mate?"

In answer, Thorn coughed again.

A sound of bolts drawn back. No sooner had the door opened than Thorn stumbled inside, his face averted from the doorman. Who shot the bolts behind him, turned, collected a lamp from a ledge by the door, and led the way through a low stone passage. It was Lippy, as Denny had said, with his sparse hair and squat frame. The lamp was powerless to illuminate the room at the end of the passage; its dimensions were lost in darkness. Here stood a wooden cubicle. Inside this makeshift guardhouse were a table, a chair and a couple of blankets – presumably so the guard could wrap up on cold nights. A second lamp burnt on the table, distilling a modest haze.

"For Godsake – what happened to you?" said Lippy. "And where's Blacky?"

Thorn began to cough again.

"Dead. Fight at the bridge. Tell you later," he managed to say.

"Dead? Blacky? This is a shambles and no mistake. The bosses aren't going to like it." Lippy patted Thorn on the shoulder. "I wouldn't want to be you and have to tell them about it tomorrow."

Thorn coughed again. "To Hell with them," he said.

"You're in a terrible state, Denny. Best get yourself to bed. Here – take this night-light."

"Thanks," said Thorn, as he took it.

Have I passed muster? he wondered as he slowly shuffled away. Would a hand descend on his shoulder, his hood be yanked back? He slipped his knife out of its sheath and held it against his chest. The space between himself and the doorman grew.

His lamp cast a halo of light as he walked. Monstrous cabinets materialised to be swallowed again by blackness. This had been some kind of storeroom when the giants ruled the world. He passed a stack of wooden crates, a tangle of chairs with broken legs and backs, a jumble of battered utensils. Beyond them a huge machine slumbered, never again to wake.

He was searching for the curtain that marked the exit from the room. And there it was, a grubby greenish drape covering a hole hacked in the bottom corner of the door. Crude but functional. He pulled it aside and went through.

This room had been Roydsal's kitchen. Once upon a time, people (servants?) had prepared food and cooked here, then washed up afterwards. But his tiny light showed him nothing of the room's fittings. Huge tiles covered the floor, rust-red, cracked and lifting in places, and he had to take care not to trip. He passed between the sturdy, lathe-turned legs of a long table – a false ceiling above him. A faint smell of onions came to his nose . . . Was he imagining it, or could ancient odours linger, encrusted in the surfaces of tables and furnishings?

He scanned the murk for the way out – another door – but his lamp lit only the floor with its unchanging pattern.

A scraping sound came to his ears. He stopped dead, and in a reflex action pulled his knife from its sheath. The noise came again, carried from somewhere in the dark ahead of him. He moved forward carefully, as if treading on broken glass.

And found himself staring into the startled face of a mouse. Its pupils gleamed in the light. He thrust his torch towards it and the timid creature swung to one side and lolloped away from him. The sound of its patter receded; then was gone. Silence again.

It was more frightened than I was, he thought.

Thorn slipped his knife back into his sheath and moved on.

At last, he came to the door. Here there was no drape. Instead, a resourceful carpenter had cut a corner out of the door and fitted it with hinges to form an entrance of human size. He opened it and went through.

He'd have liked to douse the light, but that would mean advancing blind. He moved along the wall, keeping the skirting-board in sight. As he crept forward, he felt suddenly like a thief.

But I'm not a thief, he thought: I'm here to take back what's been stolen from me.

This had been Roydsal's dining-room. Here, Denny had said, was a great table where feasts might have been held. Underneath it now, separated by makeshift partitions, their backs sawn off, each leg cut down to a few inches in length, were five ancient chair seats. Each of the Spetches' hired men was allotted one. Here they rested with their feet up, free to study the underside of the table high above them; here on pallet beds they snored when not on duty or away on some nefarious business of their masters.

And here, he hoped, right now, deep in satisfying dreamlands, were Leech and Rafter, the men unaccounted for. And here, he hoped, they'd stay till dawn came up.

So: down to the corner; right turn; then along again. He walked under a side-table, and as he emerged beside an elegantly curved leg, a black spider, fat and hairy, dropped down without warning, no more than an inch from his face. For a moment it hung there, assessing him with its inhuman gaze, then lifted up and away on its self-spun cable and vanished. He came to a door – another one with a human-size entrance built into it. But it wasn't the one he wanted. On he went to the next corner; right turn again.

So far, everything was as Denny had said it would be. The next door, let it come soon –

– and here it was.

The quality of the darkness in the next room felt different. It wasn't that in the other rooms he hadn't sensed great spaces above him, but this one . . . He shivered. Here was real emptiness.

It seemed to gather and press down on him from an intolerable height.

The entrance hall. Somewhere – according to Denny – a great staircase curved upwards.

He willed his legs into motion, and struck out into the blackness. The soles of his boots mutedly slapped the stony floor. From somewhere a draught wafted in and a leaf, brown and dead, hopped like a frog straight towards him, making his heart jump in his chest. His flame fluttered and flattened. He stopped and watched it unbend itself, then off he set again.

A shape began to define itself in the thicker obscurity: a wooden cubicle one and a half times his own height. This surely was it. He moved around the outside. It had no windows. Solitary confinement for the most harmless creature in the world . . . Abruptly he felt a surge of rage against the men who'd kidnapped Haw, the men who were now her jailers. How dare they do these things?

Here was the door. It was secured by heavy bolts set at top, bottom and centre. He slid them back. They were well oiled, and moved almost noiselessly. Then he pressed the handle down and pushed on the door. It creaked ever so slightly as it swung open. There, on a truckle bed, was Haw's small figure, the covers pulled up over her head.

"Haw?" he whispered.

But she did not move.

He set his night-light down on the table, moved to the side of the bed and took hold of the covers. Ever so gently, he pulled them back.

Beneath was the grizzled face of a man, his eyes open.

Only Thorn's journey-honed reactions saved his life. As the point of the man's knife jabbed up through the covers, Thorn twisted aside. The knife stabbed vacancy. Then Thorn seized the man by the hair and thrust his own knife under his chin.

"Try that again and I'll cut your throat."

Involuntarily, the man twitched. Thorn's knife pricked his throat and a thread of blood ran down his neck. Thorn saw fear in his eyes.

"Bring your knife slowly out from the side of the cot. Drop it on the floor."

The man obeyed. The knife hit the floor with a clunk.

"So I was expected," said Thorn. "This was a set-up all along."

The little man said nothing.

More blood sprang under Thorn's knife.

"Yes, yes!" Leech replied.

"Where's Rafter?" demanded Thorn.

"In bed, sleeping. He – he and I take turns in here."

"What have you done with my sister?"

"She – we moved her . . . last night."

"Moved her? Where?"

"Outside – to the rattery. She's in one of the stalls."

"Is the place locked?"

"No."

"And the stalls?"

"Just bolted."

"Keen on bolts here, aren't you?"

The man said nothing.

"How many rats in there?" asked Thorn.

"Three – including the masters' saddle-rats. Fine animals."

"Is that right?"

Suddenly into Thorn's mind had come a vision of himself and Haw riding into the wood, leaving the Spetch brothers fuming . . .

The man's eyes glinted. "Don't think you can ride *them*, kid. You'd never get on their backs."

"What do you know about it?"

But Leech was very likely right. Thorn could ride pretty well, but Haw had only ever ridden young rats under the supervision of the settlement's ratman. Fully-grown pedigree animals could be a tough proposition, and some were trained to accept a single specific rider.

"And my sister – how is she?"

"She's all right. But she's been drugged."

"Drugged?"

"Yes."

Anger flared once more in Thorn. He felt an urge to ram the knife deep into the man's throat.

"You're Leech, aren't you? . . . one of the men who kidnapped her."

"Whoever told you that lied to you." Leech gasped out the words, seeming to realise that his life at this moment hung by a thread. "I'm the ratman here . . . strictly home duties."

Thorn stared at the frightened man. Denny had lied to him. Denny was one of the kidnappers. Unless Leech was lying in an attempt to save his skin. Nothing would have been easier than to slash his scraggy neck.

Abruptly he drew back, threw the covers over Leech's face, seized the lamp from the table and moved out of the cubicle.

Pulling the door shut, he slammed the bolts into their keepers. The man could yell himself hoarse in there, but who in this dreary vault of a place would hear him?

The rattery . . . That meant he had to go all the way back to the door . . . and pass the guard again.

He thought for a moment, then circled the hut until he reached the point where he'd arrived. Then he struck out across the floor. The draught came again, puffing dust into his face. He closed his eyes, then beat the dust from Denny's jerkin. Behind him now he could hear Leech calling and banging on the door with his fists. But his cries were muffled by the walls of the cubicle, then dispersed in the hollow shell of the hall. By the time Thorn reached the door, they were barely audible.

And so back into the dining room. Let Rafter still be sleeping.

As Thorn moved along the wall, reversing his earlier journey, it struck him that if the brothers had set one trap for him, they might have set another. In the rattery, perhaps? Rafter was still unaccounted for, not to mention the twins themselves. He'd have to tread carefully . . .

He reached the exit without incident and went through into the kitchen. This also he safely negotiated. Now for the green drape. Setting the lamp down on the floor, he carefully drew the material back and peered into the storeroom.

The light in the far guardhouse was too distant to be seen. The night was well advanced.

He considered dousing the flame, then decided against it. Lippy would be in his cubicle. Its single window did not give a view this way. He started across the floor.

At last the dark shape of the guardhouse came into view. Wan lamplight shone from its window. Thorn blew out his own light and began to creep forwards. When he got within twenty paces of the structure, he stopped and listened; but heard nothing. Reaching its windowless side wall, he set his lamp carefully down on the floor and listened again. Still nothing. He rounded the corner. The door was closed: he would have to risk the window. Sidling up to it, he listened again. No sound reached his ear.

He peeped into the makeshift room.

Slumped in his chair next to the table where his lamp steadily burnt, Lippy was fast asleep.

Thorn went back for his night-light, crawled beneath the window, then went down the stone passageway till he came to the outer door.

It was bolted at top and bottom. Beside the door was a small ledge, and on this he put his lamp. He propped Denny's bow against the wall.

Upper bolt first. He grasped the handle. The bolt was tight, and he couldn't afford to make a sound. With a mild grating sound, the bolt retracted into its keeper.

He turned and listened, but no sound came from the passageway. The gloom beyond his lamp's reach seemed filled with invisible eyes.

He squatted and took hold of the handle of the second bolt. He pulled on it, but it wouldn't shift. He leant into the door, trying to ease the pressure on the bolt, and tried again. It moved a little, with a rasping sound, but then stuck. Gripping the handle with both hands, he tried again, still exerting less than his utmost strength. It refused to budge. Now there was nothing else for it. In desperation he tugged at the bolt with all his might. There was a screech as the bolt shot back, then a metallic clap as it rammed its buffer, jarring his fingers.

Even as he straightened up, Lippy's voice sounded from behind him, "Denny? Is that you?"

With the sound of approaching footsteps came a brightening glow. Thorn pretended to be fiddling with the door. There was a scrape as a second lamp was deposited on the ledge.

"What the hell are you up to, Denny? You know the rules."

Thorn coughed. "Didn't want to wake you. Got to slip out."

"Slip out? At this time of night? Have you gone crazy?"

But Thorn could think of nothing to say. He stood with his face averted.

A hand touched his shoulder. Pivoting on his heel, he jabbed with his upraised elbow at where he thought Lippy's head might be. There was a satisfying crunch as bone met flesh, and a sharp pain jumped along his arm.

Lippy was staggering backwards, blood running from his mouth.

"What the hell—" he gasped.

Then he took a step forward and swung a foot at Thorn's groin. But, like all men in Norgreen, Thorn had been taught how to fight. Instinctively he swivelled, and the boot flew past his hip. Then, while Lippy's foot was in the air, he kicked sharply out at the knee of his opponent's supporting leg. Lippy gasped as Thorn's toe whacked into his kneecap, then toppled sideways towards the wall. He flung out a desperate arm, but to no avail.

There was a crack as his head met a stone and he slid to the ground.

Thorn bent over the doorman. Lippy was still breathing, but out for the count. Taking his lamp from the ledge and retrieving his bow, Thorn opened the door and went out.

Stars spangled the sky above the silent rattery. A faint breeze fluttered the flame as Thorn crossed to the building. A simple latch secured the door. As it swung inwards away from him, Thorn drew his knife and stepped forward, holding the lamp in front of his body.

Set in the building's interior wall – brick-built like the outer walls – were the doors of six stalls, each wide enough to allow a rat to go through. At the end of the row was a narrower latched door. That would be the tack room.

A small window set in the door of each stall allowed the ratman to keep an eye on his beasts without entering. Thorn hurried down to the stall furthest from the tack room door and, holding up the lamp, peered through the window.

The stall was empty.

So too was the next.

Rats occupied the third, fourth and fifth. Two, curled up on their bedding, appeared asleep; the third lifted a questing snout and stared up at Thorn.

He moved to the final stall and peered in. His light was just sufficient to show, on a cot, the sleeping figure of his sister. She lay on her side in a familiar posture, hair straggling over the pillow, her left arm motionless on top of the bedclothes.

Now to wake her, if he could. If he couldn't, he'd carry her.

Put some space between them and Roydsal before the Spetches discovered her missing.

Laying his bow down on the floor, he slid back the bolts and stepped into the stall.

"Haw!" he called as loudly as he dared: "Haw!"

But she did not move. The drug must have her in its grip. He moved towards the cot.

He was halfway there when the world began to tilt. He halted, teetering in amazed disbelief . . . then slowly keeled over as, underneath his feet, the floor slid away. In a dreamlike silence, he dropped into space.

Haw's cot, against the wall, was on a fixed part of the floor and did not come after him. Thorn braced himself for the crash but now landed on something springy – a mattress perhaps – which bounced him back a little way. The lamp had slipped from his fingers, and the impact put it out. He struggled to his feet, but already above his head, in the teasing darkness, he could hear the floor's wickedly hinged halves swinging shut.

When some time later they parted again and the darkness shrank away, he looked up expectantly.

A pair of heads appeared in the lit space at the pit's brink. One had yellow-gold hair, the other red.

"Thorn Jack, welcome to Roydsal!" said the redhead ringingly. "What a time it took you! We thought you'd never get here!"

The blond shook his head and clicked his tongue disapprovingly, "But what appalling manners to drop in on us unannounced!"

355

22

BLINDFOLD ARCHERY

Jewel was drowning and she knew it. Her mind sent out instructions: to her arms to push down the water, to her legs to kick upwards. Yet nothing got through. Her limbs refused to respond. Arms outstretched, she sank down, a mote in a liquid wilderness.

A dream-memory flashed on her: of swimming, breathing water, twisting lithely through shoals of fish. There had been blue radiance, sunlight. Reality was different: as she sank, the greyness deepened – twilight moving towards night. Before too long she would open her mouth, suck in lungfuls of water and belong to the cold lake.

Not yet, not yet! urged a spiky voice in her mind. Remember what you are. Fight, hold on, don't give up!

Surrender! said a second voice, caressive and comforting. Let go. Breathe and sleep. Nothing could be easier.

Voices, voices . . . Which to ignore, which to obey?

She fought, she held on. But her chest was hurting now.

Something encircled her waist. There was a flurry of movement. A body had joined itself to hers. Vaguely she was aware that her motion had been reversed. She was moving upwards again.

Too late. Her chest was a mass of fire, her heart near to bursting. Only water could quench the flames. She fought, she held on, then could hold on no more. Her mouth opened, the lake rushed in, and with its invasion came the night.

Jewel convulsed and vomited water. Consciousness leaked into her. With consciousness came feeling. Powerful hands were pumping her chest. She coughed, spewed up more fluid.

"Good girl!" said a man's voice.

Still the hands pumped her. Still she coughed, dribbled out streams of what she'd stolen from Harrylake.

At last she opened her eyes. They stung, her vision was blurred. A man was bending over her. She blinked. He seemed familiar . . .

"Jasper . . .?" she managed.

"Yes, it's me," said Jasper Tallow. "You're going to be all right."

A second face looked down at her from a little further away.

"Parker . . .?" she said.

"The same," said Parker Catt, and grinned the broadest of grins. He seemed enormously pleased with himself, even though he was soaking wet.

Wrapped in blankets and sipping tea from steaming mugs, Jewel and Parker sat by the kitchen range in Rotten Pavilion. The fire blazed merrily. Jasper and Rainy had drinks too. Harry the Wag stood behind them, studying Jewel thoughtfully. Nog was hovering in the background.

"I can't believe my luck," said Jewel. She felt better already, although her throat was sore. "The two of you turning up when you did."

"Luck wasn't involved," said Jasper.

"Thank Elphin Loach," said Parker Catt.

"Elphin?" queried Jewel.

"She turned up," Jasper explained, "early this morning at Luke's door. She'd had a dream-sending: you were drowning in Harrylake. It was too vivid to ignore. Then she and Luke woke us and we came as fast as we could."

"Not fast enough to stop Brace," added Parker ruefully. "But in time to fish you out of the lake – just."

There was a silence. Jewel stared into the fire. The slenderest margin of time had divided her from death. If she'd obeyed that soothing voice . . .

Rainy turned to Harry the Wag. "Brace – is he still here?"

"Gone," replied Harry. "And his master and mistress with him. They'll be well away by now."

"So, will you go after them?"

"What, with the few men I've got, the Pavilion to run? Much as I'd like to, it's impossible."

"I'm disappointed in you, Harry. I thought you were made of sterner stuff."

"My stuff has nothing to do with it. Minral How's a virtual fortress. It's surrounded by high walls. You'd need an army to break in. And Crane Rockett will shield his man."

"But Rockett's guilty too."

"How do you know? Brace is a law unto himself. Killing Tarry, half-killing Jewel – I don't believe Rockett would have authorised these things. He's a man for the quiet life, unless his interests are threatened. Tarry was nothing to him. An idle moment's amusement. Even so, Rockett is sure to protect Brace: he's too useful a tool to lose."

Jewel said, "I suspect Brace only set out to frighten me. But then I insulted him, and he lost control."

"I don't believe it!" exclaimed Rainy. "Are you defending Deacon Brace?"

"Not defending. Explaining."

Despite herself, Rainy had to admit that Harry was right. Brace was beyond the Wag's reach. That he'd never again dare to set foot on Lake Island was the only satisfaction they could take from the morning's events.

It was afternoon before Jewel felt well enough to travel. Once again, she and Rainy said their goodbyes to Harry; then – together with Parker and Jasper, who'd hung around till Jewel was ready – the two women set off. This time they crossed the island uneventfully.

As the terrain rose virtually all the way to Luke's house, they went slowly, with frequent halts. Jewel walked in front with Rainy; Parker and Jasper strolled behind.

Jewel seemed disinclined to talk. It was Rainy who broke the silence.

"Jewel," she said, "when do you intend to leave Harrypark?"

"Tomorrow morning, first thing."

"I thought you'd say that. Well, I'm coming with you."

Jewel turned to look at her friend. "I can't let you do that, Rainy. You've your father to consider."

"I've already talked to him. He likes you and he didn't even try to dissuade me."

"Even so, it's not right. I can't let you come with me."

"You can't stop me, Jewel. I'm coming, and that's that."

They found Elphin sitting with Luke. Jay and Linden appeared, and enthusiastically joined in the chorus of greetings and round of hugs.

"I'm told I owe you a big thank-you," Jewel said to Elphin, and gave her a kiss.

"It wouldn't have done at all if you'd got prematurely drowned." Elphin spoke lightly and with a touch of complacency. "We'd never then have found out what you're made of, Jewel Ranson."

Jewel considered this. "If I'm as gifted as you think I am, why didn't *I* foresee what was about to happen?"

"Foresight's an unpredictable thing – even for a Magian. You can't choose what to see. It's the seeing that chooses you. And it doesn't care how inconvenient its manifestations are."

"I see," said Jewel. "I've got another question for you."

Elphin affected surprise. "*Another* one? What's that?"

"You saw me drowning. Did you see me getting rescued?"

"No. That depended on a number of things. If I'd chosen to stay in bed . . . Or if Parker and Jasper had been away, or arrived too late . . ."

"I see . . . Well, I'll never be able to repay you – or them for what they did."

360

"That remains to be seen," said Jasper.

"And in any case," said Parker, "virtue is its own reward."

"However," said Jasper, "there *is* something you can do for us."

"Name it."

"Tell us the story of last night."

"It's a long story," said Jewel.

"So much the better," broke in Jay. "The best stories are meaty, you can worry them with your mind. So here's what Linden and I propose—"

"What *we* propose," corrected Linden, patting her stomach significantly.

"Naturally," agreed Jay. "Everyone here must come to us this evening for dinner. We've got a bed for you, Elphin. Then we can *all* hear Jewel's story. *And* knock back a drop of ale."

"More than a drop, I suspect," said Luke.

"More than a drop, but less than a barrel."

"Don't bet your life on it," said Luke.

Despite her eagerness to be gone, Jewel was sorry next morning to have to say goodbye to Luke. She gave the blind man a big hug.

"Look after my daughter," Luke told her.

"It's Rainy who'll be looking after *me* – as I'm sure you know."

"I doubt it," Luke said, smiling, "after what I heard last night."

Jewel picked up a longbow. "Rainy's going to teach me how to shoot," she told Luke.

"Then I hope you turn out a better archer than she is. She's not much better than me."

"That's a scandalous lie," said Rainy with mock indignation.

"When rabbits see Rainy taking aim, they waggle their ears at her and stick their furry bottoms in the air. They know they'll still be chomping grass and hopping about tomorrow."

"Come on, Jewel, let's be gone. All I get at home is insults."

But she seized Luke, and father and daughter embraced tenderly.

Jewel and Rainy went past Round Pond and turned west along the avenue that sliced across Harrypark. The sky was overcast, and to the south the waters of Harrylake showed grey through a break in the rhododendron plantations.

They came to a gap in the ancient walls. The massive gates that had once stood here had long since fallen, and their proudly spiked uprights were now a riot of rust.

Beyond the broken walls, a different world asserted itself. Lowmoor Barrens, which cupped Harrypark in its open palm, extended here a thin finger, compelling southbound travellers to skirt its rim. In the grainy afternoon even the Barrens seemed subdued, content to slumber till the sun emerged, when – as Jewel knew to her cost – the air above its surface would glow with seductive, virulent light.

As soon as they'd put the Barrens behind them, they came to a crossroads. Here they went westwards. Later, when this new road forked, they chose the southernmost route.

They set up camp early that evening. Jewel admitted to feeling tired but, to take advantage of the last of the day's light, professed herself eager to have her first archery lesson. Despite what Luke had said, Rainy proved a competent shot. In sharp contrast, Jewel's shafts flew all over the place.

"I'll never get the hang of this." Disgust at her feeble shooting was only too evident in her voice. "I'm all fingers and thumbs."

"Patience. You'll improve. You should have seen *my* first efforts. Dad said the only safe place to stand was right in front of the target."

Next morning, Jewel woke restored. The weather was much as before, the landscape – so far as she could tell – rolling and featureless. They made good time and in mid-morning came to another junction. Here Rainy called a halt. The road they were now joining took traffic from Wibsy, Shelf and beyond in the north-west to settlements in the south and east.

"What lies south-east?" asked Jewel.

"Wyke and Norgreen," answered Rainy.

The names meant nothing to Jewel.

They were getting ready to move when a cart hove into view, pulled by a muscular grey-furred rat. They waved at the carter, who waved back and came to a halt.

"Don't I know you?" he said to Jewel – blunt but friendly, she thought.

"Perhaps," said Jewel hesitantly.

"I know – you're the lass whose father was murdered at Shelf Fair. Terrible thing. Bad for everyone, but worst of all for you . . . And you –" turning to Rainy "– you're the juggler woman, yes?"

"My name's Rainy Gill. And this is Jewel Ranson."

"My wife bought a dress from you and your dad. Classy item. I'm going to Wyke. Want a lift?"

Rainy and Jewel exchanged a glance.

"If you're offering," said Rainy, "and it's not too much for your rat."

"Nothing's too much for Grizzle. He's the best rat I've had and I've had some good uns. Hop on, girls."

They climbed onto the cart and disposed themselves among a number of cube-shaped bales. They held flax, the carter explained, grown in Shelf. He intended to trade it in Wyke for pottery and ironware. He made this trip twice a year. His name, he said, was Jimmy Stoker.

As Jimmy's cart rattled on so did its driver. "My father was a carter, and his father afore him. There's no life like it; you get to see the world. I go to Hippam, Nowram, Queeby, Shibbin and over as far as Hallax. It beats staying at home." He twisted round to look at Jewel. "But you'll know all about that, lass. You've been places I'll never get to. Seen some life too, I'll be bound."

"Not really," said Jewel. "We spent our time buying and selling. People are much the same everywhere."

"That's true, in a way," said the carter, "but in another way, it's not. So where are you off to?"

"Nowhere in particular," said Jewel cagily.

The carter shrewdly sized her up.

"Is that right?" he said at last. "Well, it's none of my business, lass. But all roads lead to reckonings, as my father used to say. Grow a third eye in your back."

It wasn't clear whether this had once been Jimmy's father's advice to Jimmy, or was Jimmy's advice to herself. What if the third eye's in your mind? she felt like asking. But didn't.

The ground began to rise. High above them on their right ran the crest of Roydsal Ridge. To save Grizzle unnecessary strain, the three humans got down and walked. Jimmy led the rat, his hand loosely holding the harness.

"Is Grizzle friendly?" Jewel asked Jimmy.

Jimmy grinned. "Here, take the rein. If he doesn't fancy you, you'll find out soon enough."

Jewel wasn't quite sure what to make of this. Nevertheless she took the rein and walked alongside the rat, addressing occasional words to him. It seemed to her that when their eyes met, Grizzle inclined his head, as if to say: I quite agree.

"I think he likes me," she said to the carter.

"Good judge of character is Grizzle. Know what I think?"

"What's that?"

"A clever rat can tell a person's nature by his smell. If you don't smell right . . . You can fool a man, but you can't fool a rat."

Jewel nodded. This made good sense to her.

When the ground levelled out, they remounted the cart. Along the northern edge of the road ran an ancient dry-stone wall. It was broken and tumbled in places, and from time to time they sighted, stretching away in the valley bottom, the steely waters of a great lake.

"Roydsal Dam," said the carter to Jewel. "There's a little group of islands in the middle. See 'em?"

"They look like a single island," she said.

"That's 'cos they're close together, pretty small and a long way off. They call them the Arkypelly-something."

"Archipelago," prompted Rainy. "I've heard there are Sybs living there."

"That's what they say. Two sisters – a rum pair. Odd place to live, middle of a lake. You wouldn't catch *me* stuck out on an island. Not much call for carting *there*."

With a nonchalance she was far from feeling, Rainy said, "I imagine we're not far from Roydsal now – I mean the house."

"It's up on the ridge above us. There's a track to it further along." Jimmy scrutinised Rainy and Jewel. "But surely you're not minded to take yourselves up there?"

"What if we are?" responded Rainy.

"That's a bad place, mark my words. And bad folk live in it. I wouldn't let women of mine up there."

"Then it's just as well, Jimmy, that we're *not* women of yours."

The carter produced a wry smile and shook his head wonderingly. "Women today . . . I don't reckon to understand 'em."

"That's hardly surprising. We don't always understand ourselves."

"Now you're having me on."

"Cross my heart."

"At least you've got a heart to cross – unlike some others I could name."

"That's the road to Roydsal."

Much overgrown with grass and weeds, and bounded on both sides by tumbled walls, a broad giant-built track slanted away up the hill.

"Then this is where we part company."

Rainy and Jewel got down from the cart. They exchanged

warm farewells with Jimmy and Jewel scratched Grizzle under the jaw. The rat licked her hand.

"Really taken to you, he has. Must be something about you, lass." The carter glanced up the hill. "There isn't money enough in the world to get me up *that* road. But something tells me it's not money that you're going up there for. Well, good luck to the both of you."

Then, with the command "Get on, Grizzle!" Jimmy Stoker was on his way.

But Jewel and Rainy, just now, were not. They sat with their backs against one of the stones that had fallen from the wall.

"We need a plan of action," said Rainy. "We can't just go and knock on the door."

"I agree. I've been thinking what to do. I think we should watch the place for a time. Perhaps we can learn something, slip inside."

"Well, unless we can take the Spetches by surprise, we've no chance. If we're going to kill them, we need two clear shots – one for you, one for me."

Rainy spoke with a cold detachment she was far from feeling. For one thing, Jewel couldn't shoot straight. For another, she had her doubts whether, remarkable as this fifteen-year-old was, Jewel had it in her to kill a man in cold blood.

"You don't think I'm up to it, do you?" said Jewel sharply. Then, in a softer tone, "Well, I don't suppose I can blame you . . . Have *you* ever killed a man?"

"No. But I think I could. If someone killed Dad – deliberately, I mean – I would kill him just like that. A life for a life: that's justice. The Spetches killed your father: that's exactly the same thing. I'm your friend; you can count on me."

Jewel looked away. "But can I count on myself . . ."

For a time there was silence. Then Jewel picked up her bow and said, "How about an archery lesson?"

They practised shooting at the bole of a bush that grew in a crack in the wall. The breadth of an average man, it was a realistic target. But Jewel missed it every time and got more and more frustrated.

"You're trying too hard," said Rainy. "You're tightening up. Try to relax."

Jewel tried, but without success. At last she threw her bow on the ground.

"I'm hopeless," she declared. "I'll never get the hang of this. I couldn't be any worse if I shut my eyes."

Rainy looked at her thoughtfully.

"Why don't you do just that?"

"Are you serious?" said Jewel.

"Deadly serious." Taking a scarf from her pack, Rainy blindfolded her.

"I can't see a thing!" Jewel complained.

"That's the idea!" said Rainy.

She picked up Jewel's bow and restored it to the girl. "Nock an arrow. Aim at the target, but don't worry about precision."

Jewel followed her instructions.

Rainy went on, "Right. Shut your eyes. Next, picture the post. Imagine it's Lanner Spetch, the brother with red hair. Then fire – *and guide the arrow into his heart with your mind.*"

Jewel shut her eyes, held for a long moment, then fired. The arrow flew fast and true and thunked into the bole – right where a man's heart would have been, if the wood had been flesh.

"It seems I can do it," she said.

"Yes. Now do it again."

And she did, ten times in ten.

They made their approach to Roydsal by way of the fields that stretched up to the brow of the hill, sticking close to the broken walls. Had they attempted to cut across, they'd have struggled in no time, swallowed by floods of grass that rippled, wind-shot, across the exposed slope. It was slow, arduous going, but the last thing they wanted was to be spotted by the Spetches' men. By the time they reached the hilltop they were tired, and the light was failing.

They rested briefly, then went prowling round the house. They peered round corners, slipped along walls, their bows nocked and ready. Conspirators double-dreaming of the perfect assassination, they whispered like oat-stalks twisted together in the wind.

It was easy enough to locate the sole entry-point to the building. Noting the newness of the rattery that stood opposite it, they stationed themselves at the corner furthest from the overgrown garden. From here they had a view down to the arch at the opposite end. That was the way anyone would approach or leave the house.

The first person they saw came out of Roydsal, not to it. He was carrying something – a tray. He crossed to the rattery, unlatched the door and went in. A little while later he came out again, this time carrying nothing. He knocked on the house door and said something. The door was opened from inside and in he went.

"There has to be someone in the rattery," said Jewel.

"The ratman?"

"I expect so, but why doesn't he go into the house to get his food?"

"Perhaps he can't leave his post. A sick animal?"

Jewel nodded. "Could be."

There was no further activity. They crept along to the rattery. A lamp shone in the end window.

"It's the tack room," whispered Rainy.

A man was sitting at a table, cleaning the metal parts of a harness. In front of him lay a heap of stirrups. The women withdrew quietly.

"I didn't see a tray on the table," said Rainy. "Did you?"

"No," confirmed Jewel. "And the ratman looked relaxed to me."

It began to drizzle. They pitched their tent under a bush in a corner of a field, then lay in their sleeping bags, listening as the drops pattered down on their thin ceiling.

The rain has gone away and a pale half-moon hangs in the treetops. Jewel, up on the rattery roof, crouches, bow in hand. Lanner comes out of the house, and she shoots him in the head. Zak comes out of the house, and she shoots him through the heart.

This is easy.

This is a dream.

*

Early next morning, as they ate, they exchanged ideas. Then, with their weapons, they returned to their corner post.

The rain-clouds had blown away, and the early morning sun burnt fiercely on the horizon, as if to celebrate its rebirth.

Time passed, but just when they'd begun to think that nothing was going to happen, the door of Roydsal opened. A man came out, crossed to the rattery and went inside. A little later he re-emerged, pushing in front of him a blindfolded man whose wrists were tied behind his back. There was a brief exchange at the door, then it opened and sucked them in.

"So," said Rainy, "that's who the tray was for last night. It looks as though we're not the only enemies of the Spetches."

"And if they've called that man in for questioning, they'll be preoccupied."

"Plan number one?"

"Definitely."

Sprawled in the guard room chair, Rafter picked his nose and puzzled his head about the bosses. The brothers baffled him; made him angry, too. Denny and Blacky had never come back and Lippy said this brat they'd caught had told him Blacky was dead. Maybe Denny was too. But the Spetches didn't give a damn about either of them: they'd left the brat overnight in the trap without troubling to question him. What's more, no one else was allowed to. What if, Rafter wondered, *I'd* been the one to go missing? Then I'd be the one to get ignored . . . The notion got right up his nose. As if to rid himself of the thought, Rafter rooted in a nostril and was rewarded with a stab of pain. He withdrew his grubby finger and rubbed the soft flange of his nose. He was disillusioned with the bosses and was frustrated with the set-up. His knife-hand itched, closed around the bone hilt. He'd just love to cut some patterns in that surly brat's skin. *He'd* find out where Denny was. But now the brothers had sent for the prisoner. Maybe when they'd finished with him he, Rafter, would get his turn . . .

A fist was banging on the door. Leech. What the hell did *he* want? Leech was pretty good with rats, but not much good for anything else. The brat had made a fool of him. Leech was only heroic when his enemies were flat on their backs or down on their faces, licking his boots.

Rafter got to his feet with a curse and ambled through the stone passageway to the outer door. He slid open the spy-panel. Leech's features filled the circle.

"Password!" demanded Rafter.

"B – blood!" came the reply.

"What do you want, Leech?" he said, not bothering to hide the irritation he was feeling.

"I'm hungry. I haven't had my breakfast yet today."

"Food! Is that all you can think of?"

"Right now, yes. Come on, open up."

Sighing, Rafter closed the panel, slid back the bolts and drew back the door. Then found himself looking at the business end of an arrow. That was the first outrageous thing. The second was, the archer was a woman of his own age. She looked determined too.

Leech shrugged his apologies. His arms, Rafter saw, were tied.

A young girl stood off to one side, and she too held a nocked bow. He thought of launching himself at the woman. He could probably knock her over before she could fire: but if the girl shot . . . He scrutinised her face and saw the passion in her eyes. This one was on a mission; this one would shoot all right. Well, he thought, this is a first. Outwitted by two females. I'll never live this down.

If I get out of this alive.

"Inside the house," ordered the woman.

They bound Rafter's arms and legs, stuffed a gag into his mouth and left him lying in the guard room.

Then Leech led them through a sequence of huge rooms – spider-webbed, mouse-droppinged, dust-ridden, echoing, scattered with giant furnishings – through doors within doors that were deceptive to the eye. Roydsal was on a scale that dwarfed Rotten Pavilion, the whole of which would have fitted into any one of its rooms with space to spare. Jewel did not look up, but kept her eyes locked on Leech as he clod-hopped along in front of them.

At last, at yet another door, he came to a halt.

"That's the room," he said flatly.

They gagged him, bound his ankles and roped him to a table-leg. Jewel thought: we're leaving a trail of trussed bodies, like spiders . . .

Rainy opened the door a crack and peered into the next room. Turning, she nodded at the girl and the two quietly slipped through.

23
SMOKE RINGS

When Lippy removed his blindfold, Thorn blinked in the sharp light. The sun was blazing into the room. He looked upwards and his head swam, whirled up into a void.

Nothing was of significance but space: height, volume. The grey-white ceiling seemed to float cloud-high. Something was falling from it – a gigantic shower of droplets . . . But no, it was suspended there, a cluster of crystal fruit, gem upon gem, too many to count. Awe-stricken, he turned for reassurance to the nearest wall.

But the cluster was there too, caught in a gilt-framed rectangle that flaunted its mad glitter . . . A mirror, a massive mirror. Had it been horizontal not vertical, made of water not glass, he could have dived in and swum to and fro in its liquid light.

The walls surrounding the mirror were lined with great panels of wood as dark as the mirror-lake was bright.

He looked down at the floor. It bounced up to meet him, paved with square-cut tiles of stone, whitish and greenish, streaked and mottled. Was all this, then, the creation of a race of super-beings – the perfected ones that Manningham Sparks believed had gone to Heaven . . ?

Lippy prodded him in the back with the hilt of his knife. "Up there. That's where you're going."

"Up there . . ?" For a moment Thorn imagined himself caught up by the invisible hand of a giant and borne aloft, dazzled and overwhelmed. Then he saw what Lippy meant, and focused on what occupied the centre of the floor, earthbound under the intricate, impossible star-cluster.

It was a great table made of a wood as dark as that of the walls. It had six massive legs and an outjutting upper lip. Slung below each corner, underneath its centre too, were curious frazzled, straggling nets. The table, which had to be two and a half feet high, would have been useless to a human had it not been for the fact that a wooden staircase had been constructed beside it. Carpentered from pale, unvarnished wood, it looked utterly out of place, rising up there alongside something ancient and noble.

They crossed to the stair and began to climb. Thorn's boots clumped on bare wood. But the stair had been solidly built, and there were handrails at each side – not that his hands were free to use them. The longest staircase in the world! Lippy followed, keeping a judicious dozen steps to Thorn's rear.

At the top, the staircase made a right angle and became a walkway of sorts in order to cross the high-ridged gleaming lip; after which a few steps led down to the table. Its surface was carpeted with some green material, now a little the worse for moths.

But his eyes were drawn elsewhere.

From the middle of the table rose the swags of a marquee. It was big and yellowy-orange – the sort you found in a travelling fair. The triangular segments of its roof gathered themselves to a point, and above this rose a mast from which a little flag flew. Or rather, did not fly; it was a painting of a flag, its wind-folds suggested by the painter's deft hand. But the flag was sufficiently extended to show off its design. This consisted of a pair of scales, its cups perfectly balanced: on one lay a nugget of gold, on the other a fat ruby. The symbol meant nothing to Thorn; but its meaning would strike him later.

Lippy now went ahead. The entrance to the marquee was positioned centrally. To its left was a glossy red sphere, to its right a yellow one – each perhaps an inch and a half in height. They looked solid and weighty, as if propelling them into motion would require quite an effort. Unhooking the entrance-flap, Lippy drew it back and brusquely ordered his captive in. Thorn obeyed, Lippy followed and rehitched the flap behind them.

The marquee was a maze of coloured curtains and screens – scarlet, pink and sky blue; purple, green and gold. But Lippy knew his way round; he threaded his way through until they came to a yellow drape. This he drew back, and Thorn was ushered inside.

Lamps burnt on pillars; the room was a riot of colour. At its centre rose the mast that flew, outside, the motionless flag. And there, propped on cushions on a scarlet and gold couch, their slippered feet on footrests, were the two men whose machinations had drawn him to this place.

Lippy gestured Thorn forward, and the young man advanced to within a foot of the sprawling twins. He could get no closer because of a long, low table. On the table sat a mechanism of outlandish appearance. A large, glass bowl was held in a trellis-work of metal. Inside was what looked like water. The bowl rested on a flat base and had a stretched-out neck that culminated in ornamented, elegant metal knobs. From its top came a curl of smoke.

Thorn studied the Spetches, the Spetches studied Thorn. No one spoke. The brothers had uttered no more than a handful of sentences in the rattery, and the light there had been less good. Smartly dressed and – he supposed – quite handsome, they differed physically only in the colour of their hair: long and wavy, it was flame-red in one case, yellow-gold in the other. The blond wore a scarlet shirt and trews and matching boots, and a bright yellow jacket. Out of his breast pocket peeped a floppy red handkerchief. The redhead wore a similar outfit with the colours reversed.

"Sit over there, Lippy." This was the redhead. Lippy withdrew to one side. Thorn had not been offered a chair.

Seize the initiative, he thought. "What have you done with my sister?"

The words died away. Still the men appraised him. You could have heard a mouse squeak in any corner of the room.

The blond man reached out towards the object on the table. Picking up the end of a long tube that protruded from the upper part of the bowl, he sucked on its mouthpiece. The water bubbled, emitting a deep gargling sound. The man leant back and after a moment expelled some smoke from his mouth. It hung in the air in front of him, a perfect ring. He smiled to see it.

"Splendiferous, bro," said the redhead.

Slowly the smoke-shape lost definition, drifting and dispersing. Below it, the eyes of the blond man had seemed for a moment unfocused; but, as Thorn looked into them, they returned to normal.

"Fancy a puff, kid?" the twin said, gesturing with the tube.

"No, thank you," said Thorn.

The blond laughed. "What a polite young chap he is."

"Well brought up," said the redhead. "Not like you and me, bro."

"Not like you and me at all. Much too young to acquire vices."

"I disagree. You're *never* too young to acquire vices."

"Funny. I could have sworn I'd heard that before."

"You have. It was you I got it from . . . together with the vices."

They laughed, a manic double chortle, echoing one another. Then the redhead took the tube from his brother and drew on it in his turn. The water foamed up again. The man smiled at Thorn, or through him as if, all at once, he'd acquired transparency.

"What is it?" asked Thorn, indicating the mechanism.

"We call it a water pipe," said the blond. "The only functioning water pipe in the world."

"How can that be?"

"How *can't* it be?" The blond turned to his brother. "Cheeky fellow, isn't he?"

"Nosy, too," said the redhead. "And it's not even much of a nose."

"I've seen bigger noses on bumble-bees."

"Black bats."

"Brown rats."

They grinned in unison.

"Even so," said the redhead, "curiosity ought to be fed. Tell him, bro."

"It's a copy of one the giants made," the blond said wearily. "We found the original in this house, soon after we moved in. There was still some water in it. We got a friend to look at the thing. She told us what it was for and described how it worked. Then we got a craftsman to make a copy – *our* size."

"It made your eyes go funny," said Thorn.

"Did it now?" said the blond. "Hear that, bro? The kid says I've got funny eyes."

"Perceptive lad," said the redhead. "I've always thought your eyes were pretty funny myself."

"But my eyes are just like yours."

"That I readily concede."

They looked solemnly at each other, then burst into laughter again.

"This little chap is good for us," said the redhead, when he'd recovered.

"Almost as good as his sister."

"But then, little girls were always good for us, bro."

"Little . . . big. Any size."

"Speak for yourself, bro. *My* mother taught me to *discriminate*, not like yours."

"Hmm . . . wish like hell *I'd* had a mother like that."

"You did. And Hell's exactly where she left us, bro!"

They were off, laughing again. They laughed so much that tears started to leak from their eyes. Until, as if on a prearranged signal, each plucked the handkerchief from his pocket and wiped them away.

We're getting nowhere, thought Thorn. They're completely round the bend.

"What have you done with my sister?" he said forcefully.

"*What have you done with my sister?*" repeated the blond in a shrill voice.

The twins looked blankly at Thorn.

"All right, since you won't answer that question, here's another. Which of you is Zak, and which Lanner? I want to know now, before I get to kill you. It'll be too late when I've done it."

"Ooo!" said the blond. "Proper scary, isn't he!"

"Terrifying," said the other. "I'm shaking in my trews. Can you hear my knees knocking?"

The brothers listened intently. Even Thorn was listening. The quiet was absolute.

"Can't hear a thing," said the blond.

"In that case," said the redhead, "they're knocking silently. Quick! Comfort-bubbles!" He took a deep drag on the pipe.

"Well?" demanded Thorn.

"Well, what?" said the blond.

"Which of you is which?"

The brothers looked at one another. "Are *you* Lanner?" said the blond.

"*You're* Lanner . . . I think," said the redhead.

"So you must be Zak . . . ?" said the other tentatively.

"Not likely!" said the redhead. "Still, what's in a name?"

"N, A, M and E. Not many people can say that. It's known as

spelling, bro. Or *not* known, as the case may be, in this ignorant country."

"So, how many of us are there?"

"That's a very deep question . . . I've been pondering it for years, and I still haven't an answer."

"Not true. You've many answers. I've heard every one of them."

"You calling me a liar?"

"Yes."

"It's true, I am a liar. I've been lying since the cradle. My mother remarked on it. 'What are you doing, lying there? Why don't you get up and go to work?' And what did I reply? 'Wurble-burble gurgle-goo!' No wonder she whopped my bottom."

"It was *my* bottom she whopped."

"She whopped mine harder."

"She whopped mine longer."

"Oh, have it your own way."

"I did, bro, and I do."

"So," said Thorn, "you've no intention of telling me?"

"Telling you what?"

"WHICH ONE OF YOU IS WHICH!!!"

"I'm Witch – I think," said the blond. "At least, I was yesterday."

"Ah, yesterday," said his brother, with a shake of the head. "Yesterday, today was tomorrow. Now it isn't. That's the trouble with the world. Things simply don't stay the same from one day to the next. From one *instant* to the next. And words are worst of all. They slip and slide, young man; they wobble, they turn cartwheels, stand on their heads and do the splits. No sensible person trusts them."

"That explains it!" cried the other, with an air of discovery.

"Explains what?" said the redhead.

"Why, brother dear, I've never been a sensible person!"

The twins looked back at Thorn.

"One thing we *can* be sure of," said the redhead confidently: "there's only one of *him.*"

"One's enough," said his twin.

"Enough for what?" asked Thorn.

"Now you're talking," said the blond. "Now he's talking," he said to the redhead.

"Oh, he's talking all right. He could talk the legs off a table."

"Off a crayfish."

"Off a sausage."

"Are you always as silly as this?" said an exasperated Thorn.

The blond got unsteadily to his feet and glared at him. "Sometimes, we're a world away from *silly*, little boy." His voice was as sharp as a scythe.

"Take it easy, Zak," said the redhead. "The kid hasn't a clue."

So Zak's the blond, thought Thorn. That means Lanner's the redhead.

Zak glowered at Thorn, then sank down again on the couch. Noticing that Lanner still held the tube of the water pipe, he snatched it from him, giggled, and took a long suck on it. The water bubbled gaily. His eyes glazed over. This time, he blew twin plumes of smoke from his nostrils.

Thorn turned to the redhead and shouted: "WHAT HAVE YOU DONE WITH MY SISTER?"

"She's dead," said the man. His blue eyes were cold as ice.

Thorn's legs went weak, as if their sinews had been slit.

"Dead? That can't be true." His voice came to him from far away, wraith-like, a voice heard in a dream.

"Why can't it be true?"

"Because . . . it doesn't make any sense . . ."

"It doesn't have to make sense. Everybody dies."

"But she's a child . . . Why kill a child?"

"Who said we killed her? We didn't kill her. She did it all by herself."

"By herself? When?"

"Yesterday," said Zak. There was a malicious gleam in his eyes. "She jumped off the top of this table. Not a word of warning. No way could we have stopped her. We had to scrape her up off the tiles."

A blood-splashed image exploded inside Thorn, burning a hole in his mind.

"You – you murdering monsters," he whispered. He wanted to say more, but the words wouldn't come. There was a blockage in his brain, as if, all at once, its processes had silted up.

Lanner took the pipe from Zak and blew a leisurely smoke ring. It was perfect, a hoop you could have poked your finger through, a passing absence, a glorious nothing.

"Marvellicious!" commented Zak.

"Isn't it just?" Lanner agreed.

"Just or unjust," said Zak. "Who's to know, who's to say?"

There was movement behind Thorn's back. He turned, and to his amazement saw two women coming towards him. Or rather, one was a woman and one a girl of his own age. Both were armed with bows, and these were pointing at the brothers. Lippy got up from his chair.

"Sit down!" commanded the woman. "Or I'll put an arrow into you."

Lippy sat down again.

The woman and the girl reached the table. The girl looked at Thorn. Her face was a furious mask, like a carving in pale wood.

"We've been listening," she told him. She nodded towards the twins. "Killing people – that's all they do. They murdered my father. But now it's my turn."

Thorn could think of nothing to say. Events had leapt beyond him now.

Jewel stood over the brothers. They were overgrown boys. They had plump, rosy lips, beautiful hair and blue eyes.

The one with red hair said: "What's this rubbish about your father? I don't even know who you are."

"You know all right," said Jewel. "Shelf Fair – you were watching us. You saw us making good money. You murdered my father in the mirror maze. You'd have killed me too if people hadn't come on the scene."

Lanner turned on Zak a mask of bafflement and said: "Shelf Fair, the mirror maze . . . Ring a bell with you, bro?"

Zak pursed his lips and frowned. "Not a teensy tinkle, bro. But you know the kind of memory that *I'm* blessed with. Takes me all my time to remember what I had last night for dinner."

The pair turned faces of utter innocence on Jewel, but she was sick of their foolery. Lifting her bow, she aimed the arrow straight at Lanner's heart. When she let fly, the man would die. It was the moment she'd longed for, but now it had arrived she felt a strange dissatisfaction, a sense of defeat rather than a sense of triumph. As she stood there, an uprush of pity overwhelmed her: pity not for these men – who deserved no such gift – but for her father, for herself, for the young man and his dead sister.

Yet she must shoot, and end this thing.

Rainy had drawn a bead on Zak. She would fire when Jewel fired. The blond sat utterly still, a half-smile on his lips.

Lanner grinned at Jewel. Then, raising a hand, snapped his fingers.

"*Look this way, all of you,*" commanded a masculine voice.

Thorn would have known it anywhere. He swung round.

Haw was standing away to their rear – might have materialised there. She stared at Thorn as if she couldn't believe it was him, then cried out his name in both hope and despair.

Thorn's lips moved. "Haw . . ." He barely breathed her name. It might have been a thing of wonder.

Behind Haw, one arm around her chest, stood Racky Jagger. He held a knife to her neck, its point almost touching an ear.

He said, "Lay your weapons down. Don't make me cut the girl's throat."

It's the sister, thought Jewel. The brothers were lying; she's not dead. Why didn't I *see* this?

She threw her bow down on the floor.

We've lost, thought Rainy, and let her bow drop from her hands.

Zak tut-tutted and said, with emphatic disapproval: "It's *awfully* bad manners to point arrows at people. Somebody could get hurt."

Lanner shook his head sadly. "I blame the parents, bro. Today's young – they don't get the *discipline* we had."

Zak waved a hand at Lippy: "Secure the weapons, Lippy. And you two – let's have you both down on your knees."

Jewel and Rainy knelt. Lippy kicked their weapons away.

"Now, Lippy," Zak continued, "tie their hands behind their backs, and put a knife on the big one."

Lippy roped the women up. Then, standing behind Rainy, he gripped the collar of her jacket and held his knife to her neck.

As the Spetches' man was doing this, Thorn said to Lanner, in a voice that was almost lifeless, "Why did you tell me she was dead?"

"Why not? It amused me. But cheer up, she's alive again. Astonishing, isn't it?" He snapped his fingers. "Dead!" He snapped them again. "Alive!" He grinned winningly. "Behold, Thorn Jack, your little sister's resurrection! Just like that! Easy as pie! Let this be a lesson to you."

"You're a miracle-worker, bro!" Zak said admiringly.

"I have my good points!" Lanner admitted modestly.

"But why kidnap her?" asked Thorn. "Why bring her all this way?"

"Flip my giblets, you're slow! Snails are quicker than you, lad. Enlighten him, bro."

Zak said, "So that you'd come after her, of course. So that, when you arrived, we'd have a lever to lever you."

He cranked an imaginary lever with his hand.

"We've got a job for you, young man. A nice little job," said Lanner. "If and when you complete it, you'll get your sister back."

"All in one piece, good as new!" added Zak. "Though if you fail, I hate to think how many pieces she might be in!"

"We're life-long believers in *incentives*," Lanner explained. "Carrots for rabbits!"

"Beetles for voles!"

"Maggots for fish!"

"Ants for pants!"

"But why *me*?" asked Thorn. "Why *me* of all people?"

Lanner smiled mysteriously. "Now, wouldn't you like to know!"

Thorn was baffled. "You mean . . . after all this, you're not even going to *tell* me?"

"It's best if you find out – when you find out!" Lanner quipped; then added mockingly, "And we wouldn't want to deprive you of the pleasure of the surprise."

Surprise? thought Thorn. What is the man talking about?

But it was clear that the brothers were in no mood to enlighten him.

"What do you want me to do?" he asked.

"A certain object," Zak informed him, "was stolen from us." He spoke seriously now. "A *unique* object," he added, "an *irreplaceable* object. We want this object back. *You* will go and get it for us."

"What object?" Thorn asked weakly.

"A key," supplied Lanner. "A key made by the giants."

Jewel, who'd been gazing at the floor and thinking that no self-respecting Magian ought to have let herself be reduced to the state that *she* was in, roused herself.

"A *brass* key?" she said.

Thorn twisted to look at the girl. Despite her servile posture, she'd recovered some of her poise, and on her taut, boyish face was an expression of contempt.

For once the twins showed surprise. Zak was the first to recover.

"How the hell do you know that?"

But Jewel was not in any mood for explanations.

"That key wasn't stolen," she said with vehemence. "You lost it in a fair wager – to Briar Spurr, at Harrypark."

Zak leapt to his feet.

"If I say the key was stolen, it was stolen!" he shouted, like a child in a tantrum.

Jewel replied coolly, "You can say what you like, but it won't alter the truth – something you wouldn't recognise if it smacked you in the teeth."

Zak was incandescent. "Take her away," he yelled at Lippy, spittle jumping from his lips. "Stick her in the rattery. Put the woman in there too."

But Lanner had risen now.

"Stay where you are, Lippy," he ordered.

The underling obeyed. The redhead laid a calming hand on his incensed twin's arm.

"Easy, bro," he counselled.

"*Easy?*" cried Zak. "You're telling me to go *easy?*"

"Not *telling* you – *asking* you. Let me talk to this girl." He turned to Jewel. "Where are our men – Rafter and Leech?"

With a tight smile, Jewel said, "Just like us, they're tied up at the moment."

"Tied up? Really . . .? How resourceful of you." His tone trod a tightrope between respect and sarcasm.

Jewel made no reply.

Lanner went on, "And Crane Rockett and Briar Spurr, and their man Deacon Brace. What do you know of them?"

"Enough," said Jewel dryly.

Rainy, who thought she saw where the red-haired twin was going, said, "We bumped into them in the same place you did – Harrypark. While we were there, Deacon Brace murdered a man, a harmless gambler."

"And got away with it?" asked Lanner.

"What do *you* think?" said Rainy.

Lanner thought Deacon Brace was the stuff of nightmare, but he wasn't going to admit it.

"To know 'enough' about those three is to know more than enough," he said. "You say you *bumped into* them . . . meaning you didn't just *see* them, you *got involved* with them?"

"That's one way of putting it."

"Interesting . . ." Lanner turned to Thorn, who was clearly bewildered by the rash of strange names. "Now *you*, Master Jack," he said, "*you* don't have a clue who these people are, do you? Correct me if I'm wrong."

Thorn's expression was more than adequate reply.

Lanner turned to his twin.

"Do you see what we have here, bro? *Do you see?*"

Zak nodded. Now that he was cooling down, he'd got the point too.

"Yes," said Lanner smugly, "what we have is Master Jack, who hasn't a clue what he's going to be up against, and a girl and a woman who don't need any telling. *And* they're handy with bows and arrows. Conclusion: three have a better chance of success than one."

Zak murmured, "And I was looking forward to getting to grips with pouty little miss – you know, doing what I didn't get to do to her last time. Still, *priorities*, bro. The key must come first."

"Right – that's decided then—"

"Nothing's decided," Jewel cut in. "If you think I'm helping *you*—"

"I don't *think* it, I *know* it." Lanner's tone was brutal now. "Looks like you need a little reminder of just who's in charge here. *Cut the woman, Lippy.*"

The shock of Lanner's order struck Jewel rigid, but elsewhere in the room another voice cried out, "No!"

It was Haw. Thorn saw anguish in her face.

Rainy tried to struggle but Lippy had her in a vice. His knife was almost at her cheek when Thorn came barrelling into him. The men went sprawling, Lippy dragging Rainy with him till he let go of her; his knife was sent spinning. But, wrists tied, Thorn was no match for anyone, and Lippy soon had him subdued.

Lanner was round the table now. Picking up the knife, he looked down at Thorn.

"Perhaps it's *you* that needs cutting," he said thoughtfully.

"Leave him alone," said Jewel. "Leave both of them alone. I'll go. I swear it on the grave of my father."

"Now you're talking," said Lanner. "And you?" – looking at Rainy.

"Where Jewel goes, *I* go," the juggler said in a firm voice.

"Excellent!" said Lanner. "The three of you will leave today."

The twins grinned in unison – grins that stretched from ear to ear.

You've won this round, thought Jewel. But there'll come another day, and you'll not win the next.

The adventures
of Jewel and Thorn
continue in
The Brass Key.

ISBN 0 689 87290 9